MY WILD HORSE KING
THE RUSSIAN WITCH'S CURSE
BOOK IV

BRIDGET E. BAKER

For Chewy
You're the world's worst dog, but look!
You still got your own book.

❧ I ❧

GUSTAV

When I was in grade school, Latvia experienced the worst recession it had ever known. In fact, the country lost a quarter of its gross domestic product in under two years.

Things were pretty dire for most everyone.

People don't handle stuff like losing their job with no hope of a new one very well, and many, *many* of my friends had already lousy fathers who only got worse thanks to the turn in the economy. Alcoholics. Abusive jerks. Depressed souls who stopped even trying to support their families. I think that's why it took me so long to notice. In fact, it wasn't until I walked in on my little sister Kristiana watching *The Lion King* that it hit me.

That father *died* for his child. My dad was nothing like that.

My dad sucks.

Dads are supposed to protect you—it's the central part of the gig.

They're supposed to teach you and shelter you while you grow.

Mine never did that.

He was too busy gambling, and while he may have won sometimes too, I never really saw a difference when he did. Whereas, I do vividly recall nearly every time he lost.

But even more than me, it always wrecked my mom's life.

My very earliest memory is of my mother, the phone pressed against her ear as tears rolled down her face, begging her parents to send her money so that we wouldn't lose Liepašeta, Dad's family farm.

That wasn't the only time she begged, though. In fact, I remember countless instances where my mom was forced to bail Dad out. But the last time. . . It was long after Grandfather and Grandmother had refused to send another dime, long after Mom had been turned down for any additional loans by every bank in Latvia, and long after Mom had exhausted the contents of her own trust fund and personal savings. That last time, Mom set out to repair the damage done by Dad's gambling debts herself, by riding in the Grand National and betting on her own horse to win. I still recall her telling me, her eyes shining, that she meant to be the first woman to win the Grand National, and that when she did, she was going to insist that Dad put the farm in her name— so he couldn't ever put it at risk again.

She did make the history books.

Just, not in the way she hoped. She became the first woman to die as a result of that wretched race. That was the day I started to hate horses, gambling, and my father—in that order—but it took me three more years to get away from it all.

Leaving Latvia was a bonus.

In the end, when I finally escaped, I had even less money than Dad before that last fateful race. I barely scraped together enough for a plane ticket, which is how I found myself on the front porch of my estranged American grandfather's mansion, knowing they barely knew me and guessing that they didn't like me. Dad had seen to that, with all the times he'd forced Mom to call and beg for money.

To my grandparents, I was part and parcel of exactly what had killed my mother—my grandfather's beloved only daughter. I couldn't even blame him for cutting us off. I was Latvian, through and through, and Latvia had burned Mom right down to the ground.

But this was my only play.

Because I didn't want to *be* Latvian. It had come to stand for failure, for loss, and for the promise that I would never amount to any more than my own father had. More than anything, I wanted a new start in a new place where no one knew me. I wanted to leave racing, horses, gambling, and my pitiful little country behind forever. Mom had gifted me a comprehension and fluency in her native tongue, and I meant to put it to good use. I'd secured admittance to an American school, but the only way I'd be able to stay without any funds of my own to pay for my schooling was with the support of my very wealthy and very judgmental grandfather.

After banging on the door and doing my best to schmooze a very disgruntled butler, I was starting to worry I wouldn't even be allowed to see him. But when the door opens abruptly, I straighten.

"It is you." Only the slight widening of Grandfather's nostrils betrays his feelings about seeing me here, on his porch, without an invite. Ironically, it's Dad's cursed poker training that makes me capable of recognizing these types of tiny tells. Now I just need to convince him to bankroll me for the next four years. According to Mom, Grandfather's absolutely famous for only making solid investments, no matter how ill-fated they may at first seem.

I just have to convince him that I am one.

"I know it's late," I say. "My flight was delayed, and by the time I navigated the public transportation system, well. I'm sorry if I woke you up."

"It's ten thirty," Grandfather says. "And I'm sixty-one, not ninety-five."

I frown. "I'm not sure whether you saw the letters I sent, but I was accepted to New York University, and I'm starting there next week." I force a smile. "Now that I'll be in New York City, I was hoping that—"

"No," he says. "I won't pay for your education."

Well, that's unfortunate. I wonder how long they'll let me attend before booting me for nonpayment. Maybe I could find a part-time job. Or, there has to be some kind of loan system, even for foreign nationals, right?

"I'm sure your father sent you here to—"

"He told me if I left Europe, he'd never speak to me again." It's harder than I thought it would be, repeating my dad's angry threat.

"You're assuming he doesn't really mean it." Grandfather raises one bushy white eyebrow. He may not be more than sixty-one, but his full head of hair is the color of cotton balls, and his eyebrows are twice as thick as a normal person's.

"On the contrary," I say. "I made him promise that he'd stand by it."

Grandfather stares at me, frozen, for three beats. And then he throws his head back and bellows, like a bull that's just run into a barbed wire fence. At first, I try to figure out how he was injured, standing stock still as he was.

Then I realize that he's *laughing*.

When he stops, it's equally unexpected, and it's just as disconcerting. "Have you ever read the Bible, boy?"

I can't help my frown. He keeps changing the subject in ways that make no sense. I shake my head, tightly, sensing this is not going well for me.

"That's a pity. There's a great story in there—a boy who sold his birthright."

What's he talking about?

"He sold it for a bowl of oatmeal." He shuffles just a bit closer. "A bowl of pottage, they called it."

"Why would he do that?"

Grandfather tilts his head. "Your mother sold your birthright, you know, for that parasite husband of hers. Sold it four times over."

Oh.

"I know you're here because you need money. It's the only time I ever hear from anyone with the Liepa surname, but here's the thing. I'm done giving money to all of you. You hear me?"

I nod slowly.

"But you are my grandson." He sighs. "I imagine you need money for school at least, and that's one thing I can respect— wanting to better yourself."

A tightness in my chest eases. Mom always said Grandfather acted tough, but he would sometimes yield, if you didn't push. I was counting on that still being true.

"I'll loan it to you," he says. "How about that? Market interest."

I'm not exactly in a position to argue. "Yes," I say. "I do need money for tuition and housing."

"And, as long as you're getting As, I'll waive the interest," he says. "When you graduate, if you graduate, you come to work for me. If you prove to me that you're nothing like your father, I might even consider giving you back your bowl of porridge." His snort is sharp.

"I plan to prove myself to you in any way I can." I shake my head slowly. "And I'm sure that I'll get all As, but I can't promise to work for you."

His scowl is terrifying, but I hold the line, because if my mother was right, this may be the most important bluff of my life. "Why wouldn't you work for me?"

"I'm sure your company's amazing, but it's too risky, working for someone else. If I'm going to work my hardest to impress you, I'll do it while building something for myself. Then if you decide that I don't measure up, I'll still have something to show for all my hard work."

His lip curves upward very, very slowly. "You're hedging your bet."

I shrug. "My dad never bothered, but I'm not like him."

"No." He harrumphs. "Perhaps not." He runs his hand over the bristle on his face. "New York University." He shakes his head.

"I've read that it's a good school, and New York City is in the middle of everything."

He shrugs with a slightly pained expression. "It's not bad, but it's not Ivy League."

"I can't get into an Ivy League," I say. "And paying for it would destroy me."

Grandfather whips a phone out of his pocket and presses a few buttons. "Hey, Ulysses." He pauses. "Uh-huh. As if I'd let you get away with that. I'll show you on the back nine on Tuesday." Another pause. "But that's not why I'm calling." He grunts. "No, not about that either, though I haven't forgotten. Actually, I'm calling to tell you that my tall, handsome, brilliant grandson is about to start school at NYU. It looks like I may have to realign the Belmont Endowment."

I can't tell what the man's saying, but the person he's talking to just got much louder. It almost sounds like he's shouting.

Grandfather smiles. "Why yes, perhaps his admittance letter was lost in transit somehow. You can send it to my address. I'll text you the details."

"What was that?" I ask.

"Yale," Grandfather says. "You were just accepted to Yale."

"I'm not sure that's a good idea." I cross my arms.

"Worried you'll fail?" He's smirking now, and it's irritating.

"It's not that," I say. "But Yale sounds very expensive, and you said I have to repay everything but the interest. I imagine I'll get more bang for my buck at NYU."

"You're intriguing, Gustav Liepa." But Grandfather's frown returns. "You know, I've always hated that name. You have no idea how much I hate it now." He narrows his eyes at me. "If you change your name, I'll give you the money for tuition for all four years. You'll only need to borrow money to cover your living expenses."

"Done," I say.

"Just like that?" He raises both eyebrows.

I shrug. "I've never loved my name. You overpaid."

I made him laugh twice in one conversation. At the time, I had no idea how rare that was.

And that's how I came to be known as Daniel Belmont. Unlike my father, Daniel Belmont makes the smart play every time. He never gambles. He never so much as buys a lottery ticket. He's smart, he works hard, and he doesn't cut corners.

It takes every bit of my time and one hundred and ten percent of my effort, but ten years later, I've actually built a company that Grandfather's proud of.

Forget Grandfather, it's a company that *I'm* proud of.

And in two months, Grandfather will finally retire, and he's going to name his successor, the person who'll inherit control of his entire estate. A decade ago, I had a snow*flake*'s chance of being named, but now? I'm neck and neck with my cousin Prescott. I knew this day was coming—Grandfather's seventy-second birthday—and I'm prepared.

So when my legal team calls and tells me they hear my IPO's about to go live, I'm ready. My road show presentation is polished, my books and numbers are immaculate, and I've got a bombproof team in place.

My mother let my father and her obsession with horses destroy the life she was born into, but I'm about to win it all back and more. All that stands between me and success is taking this company I've built public and showing my grandfather that I have what it takes to go all the way. I'll finally escape my father's legacy once and for all.

Of course, that's when my irritating little sister starts calling. I feel a twinge of guilt, but not nearly enough to answer her. I hear she married some rich guy. She's his problem, now.

She'll be fine, even without my help.

Because any help I give her just enables Dad. I'm not the bad guy here. I'm the smart one. The safe one. The one who will never, not ever, wind up like the rest of the Liepa family. I'm free of the name, the gambling addiction, and anything else that family ever tried to foist off on me.

Free.

That's what my cross-continent move was all about a decade ago, and it's still true today. The only way I stay free of the Liepa plague is to hold my ground and play it safe. Kris will figure things out without me.

She always does.

2

KATERINA

In Russia, you can't throw a rock without hitting a half dozen princes or princesses. Or at least, people claiming that title. It took the monarchy far too long to apply principles of primogeniture. But in my father's case, his title was at least backed up with both land and power. My father felt guilty, I think, that my mother died giving birth to me, and he denied me nothing. What I really wanted, however, I never quite got.

In almost seventeen years, my father never once spoke kindly to me. No matter what I mastered, or how I behaved, he never seemed to care. But today, I ripped my brand new gown while visiting my favorite horse, and he's never had any problem yelling over that kind of waste.

"Someone's going to notice," my father's saying when I reach the end of the hall.

I slide to a stop on the thick rug before he could possibly see me. My room's at the end of the main hall, but there's no way I'm marching past him like this. I need my lady's maid to try and repair the rip before he sees me—before tonight's ball.

"If we don't take the portraits down, someone will eventually notice that her eyes are the only blue ones, amid a sea of deep russet."

I'm not his child.

That's my first thought, and it would fit. If my mother had been unfaithful. . . But that can't be. I've been mastering my powers, and last week, I shifted into my equine form for the first time. That's a magic unique to the Yurovsky line—my father's magic.

But he's still talking.

He's arguing with someone who doesn't speak nearly as loudly as he does, perhaps Mrs. Cerny, our housekeeper. "Of course not," he mutters angrily. "But no one must know that her mother wasn't legitimate. Even her grandfather doesn't know, or he'd never have given her mother that dowry, and then I'd be in even bigger trouble than I am."

Legitimate?

My mother—whose dowry famously saved my father's estate—was not actually my grandfather's child? And my grandfather's struggling now, after a dispute with the czar. I'm sure if Grandfather had an excuse, he'd demand all that money back from my father in a heartbeat.

"But of course," my father bellows, clearly growing more agitated. "Not a single war to wage since the cursed Turkish mess that stupid San Stefano destroyed, which means our powers are essentially useless. The only way to clear the current debts is with another well-planned marriage. And when this fell right into my lap, it must be fate." He guffaws. "Seventeen's more than old enough."

I can't help the squeak I make. No one has spoken to me about marriage at all—this is to be my first ball.

But when Father's head pokes around the corner, his eyes widen and his nostrils flare. "Katerina."

I swallow.

"You should not be listening in on adult conversations around corners."

"Why not?" I can't help myself. "If I'm old enough to get married, aren't I old enough to find out about it?"

Father steps into plain view, his eyes flinty, and he straightens his coat. "I think you'll find that not much changes for women, when they become old enough to marry. Instead of listening to me, you'll simply be expected to listen to your husband."

"I don't have a husband." I frown. "And sometimes it barely feels like I have a father."

My dad's hand moves so quickly that I barely see it before his palm striking my cheek sends my entire body flying toward the wall. The sound of my body slapping into the wall is so loud that I can't tell whether it was the force or the sound that sets my ears ringing.

"My Lord, beating her just before a ball is not a good plan," Mrs. Cerny says softly. "It begins in less than two hours."

Once the spots clear from my eyes, I see our housekeeper standing a suitable distance behind my father, her head bowed. She may not dare to defy him, but she did defend me in her way. I appreciate the effort, however feeble.

"You will go to your room and rest until the ball," Father says sharply. "And when you come down, you'll be reconciled to the idea of marriage." He drops his voice. "It should hardly be a new one. You've known that proper ladies marry since the day you were born."

Thankfully, he doesn't even notice the rip in the dress, so that feels like a small win. The bad news is that my lady's maid insists she can't repair it quickly enough for the ball without leaving visible lines, so I'm stuck choosing. I can wear a gown from last year, with skirts that are noticeably too short, or I can pin a strange sash over the clumsy repair.

I opt for the sash.

Who knows? Maybe it'll start a new trend, even if the

gown is pale cream with green flourishes while the sash is bright blue.

I've certainly seen stranger things.

As I walk down the stairs, I notice that Dad and Boris are both waiting at the bottom for me. "You, too?" I lift my chin. "And you're fine with it?"

Boris—ten years older than me—has never been much of a brother, but I always thought that if it came down to it, he'd do whatever it took to keep me safe. "Lord Engelhardt's respectable. You shouldn't fight Father about this."

As I step onto the main floor, my jaw drops. "You—not only do you approve of marrying me off, but you've already picked out the man?"

Father and Boris wear nearly identical expressions of immutable resolve. I pelt them with questions the entire carriage ride to the Winter Palace, but they either deflect or outright refuse to answer all of them.

"At least tell me about this Lord Engelhardt," I say. "Is he my age? Is he tall? Short? Where does he live?"

Father compresses his lips, glancing out the window of our carriage and watching resolutely as we pull up in front of the massive, three-story-tall green and white palace. The windows appear to be practically endless as we roll past, but eventually our carriage comes to a stop in the front.

"He's very wealthy," Father finally says. "And he's delighted to meet you and finalize your engagement tonight." As if that's all the information I could possibly want, he climbs out of the carriage and strides toward the massive front doors, leaving Boris and me to scramble along behind him.

"I checked," Boris says. "He's not a terrible person."

Not a terrible person.

Four words to describe the man they're marrying me off to—hardly reassuring. I gather up my skirts and race after him. "But have you spoken to him? Do you know him at all?"

"I can't say that I have," Boris says.

"Why not?" I know I sound like a whining child, but I can't help it. Boris will never have a moment in his life where critical things are being decided about him without his input —he's a man. They get to make decisions for themselves. As my brother, I thought he might show a bit more of an interest in what happens to me.

"Listen." Boris stops, grabbing my right arm and spinning me to face him. "You didn't have a mother to teach you anything, and people have made accommodations for that, but you will not embarrass Father and me today. Am I clear?"

I open my mouth, and then I realize I'm not sure what to say.

He shakes me.

"You've made no promises to me," I finally say. "So why should I promise anything to you?"

Boris sighs, releasing my arm. "You're a disaster. Let's hope Lord Engelhardt is too dumb to care."

"I don't see how you could not know him," I say. "You've been coming to these balls forever."

"He's not often in attendance," Boris says. "He happened to see you at a picnic last week, and he reached out to Father with a proposal."

I caught *his* eye somehow? But how? And when? I don't recall ever dancing with a Lord Engelhardt.

As we pass through the open doors, Father's already talking to someone. Someone older than he is. Someone with slate-grey hair. Someone who's smiling—beaming, really—and gesturing in my direction.

Boris doesn't know him, because he's *older than our father.* They don't move in the same circles—not even close. "Is that Lord Engelhardt?" I hiss.

"It is," Boris says. "Now, be polite."

I've watched, each spring, as the shepherds lead the little sheep through the gate and into the barn to slaughter them.

I've always wondered why they didn't struggle, or even try to flee.

Not me, I think. *I won't walk toward that man with an insipid smile on my face. Father will have to chase after me with a whip and a rope if he means to kill me for the good of his estate.*

I spin on one heel and sprint to the right, colliding painfully with another person wearing a large and voluminous gown.

"Ow." As I straighten, I realize that the blow dislodged my sash and the strain reopened the tear that was rather hastily repaired.

The woman I collided with is wearing a large headdress, and she looks angrier than I imagine my father must be. Her eyes are flashing, and her rather ample bosom is trembling with rage.

"Katerina," a loud, clear voice calls. "I'm so sorry."

Alexei Romanov steps closer, one hand extended. "I must have bumped you. This is all my fault."

I drop my hand into his, which seems much larger than it was the last time I saw him, only a year ago. "Oh."

"Come with me, and I'll see whether Mother can find you a suitable gown to wear until yours can be repaired."

The woman who was about to destroy me forces a pained smile. "Your Majesty, what a delight to see you. You know this girl?"

"She's an old family friend." His smile's genuine.

As if I'm seeing him for the first time, I stare. His shoulders are broad. His eyes are sky blue. His brow's wide and clear, and his jaw's square and decisive. His hand tightens around mine.

"Let's go," he whispers. "Before more guests arrive and Mother starts shoving me in front of all of them." He tucks my arm inside of his elbow and begins expertly shifting us through the crowd, acknowledging everyone, but stopping to talk with none of them.

I glance over my shoulder, and notice that my dad's standing beside my brother, both of them scowling at me angrily. They can't do much about the czar's son whisking me away, though.

Alexei's like a trump card.

He's young, handsome, polite, and chivalrous, judging by the way he hauls me all the way upstairs and finds a maid to locate one of his sisters' gowns.

"I can't possibly borrow one of their gowns," I say. "My father would—"

"No sister of mine would ever even notice," he says. "Trust me. They have enough gowns between them to clothe all of Saint Petersburg. It's practically a crime." His eyes are dancing.

A crime. I can't help thinking of the true crime— marrying your daughter off to pay your own debts. I wonder whether this is what happened to my mother.

"You were always so happy—bubbly, really," Alexei says. "Is everything alright?" His eyes study mine. "You look. . .morose."

"I'm fine." I can't quite make the words sound sincere, but I did manage to say them.

"You know, Tatiana sounds just like that when she's lying." He's narrowed his eyes. "You may as well tell me. I won't stop prying until I discover the truth."

"Did you happen to notice my father earlier?" I ask.

He frowns. "You were moving toward him—with Boris, were you not?"

Alexei and my brother don't get along. That I recall. "They brought me here—my very first ball at the royal palace —for a reason."

Alexei's frown deepens. "Don't tell me."

"The man my father was standing next to. . ."

"With the grey hair?" Alexei arches one eyebrow. "No. It's not possible."

"We're supposed to finalize our 'engagement' tonight, only I just found out."

Alexei groans. "I'd heard that some families—you must refuse."

"Really," I say. "I do appreciate your help, but there's not much you can do." I pull the sash around my dress, wrapping it around twice, spreading the fabric out, and tying a large bow. "Just like this rip in my dress—I'll cover up what I can, and I'll figure out how to deal with the rest."

As if summoned by my statement, the lady's maid returns, her arms laden down with heavy dresses. "I've located three gowns none of them will ever miss." She eyes me. "I think at least one of them will work."

"You go change," Alexei says. "I have an idea for the rest."

I try to argue, but between him and the maid, I'm bundled off to the back room before I can compose a decent explanation as to how I'll handle things. Alexei disappears immediately, and then I'm half-undressed by the maid with lightning fingers two minutes later.

"This one, I think." The maid holds out a stunning, sky blue gown, embroidered with silver thread. "Your coloring is so similar to Miss Tatiana, and this one was made for her. She hates birds, or she'd probably be wearing it now."

"I can't possibly take her gown." I brush my fingers across the rip in mine. "If you could just sew up this section—"

"It'll only tear again," the maid says. "The fabric's too sheer to be sewn in that way. The only hope for that is a patch."

"But this gown—"

"Did I mention that Miss Tatiana has also gained a bit of weight." The maid's lip curls. "Trust me. She won't be missing this one—it no longer fits her properly."

I finally allow her to button and tie me into the gorgeous dress. A few moments later, I'm marching back out into the hall, ready to take on my father with renewed vigor. Surely, once I tell him that I'm not ready for marriage, Lord Engelhardt will agree to wait. Or maybe he'll move on to someone else who is ready now.

But when I reach the stairs, Alexei's waiting for me. He's beaming. "You know, we could do one another a favor."

I freeze. "What do you mean?"

"Mother has been after me to meet someone eligible."

My heart races. "Oh?"

"I'm not keen on marrying—not for a while yet. I'm far too young."

"I feel the same way," I rush to say.

"Perfect." He beams at me. "What father would force his daughter to marry an old man when the future czar of Russia is courting her?" He shrugs.

"And then what?" I ask. "I'm fine to wait as long as you'd like." I'm younger than he is. Even waiting ten years would be fine, if that's what he wanted.

"Oh, I couldn't possibly ask you to pretend for more than a season," he says. "Or however long it takes for that old man to find someone new." He winks. "So once he's otherwise engaged, we'll announce that we're nothing more than friends, and we'll both have been spared some family grief."

My heart sinks. "Oh. Right." I nod woodenly. Pretend. I force myself to do it now, too. It's good practice, apparently. "Perfect."

But from that moment forward, I make myself a different promise. It may be pretend to Alexei—a favor to an old family friend who shares a similar magical secret. But I plan to win him over this season, and by the end, he won't want to call our courtship off.

Not ever.

3

KRISTIANA

Perspective's a funny thing.

While I was growing up, a lot of my friends spent their free time shopping and watching television. I, meanwhile, was busy mucking stalls, cleaning tack, sweeping aisles and tack rooms and porches and the area behind the various cross ties. The bathrooms had to be cleaned twice a week, the trucks and trailers were always dirty, and there was always a horse that needed some kind of special care. Usually, there were several.

The work when you own a stable is never ending.

I didn't think of myself as a pampered princess. I mean, sure, we had a really nice farm, and we also personally owned a lot of horses, but we worked really hard for what we had. Maintaining it, paying taxes, all of it was a chore, and sometimes it was an axe hanging over our heads. But when I met Adriana and Mirdza, when their mother came to work for our mom, well. Compared to them, we were living in complete luxury.

I try really hard not to look at other people and judge them. I really, truly do. It's hard to know quite what someone's history is, and without knowing about the ins and outs of their life, it's unfair to make assumptions. But I know that Katerina was raised during the early 1900s, and I know her family was wealthy—Aleksandr has told me a little about his life then, and it was different than the world today, but not *that* different.

After hiding in her room for days, the pampered princess finally emerges, and the first thing she does is demand that we buy her a ticket to come with us to America.

"The thing is," I say, "I think the seats on the plane are sold out."

It's a lie.

I have no idea whether there are tickets left, and even if a last-minute ticket costs a fortune, it won't put a dent in Aleksandr's money. I know this to be true.

But I don't trust her.

She escaped from Leonid's a little too easily, and she's done nothing to connect with any of us. I wouldn't put it past them to have worked out a plan that she should come with us, inveigle herself with our group, and then report back.

"There must be other flights," Katerina says. "Can I call to place one? I have a phone."

She's clearly already watched too much television. Why can't she be more like Aleksandr was at the beginning, before he became addicted to the internet?

"I need to ask Aleks what he thinks," I say. "Who knows? Maybe he can convince someone at the airline to sell us their spare ticket."

Her eyes light up, making her already stunning face even more beautiful. I suppress the female urge to dislike someone just because she's prettier than me. It's unkind, and I've always hated it. I try never to give in to those baser impulses, but some people make it particularly hard. "That would be amazing. I'll just duck back in here and pack." She nods slightly. "Just in case."

Her acting all cute and grateful makes me feel horrible for

doubting her. What woman in her right mind could possibly be on Leonid's side?

I decide to do just what I said I would. Aleksandr knows her. I'll tell him she wants to come and let him decide whether she's trustworthy. But when I track down where he's gone, it's the stable. What on earth he's doing there, I have no idea. The man doesn't even like to ride. He loves when *I* ride him, but he almost never gets on a horse himself. He insists they're too unreliable, which I find hilarious.

I'm trolling around the barn, distracted by three or four different horses who need my attention, when I finally see him way past the stable walls. He's coming in from a run, which makes way more sense. Most of the staff isn't sure *why* the black stallion's allowed to roam free, but they all know it's true by now. The exterior perimeter fence is somewhat helpful in assuaging their concerns, but not entirely. Only a handful of them know his secret, and so far, they've all done a good job of keeping it.

I think it helps that we're in Russia. People here seem to do way better with things being *weird*.

I can't help myself. I stare transfixed, even now, every time I see him out running. His coat glistens. His mane ripples beautifully like waves on the ocean. And his tail streams almost straight back as his hooves fly over the soft sod, throwing chunks of grass and dirt in all directions.

"Really?" I yell, as he draws close enough to hear me. He slows down and arrows toward me, and I can at least drop my voice. "I'm panicked about finding my brother and warning him before Leonid can, and you're just. . .out for a run?"

He tosses his head, but even without words, I know.

"You'll miss it." I press one hand against the flat part of his head, between his eyes. "Russia. You love it here."

I even get it. His run was a goodbye of sorts, at least for now.

When I'm away, I also yearn for Latvia. It's home. I'm

sure it feels the same to him, and moving our assets and shifting things out and away has been a relief for me, but not for Aleks. He's finally back in his ancestral home, after being cursed and locked who knows where for a hundred plus years. Fleeing can't be comfortable.

"We'll come back," I say. "I promise we will. The bad guys never win, not in the long run."

He snorts, because he knows, after watching countless movies with me, that Hollywood isn't the real world. Americans can't seem to tolerate tragedy, which is fine for them, but the real world thrives on it. There aren't 'happy ending guarantees' in life. Depressing, exhausting, and unlucky are far more common than shining, smiling, and joyful.

He drops his head against my shoulder and I wrap my arms around his neck and squeeze. I let him lean against me —or rather, I lean against him—for one moment. Then another. But eventually, I have to tell him what's going on.

"As you know, our flight leaves in three and a half hours, and we need to go to Saint Petersburg first."

He huffs.

"And there's something else."

He lifts his head, his big, dark eye studying mine intently.

"You know how Katerina has basically been hiding since we rescued her?"

He bobs his head.

"She wants to come with us, and I lied and told her that the flight is full, because I'm not sure whether we can trust her. If she's not really on our side, she could tell Leonid more than just Gustav's American name. She'd know his address, too." I sigh. "She could lead Leonid right to him."

And that feels like the worst thing that could happen to me. Leonid already has the powers of fire, electricity, and water. All we have over on him is air and earth—and it's not really an advantage since he has three powers we don't. Water combined with really anything else would already be overpowering—but Gustav has no idea what's going on or how to use any powers he may acquire. Without any powers, he'd be an easy target. The fact that he changed his name for Grandfather—well, I'm sure that it's the only thing keeping him safe right now.

"We don't know her very well, and this is her first time to even leave that room. She's been having food delivered on trays like she thinks she's an honest-to-goodness queen." I rub Obsidian Devil's nose. "So you guys will have to decide whether to bring her or not."

Obsidian glances around, clearly checking to see whether we're alone.

"It's fine. The groom went home around lunch," I say. "You can shift." It helps that now, with his power fully restored, he doesn't shift entirely naked. Only when he was reliant on my help did that happen. "Go ahead."

I should be tired of seeing it, or at least, not in awe of the change anymore, but every single time Aleks shifts, I watch like a slack-jawed idiot. It's just so. . .*unbelievable* that a human can turn into a stallion and vice versa.

Only, this time, as my gorgeous husband shivers and straightens his shoulders, someone else is shouting loudly in Latvian. The words this person's saying should *not* be said out loud, at least, not in polite company.

Aleks and I turn at the same time to stare at. . .my dad.

"What are you doing here?" I ask.

My father's eyes are wide, and now that he's done shouting, it appears he has no idea what to say. It seems that all he can do is splutter.

"I can explain," I say, with no real idea of where to even start.

You'd think, after explaining this to Mirdza *and* Adriana already, that I'd be better at this part. I should memorize a speech or something.

"You see, I was cursed," Aleks says.

"It's true," my father says, his face pale. "All of it was *true*."

"What's true?" I ask.

Dad's shaking his head now. "I can't believe it. My uncle would be absolutely *giddy* to meet you, if he were still alive."

I blink. "Your uncle?"

"Technically, he's my great-uncle—your great-grandfather's younger brother. He moved to America before I was born," Dad says. "Father told me that he was always going on and on about how our family had the power to change into a horse." Dad laughs. "We all thought he was insane."

"Wait," I say.

"Tell me all about it," Aleks says.

Could my dad have been sitting on the answers we needed all along? My clueless father? It can't be true. Right? Surely if he knew anything helpful, he'd have noticed something about Aleks and Grigoriy and Alexei long ago. Surely.

But who would assume that any stories they heard about magical powers and shapeshifting horses were true?

"I don't really know anything," Dad says.

My heart sinks.

"Your grandfather thought it was all the worst kind of nonsense, and his father did as well. They never listened to him, and when he emigrated to America, he took all the old journals that mentioned it with him."

Journals?

"What journals?" Aleksandr sounds even more desperate than me.

"All I know is that when Grandfather's brother insisted on taking them, Grandfather put up a token fight and then caved immediately. He said he always thought they were strange, so if his brother was willing to sign away his inheritance as long as he could keep them. . ." Dad shrugs.

I close my eyes. "But we need those."

"I think I have a cousin or something living in the United

States, somewhere out west. I can rummage around and see whether I can find her address."

"Is this cousin's last name Liepa?" I cringe. With Gustav changing his name, Leonid could find and kill this cousin before Dad even gets back to Latvia, just to prove that he can.

Dad shakes his head. "I think my great-uncle changed his name—he fled because he deserted from the army. The Russians were—" Dad freezes.

Aleks laughs. "Go ahead. I won't get offended."

Dad winces, but he continues. "They were attacking, and we were stuck, drafting anyone we could to fight them. But then when they won. . ."

"I get it," Aleks says.

I'm sure he doesn't, but it's nice of him to say.

"My great-uncle wasn't someone who was overly brave," Dad says, "or at least, not according to my Grandfather. And he certainly felt no loyalty to Russia. He was done with war, so I heard he changed his name, but I can't recall what he changed it to." Dad taps his lip like that might help.

I'd like to badger him and press him and push until he comes up with an answer, but it won't help. If he doesn't know, he doesn't know. "Please, Dad, please find out as much as you can as fast as you can." It occurs to me that he's in *Russia,* for some reason. He didn't announce his visit, and it's a turbulent time, which makes it odd that he came now. Frankly, all of that is already not promising. Historically, he would only come to see me in a strange place. . .if we were about to lose the farm. I can barely force the words out. "What are you doing here, Dad? Is everything okay?"

"I've been watching the news," he says. "Things aren't safe. I worried that maybe you'd gotten trapped, and you weren't returning my calls."

I'm as bad as Gustav. Assuming the worst about him when, for once, he was actually being a dad. Or at least, maybe he is. I decide to press one more time. "Everything's fine back home?"

Dad winces.

I knew it. "What?"

"John had a heart attack," he says. "He's alright, though. He's recuperating at the hospital, but the barn's a bit of a mess."

I should fly straight home.

Gustav's the brother who ran away—like Dad's uncle, apparently, but John's been like a second father to me. Plus, he's never almost cost me the farm.

The thought of him in a hospital. . .

"Do you want to go home?" Aleks whispers. "You can look for the journals, and—"

"No," Dad says. "I came to make sure you were alright. John *insisted* on it."

Of course he did. He'd have come himself, if he wasn't stuck in the hospital. "I should at least stop there."

"I can go to America," Aleks offers. "You can meet me there." I can tell the offer pains him. Aleksandr hasn't been great about letting me out of his sight for more than half an hour lately, and even knowing that Leonid's powers, or any of their powers, can't directly hurt me, he's not taking any chances. "If that's what you want."

We argue back and forth as we walk back to the house, making no progress. I know John would come and check on me, whereas I'm positive Gustav wouldn't. He hasn't looked back once since leaving us. It would serve him right if his past came back to bite him on the backside.

Although, not if that bite kills him.

I'm leaning toward flying through Latvia on our way to America when we reach the kitchen. Grigoriy, Alexei, Mirdza, and Adriana are all staring at the screen. It always takes me a split second to switch gears into a new language after slipping back into Latvian.

But once the Russian clicks into place, I find myself staring, too.

A blonde woman with a frozen smile's saying, "—reports of large-scale executions are unusual, but they're only happening after purported trials. We should keep in mind that these executions are not like Stalin or Hitler—they're criminals who are being punished rightfully."

"Still, the reports we've received show that they're not receiving what anyone could consider to be proper trials," the man on the split screen says. He looks like he's reporting from another country. "Are we sure those who have been executed are actually criminals? No reports or evidence have been made available in any of these cases."

"The leadership was quite clear that they have seen the evidence and it's incontrovertible. Those individuals whose lives have been terminated presented a clear and present danger to the safety of Russia. We've always known that our new leader had a tough stance on the Red Mafiya. He has a zero tolerance policy, and he's promised to eliminate the crime syndicate in Russia within the year."

I blink.

"Well, if that's possible, it would be miraculous," the man says. "But it hardly seems likely that—"

"I spoke to His Majesty myself yesterday," the woman says.

She does look a little unhinged.

"Oh?" the man asks. "And what did he say?"

"He promised me that by this time next year, I'd be able to walk the streets in my underwear without fear that anyone would threaten me." She beams. "He said he intends to rid Russia of every single evil person residing within its borders." She leans closer to the camera. "And you tell me, Filip, if you found a colony of cockroaches living in your house, what would you do?"

Filip looks nervous. He shakes his head, blinking.

"You'd exterminate them with extreme prejudice." She nods slowly. "I can't fault our new monarch for doing the same. This country is his home, and he means to clean it up."

The screen cuts to a bizarre display of rainbow stripes.

"What happened to the feed?" Dad asks.

"Mr. Liepa?" Mirdza leaps to her feet—it still surprises me every time she does that, now that she's healthy and hale—and spins around to face us. "Are you okay? Is Liepašeta alright?"

Dad waves his hands, telling her to sit. "It's fine. I'm fine. I just wanted to make sure you and Kris were alright. The news has been. . .alarming."

"So you *flew* into Russia?" Adriana tilts her head. "You should have stayed put."

"Tell my daughter to call me occasionally, and I will." Dad's frowning now. He's probably tired of being scolded like he's a child. I suppose I can't blame him for that.

"John had a heart attack," I say softly. "I was going to fly through Latvia to see him, but. . ." I glance at the television. If Leonid's executing people without real trials, I'm not sure I can delay going to see my brother. He deserves to know what type of person is coming for him.

"I told her to go straight to America," Dad says. "I know you're worried about Gustav."

Mirdza and Adriana both glare. I can't blame them. My dad has not, historically, been the most trustworthy. Spilling our plans to him wasn't ideal. "He saw Aleks shift," I explain. I fill them in on the existence of journals that are possibly still in the custody of a cousin in the United States.

"Or they were thrown out decades ago for sounding insane," Adriana says.

"You can't really expect people to believe any of this without seeing it first," Mirdza says. "They probably thought their ancestors were profoundly crazy." She cringes. "No offense."

"None taken," Dad says. "They all thought my great-uncle was mad for even reading them, much less believing any part of them."

"We do need to leave soon, if we're going to try to make that New York flight," Aleks says. "Speaking of that, apparently Katerina wants to come with us to the United States."

"Absolutely not," Adriana says. "She's untrustworthy, and frankly, she creeps me out."

"You're just saying that because she keeps gazing longingly at your fiancé." Mirdza's smirking.

"That's not the only reason," Adriana says. "We freed her, and she's done nothing but spend days and days hiding in her room." She arches one imperious brow. "It's not normal, and it's certainly not the behavior of someone trustworthy." She glares at me. "I'm not sure why you told her we were even *going* to the States."

I sigh. "I shouldn't have said it, I suppose, but she surprised me."

Adriana leans forward, her eyes crazy, and makes a clawing motion in my direction. "Like a spider," she whispers. Then she shakes her head. "She can't come."

"I think she might have information we need," Grigoriy says. "She was with Leonid for a long time, and she may understand things we would miss."

"But she's right that we can't trust her," Mirdza says.

"I agree," Grigoriy says. "But you don't have to trust someone to learn from them."

I hate the idea, but after a few more minutes of talking, we decide to send my dad back to John with the promise that I'll follow as soon as possible, and the six of us rush to catch our flight.

After buying a ticket for Katerina Yurovsky, the enemy in our midst.

She's packed and ready to go as we rush to the vehicles, and we're stuck taking two, since we have eight people who all need to head for the airport. Dad comes in our vehicle, and I'm legitimately worried that Adriana might try to claw Katerina's luminous eyes out, so I suggest that Katerina ride with us too, leaving the twins to take Grigoriy's car.

"They're a strange pair," Katerina says, watching Alexei and Adriana loading their belongings into the back of the SUV.

"I don't think so," I say.

"They are," Aleks says. "But I think that's why they work." He's smiling.

"What does that mean?" Katerina looks ready to pounce on him from behind, and I regret suggesting she ride with us.

Aleks responds half-heartedly, the majority of his attention on the drive as we head out for the airport. "Alexei's always been too serious for his own good, and he's inflexible. His whole world has been black and white, good and bad. Adriana drags him by his collar into the real world."

"The world should be black and white," Katerina says. "And Alexei was one of the good ones. He made things better." Her lip curls. "She makes them worse."

"She's my best friend's sister," I say. "Watch what you say."

When I turn back, Katerina's watching me with a disturbingly blank face. "You think Adriana makes the world better?" The way Katerina says her name. . .like it's being pulled out of her with great pain. It makes me wonder why she loves Alexei so very much.

It also makes me really think about my answer before giving it. "Adriana takes a very imperfect, very inequitable world, and she forces it to make space for her," I say. "I think someone like you, someone for whom the world has always been paved in gold bricks, will struggle to understand her or the way Alexei and Adriana fit together."

I wonder what kind of training allows her to remain so expressionless. "Gold bricks." She frowns. "You think someone who twists the world for her own gain is a good match for the rightful leader of Russia? He's our shining golden prince, and he has a responsibility to his people, to keep them safe and make Russia the best place it can be."

I roll my eyes. "And that's your problem." I crane my neck around so I'm staring right at her. "To you, Alexei Romanov is some kind of totem, honor bound to fulfill his great destiny. To Adriana, he's a *man*."

Katerina looks sideways, now staring at Aleksandr instead of Alexei. "She's a perfect match for you, Aleks." Her sideways smile creeps me out even more than her impassive expression did. "She's impartial while still giving no quarter, and remaining loyal. I like her."

It shouldn't, but somehow, her assessment of me makes me hate her a little less.

I'm not exactly looking forward to the long flight to New York City, but I'm prepared to try and pry out whatever information I can along the way. If Katerina continues to surprise me, perhaps it won't be quite as bad as I thought. By the time we reach the airport, I've started to come up with the rough elements of a plan. We'll land in New York, check into a hotel, and while Katerina's recovering from jet lag, I'll go to see my brother. That way, she won't need to find out anything that she doesn't have to know, like where exactly he lives.

"Once we reach New York," she says, "do we have far to travel? I know the United States is very large."

"No, Gustav's in New York City," my dad helpfully offers. "In fact, you'll probably see signs for his company all over."

Before I can stop him, my dad goes and does it.

"Although, he goes by Daniel Belmont over there. His grandfather insisted he change his name or he wouldn't pay for his school." Dad's beaming with pride. "My son went to Yale University—which is the best school in the United States."

"You don't say." Katerina's impassive face is starting to irritate me enough that I just may punch her.

"Not that it matters to you," I say. "I'm still not sure why you're coming with us."

"If you're leaving Russia, who will protect me?"

She has a point there. If I were her, the last place I'd want to stay, if my rescuers were leaving, was the country where the person I'd fled was executing people without any kind of fair trial. Even so, I'm relieved when we reach the airport, and I get a little break from seeing Katerina's face. It takes a bit to walk my dad to the front counter, pay for his flight, and convince them to add Katerina to the flight with us.

I wish we were taking Aleksandr's plane, but it's not large enough to go direct to New York, and the paperwork involved is a nightmare. We decided it would be better to fly commercial this time. It's also nicer for my dad, because we can take him right to the gate this way.

But by the time that's all done, as we begin to board the plane, I'm ready to confront Katerina. I'll just ask her, point blank, if she's on our side. You can tell a lot from people when they're surprised, and I aim to knock that impassive look right off her face.

Or at least, that was the plan.

Only, she's nowhere to be found.

Somewhere between arriving at the airport and preparing to board our flight, Katerina disappeared.

❧ 4 ❧

KATERINA

I don't trust Leonid. Trusting him was the dumbest thing I've ever done. But I've also learned not to underestimate him. That was the second dumbest thing I ever did.

So when I hear that they're flying to the United States to warn Kristiana's older brother of the risk Leonid poses. . .

I'm torn. I want to get away from that lunatic and never look back. I want to run with them as far and as fast as possible. The only thing that might keep me safe from Leonid in the long run is distance. He might decide he wants to take over the whole world, but I'm hoping he'll be busy with Russia and other nearby countries, at least for a while.

And if this Gustav person never challenges him, maybe he'll let sleeping dogs sleep.

But Alexei. . .he's already lost his powers. He has no way to protect himself, no matter where he may run. To make matters worse, he's gotten confused by this woman, and he thinks he's in love with her. She's the trashiest, most irritating and base woman I've ever met.

I hate her.

If I'm being honest with myself, my dislike is probably

32

directly proportional to the magnitude of Alexei's love for her. I'm smart enough to know that, at least, but I still dislike her. And I think if Alexei's mother were here, she would agree with me. The two of them are a disastrous pairing.

Even so, she's what he wants.

Above all else, I want Alexei to find the happiness I never have. I want him to have everything his heart desires. He deserves it. He's only ever done the right thing. He brings joy to everyone around him. He's Russia's golden boy in looks and actions.

So I've pretty much resolved to run with them—and if he and Miss Trashy go south, well. I'll be there to pick up the pieces. But after I pack my bag, I leave my room to find out how soon everyone's leaving. No one's anywhere to be seen, so I walk outside. The voices I hear in the garden are male, and I don't *try* to eavesdrop, but I've always been pretty good at it.

I can't seem to help myself.

"—how long you can go without talking." It's Grigoriy.

"Oh, stop," Alexei says.

My heart jumps, just hearing his voice.

"I'm just saying, for sisters, they aren't very similar. Mirdza's so much more reserved. Polite. Calm."

"Adriana's passion is one of the things I love most about her." His words are like a dagger in my heart.

"Not when she's mad at you," Grigoriy says. "And I hear she's really ticked that you ignored her for days and days."

"I still think she should dump me," Alexei says. "I'm powerless now. I can't protect her. I can't protect anyone."

If saying he liked Adriana was a dagger, this feels like an evisceration. It's partially my fault. If I had done something, could I have warned them off? I knew Leonid wanted the water powers most of all. I knew he meant to gain enough leverage to take them. It was all he wanted that night, and he'd have given up most anything to get them.

"You're still strong," Grigoriy says.

But even I can hear the lie.

I can't change the decisions I made in the past. I can't fix things I broke. But I might be able to convince Leonid to trade information about the man who poses a threat to him in exchange for releasing Alexei's powers. I know he can do it —he granted my brother and Mikhail their powers back.

So it's possible.

If I go back to Leonid on my own with useful information on Gustav, it might be enough. He might agree to release Alexei. With his powers back, would he look at me again? Smile at me again?

When he tires of Adriana, when he realizes how *wrong* for him she is. . .it wouldn't hurt to be in his good graces. It wouldn't hurt to be the one who restored him to his former strength and abilities.

But to do that, I have to see Leonid again. After betraying him.

The very idea terrifies me. Leonid can't be predicted. No one ever has any idea what he'll do. Normal people can't comprehend how he'll react to things. It's not even entirely his fault. His father was. . .

No one who was raised as he was turns out to be healthy.

Would he even agree to see me? He let me leave. I know he could've stopped me from leaving, and I know why he didn't. I know all his biggest weaknesses, and I know the depths of his strength too. Will he let me back in? And how will he react when I tell him why I've come?

It takes me a few hours, and I'm worried I'll wind up on a plane to New York before I finally get the information I need, but then I hear it.

Gustav's legal name.

That's information that Leonid could flail around for weeks and weeks before discovering himself. With this, I'll be able to generate some goodwill. It's not easy to escape—there are so many of them that it feels like someone's always watching—but even Adriana's distracted during the security line.

And after I duck away, the rest is simple.

Stupid Aleksandr made it simple. He gave me identification and money on my third day with them. He told me that no one should ever feel trapped. And thanks to him, I'm not. I waltz right out of the airport and hail a cab.

It's shockingly easy to get from the airport to the new czar's palace. Of course, once I'm outside, I realize how far I am from Leonid's side. The place is even more heavily guarded than it was before, with external patrols of men with guns making sweeps, and as I sit and watch, I realize there are cameras *everywhere*.

The cameras are still new to me.

Everyone in this time period is used to them. They're no big deal to everyone now, but to me, taking exact recordings of everything that happens so you can watch it as many times as you want?

If I had been able to record that first night with Alexei, and if I could replay it over and over, how much would that mean to me? How much would he recall of our time together? Would recordings have made a difference? I think back to the first ball—how surprised my dad was—how beautiful Alexei was—how I cherished that silver and blue ball gown. . . Even a single photo would mean the world to me now. Reliving it in my head just isn't the same.

A hand grabs the hair at the nape of my neck and yanks backward. "Katerina. I didn't expect to see you." It's Mikhail.

I would know who it was even if his hand wasn't blisteringly hot. Even if I couldn't smell the faint whiff of brimstone that always clings to him. No one else has quite the same level of glee in his tone when he's caught someone unawares. When we were younger, he used to do the same thing with lizards.

"I wish I could say Leonid will be happy to see you, but I'm not sure that's true. He wasn't pleased that you left when you did."

I square my shoulders and send a little zap through my entire body—not a lot, but enough that he drops my hair.

"You've always been such a b—"

"Watch yourself," I say. "You can't really go around flaming people in broad daylight, whereas I could fry you like a bug in a zapper and play it off as the effect of a taser."

"We're about to go inside where there's far worse than me, and he's very unhappy with you." Mikhail tilts his head. "I don't have to fry you. I can just sit back and watch what he does."

"Alright, you two," Boris steps through the gate. "No more bickering. Leonid heard you're here." My older brother really should be on my side, but he never has been. He's always and forever only on his own side.

"I came here of my own volition," I say. "I don't need a police escort."

"Alexei turned you down again?" Boris asks.

"Lurking around and peering at what kind of security measures are in place is hardly a surrender," Mikhail says. "Did he really turn you down again?"

"He's already upgraded." Boris frowns.

I kick dirt at them so hard that it flies up in their eyes, and then I march past them both.

The guards on this round of patrols were here when I left—they know me. At least, they know enough to be afraid of me. I'm not really proving anything, but it feels nice to be walking in a few steps ahead of idiot one and two. I breeze down the main hall, only having to zap one guard who decides I may not be authorized. He jumps back quickly, which is always a little gratifying, and I continue on my way. But when I reach the throne room, it's irritatingly empty.

Boris is practically huffing when he catches up to me. A

little dirt shouldn't have set him that far behind, so maybe he's let himself get out of shape.

"He's not here."

"You've always had a knack for stating the obvious," I say. "Just tell me where he is."

His mouth twists in irritation, but he mutters, "Follow me," as he turns on his heel and storms out.

I don't expect to wind up outside, but that's where we are after I follow Boris down a long hallway I've never walked and through the side gate.

In fact, I'm staring at the barn. Leonid didn't grow up wealthy like we did, and he knows almost nothing about horses. In spite of his best efforts, he's never been able to shift into his horse form, since he hasn't mastered all his magical abilities yet. I think that's why he's never been too keen on horses. He avoids stables and riding, as a general rule.

This is the last place I expected to see him, but as we walk up, I can't help noticing what he's doing.

Blowing things up.

Spectacularly.

And then, more surprisingly, he's putting them back together. It's not quite as elegant, but it's working disturbingly well.

First, he stares intently at a large, round bale of hay. Then he spreads his hands and shoots his fingers outward. The bale of hay explodes, but before the pieces can even flutter to the ground, his hands flex and then come together, and as he tightens them back into a ball shape, the hay sucking back in, the broken pieces knitting together and reforming into a bale. Even the string tightens back down, the threads weaving together and retying.

I've never seen anything like it.

"The elements work together, you know," Leonid says, his eyes still trained on the bale of hay. "All living—and unliving —things have an electric charge, and most living things are made with at least some component of water. Add in fire, and you know, there's not much I can't do." He drops his hands and looks at me. "Not *much*, but soon, there won't be *anything*."

"I'm not sure," I say. "The only people who can use wind and earth just left the country."

Leonid smiles. "It will take me some time to fully master my abilities here. As you know, once I gain a new affinity, I'm wiped out for days."

I did know. I debated telling the others—they seemed to be struggling to grasp why he let them leave. They had no idea that their departure was exactly what he needed. Had they stayed, he'd have collapsed in front of them. They might have caught him and caged him while he was down.

"I didn't share your secret," I say. "Instead, I came here, offering to share one of theirs."

"But you want something for it." Leonid sighs. "That's the problem with you, Katerina. It always has been. You've had countless opportunities to *be* on my side, but you never take it. In your heart of hearts, you've always been *his*."

We both know who he means. He's the only man I've ever really loved. Even if to Alexei, it was always fake.

To me, it's always been real, and Leonid has been the only one who saw that. "You won't be shocked at what I'm here to offer."

Leonid raises one eyebrow. I find it hard to look at him sometimes. He's so beautiful, like a work of art, or someone out of a painting. Even when he's wearing a look of displeasure, his beauty cuts like a knife. "Go ahead." He waves his hand through the air. "Offer it already."

"I'm sorry. Did you have a full day of exploding things planned, and I'm interrupting?"

He laughs. It actually makes his face even more unbearably perfect. But it's not the same kind of beauty that Alexei has. No, Alexei's like the horse, running through the field.

He's like a shining golden retriever, smiling at the world. Leonid's beauty is different, deadly—like nightshade, or a blue-ringed octopus. He's a poison dart frog, or a leopard that's half-starved. He's as likely to destroy you while you ogle him as anything I've ever seen.

"You know what I'm here to ask for." I cock my head. "You know what I want."

"I can't give you Alexei, even broken though he is. Someone else already wandered along and snatched him up." He looks as irritated by that as I am.

I scowl.

"Ah. That's it. You think if *you* can be the one who fixes him. . ." His smile broadens. "You have never been creative, not a day in your life. Ah, Katerina. You're so predictable, and just like the dozen other times you've sacrificed yourself for him, you could serve him his powers on a silver platter and he still won't even *notice* you."

I set my jaw. "Will you release his powers or not?"

"It doesn't really matter to me, you know," Leonid says. "My power is unchanged, whether I release his back to him or refuse."

"Right," I say. "Giving them back costs you nothing—you'll still be the only person who can wield all three powers combined." I can't help thinking of the bale of hay—which could be most anything on earth—and shuddering.

"You know that I don't do things for nothing." Leonid steps toward me, the angle of his mouth sharp, and the glance in his eyes predatory. "So what are you offering that I need?"

"I—well."

He steps closer still, and as he draws right up next to me, a chill runs up my spine. "Nothing." His voice is a bare whisper now. "There is nothing you have, Katerina, that I want."

"The one person who could ruin your plans, the one person who could take it all away. . ." I swallow.

His eyes go hard. Dead. "You should not bring him up."

"If his claim has priority. . ."

"She didn't say it did," he says. "She said it *might*."

"But if it *does*." I wait. He must have been thinking about that night, the pleading with Baba Yaga, and how pathetic he was. The trouble, she told us, was that she's gifted her power to humans twice, and she's not sure exactly how the magic will interact. . . And if it was Gustav's family that had supervisory access to all five powers, which it must be since Kristiana's a null, then they won't know who draws from the higher point until they go head-to-head.

"You may struggle to believe this," Leonid says, "but I don't want to attack him. I hope he stays hidden away, head in the sand, forever."

"You're right," I say. "I don't believe you." That's not something Leonid would ever count on. Nothing in his life has ever gone his way. He's the kind of person who takes care of problems before they can attack. "I know you've been looking for him, but you'll never find him."

"Oh?" He drops to his seat next to me then, putting all his weight on the bale of hay he recently reconstructed. "Then you tell me what exactly you're offering in exchange for the restoration of your boyfriend's magical powers."

"He isn't my boyfriend, as you well know." I sigh. "But what I'm offering is the information you need to locate and eliminate the threat. I'm offering Gustav's *real* name."

Leonid's face doesn't shift a single hair. "His real name." He snorts. "And you'd give that to me? I doubt Alexei would thank you for it. In his mind, this man is the only one who might restore his magic. No?"

"We both know you're going to find him eventually. What I'm really offering you is *time*. You'll be able to locate him before they can prepare him. You could reach him before they hide him or teach him or. . ."

"You tell me his name, and I can fly to America and

explode him into a million tiny pieces. Is that what you're suggesting?"

"Or something less grotesque, yes." I can't help cringing a little.

"His death would be on your hands." He frowns. "You're really fine with that?"

"Like I said." My tone is tight. "He was going to die from the moment he was born. I'm just accelerating the timetable a bit."

"But think how upset your boyfriend will be when. . ." He stands. "Oh. You don't want me to restore his powers *right now*, do you?" He smiles. "You want me to do it. . .when you tell me to do it. You want to take the credit for saving him."

I shrug. "I mean, it helps you too. Think about it. Alexei has been using the water powers for years and years, taught by his father who was an expert as well. He's proficient. And with Aleksandr and Grigoriy, they'd make a formidable opponent. But if you can attack now, eliminate their possible trump card, and then return to Russia, leaving Alexei his powers as a show of good faith. . ."

"Then you could claim credit, and you'd be a hero, and you'd be able to keep him away from me to keep him safe." He shrugs. "It's not your worst plan."

"So?"

"I'll do it," he says.

I wanted it to work. I thought it might, even. But I'm still a little shocked when it does. I mean, he's actually saying that he'll just give Alexei his powers back, and more than that, he'll let me claim credit for it. A bubbly sort of joy escapes in the form of a giggle-laugh.

"Wow, that was a strange noise," Leonid says. "Well, you better pay me."

"The name of the brother is—"

"Daniel Belmont," Leonid says, "and he lives in Manhattan. His company's about to make an initial public offering."

I freeze. "You already knew."

He shrugs.

"So you won't give Alexei his powers?" My heart sinks. How did he already find out? Being the czar of a large country must come with some perks, I suppose, but I hate thinking that he already has this kind of power. "Is he already dead?"

"I said I'd give Alexei his powers back, and I meant it. You were willing to tell me the name. I'll hold up my end of the bargain."

"No way," I say. "You're not that kind of guy."

Leonid leans closer to me, his breath brushing warmly over my ear. "You have no idea what kind of guy I am. To you, I've always been the *wrong* guy. I've always been a piece on your chessboard, a pawn you didn't care about. But it doesn't matter. I'll do this anyway, because it amuses me."

"Amuses you?" Now I'm shivering, and it's not at all cold outside.

He steps backward, retreating down the same path he took toward my side. "Yes." He holds out his hands. "The idea that every single time your little boyfriend uses his power, he'll know it's because I allow it? That his magic exists only because of my generosity? That's why I'll do it." His smile is genuine.

Genuinely irritating.

"But you can take it back at any time." My voice is too flat. He can tell I'm displeased.

"That's always been true. For him. For you." He tilts his head, and I can feel it, like a light switch going off. My power's gone.

"So that's the payment, then? I can have my power, or he can have his?"

Leonid shrugs. "Everything has a cost, and what you brought me, I already had."

"Fine." My nostrils flare. "Fine. If that's what you want, you can have my power."

"Oh, I already do," he says. "What I'm trying to gauge is how badly you want this for *him*."

"I'll make the trade," I say.

Before I can storm off, Leonid speaks, and his voice is so calm, so quiet, and so stark that it once again makes me shiver. He's like this sometimes, like the striking of a viper, like the flick of acid rain, deadly earnest and unforgiving. "And Katerina, if you happen to come in contact with this Gustav when you run back to Alexei?"

I swallow, forcing myself to ask. "Yes?"

"Do your best to keep him in America," he says. "Because if they advance toward me, if they make a move of *any* kind to work against me?"

I stay upright, forcing myself to hold his gaze.

"I really will take it personally. And if I have to come after them, if I feel like they're a threat, I'll raze them to the ground. That's a promise."

I'm not sure, in that moment, what comes over me. I'm not usually the kind of person to yank on a tiger's tail. I'm certainly not someone who would taunt a cobra. It's just not how I behave. But I can't help myself. "What are you doing, Leonid, with all these executions? You may be powerful, but if you let everyone find out you're a psychopath, they'll be forced to do something about it."

He nods slowly. "I'll keep that in mind. I shouldn't let anyone else find out the truth about who I am."

For a split second, it almost feels like I've offended him— or stranger, hurt his feelings. But there's no way. . .Leonid doesn't really *have* feelings. Not like a normal person.

"Don't worry, though, princess. They're a necessary evil, no more, no less. They'll be done soon enough, and then things will be much simpler all around, I assure you."

"I'll text you when I want Alexei's powers restored."

Leonid just nods, but as I'm exiting the palace, one of the guards hands me a phone. "It's from His Majesty. He said to text or call him from this phone, or he won't get your message."

I'm distinctly uneasy as I head back to the airport, again bound for New York City, but not because of Leonid, precisely. No, I'm uneasy because, other than losing my powers, I got what I wanted with almost no sacrifice. Leonid *never* does something for nothing. Never, ever.

Which means there's something I'm missing.

And it's big.

I just can't figure out what it is.

5

GUSTAV

I hate horses.

From the moment I was born, they were foisted upon me. My mother loved them. My father's obsessed. Our entire family, I was told as soon as I could understand words, are *horse* people. We love them. We raise them. We race them. We live and breathe them.

Only, I never really got the draw.

They're large. Clumsy. Stupid. They stink. They eat between twenty and thirty pounds of grass or hay a day, and where does all that go? Poop. Poop that humans idiotic enough to keep them constantly have to deal with. From the moment that Daimler invented the car, we should have retired the less reliable, more costly, and less useful version of transportation. Forever.

Who wants to ride a motorcycle that spooks at trash and tries to kill you?

It's a stroke of irony, really, that my company revolves around horses. Or maybe it's not. They do say that you should do what you know in business, and I knew *nothing* as well as I knew horses. It makes sense that when I decided to start a company, I'd focus on one that siphons off an industry

I already knew and hated. I have no guilt taking money from people dumb enough to gamble it all away. It feels, for once, like I'm getting a little of my own back. I make money off people who can't keep from betting on horses, and I do it in three ways, hence the company name, Trifecta.

Jean walks in during my call and hands me a folder. Her face is totally neutral, as always. "Thought you might want to see this."

I finish up my conversation with our in-house lawyer before hanging up and flipping the folder open.

It's one piece of paper.

But it's kind of an important one. "Hey," I shout at her retreating back. "The SEC approved our filing?" I stand up, a half-smile stealing its way across my face. "You're kidding."

One of my friends told me three days ago that he'd heard I was about to be approved. After the initial adrenaline surge —nothing. We waited. Waited some more. But finally. . .

"Start calling to set up—"

Jean shifts so I can see her, and she's already on the phone, smiling and talking at the same time, clearly anticipating my next step.

I swear under my breath, pick up my phone and start making some calls myself. It's roadshow time. My hands are shaking as I line up our first appointments, blocking the time off in our shared calendar, which is stupid, because I'm totally prepared for this. We already decided to do New York appointments for the first three days and then start traveling. Our video's spot on—we tested it on a few friends of mine who are also decision-makers with big firms. I've already spoken with most of the biggest investors, and based on our planned initial stock price, which is rather conservative, and our modest percentage for sale, success should be a lock.

Even so, I need this to fund and hold, because Grandfather turns seventy in two and a half weeks, and he's going to announce his successor at that party.

My contact at Black Rock calls me fifteen minutes later. "Danny boy—we had a deal fall through, and I just got your message that you got your approval." I hate that he always calls me Danny boy, but you don't quibble over anything with the people who run the big funds. They make or break IPOs.

"I did," I say. "Wow, you must have found out as fast as I did."

"You probably wanted to start your presentations with a few softballs, but Evan has time in two hours. How'd you like to come in with a bang?"

"Of course," I say. "The boardroom on Hudson Yards?"

"Yep," he says. "See you at three."

So much for grabbing lunch. Still, better to nail our first presentation, even if I wind up a little hangry by the end. It's a little bit of a frenzy when I hang up, but we had most things ready to go, and I'm heading downstairs, briefcase in hand, my team assembled with thirty minutes to spare. Their boardroom is six minutes away by cab, or it's an eleven-minute walk, so we're good even if we can't hail a cab easily.

Except it's raining when I reach the lobby.

I don't see any cabs, but I'm ordering an uber—with room for six—when someone calls my name from across the lobby —not my real name. My former name: Gustav.

Whoever it is clearly came in through the tenth street entrance, which is where normal foot traffic enters, but for them to know that name, I would expect them to come in off the street. I turn slowly, after clicking approve on the uber, which will arrive in four minutes, and that's when I see who's calling me.

She's the last person I want to see, or at least, the second to last. It's not really her fault that she looks *exactly* like our mother. I'd forgotten how much it hurts, seeing her face. It's also not her fault that she's a direct line to Dad, the one person on Earth I'd really rather never see again.

But when Kristiana spots my face, she brightens noticeably.

That makes me feel terribly, terribly guilty. When she jogs toward me, people are following her. So many people. One of them I recognize from her wedding announcement—her husband, the Russian nobleman. The others are complete strangers, until I realize that the girls, I know.

"Gustav!" Kris is a little out of breath from running across the lobby. "I can hardly believe I'm here—or that you're here. It's been *years*." She doesn't look angry that I've been ducking her calls. She doesn't look annoyed that she had to travel to the United States and hunt me down. She doesn't even look upset that I missed her wedding.

She looks. . .delighted to see me. Is she faking?

"And look!" She gestures behind her. "It's Adriana and Mirdza. Can you believe how old everyone is now?"

She's speaking in Latvian, which is somewhat helpful, because at least the people around me have no idea what's going on.

"This poor woman thinks she knows me." I glance at my phone and hand it to Jean. "Go and wave the uber driver down. I'll be out in a moment."

When I turn back, Kris looks annoyed. Of course she does. Her English is as good as mine, one of the joys of an American mother combined with her education at Oxford. But what shocks me is that *everyone* in her group looks annoyed. Surely they can't all speak English, too?

But then I vaguely recall Mom teaching Adriana and Mirdza to speak English like it was some kind of lark—the four of them would all chatter along while riding. . .in English. Still, it's not the girls who are glaring the most.

It's the three men, and they're disturbingly large, nerve-wrackingly aggressive men. One of them looks ready to run me through with a sword. If it was still the eighteen hundreds and people actually used swords.

Kris compresses her lips, but she waits to speak until my team's gone. "Poor woman?" She arches an eyebrow. "Really?"

"They don't know me as Gustav," I say. "And none of them speak Latvian. I'm Daniel Belmont."

"I'm aware," she says. "I've let you hide over here for a decade and change, and. . ." She frowns.

I think she was about to say she's never asked me for anything. At least she didn't have the audacity to say that out loud.

"Listen," she says, recomposing herself. "I'm not here to ask for something. I don't need money."

"That's a first," I say. "And this one time, I'd actually give it to you, but only if you *go away*."

The man I think is her husband, the one with hair so dark it's almost black steps toward me, his face a veritable storm cloud. "That's more than enough rudeness for one lifetime. You will speak to her with respect, and you will—"

"Grandfather turns seventy in two weeks," I say, ignoring her high-handed spouse. "I've timed my IPO perfectly—do you even know what that is? It's an initial public offering, and it's something you do when your company's going public. I've timed it to happen right before Grandfather's birthday. When it funds, he's going to name me his successor, and then, after that, I'm all yours."

"You always say you'll call me later. You always say that, soon, you'll have more time." Kris doesn't look composed now. She looks close to tears.

"This is different," I say, feeling a little guilty. I have put her off a lot, and she didn't gamble our money away or leave me motherless. "We can take some time off and tour around the United States in a few weeks. I'll buy you a house in Maine with a barn and you can live here during the summer. Whatever you want, whatever you need, I'll make it happen in a month. But right now, you have to go away and leave me alone. Okay?" Because if Grandfather even so much as catches a glimpse of her, it's going to remind him of the misery I've spent a decade disassociating myself from. His daughter's death.

I expect her to be proud of me, or at least willing to wait just a little longer. Instead, my sweet little sister who has always accepted my excuses, my delays, and my refusals leans toward me and slaps me hard, right across the face. The crack's almost deafening.

Everyone in the entire lobby turns to stare.

"You will come with me," she hisses in Latvian, "or I will start to scream, loudly and in English, about all the ways in which Daniel Belmont sexually assaulted and violated me."

She has *got* to be kidding. "I have a meeting right now. If you *insist,* I can see you after, but not for very long."

"This man right here," she screams, in English, "Daniel Belmont, last night, he got drunk and—"

I clap a hand over her mouth. "Knock it off." I didn't grab her hard, but apparently any sort of touching is too much, because her broody husband grabs the lapels of my coat and lifts me up until my feet are dangling off the ground.

I consider defending myself, but building security's coming, and if I take his head off, there's no way I'll get out of this building and make my meeting in time.

"Put him down," Kris whispers.

Strangely, her attack-dog listens. Maybe he's not her husband after all. Maybe he's very devoted hired help.

"Your team can handle your meeting," Kristiana says. "I'm not being melodramatic when I say you must come with us. This is truly a matter of life and death."

It always is, with her. "What did Dad do this time? Ostrich races?" I shake my head. "No, wait. I know. Card game with his friends that got 'complicated'?"

"It's not even about Dad," she says, clearly lying.

It's always about Dad. "It doesn't matter. Listen, I have your number, and I'll call you when this meeting's done.

Okay?" I don't wait for her to answer, and I certainly don't stand around to give her time to sic her whoever-he-is on me again. I pivot on my heel and head for the door.

That's when *something* wraps around me, no idea what because I can't see it, and I'm dragged backward.

My brain tries to make sense of it but can't. I really have no idea what's happening. One minute, I'm reaching for the handle of the door, my eyes making contact with Jean's where she's holding the uber, and the next, I'm sliding across the floor at a forty-five degree angle, my heels dragging against the marble tile.

"What in the world—" My sputtering's cut off by, well, it *feels* like a gag, but I can see that there's nothing there. No one came close enough to even touch me, either.

People all around me are staring, their faces scrunched up, and building security, which had finally drawn close and then backed off when Kris had the guy put me down, is staring at me blankly.

Like me, they have no idea what to do.

One of them picks up a walkie talkie, at least, and he's muttering something. Another person has their phone out, and they're recording. Just as quickly as I was whipped back, the phone and walkie talkie fly out of the people's hands and smash simultaneously into the wall.

"No recordings," the stocky man near Mirdza says. "This is a private issue."

Jean has rushed through the front door, and she's staring at me, wide-eyed.

I lift one hand and wave her off, hoping they'll muddle through the meeting without me, because it's looking less and less like I'm going to successfully break away. But I'm much more alarmed than before. I'm really not sure what exactly Kris has gotten herself into, and maybe she's not wrong. Maybe it really *is* life and death if she's wrapped up with someone who has the kind of technology that can drag people through lobbies without even touching them.

A moment later, I'm being pulled through the back doors into the stairwell, and after Kris and her posse have followed me, instead of being dragged farther, I'm lifted into the air.

I'm floating.

Mid air.

It's like I'm in the middle of some kind of strange sci-fi movie.

That's when I realize the gag's gone. "What on earth is happening?"

"I'll explain all of it," Kris says. "But as you may finally believe, it's going to be a bit of a fantastic tale, and it would be better if we weren't explaining it in a public place."

My mind's spinning like a pinwheel. The Black Rock meeting is already a disaster. I have to assume they won't buy any shares at all. And if they don't purchase any. . . The bigger issue is, who might they tell that we're unreliable and disorganized? The lead not making it to the very first meeting is bad.

Very bad.

But what on earth is happening with Kristiana? If she really is in physical danger. . .I feel terribly guilty for dodging her calls. If I weren't such a lousy brother, we might not have wound up here.

"Alright," I say. "Release me, and I'll go with you."

Kris narrows her eyes. "Do you mean it?"

"You've made your point," I say. "Something strange is clearly going on, and if you insist that it can't wait for my Black Rock meeting to happen first, well. I'll follow you and hear you out right." Not that I have much choice, apparently.

In that very moment, the doors to the stairs burst open, and an already overcrowded landing area is crammed tighter when two armed officers shove through, pointing their guns at Kristiana's tall attack dog and the big, burly one. Those are the two I'd aim at, too, if I had a gun. The pretty boy with

Adriana looks. . .non-threatening, like he used to be a Calvin Klein model and hasn't found his calling in life as an adult yet.

"Identification," the first officer says. "Now."

Kristiana's dark-haired body guard man holds up one hand. "I have to reach into my pocket for it. Unlike you, I'm not armed. So don't be alarmed."

I doubt his Russian accent reassures them, but after the two officers exchange a glance, the one with a gun on tall-dark-and-Russian nods.

He fishes out a passport—bright red and gold, clearly Russian—and hands it over. "This woman is my wife, and she is that man's sister."

So he is Aleksandr—I think that was his name.

The first officer lowers his gun to take the passport, reads it, or at least tries, and says, "Alessander Volonsy." I recall from the wedding invitation that it was Aleksandr Volkonsky, but it's probably close enough for an American.

"This was a domestic dispute," Aleksandr says. "I assure you, your interference is not required."

"Interference?" The other officer raises his gun an inch and frowns. "We were told that you dragged this man—" He tosses his head in my direction. "—across the lobby and shoved him into this stairwell."

"That's what happened." Kristiana's smiling. "But if you have a brother, I bet you've wanted to drag him around from time to time."

The officer's hand wobbles a little.

"My brother has been ignoring my calls for weeks, and lately, I've been calling more and more. We have some complicated family stuff to work out, and he refused to listen." She tilts her head and sighs dramatically. "Not a good time for him apparently, but then, it never is."

The second officer glances at me, and I don't argue. He drops his weapon. "In the future, you shouldn't drag people, especially tenants of this building, through public places. I can't speak for Russia, but we frown on that in America."

"I'll remember that," Kristiana says. "I'm so sorry to bother you."

"Someone in the lobby claims you smashed their phone," the first officer says as he returns Aleksandr's passport.

"I did," the stocky man beside Mirdza says. "I'm sorry about that." He reaches for his pocket and both officers lift their guns again. "I'm just grabbing my wallet."

They relax a bit, and he pulls out a wad of cash. "Can you offer this to the person whose phone I destroyed and tell them that I'm very sorry?"

"That's not really how—" the first officer starts.

But the second one takes the cash and nods. "We'll take care of it."

I don't have the heart to tell the stocky guy that the person who lost their phone will never see a dime of that money. It is New York, after all. Hopefully that guy had insurance on it. The wad of cash does get rid of the officers, though, thankfully.

Before Kris can start ordering me around again, my phone rings. It's Jean, of course. "Yes," I say. "I'm delayed, so you're going to have to start without me."

"I've never—I can't lead the meeting."

"You can," I say. "You know this stuff better than anyone other than me. But if you don't want to, that's why we're paying the lawyers and that stupid investment bank so much money. Tell them I've had a family emergency and let one of them take lead. They came up with half the content."

"Daniel, we need you—they want to hear from Trifecta's Founder and CEO about our vision."

"And starting tomorrow morning, everyone will hear from me. Tell them that, thanks to an unforeseen emergency, I'm detained and they're still getting the first pass—no other calls or meetings today. At the end of the day, if they aren't interested, it's fine. We have two dozen other meetings set up already with more to come."

"But if they don't commit to buying any," Jean whispers, trailing off. "They're *Black Rock*."

"You can do this," I say. "I believe you can." Then I hang up, because there are six people staring at me, and I'm still standing in a stairwell after being dragged here by, well, by *air*. Kris has some explaining to do, and quick. "I really do have two weeks of solid meetings. The roadshow is the single most important moment in the entire IPO process. You have some truly horrific timing."

"You're not safe," Kristiana says. "I'm not here for me. I'm here for you."

I roll my eyes. "I think I'll take my chances."

"Have you been following Russian politics at all?" Aleksandr asks.

Knowing he is my brother-in-law, and that he's fully Russian, I'm actually impressed that his accent's so slight. "I know the Russians have gone entirely mad and voted to return to a monarchy."

"Britain has a monarchy," Mirdza says.

"Britain has a frosting monarchy," I say. "They're a social nicety. The monarchs are trotted out for photos and to keep bored people happy. They're not involved in the government in any way." But something that was digging at me before hits me then. "Wait." I turn toward the pretty, wannabe Calvin Klein guy. "You—the Latvian citizen named Adriana who was dating the would-be Romanov czar. . . Was that *you*?"

The blond man with bright blue eyes shrugs. "Alexei Romanov."

I can't even speak when I feel my phone buzzing this time. I whip it out and press it to my ear. "What, Jean? I told you, you can do this, and I'm really busy."

"Jean?" a man's voice asks. "Who's Jean?"

"Oh." Almost no one has this phone number. I assumed. . .incorrectly, clearly. "I'm sorry. Who is this?"

"I was given this number by the secretary at your company, one Kalinda Roth."

Kalinda never passes out my personal cell phone. It's basically the entire first day of training. She's been with us for four years. "I'll be sure to talk to her. In the meantime, is there something I can help you with?"

"This is Daniel Belmont?"

"Speaking," I say.

"My name's Theodore Price, and I'm an agent with the Department of Homeland Security. Your name has been given as a sponsor for a visa for a young woman named Kat—"

"Ho there, Theodore. I can save you some time. I have exactly *zero* non-US citizens I would sponsor for a visa. So you can go ahead and cross their name off. Or do you cross mine off? Either way, I'm really busy. You either have the wrong Daniel Belmont, or there's been some other mix-up." I hang up.

It's probably a scam, but on the outside chance that the Department of Homeland Security is confused, it's really not something I have time to deal with today. They can mark my name off and keep calling whoever they need to call about this illegal immigrant or whoever.

"Where can we go to talk that people will not see us?" the stocky man asks. "I'd rather not drag you somewhere, but I will if I must."

"Destroying phones the entire way, no doubt." I sigh. "My apartment is only two blocks from here. Let's go there."

They follow me through the stairwell into the main lobby and out the tenth street exit. They wouldn't all fit into my car in any case, so we may as well walk. It occurs to me that I might be able to slip away from them, but my sister appears to be deadly serious about all this. I wonder what kind of mess she's found herself in for it to be life and death, and for her to have the kind of tech I have only seen in science fiction movies.

"While we walk, why don't you tell me whose life is at risk, exactly," I say.

"Yours," Kris says. "You couldn't be bothered to answer the phone, and John just had a heart attack, and you practically ran away when I flew all the way out here."

"John what?" That makes me freeze. "Is he alright?"

"He's recovering," she says. "I wanted to fly home to deal with him, but I came all the way here to save your ungrateful life instead. Because that's what family does."

She seems utterly serious. That gives me something to think about for the last block.

"This is a pretty nice building," Mirdza says.

"Thanks." I wave at my doorman, Norm. His eyes widen as we walk in, and I shake my head. He's a pretty chatty guy, which is fine usually, but I don't have time or the words to even try to explain my entourage this time.

"You've done well for yourself in America," Adriana says.

"I'm sorry," I say. "Did the three of you get some kind of Russian package deal? Or, like, how did you all wind up with Russian boyfriends?"

"Fiancés," Adriana says. "Not that you asked."

"Right," I say. "Sure. Fiancés."

"There *was* a deal on Match dot com," Kristiana says. "Too good to miss. Buy one hot Russian lord, get two free."

I tried to surreptitiously google Alexei Romanov as we were walking, but for some reason my phone wouldn't load the page. Now that we're not walking anymore, it finally shows up, and I can't believe it. The Calvin Klein model really *is* the failed Russian prince—standing right in front of me. "You really are Alexei Romanov."

"I am," he says. "Not that it means much. I lost the vote."

The elevator doors ding before opening, and I step onto my floor, waving them all through.

"Whoa," Kris says, looking around with wide eyes. "Is this entire floor yours?"

"Penthouse," I say. "Gift from Grandfather when I graduated third in my class."

"Wow," she says. "Maybe I should've come to America, too."

"You wouldn't have met me if you had," Aleks says softly.

"Which brings us back to our point." Kristiana folds her arms. "Gustav's never going to believe us unless you just show him."

"Show me what?" I ask while the entire group of them exit the elevator.

"There's something about our family that we didn't know," Kris says. "Dad says there were old journals, but our great-great-uncle or someone took them when he left Latvia for the United States. It's unlikely we'd have believed them in any case."

"Journals?" Some old family illness or something better not be why they just torched my Black Rock meeting. I wouldn't put it past Dad to send them here asking for money for expensive genetic tests or something. It feels like I've been duped once again.

"The journals probably go more into our connection to the Romanov family and the other royal families of Russia that had special magical powers."

Oh, no. This is not going anywhere good.

"Yeah, see, we lost him." Kris turns and looks at Aleks. "Just do it."

"Do what?"

But instead of answering me, something very, very strange happens. There's a churning blur my eyes can't make any sense of, and then suddenly, standing in my entryway, alongside the five uninvited guests, instead of Aleksandr, my sister's new Russian husband, there's an enormous black stallion.

My phone rings again, in this bizarre moment.

The horse's nostrils flare and he looks right at my phone, then back up at my face, as if to say, "Are you going to answer that?"

I can hardly believe it's happening, but the giant black horse actually tosses his head at my phone and whinnies.

"Fine." I snap my phone against my ear. "Yes, what?"

"Mr. Belmont. We must have been disconnected before. This is agent Theodore Price with Homeland Security. It's rather urgent that we speak. You're currently the only contact we have for Katerina Yurovsky, and she has now gone missing. Instead of needing a sponsor for her visa, we're beginning to believe she might present a direct threat to our national security. If you don't voluntarily submit to questioning, I'm afraid we'll need to track you down and detain you. Trust me. That won't be good for either of us."

"Did you say you *lost* some woman named Katerina Yurovsky?" The wheels in my head are spinning a hundred miles an hour. Could this be connected to the three Russians in my room right now? What would they find when they interrogate me? And how could this destroy my IPO more thoroughly than Kris' uninvited appearance already has?

"We had an. . .incident unlike any we've ever experienced before," Agent Price says. "But we're going over all the details. You can be sure of that."

"Under what circumstance did this woman disappear?"

Kristiana looks decidedly uncomfortable, and I'm almost positive that she knows this missing criminal.

"I'm happy to fill you in on additional details when we meet," he says. "But for now, can you confirm your address? I'll be coming by myself in the next hour or so." He rattles off my home address, and if I weren't freaked out, I might be impressed. It's not listed.

"Is a home visit tonight really necessary?" I ask. "I'm happy to come to you tomorrow." Which is a complete lie.

"We feel it is both necessary and urgent," Agent Price says, "yes."

"Alright," I say. "Fine. Yes, that's my current address, and I'm home now." I glare at Kristiana. As far as I can tell, this whole thing is her fault.

"—still can't find the horse, sir," someone says in the background.

"The *horse*?" I ask, my gaze cutting sideways at the mighty black stallion still watching me carefully.

"Yes, as I said, I'll give you more details, but somehow this missing person, this Russian national, managed to summon a horse or something, and while we were dealing with the appearance of that rather large and untrained beast, she escaped."

"I'll be waiting for you." I hang up. "Who wants to tell me what in the world is going on and who this Katerina Yurovsky is?" I glare at the stallion. "Because there's no way that it's a coincidence that you're suddenly a horse, and that she somehow escaped US custody with the help of a horse."

"It wasn't with the help of a horse," Kristiana says. "Like Aleksandr, she *is* the horse." She shrugs. "We have a lot to catch you up on."

6

KATERINA

I'm not a total idiot.

This may not be my century, but I've done an alright job figuring things out. I can use the internet, now, kind of, and I know some things. Before leaving Russia, I went back by Aleksandr's house, and wonder of wonders, the staff let me inside. They must not have gotten a message from Aleksandr saying that I'd run.

I'm also delighted to find a list of addresses among Kristiana's personal belongings—the servants are too afraid to stop me from rummaging around when I tell them it's a favor for Kristiana, who left something behind—and it even has an address for this elusive Daniel Belmont. The internet says the address is in New York City, and I press some buttons and the phone magically locates it.

Maps may be the most wonderful thing on the internet.

Which I have access to all the time, thanks to a very nice man who helped me figure out how to work my new phone and download a few pictures called apps. Everything looks good, and with the money Aleksandr helpfully left for me, and the passport, I book a flight to New York City.

I board easily, actually. Most people are so *helpful* this century, especially the men.

It's a little unnerving that I can't use my powers. I've grown accustomed to always having them as a fallback, but even without them, no one really seems threatening.

Until I reach the United States.

My biggest hurdle should have been the language, but before we went to the airport, Kristiana explained something, something amazing. You see, somehow she was the key to freeing all the shifters who were stuck by Leonid's actions in their horse forms. When she forgave us? Or something like that? We could suddenly shift freely again. And tied up in all that, somehow, we're all connected to her. We can all speak the languages she can: English, Russian, and Latvian.

I never knew Latvian, but I understand it now.

I'm hoping it's true of English. . .and thankfully, when I land, it holds. I can't read the letters on any of the signs, but I understand what people are saying, and I'm able to respond in kind. Most people would probably be freaked out by something like that, but as a child who was taught to shock things early, I've always accepted magic in stride.

More concerning was the man who practically pounced on me when we landed. He has a big head of bushy white hair, and he really, really likes to yell. I start tuning him out about the third time he tells me the same thing, but I can't seem to ignore one word. He says it over and over and over: visa. It's the reason he's so hot under the collar, apparently.

See, I didn't get one, and everyone from Russia needs one.

"In order to even apply for a visa, you need a sponsor," chick-fluff-head says. "So you'll need someone in the United States who will agree to sponsor you, or you'll have to turn right back around and fly home to Russia." His lip curls, and he sounds like, instead of saying *Russia*, he meant to say *raw sewage*.

"But I'm not from the United States," I say. "I'm from

Russia. So how would I get a sponsor who lives in the United States?"

"Without contacts, you would have no reason to visit." His tone is flat. "If you don't have any, you never should have come. I'm not sure how they even let you on the plane without a visa."

I can't very well tell them that I had one, but when I ditched the chumps who booked this ticket in the first place, they kept it. I figured we'd sort it out on this end, once I was already here. In retrospect, I possibly should have looked into that part a little more.

Another man shows up, this one with dark skin and a less angry face. He speaks slowly, and he's very intent, looking at me the whole time. "Miss Yurovsky. If you don't know anyone here who can be your sponsor, you can't get a visa. Think very carefully about why you came to America. Isn't there someone we can contact here who could be your American contact?"

It finally hits me that I do know someone here, sort of.

Daniel Belmont.

He doesn't know me, and I've actually tried to betray him spectacularly, but with the information I have, I could save his life. Also, if Kristiana and Aleksandr have already reached him, they could have told him who I am. There's an outside chance he might actually vouch for me, and then I wouldn't have to turn around and fly back to Russia.

I give the man his name, and I tell them his company name, which I also overheard. "Can you look him up, do you think?"

"You said he's the president of a company named Trifecta, and that it's a horse gambling company?"

"Not a horse gambling company," I say. "A horse race betting company."

The dark-skinned man sighs. "I'll search for him and give

him a call. We'll wait to see what he says until. . ." He glances at his watch. "Close of business tomorrow, anyway."

Chick-fluff-head explodes. "Who exactly is paying for her hotel tonight? The US Government? Do you think that's appropriate?"

"She's a young woman, clearly a little lost, and she's scared." The dark-skinned man shakes his head. "She can't leave the premises until she's been cleared, so she'll have to stay in one of the interrogation rooms."

"Oh. Well." Chick-fluff-head nods. "That sounds miserable."

Apparently he's only satisfied if I'm uncomfortable. I'm not gum on his shoe. I'm a person. "I'll be fine to sleep here." I point at the floor behind the small table and chairs in the room. "I can use my bag as a pillow."

The dark-skinned man frowns. "I'll have a sleeping bag sent in, and a meal tray, too. And hopefully this Daniel Belmont will rush right over."

I'm not holding my breath for that, but it would be nice.

Although, if he is the kind of guy who rushes over to help damsels in distress that he doesn't even know, I'll feel especially bad for trying to trade his life to Leonid, not that anything I did even mattered. Leonid already knew everything, as usual. And on top of that, even if he hadn't already known everything, it was always only a matter of time before he discovered who Kristiana's brother was.

I shove my guilt down deep and let my little shred of hope expand instead. That's a lot more comfortable, at least.

I'm tugging things out of my bag to make do until tomorrow—a toothbrush, deodorant, which is new to this time period, and basically magical, and some toothpaste, when the chick-fluff-head walks back in my room.

He's smiling, so that means he has bad news. "Agent Price is soft." His grin widens. "I'm not. I called my supervisor, and he's ready to send you back now. I've talked to the airline, and they have a spot for you. Get your junk together. It's time to head back to where you belong."

But if I'm not here, I can't warn Daniel Belmont to stay away from his powers. I can't tell Alexei about his restored powers or see how he and that girl are doing. I have no idea how long it'll be before they all come back to Russia—if they ever do at all. With Leonid in charge, they may flee, and Latvia might be the closest they ever come again.

With my Russian passport, Latvia's not going to be too keen on me emigrating, either.

I can't get on that plane.

But they're about to force me.

"Be back in five," chick-fluff says. "Be ready to go." He leans closer. "That means go pee now so you aren't squawking when it's time to board about us mistreating you."

He closes the door behind him, and I run through my options. I could hope that Agent Price will intervene. I could get on the plane to Russia, or. . .

An idea hits me.

I don't have my powers, thanks to Leonid's perverse sense of humor or desire to punish me or whatever. But I do still have the ability to shift into my horse form, thanks to Kristiana restoring that power herself. Which means. . .

Before I have time to agonize over my decision, I shift into a horse. It's really a shame, because now I'll be stuck leaving all my stuff behind. Unless. . . In the split second between when I hear the doorknob turning and when the door opens, I snag my bag between my teeth.

When it swings open, chick-fluff-head staring at me with wide eyes and an open mouth, I surge forward, slamming my bag against his face. He leaps backward, shouting something nonsensical.

I can, however, make out his next words clearly. "There's —there's a—there's a *horse* in here." He grabs handfuls of paper off the desk next to him and flings them at me.

If I were a real horse, that might work. I'd probably backpedal into the room, eyes wide, nostrils flared, hooves scrambling on the tile, absolutely terrified of the horror of fluttering paper. But I'm *not* a real horse. I have more than a third of a brain, and I know how to use it. I surge past him, kicking up fluttering papers as I race for the door marked "exit."

Of course, it's not that easy to escape, merely finding a marked exit.

America's Department of Homeland Security is full of people, and all of them mobilize pretty quickly. Apparently one palomino pony poses a pretty dire threat to their country's well-being. But that's when I have my stroke of brilliance. I brought my bag, which I figured I would need when I shift back, but maybe since I can shift, I can come up with something a little better.

When I shift, I can manifest clothes. Usually. I'm not sure whether that's tied to my powers, or tied to my ability to shift. Back when I couldn't shift right after we woke up— when Leonid had to touch me to shift me—I couldn't make clothing. But when I was younger, I always could. I pound my way around the corner, watching as personnel scatter, including two people in tan coveralls with name tags, marking them as janitorial staff. I finally shove past a turn in the large hall and see what I've been looking for.

A janitorial closet.

I drop the bag and use my lips to open the door, kick the bag through, and then I shove through myself, barely getting my butt inside. Once in, I shift, trying with all my might to make clothing like the coveralls with the name tag 'Edith.' It's one of the few American names I can think of off the top of my head—the name of President Wilson's wife, the 'first lady,' back before we all got cursed to sleep for a hundred years.

And, it works.

Mostly. My coveralls are blue while theirs were tan, but

hopefully it's close enough. I grab my bag duck out of the closet, head bowed.

"Did you see a horse?" a woman with a long, poky stick with a loop at the end asks.

What on earth do they think they'd do if they got that loop around a horse's neck? Be dragged to death? "A. . .what?"

"A horse came running down this hall." The man beside the woman is holding a dart gun, ready to tranquilize the terrible, horrifying horse that's running wild.

I didn't shift back a moment too soon.

"Keep safe," the woman says. "It's crazed, probably sick."

"Where did it come from?" I'm pressing my luck. I should have stayed quiet—who knows when they'll notice a hint of my accent.

The man frowns. "No one knows. Head back to the central office. They'll tell you when it's clear to be out again."

Since I have no idea where that is, I wait for them to move on before following more signs to the exit. Once I reach a door out, I realize I'm in the employee parking lot. Now, if only I owned one of these cars. . . I can't help staring at one longingly.

"Car won't start?" A young man with big teeth tilts his head. "It's been a bad day all around. I can give you a ride to the metro, if you want."

I'm not totally sure what the metro is, but any kind of ride would get me out of the airport complex, I hope. "That would be great."

As we leave, the young man flashes a badge at the security guard, who's on the phone, yelling. "Of course I haven't seen a *horse*. Do you think I'm drunk at work? Is this some sort of joke?" He waves us through without even checking our faces.

"What a weird day, right?" Big teeth keeps smiling at me.

I nod, learning from my past mistakes. I won't be overly gregarious this time.

The guy takes the hint, luckily, and stops trying to make small talk. "Is Jamaica Beach okay?"

I have no idea what he's saying, so I just smile dumbly. A few miles from the airport, he drops me off. I think it's some kind of train station. Unfortunately, I have no idea how to get on the train or what the rules are for riding it. Then I see someone hop over the barricade. . .and no one says a thing. I wait a moment or two, and I do the same thing. Thankfully, it works. No one chases me or shouts, and pretty soon, I'm staring at a bunch of maps while trains lumber past, the air from their movement blowing my hair in every direction.

"Confused?" An older woman with a magazine in her hand tilts her head and looks up at me. Her accent sounds strange, but I can't place why.

"It's my first time in New York," I confess. "I'm not sure how to get to my friend's house, and the phone I had with a map on it. . .well, it's been a weird day." I echo what the nice guy said.

The woman smiles, showing a mouth full of missing teeth. "You tell me about it. My dentures broke, and now I'm stuck traveling all over creation to get them fixed. You know they wanted seven hundred dollars for new ones?" She shakes her head. "No thank you."

I realize it's not an accent—it's a lisp because her teeth aren't quite right. "I'm sorry about that."

She shrugs. "Not your fault. But you're in luck, because I do have a phone with a map, and it even shows subway routes. Tell me where you're going, and I'll tell you how to get there."

Three minutes later, I have a plan. I take this train, she points me at the right platform, two stops, and then I transfer. After that, I'll go straight up, and I'll walk three blocks, and then I'll have reached Daniel Belmont's home. He may not have wanted to sponsor me, although who knows? Maybe he did.

But he's about to have no choice.

He's really my only tie to finding Alexei in America, so if I have to camp out on his front step, I'll do it. Unfortunately, when I reach the stop she said, getting off and up to the top level isn't as easy as I thought it would be. And when I finally make it topside, it's raining. A lot. I'm completely soaked by the time I find the right street, and people keep striking me in the head with their umbrellas by mistake—one of the downsides to being tall, I suppose. By the time I know which direction to go, my stomach's rumbling like a bus engine. The kind that pumps out a lot of dark smoke.

Luckily, there's a little stand selling sausages wrapped in bread—the signage calls them 'hot dogs'—and since I managed to salvage my wallet, I can get one. Or at least, I thought I could. I didn't think about the fact that their money would be different here. It's pretty frustrating, watching other people buy these 'hot dogs,' which have amazing yellow and red sauces and small, green, pickled cucumber pieces. The smell's tantalizing, and I can't help looking at them longingly.

"You poor thing," the man making the hot dogs says. "Oh, fine. Once you get that money changed over, you come back and give me eight bucks. Got it?"

I nod, rendered mute by my hunger.

My stomach actually growls as he hands me a hot dog, which is a little embarrassing, but he smiles. There's nowhere to stand out of the rain, so I eat as I walk.

Unfortunately, a blob of yellowish-reddish goo drops on my already unimpressive coveralls, and even in the rain, it manages to stain the front. Luckily, I'm right around the corner from Daniel's apartment. Surely Kristiana and Aleksandr have already found him, and they'll be able to help me locate Alexei. Then I just need to come up with a way to take credit for restoring his powers that doesn't give away that I bargained with Leonid, or tried, and I'll be back on track.

Or as close to it as I can get.

I've been trying to come up with a way ever since Leonid said he'd give Alexei his powers back, but so far, every idea I have circles back to me bargaining with Leonid. That will not endear me to Alexei. I'm going to try and just find a natural time and way, I suppose. And if I manage to convince this Daniel Belmont to keep his nose out of Leonid's plans and Russia's politics in the process, well, even better. That should keep Alexei and Daniel safe.

I'll also feel better about trying to trade his life for Alexei's powers.

I finally reach the building, but when I walk inside, some guy with thick glasses and greying hair, wearing a very formal looking navy uniform with red and gold trim, holds up his hand. "What's your business in the building, Miss?"

I blink.

"You have to tell me where you're going."

"Why?" I ask. "Are you a guard?" I didn't think most people used guards in America, or at least, in the movies I've seen, I didn't see a single one.

"A guard." The man laughs, and then he straightens, brushing his hands down his uniform. "I'm the doorman for this building." He smiles.

"But, the door opened itself." I frown. "So what do you really do?"

Now the man's frowning.

"I'm sorry," I say. "I'm not trying to offend you, sir. I just don't understand what a doorman does, clearly."

"My name is Norm." He huffs. "I stand here to greet people as they come in. I help with packages. I monitor the building. I make sure if a resident is ever locked out of their apartment, they can get in."

"Uh, okay," I say. "Well, I'm looking for my friend, Daniel Belmont. He's on. . ." I glance down at the note on my phone. "Floor twenty-four."

"He's a busy man today." The man snags a clipboard off his podium stand and flips through a paper or two. "I don't see any notes about you coming." He folds his arms.

"Well, Norm, Daniel doesn't know I'm coming."

"I can call him and ask for permission to send you up." He looks at my name tag. "*Edith*."

"He doesn't know I'm coming. . ." I lean closer. "Because it's a *surprise*."

He arches one eyebrow. "Mr. Belmont doesn't like surprises, and more importantly, he doesn't allow them."

I'm sure that, thanks to the rain soaking my hair and body, the coveralls, and the big blotchy stain on the front of my chest, I'm not looking very inspiring. I'll have to gamble just a little bit more.

"Listen, my friends have already gone up to see him." Please let that have some hope of being true. "You probably saw them. A blond Russian man, quite tall. Another tall, dark-haired one, and a blockier, really muscular one. They each had their *girlfriends*—" I cringe at the word, because I hate saying it in reference to Alexei. "With them."

Norm's still frowning, but he waves me toward the elevator. "You don't look particularly scary. I suppose it's fine." He huffs again. "You better hope I don't get fired for this. I have quite a few, very bright grandchildren whose college I'm saving to pay for. I really need to keep this job."

"I'm not a serial killer," I say. "I swear."

"Which is exactly what a serial killer would say." He looks like he's thinking about changing his mind and lunging in front of me, much as a guard would do, but he sighs as the elevator opens. "Twenty-fourth floor."

I hit the button and wait.

It feels like it takes a lot longer than it should to reach the top floor, but the elevator never stops. When the doors open, I know I'm in the right place.

Because Alexei and his stupid girlfriend, her sister and

Grigoriy, and Kristiana and Aleksandr are all standing in the entryway. The only person I don't recognize. . .*must* be Daniel Belmont.

"Daniel," I say. "It's so nice to finally meet you."

"Is it, Miss Yurovsky?" The same dark-skinned man from the airport steps into the entry from behind a short wall, and he tilts his head. "Tell me again, Mr. Belmont, how you don't know her." At the airport, he seemed like the reasonable one, but right now, his expression is practically diabolical.

I had almost forgotten how quickly the Liepas can drag someone down and drown them.

"I've been here more than ten years," I mutter. "*Ten years*, and you show up now, when I'm two weeks away from the end zone."

"You said you've been planning this for ten years?" Suddenly, for the second time today, someone pulls a gun.

This time, though, it's pointed at me.

"Agent Price," I say. "I haven't planned anything like you're thinking. I'm as much a victim here as you are. I have no idea how this horrible woman escaped your custody, and I've never met her in my entire life. The woman there—" I point. "Is my sister Kristiana Liepa. I changed my name when I emigrated here, legally, from Latvia more than a decade gone. My grandfather agreed to help me with school and support my business efforts, but he wanted me to look and sound as American as my mother. I agreed with his plan, and so my dual citizenship quickly became solely US citizenship."

Agent Price isn't having it. "So you have *no* idea how this particular woman, who gave me your name back at the airport office, escaped and wound up right here, somehow slipping past your doorman, and is now standing brazenly in your entryway?"

"I understand that it sounds strange, but—"

Agent Price squints and looks past me at the ground. "What the—" He cuts off, leaning toward the ground behind Kristiana. "What is that?" He uses his free hand to wave us back and then he steps forward.

A very dark, very clearly shaped muddy hoofprint on my white carpet is what he's staring at. I can't help wincing. After all, there *was* a horse at the detention center, and now there's a hoofprint here, in my apartment.

"Do you have a horse here in your apartment, Mr. Belmont?"

I laugh. "A what?"

Agent Price points.

I follow his hand to the hoofprint I already know's there, but then I feign surprise. "Wow, that's strange. You're right, it does look like a hoofprint, but I have no idea how that could possibly be. You're welcome to request footage from the lobby downstairs. There are several CCTVs there, and I'm sure you can verify that no horse has come up or down the elevator or stairwells to my room."

"Don't you think the more reasonable explanation for mud on the floor of a twenty-fourth floor penthouse is someone's shoe?" Kristiana's eyebrows are lifted. "When I was in vet school, the first thing they told us was that if we hear the sound of hoofbeats, we should assume horses, not zebras."

"So you're a vet?" Agent Price asks. "And what kind of animals do you treat?"

"If I say horses, are you going to arrest me for something that happened at the airport?" Kristiana looks like she's about to burst out laughing.

Agent Price goes on like this, being baited by my Russian and Latvian guests, for a few moments before his reinforcements arrive. That's when they cuff me and drag me downstairs, requesting the video footage, as I suggested. They take all my unwanted guests with them, to be safe, and of course, there's no chance they're going to release that Katerina lady. I still can't believe that Kristiana's husband and this girl can turn into horses.

I wouldn't believe it, if I hadn't seen Aleks do it with my own eyes.

Kris didn't have time to tell me much before Agent Price arrived, other than the fact that somehow our family's involved, and that the person who defeated Alexei Romanov in the election is a maniac, who is inexplicably interested in killing me.

All of it seems absolutely insane, but then again, the muddy hoofprint in my family room also makes no sense. But eventually, after Grandfather's lawyers show up, after they've looked over the videos from my lobby, and after they've confirmed that Kris is, in fact, my sister, and that I really did change my name, and that this Katerina person really has no criminal record, that she really did just slip out of the detention center after realizing there was a lot of chaos, they let us go.

"They're acting like a normal person would stick around while a horse is rampaging, loose, through a building," Kristiana's saying to the agent. It's impressive, how solid she is in defending her husband's friend. If I were her, and my husband had a hot friend who needed saving, I'm not sure I'd be leaping into the fray to do it.

Kristiana's acting skills are much better than I expected, honestly. She knows that Katerina *was* the horse, and that her friend caused the very distraction that freed her, but Kris lies about it effortlessly. I suppose that since she's known about the whole horse thing for a while, it's not as strange to her.

It takes a stupidly long time, but right before two in the morning, they finally drive us in a big white van back to Manhattan and release us less than a block from my apartment, surrendering the seven of them into my unenthusiastic custody. I wish I could hustle them all over to the airport and shove them onto the first flight back to Russia. I did see one of them turn into a horse, and then when there was a knock on my door, he shifted just as easily right back into a human right down to the same clothing. There's clearly *something* to their bizarre story. And I do believe Kris would not be here, wrecking my life, unless she felt this was important.

But I still want to get them gone as soon as possible.

"Now that they're releasing us, can we stay with you?" Kris asks. "It's really the only way we can guarantee your safety."

I don't even answer until we're all outside my building, breathing the brisk fall air. The idea of them protecting me is ridiculous, so I say so. "You're the only ones who have put me in danger so far."

"But Leonid—" Kris starts again.

"No," I say. "Stop with the Leonid stuff. There's no way that someone in Russia—the country's new leader, no less—cares about me or my tiny horse-race betting company. Until you showed up, my biggest concern was whether Grandfather was happy with the way I was handling the IPO."

My phone starts to ring, and it's him—his ears must have been burning. I wince as I answer, walking away from them and toward my apartment building's entrance. "Grandfather."

He may never have been a sailor in his life, but I'm pretty sure he was trained to swear by one. When, after several minutes, he finally stops ranting, he asks, "Have you lost your mind? The SEC just approved your company for the IPO, and you bail on the meeting with Black Rock that I arranged to kick this off, and then you were photographed being cuffed and dragged down to be interrogated by the Department of Homeland Security?"

It does sound bad when he puts it that way.

"Kristiana has run into some trouble." Maybe someone

else would feel guilty about throwing his sister under the bus, but I don't. She doesn't even care what our grandparents think. "She showed up—unannounced—and started shouting at me in the lobby. A friend of hers followed her here but didn't get a visa, and she needed a US Citizen to vouch for her."

"Please tell me you didn't agree to do that. You don't even know this friend."

"I certainly do not," I say. "But I do know my sister, and vouching for her Russian husband's old family friend was easier than making an even bigger deal out of this to the media or a government agency."

Grandfather grunts.

"Trust me—none of this was any part of a plan I made."

"This is the problem with all Liepas. No matter what you intend to do, your family always drags you down."

I grit my teeth. I can't even argue, because he's right.

"You, Daniel, must find a way to rise above this. It's always been your anchor—the ties you have to that place. Those people."

The one thing that has bothered me the most over the past decade is how rude and dismissive he is about Kristiana. She stayed with my father, sure, but he's her *father*. She was born and raised in Latvia, on a farm our mother loved, in a place she chose. Grandfather could be a little more understanding of why Kristiana, his only granddaughter, might want to stay with her father in the only place she ever knew. It's not like the sums of money he sent to help them at various times ever made any sort of dent in his personal fortune.

Though I suppose Mom's trust fund was probably substantial, and she did manage to use all of that in a short span of years.

One thing Grandfather *never* brooks is any kind of personal criticism. Pointing out that Kristiana is his blood won't help. Defending her is pointless. She came here and caused all this mess—she can deal with me hanging it around her neck. "I will get her to leave as soon as possible," I say. "She brought quite a few friends, and they appear to have some kind of dispute with the current leader of Russia."

"He did steal the country from one of her friends, according to my sources. The would-be Romanov heir is marrying her best friend's sister."

"Yes," I say, lowering my voice a bit. As always, Grandfather is shockingly well-informed. "He's here too."

"Get rid of all of them. Associating with them will make investors very nervous. And if they get nervous, and they look into Daniel Belmont and his background. . ."

It's bad for all of us, but most especially for business.

Russia hasn't been in good standing for a while, but it's only gotten worse lately.

And of course, politics aside, I'm well aware that Grandfather thinks any connection to my Latvian family would be the worst thing in the world. He's essentially eliminated all ties between Dad and him. "Don't worry," I say. "I won't let them drag me down, not when I'm so close to finally taking this company public. Not when I can finally show you that I'm competent and capable."

"Someone who can't manage their own family isn't competent," Grandfather says.

I'm aware he cut off his own daughter because he felt she couldn't be reliably managed. How could I ever forget that? "Believe me. I know how serious it is to you," I say.

He hangs up.

I'm standing in front of my apartment building, staring at Norm's concerned face. He's even come outside to make sure I'm alright. "Your friends are all back?" He looks nervous, and maybe he should. He must have been the one to let that Katerina lunatic up to my apartment earlier.

If she hadn't shown up *just then*, that stupid Agent Price

would have left, and I never would have been hauled down to be interrogated. Grandfather would not have lost it, and the only thing I would've botched was the Black Rock meeting. Even so, I shoo him back inside. "Give us a minute to talk out here."

He bobs his head and heads back into the lobby.

It hits me then, how catastrophically bad this whole day really has been. Grandfather always overreacts to everything, so I'm used to him yelling at me, but I'm going to be on the news and in trending social media posts and articles, and not for anything good. No, the day that should have been a coup for me, the day my IPO was approved and the dissemination of information about Trifecta began, the day I had an early meeting with one of the biggest purchasers of publicly traded companies, I bailed on the meeting, and then got arrested.

"Gustav." Kristiana's hand on my shoulder is the last straw. She's acting like *I'm* the problem, like it's *my fault* things are falling apart, or like I have some kind of bizarre obligation to help her. I spin around, my jaw muscle twitching.

"Watch yourself." Aleksandr's suddenly there, looming over me, acting like he might. . .what? Pummel me for being threatening around my own sister?

"I don't attack women." I curl my lip with disgust. "And I would never harm Kris."

"Yes." Aleksandr nods. "You'd simply ignore all her calls, texts, and messages while she pleads for your help." He's scowling like I'm a villain.

"I have my own life," I say. "Kris is a big girl. I knew she didn't need me."

"You know nothing about her," Aleks says softly. "And if it were up to me, you'd continue to know nothing about her. You're a waste of space." He turns around and starts to walk away.

Kris barely whispers his name. "Aleksandr."

He freezes, his shoulders drooping.

"Please." Her voice is so soft, I wonder whether I'm imagining it.

But Aleksandr acts like he's on a leash that's been tugged. He turns around slowly, his head bowed. "We will stay with you, and we will keep your ungrateful, unworthy life safe."

"Oh, how wonderful for me," I say. "Won't that just be a total delight?"

Aleks steps closer. "I love your sister." He exhales slowly. "I love her more than an arthropod like you could possibly comprehend." He smiles, now, but it spreads across his face slowly and painfully, like a spreading bruise, not a sign of his joy. "You will listen to her, and we will keep you safe, no matter how little you deserve our protection. But you will *not* disrespect her again, or I will bury you."

The way he says it, he will *bury* me, it sounds like he means it. "I've had more than ten years of martial arts training." I roll my shoulders. "I'm sure you're a very scary Russian man, but I assure you. I'm not easy to bury." I lean toward him, expecting him to give at least a little.

It's like I'm threatening a brick wall. He just glowers.

"He literally means that he'll bury you," Kris says, her voice still small. "He's a shifter, which you saw, but he also has earth powers. He can bury anything." She tosses her head. "Your building. All those cars. You name it, and he can shove it underground."

I have no idea whether she's serious.

I'm afraid she might be.

But perhaps more concerning than the possibility that she might be telling the truth, is the people who've begun to gather around and watch us. One of them's fiddling with his phone. He could easily be recording us. It's almost two-thirty in the morning, but this is New York City. Someone's always awake, and with the internet, someone's always watching.

"Let's go upstairs," Kris says again. "Please?"

"I have two guest rooms," I say. "And one office. I'm not sure where everyone will sleep."

"We'll figure it out," Kris says. "And in the morning, we can explain the rest of what's going on."

Or I'll leave before they do and make sure no one at the office allows them inside. I doubt Kris would really have her husband or his friends do anything truly crazy. If so, I would already have seen some kind of reports of magical horse humans on the news, right?

"Fine." I let them follow me up. How bad can it be to let them stay for a day or two?

We barely all fit on the elevator at the same time, and it makes for an uncomfortable ride.

"Sorry." The Katerina person hasn't met my eye since she walked into my apartment earlier. In fact, the only person she's even looked at is. . . I follow her gaze to Alexei.

Alexei's engaged to Adriana, I think. Before I had any inkling it might be the Adriana I'd almost forgotten about, I heard people talking about how the future czar of Russia proposed to some trashy woman on television. I know Mom loved her dearly, but that entire family was always a mess.

I refuse to get involved, but if I were Adriana's actual brother, it would annoy me that Katerina can't seem to stop staring at her boyfriend.

"What?" Katerina asks, her light green eyes looking up at mine.

"Nothing." I shrug.

"Just ask," she presses. "You're thinking something, and I'm sure we all want to know what it is."

"I'm just tired." I yawn.

Adriana, Kristiana, Aleks, the blocky man named Grigoriy, and Alexei all yawn too.

Katerina does not. She scowls. "But that's not what you're thinking. You're thinking something about me."

"I was," I admit. "I want to know why you came on a

flight after the others. How did you get caught by the Department of Homeland Security and cause this mess?"

Everyone's entirely silent when the elevator dings and the doors roll open. I'm stuck at the back, so I can't do much about it. But when the doors start to close again, I've had it.

I shove outward, my arms bumping Kris and Katerina and shoving them into the people beside them. No one exits, but it does trigger the motion sensors and the doors open again.

"Are we planning to get off?" I ask. "Or are we all going back down?"

There's a flurry of murmurs and shifting as they finally climb off. Once I'm free of the elevator, I press. "What's really going on with you? Why are you here, and who are you?"

"You're not asking who they are." Katerina narrows her eyes at me.

"Because Kris is my sister. Aleks is her husband. Mirdza is her best friend, who's marrying Aleksandr's friend Grigoriy. Adriana's Mirdza's twin sister, and while none of us liked her as much as Mirdza, she's still extended family. That makes Alexei, her fiancé, sort of family as well. But you're just the woman who stares at him too much. So I want to know why you're here and what made you later than them." I cross my arms. "Kris said you'd explain things, and that's what I want to know, because they all had diplomatic visas, whereas you landed with nothing at all other than my name."

"You're absolutely right. I am late." Katerina lifts her chin. "Instead of flying here with them, I took a detour." Her eyes flash. "I went to see Leonid, the new ruler of Russia, to beg him to grant Alexei his powers again." She winces, like saying all that was not intended.

"You did what?" Alexei asks.

She shakes her head. "I won't apologize. He even told me he'd give them to you. On one condition."

Adriana's jaw dangles open.

It's been a long time since I saw her, but I don't recall anyone shocking her when she was younger. I'm guessing that hasn't changed much in the past decade.

"Why would he?" Adriana asks. "What does Leonid want?"

"Whatever it is, he can't have it," Alexei says. "We won't negotiate with him."

"It would be nice to know what he wants, though," Adriana says. "No one knows his next move, and we have no idea why he's having these trials and executions."

Politics I don't care about and more magic I don't understand. Fabulous. At least it sparked some internal debate, even if it makes no sense to me. "I'm going to get some extra pillows and blankets," I say.

But before I can walk off, Katerina speaks. "He told me that if Alexei will renounce his relationship with Adriana and marry me instead, Leonid will return his powers to him."

Wow. Weird stuff just keeps coming. "He wants you to marry Alexei, instead of Adriana?" I can't help lifting my eyebrows. "The guy you've been eyeing like he's a vat of Ben & Jerry's all night? That's convenient."

"A vat of. . . Huh?" Katerina looks like she would happily spear me. "You have no idea what you're talking about."

"What's Ben & Jerry's?" Mirdza asks.

"Never mind," I say. "None of this is my problem."

"Why would Leonid want Alexei to dump Adriana and marry you?" Kristiana's eyeing Katerina strangely, like they're not friends at all. I suppose when she has to choose between Adriana and someone else, there's no contest. For a split second, I almost pity this Katerina person. No one seems to like her.

I've been there.

But then I remember that she wrecked my entire night, and she may have single-handedly ruined Trifecta's IPO and I'm back to hating her again.

"Leonid has known me for a long time," Katerina says. "I'm not a wild card." She shrugs. "Anyway, that's the deal. I told him you'd never take it, but that's—"

"You're right." Alexei wraps an arm around Adriana's shoulder and drags her closer. "I would never, not in a million years, leave Adriana and marry you. Not if it eradicated the threat of Leonid and restored all his powers to me. Not if the entire world hung in the balance. Not even if it would bring my family back again."

I have no idea what happened to his family, but that was a pretty savage burn. Nothing in the world would convince him to leave Adriana for Katerina. *Nothing.* I'm not sure whether it's a strong declaration of love for Adriana (which I don't really understand. She was always a high-strung mess.) or whether it's a clear message about how much he dislikes Katerina.

Either way, it's not great when your vat of ice cream denounces you entirely and completely. Katerina looks, predictably, wrecked.

"Hey, Katerina," I say. "Why don't you help me with the blankets and pillows?"

She follows me out of the family room and down the hall to the linen closet, but once we reach it, and I open a cabinet, she doubles over, her hands wrapping around her waist, and starts gulping in air in great, heaving breaths. Suddenly, she's bawling. Tears rolling down her face, sobs wracking her body.

I called her over here thinking she might want to get away from the others, not so that she could completely break down and I would be stuck here comforting her. Without any idea what to do, I awkwardly pat her back. "There, there."

My mom died when I was young. No one taught me what to do with women when they flip out. I start to try and back away slowly, but her hand shoots out and closes around my wrist like a vise. Around ragged breaths, she manages to snap, "You will stay here."

I suppose I'm her cover for this complete mental break-down. "I take it that didn't go as planned."

She straightens lightning quick, her eyes flashing. "None of that was planned."

"Look, I know you like Alexei. I doubt there's anyone who has seen us all in the same room today who hasn't cracked that puzzle. But the thing is, Adriana's—"

"Don't." She shakes her head. "You don't have to try and make me feel better."

"Oh." I snort. "I wasn't. I was going to warn you. Adriana's straight-up insane. I'd back away from anyone who likes her slowly, and I would never turn toward them again. She's likely to carve your eyes out of your skull and eat them, and if they like that kind of energy, that's not someone you want."

Katerina laughs. The sound isn't sad and desperate and painful. It's actually kind of nice, like a firm handshake or a hug. I didn't expect that kind of laugh from this woman who flies to new continents for men who are engaged to crazy women. "Thanks."

"Uh, sure." Then I remember we're supposed to be getting extra pillows and blankets. Katerina gets herself together enough to help me, and we make it back to the kitchen when I realize that everyone's huddled around some small screen, transfixed.

It's someone's phone.

The tinny sound's coming from the speakers of the device. "—who until today had been the last official dictator in Europe, leading the country of Belarus for more than twenty-eight years."

I freeze. "What is it?"

The six of them turn toward us slowly.

Aleksandr's the one holding the phone, and he looks concerned. "Leonid's not staying still."

"What did he do?" Katerina asks.

"Well, rumors say he killed Putin. But it's undeniable that

he killed Europe's last dictator—Putin's favorite crony, the leader of Belarus."

"But Lukashenko's a pretty bad man," I say. "Wasn't he? Are people upset about that?"

"He invited the man to visit him in Russia, and then after Lukashenko accepted his invite, Leonid killed him," Aleksandr says. "The execution has thrown Belarus into disarray, and in answer to that concern, Leonid announced that he'll absorb Belarus into Russia once again."

I don't know enough about the region's politics to really have any understanding about what all of that means or how it might have happened. They want me to be scared, or outraged, or upset, but it all feels very far removed from anything that might affect me here, in the United States. Surely the madman wouldn't try to come here and start any fights. His armies would be half a world away, and we're hardly Belarus.

"You need to pass this IPO to someone else," Kris says.

And that's it. That's what she's wanted since she walked into my life. She wants me to torch everything I've worked to build, weeks before the culmination of all my plans, because of something that won't really affect me in any way. "I won't do that." I shake my head. "I have about three hours to sleep before I need to wake up and prepare for a long day of meetings tomorrow. It's going to be hard to recover from today, but I think I can do it."

Kris doesn't argue, but she looks sick.

"You saw Aleksandr turn into a horse," Mirdza says softly. "You still don't believe us?"

I shrug. "I believe that *you* believe what you're saying. It's just that I'm not willing to burn my life to the ground over it. I don't think you're right about how this will affect me."

"You're right," Katerina says.

I feel validated at first, thinking that someone in this mob of lunatics agrees with me. But then I realize she's not talking to me.

"He's too stubborn. It was a waste of time coming here."

"You are also wasting your time," Adriana says. "No matter what Leonid wants, no matter what you want, you're not going to split me and Alexei up."

The two women glare at each other, and I realize I'm not the only one with no one on my side. Katerina looks just as beleaguered as me, but hers is for a one-sided love, and mine is because I walked away from a toxic family situation.

"We need to figure out what Leonid's plan is," Aleksandr says. "And fighting among ourselves won't help."

"None of us are thinking clearly," Kristiana says.

"We do need sleep," I agree.

"But in the morning?" Grigoriy arches one eyebrow. "I plan to interrogate you." He's glaring at Katerina.

I don't know her, and I definitely don't like her, but I almost feel sorry for her. "Why?" I ask. "Is she a criminal after all?"

Grigoriy's eyes when he turns to face me are dark. Shuttered. "Maybe. She's the only one who really knows the maniac, and she hasn't told us anything of value yet." He grimaces. "But she's going to."

❧ 8 ❧

KATERINA

Kristiana and Aleksandr take one room.

Alexei and Adriana take the other.

Mirdza's generosity results in the other two getting beds, but as a couple, she and Grigoriy score the air mattress in the office.

"But what about her?" Adriana's scowling at me. "We can't trust her, clearly. The last time we weren't watching her, she ran to Leonid and struck some kind of deal for Alexei to be forced to marry her."

"I didn't strike that deal," I lie. "I begged him to give Alexei's powers back, and I told him you were leaving Russia. I swore Alexei wouldn't be a threat."

"But we mean to be exactly that," Grigoriy says. "Leonid may not be afraid of us, but we plan to do everything we can to stop him from terrorizing anyone else."

"Who exactly has he terrorized?" Gustav asks. "Because I'm not nearly as upset about Lukashenko's death as you seem to be, and Russia has always had executions that we would never approve of here in the United States. Heck, the United States has executions that its citizens think violate due process. Being copacetic in America is a high bar, and dictators never clear it."

"It's not that one death that bothers me." Grigoriy scowls. "It's the reason Lukashenko's dead that should worry you. Leonid wanted Belarus, and when he wants Iran and then Syria, no one will object either, because their leaders are also bad men. But what happens when he starts taking countries you Americans care about? What happens when he starts killing good people? Is that when you'll finally decide that bad actions are wrong and shouldn't be tolerated?"

"I thought we decided to talk about this tomorrow." Kristiana shoves a pile of pillows and blankets at Grigoriy.

Surprisingly, the notorious hothead actually backs down. I wish I had Kristiana's skill at pushing the guys around. From the day we first met at magical training as children, no one has ever listened to me.

Except Leonid, I suppose, but by the time I met him, we were all much older, and his listening days were short-lived.

"Alright." Kris claps. "Katerina will sleep here." She points at the sofa. "All of us will hear if you try and sneak off, because Gustav's door has a security code, and the elevator's ding is noisy." She glances at him as if to verify what she's saying is true.

Gustav nods.

"Great, so let's sleep. Things will make more sense after we've rested—I can't speak for everyone, but jet lag combined with the late hour is making me downright punchy."

Once everyone disappears, I realize there aren't any pillows and blankets left over. Of course there aren't. At least Gustav has a throw pillow. I punch it a few times and lie down. It feels like I'm trying to sleep on a pile of slate. I tiptoe back down the hallway to the closet Gustav keeps his blankets and pillows in, but it's right by his bedroom door. I have to work hard to make sure I'm extra quiet.

And after all my efforts, I discover that the cabinets are entirely empty. I suppose he's not used to accommodating this many uninvited guests. Who would be? I close it slowly, and turn to walk back.

My foot squeaks on a board.

I freeze.

No sounds. I think I'm safe.

I sneak back to my sofa, but before I can lie down, Gustav's door opens and he emerges, looking around. "Were you over here?" He arches one eyebrow.

No one on earth is quite as perfect as Alexei, but Gustav's not actually too bad looking. He's relatively tall, and he has sandy brown hair with light brown, almost golden eyes. His nose is long and sharp, balanced with powerful—but not overpowering—brows. His cheeks are high and prominent, and his jaw's square. His hair's just long enough to fall over his eyes a bit.

Exactly like I like it.

When he's not standing next to one of the most beautiful men on earth, he's impressively good looking. I feel a little bad for not noticing before. "Sorry. I was looking for a pillow."

"At least you weren't trying to escape."

"Wouldn't that be easier on everyone, being honest?" I sigh. "I probably shouldn't have come to New York at all."

His brows draw together. "Come with me."

I consider refusing, but he's been nicer to me than anyone else in this entire country, and I did cause him quite a lot of trouble. I straighten and follow him. . .into his bedroom. I freeze in the doorway, wondering why he summoned me here.

But all he does is grab one of his pillows and the duvet from his bed. "Here." He extends his hand toward me.

"I can't take your pillow and blanket." I shake my head.

"I sleep anywhere, and I'm not at all fussy. Besides, I tend to run hot. The blanket's usually kicked off on the floor by morning." He shakes his hand at me as if to say, *come get it already*.

I finally take the four steps across the room to take it, but I can't help looking around as I do. His room looks nothing like I expected—nothing like the rest of the apartment.

The family room, entry, and kitchen are plain, utilitarian, and modern. They boast clean, straight lines, but this room is different, like it's part of a totally unrelated apartment. It's bright and warm, with wood tones and taupe paint. All the furniture, from the chest of drawers to the nightstands and the end table by the large leather chair, are made from rich, dark wood. The floor's made of a lighter color of wood. Ash, maybe. There are large, brilliant whorls that cover it. There's a huge portrait of a stunningly beautiful woman on the wall, and I can't help wondering who she is.

"Your girlfriend?" I ask, inclining my head.

"The only woman I love, other than my sister." He compresses his lips and drops the blanket in my arms. "Now, go."

I'm nearly out the door when I hear him.

"Is he really as bad as they say?"

I pause. When I turn, slowly, he's still standing exactly where he was before. "You tell me about the picture." I point. "And I'll tell you more about Leonid."

His jaw locks, and I realize he's not going to talk. I'm turning to leave again when he says, "It's my mother. She loved horses—sometimes I think she loved them even more than my father. She surely loved them more than I ever did. She loved them more than anything in her life, except maybe Kristiana. But in spite of her passion, I never wondered whether she loved me—she made that clear every day. She brightened up every room she was in, and she died because of my dad. . .and because of a horse." The muscles in his jaw work.

I realize that's it. That's everything he's willing to share.

"Leonid." I inhale and exhale slowly. "Have you ever seen a stray kitten?"

His brow furrows.

"When I met him, he was like a stray cat who had spent his entire life being kicked. He was pitiful, really. His dad was completely nuts. He had dragged Leonid from hither to yon, ranting about their great destiny and their esteemed pedigree to anyone who would listen. Leonid had been booed, mocked, and attacked by people for years. He knew his dad was insane, but he didn't have anyone else."

"You felt sorry for him?" Gustav says. "Is that why you're friends?"

"Friends is not a great word for what we were." It's far more complicated than that. "I did feel sorry for him— anyone would have. But the thing about Leonid is that. . .instead of a kitten, I should've said he's like a baby tiger. He's beautiful in a way that almost no one is." It almost hurts saying that. It feels like I'm being disloyal to Alexei.

And for some reason, Gustav also looks angry.

"Pull up his photo. You'll see what I mean. I thought he was like a kitten, but by the time I realized I'd caught a wounded tiger by the tail, it was too late."

"What did you do for him?" Gustav looks well and truly curious now. "How did you catch his tail?"

"Leonid had never really spent more than a night or two in the same place. I think his father was terribly ill, but not in his body. He was sick in his mind."

Gustav's frown returns.

"I was the one who met them when they came through our town. I had just gotten a new hat and was walking through the main street of town when I saw Leonid, defending his father near the square. I begged Father to let them stay with us. I asked him to ignore the man's ranting and take pity—find him some kind of job."

"And your father did it?"

"Father was pleased with me at the time. He thought I was going to marry the czar's son." I sigh. I'm not sure exactly what he knows about how things went down a hundred years ago. "At first, I pitied him. But later, because of his extraordinary looks, I used him to try and make another man jealous."

"Alexei."

I hate that he can see through me after knowing me all of two minutes. "It didn't work."

Gustav's expression is absurdly disapproving. "So far, Leonid doesn't seem like the villain."

"I thought I was honestly doing Leonid a favor." I do feel pretty bad when I think about it in retrospect.

"So, that's it? You used him, and now he's mad?"

"You have about two and a half hours of sleep now, if you want to go to your precious meetings," I say. "There's not even half as much time as you'd need for me to share this entire story."

Gustav nods slowly. "You're right. I need to worry about things that matter. Things in the here and now."

"But you should know that he's very dangerous, and he's very powerful, and they haven't exaggerated a single thing. He told me himself that he's coming after you, and he'll kill you. If. . ." I'm not sure how to warn him away from using his powers. It's a complicated thing, being able to use them.

"If what?" Gustav's eyes are so light in this moment that they look nearly champagne.

"If you do any of the things they want you to do."

"The things? No one has asked me to do anything."

"Kristiana's a null," I say. "The magical powers Baba Yaga gave our families don't work on her, and we think the reason why is that her older brother's the heir of the family power—that only happens when the powers aren't split."

"I have no idea what you mean," Gustav says. "You're making no sense."

"Let me put it this way. Baba Yaga gave the founder of Russia, Rurik, powers over a thousand years ago. When she thought the line died out, she granted similar powers again, but this time to a group of people instead of only to one. She spread the powers out to try and help balance things out a little better. But when Leonid showed up, she told him he could only regain his powers by retaking them from those people."

"Okay." Gustav sits on the edge of his now-denuded bed. "But you said—"

"I'm not done." I lean against the doorframe. "When she gave them to the group of people, she picked one person whose powers would control all the others. It was someone who kind of ran things, at the time."

"Wouldn't that have been the Romanovs?" Gustav runs his hand over his chin, and the tiny hairs on his face make a rasping sound.

"The Romanovs had just become the new ruling family before she stepped in. The last few families that took over for Rurik couldn't hold the throne. It had been hard on the entire country. The family behind their appointment. . .well, I thought you were Rurikid like Leonid, but now I think that person was your ancestor."

Gustav blinks.

"Which means, if you learn how to use Baba Yaga's magic, you could potentially defeat Leonid. You're the only one who might."

"Which is why he wants me dead."

"It is," I say. "If you learn how to use the powers you can control, you become a threat to him, and once that happens. . ."

"He'll eliminate me."

I nod. "Leonid's become terrible. He's extremely power-ful. He's hot-tempered and rash. But in this case, his behavior's predictable. He told me he would return Alexei's powers to him—"

"If he marries you instead of Adriana."

"So that I can ensure he's not plotting," I say.

"You're loyal to Leonid?"

"Not exactly. Let's say that I know enough to be afraid of him." I shrug. "And I'm smart enough not to move against him. I came here to try and convince Alexei to be smart, too. Even if he doesn't marry me, he needs to leave Leonid alone. But for you, I came to warn you that if you want to carry on with your American life here, you should. Never touch your magic, and Leonid will leave you be."

"But if I lift my littlest magical finger, then bam?" He lifts both eyebrows. "I'll be squashed like a bug?"

"Something like that," I say.

"Your pretty boy's in luck." Gustav's lip twists. "I happen to want nothing to do with any of this, and I have zero plans to challenge him in any way."

"Finally, someone smart."

A wave of exhaustion rolls over me. "Time to sleep."

"Past time." Gustav yawns, and I find myself yawning in reply.

I'm several steps down the hall when he asks another question from the doorway. "When you start your training, how do you learn to access this magic?"

"I thought you wanted nothing to do with it." This sort of question isn't promising.

"Have you ever had an allergy to something?" Gustav asks. "You have to understand what you're allergic to in order to avoid triggering it by accident."

It's a fair point. "In order to awaken our powers, we have to commit a selfless act."

"But if I do something selfless in order to awaken my powers, isn't that no longer selfless?"

"I'm too tired to debate with you in English," I say. "But I'll tell you this. When I was seven, I released a mouse from a trap. I was terrified of mice, and I didn't want to loose it. If I got caught, I would've been punished. But it looked so miserable, and it was shaking, and I knew what it was like to be afraid. I couldn't leave it in the trap to be killed. When I pulled the side of the trap up to free it, the mechanism broke my finger." I hold up my right hand, showing him how my fourth finger's still crooked. "If your sacrifice has no cost to you, it won't do anything."

"Should be easy enough to avoid." He nods. "Thanks. I appreciate it."

"Good luck with your meetings tomorrow," I say. "If I had any money, I'd buy some of your company myself to try and help."

"You've done more than enough." Gustav's smiling as he closes the door, and it's not the worst thing I've ever seen.

When I go to sleep, it's the first time I haven't been imagining Alexei's smiling face in a very, very long time.

9

KATERINA

A hundred years before

I never expected that Alexei's ploy would go on for *three years*.

My father was so excited about the prospect of my marrying the future czar that he didn't shove any eligible men my way. Father took me to every single ball and event Alexei was reputed to be attending, and the more time I spent, the more in love with him I fell. The only real problem was that it was all fake. Alexei liked the charade almost as much as I did, because his mother stopped trying to fix him up with nobles from other families and countries.

We were both free.

Until the spring that I was turning twenty-one.

"It's time," my father says. "We've waited *years* now, because Alexandra has these stupid ideals of a women not being forced into marriage, but you *will* set the date for a wedding while you're at the palace." My father's nearly salivating at the prospect of my marrying Alexei.

He has no idea that the groom's the one opposed, so I have to put him off in some other way.

"I'm not sure whether—"

Father shakes his head. "You're there for a full two weeks, and you're blessedly the only daughter from all the magical families of Russia. It's a real stroke of luck that we started training all the children together after your mother passed. Your brother will be there to see that things progress properly."

He means that Boris will be reporting back.

"But this year, Alexei has to—"

"No more excuses!" Father flips an end table over, sending his disgusting snuff box flying toward the wall. "Katerina, I swear that if you do not come back officially engaged, I'll find the next eligible man and marry you off this summer."

What he means is that he'll find me a disgustingly rich old man. Father has always motivated with threats. The reason they work is that I know he'll follow through.

Which means I have about two weeks to convince Alexei that after pretending to like me for three years, he likes me for real. Luckily, I have an idea of how I might encourage him to commit. Last season, my friend Cassandra had a wealthy and impressive suitor who had casually pursued her for a full season, but never committed. . .until a young and dashing baron with a nice little estate started to pursue her as well. Once the original man saw that someone else wanted her, he committed.

The trouble in my case is in finding anyone in Russia who's willing to even *flirt* with the woman the future czar has expressed an interest in. For the past three years, everyone has given me a wide berth. The last thing they want to do is alienate the Romanov family.

"I hope you have your trunks packed," Father says. "Mr. Ivanovich is prepared to load them into the boot on the car."

"Dad," I complain. "It feels like we're trying too hard. The palace isn't that far. Have the trunks delivered, and I'll just shift and run over myself."

"Absolutely not." Father's eyes flash, and I worry about the other end table.

"But—"

"You will be seen as a *lady*, not as some unrefined hooligan who gallops anywhere she'd like as a horse."

In the doorway, Leonid clears his throat. Luckily, he's already in on the family secret—he and his father have been with us for more than two years now, and they were brought in almost six months after their employment began. It's always easier for Father to trust people when they're entirely reliant on our family for support.

But no one expected Leonid to fill out and grow up like he has. He's taller and broader than both Father and Boris, and he's only a year older than I am. His handsome face has become almost disturbingly beautiful. "Father has loaded the trunks already." He inclines his head. He's wearing the nicest clothes I've ever seen him wear—Father must have bought him a new wardrobe now that he's our chauffeur.

"Perfect." Father tosses his head. "Then you should go now."

"I'm not expected until tomorrow," I say.

"You'll go today—early. Tell them you were confused. That'll give you some time to spend with Alexei, alone. Leonid will go with you as your footman, and if you leave the palace for any reason, he'll go as your chaperone and guard. The car will stay there with you for the duration."

As some kind of misguided show of wealth, I'm sure. I can't help rolling my eyes. "It's not necessary for—"

"They don't see us as equals," Father roars. "That's been the issue all along. I'm not sure whether it's Alexei or his parents who looks down on us, but we will observe all formalities. They'll see that the Yurovsky family's lacking *nothing* that the Romanovs have, and that my beautiful daughter's a perfect match for their jumped-up popinjay of a son."

When he gets like this, arguing is a total waste of time. "Yes, Father."

I'm actually glad Leonid's coming. He's smart, and the more things I teach him, the more I realize that he might even be smarter than I am. He's always insisted he was born to the Rurikid line, and maybe he was. He certainly looks the part—regal, assured, and commanding. Now that he can read and write Russian, English, and French, he actually sounds the part too. And every day, I find him reading more books that I didn't even assign.

"I think it'll be interesting," Leonid says. "I've never been invited to accompany you during the palace weeks."

"You know we'll be practicing using our powers," I say. "It's not anything to do with politics or affairs of state."

"But you said Rurik was supposed to be the first person who had these magical powers," Leonid says. "I've always wondered whether I might be able to use them."

It's not the first time he's pushed for me to show him what I can do. It's clear he's hopeful that he can learn to use magic. I even tried to help him once, more than a year ago, but nothing happened. It's hard to know whether it's that he's never done something selfless that requires a sacrifice, or whether he has no ability to begin with.

I've grabbed my cloak—spring in Russia is still brisk—and I'm almost to the front of the house when our butler answers the door. My friend Sasha didn't announce she was coming, but then, she almost never does.

"Oh, you haven't left yet." She claps. "I just wanted to wish you luck at the palace before—"

Leonid has just walked down the stairs, his dark clothing bag in hand.

"Who's this?" Sasha bites her lip and bats her eyes. "I'm one of Katerina's oldest friends."

She's certainly not old, and we haven't even been friends for that long. She is, however, quite wealthy. She's one of the nobles in town that started coming around after Alexei expressed interest in me. In my mind, that makes her a little suspect. To my father, it makes her the very kind of person we should be interacting with more often. Her father's one of the few Russian nobles who has actually grown his ample inheritance with good investments.

Not that anyone talks about wealth, honestly.

"This is Leonid Ivanovich," I say. "He's a direct descendant from Rurik himself." I'm mostly teasing, since Father doesn't even believe Leonid's dad's wild tales, but Sasha's eyes widen all the same.

"How have we not met before?" She pretends to scowl at me. "You've been keeping him to yourself, haven't you?"

Leonid's eyes dart toward mine with alarm.

"I—I suppose I have." I can't help my suppressed smile. Irritating Sasha is too much fun. "I'm not very good at sharing."

"Shame on you." Sasha shakes her head. "You already have the future leader of Russia. You can't have him *and* the most handsome man alive."

The most handsome man alive.

I suppose that might actually be true of Leonid. Alexei's beauty is just as bright, in my opinion, even if it's not quite as obvious. It's certainly more unique than Leonid's, whose beauty is classic and flawless.

I like someone who looks *real.*

"Let's go," I say. "Leonid's taking me to the palace." I don't say that he works for me, and Sasha about loses her mind that I'm traveling with my new, eligible bachelor friend, off to see my beau at the palace.

But that gives me an idea.

I've been wondering for weeks who I might use as a foil to inflame Alexei's interest, and maybe the answer has been right by my side all this time. Leonid's eager to spend time with all of us, hoping to discover whether he may fit in with us in more ways than one.

As we drive, I explain my predicament.

Leonid never knew that Alexei and I were faking, but he catches on quickly. "So he's not interested in you, but the reverse isn't true?" He quirks one eyebrow.

I sigh.

"And you think that you can somehow use me, a servant, to change his mind?" He doesn't sound very confident.

"You're a direct descendant of Rurik," I say. "That means that Alexei's actually your inferior."

Leonid rolls his eyes. "Don't say that around my dad, or he'll go back to foaming and ranting."

"He's come a long way in the past few years," I say.

"It's amazing what abstaining from alcohol and regular meals can do," he says. "I'm a little worried about what might happen while I'm gone."

Leonid's a pretty attentive son—even though his father's an embarrassing mess, he always takes good care of him. It can't have been an easy task. He surely could have abandoned his father years ago and done much better on his own.

But working as a gardener, his father has blossomed himself.

"Look, when we get there, instead of saying you're my driver, why don't we introduce you as an old family friend?" I tilt my head. "Father purchased you new clothing. We can tell them your connection to Rurik, and they'll do their best to see whether you can use magic. That'll give us a chance to see whether you might have powers." I drop my voice just a bit. "It's a win for both of us."

Leonid's eyes light up, and his hands grip the steering wheel tightly enough that his knuckles turn white. "Do you mean it?"

"It helps us both."

He nods slowly. "I pretend to be interested in you, to make Alexei Romanov jealous."

"At the end, we'll tell them that what we said *is* true, but also that you work for me, so that no one gets upset about the lying."

"What about Boris?" he asks. "He'll tell them the truth immediately."

"I lied to Father," I say. "Boris wrote me to say he's staying in France at least an extra week, maybe two." He went to try and set up some trade agreements for our family, and he's met a woman he really likes—he doesn't want to leave until she's agreed to return with him. That's why he wrote to me instead of straight to Father. He wanted me to cover for him.

It's why I wasn't overly worried about him reporting to Father.

The rest of the drive, Leonid's quiet. As we pull around the drive to the Romanov palace, he asks me a question. "What if, at the end of all this, I feel about you the way you feel about Alexei?" He shifts the car into neutral, shoves on the hand brake, and turns to face me.

"What if. . .are you asking what happens if you start to like me for real?"

Leonid shrugs. "Stranger things have happened."

I suppose he's right. "I—I don't know." Heat rises in my cheeks, because the idea of Leonid liking me is a strange one. He was my charity case. My project. The boy I met on a trip home from a ball and convinced my father to bring into our home as an act of charity.

He smiles then. "Don't worry. It won't happen."

"How do you know?" I arch one eyebrow.

He leans closer, his breath warming my ear. "Just like that," he whispers. "You need to blush like that, and talk to me like that, and look at me like that if you want to make him jealous."

I was worried. Worried that Leonid, who has worked at

our home doing odds and ends for years, would have no idea how to flirt or court or make Alexei jealous, in spite of his face. But apparently, it was for nothing.

"Who's this?" Alexei's voice is strong. Louder than usual.

I spring away from Leonid, not sure why I feel guilty. It's stupid. I swallow. "Alexei Romanov, meet Leonid Ivanovich. He's a direct descendant of Rurik himself." Before I can open my own car door, Leonid leans across me and pops the door open himself.

"Katerina invited me to come." Leonid's voice is deeper than I remembered. "She said that I might be able to learn something." His insouciant grin is *exactly* what it should be. It's almost like he'd been preparing his entire life for exactly this role.

"Learn something?" Alexei frowns at Leonid and then turns to me, offering his hand to help me exit the car. "Learn *what* exactly?"

I step a little closer, inclining my head. "The same thing we're all here to learn." I widen my eyes. "My father told him about it, so you don't have to worry. He already knows."

"Your father—" Alexei's mouth clicks closed. "He must trust him a great deal." His nostrils flare, and it's clear he's not pleased. "I don't recall reading that Rurik or his descendants were exceedingly handso. . ." He shakes his head. "Never mind. I'll talk to Maria about finding him a room."

We may have hatched our plan as an afterthought, and we may only be in the first few moments of it, but so far, it's off to a promising start.

10

GUSTAV

I pulled quite a few all-nighters at Yale, and I wound up doing even more during business school. It might be because I'm older, but waking up after sleeping only two and a half hours feels harder than any of those. All I want to do is roll over and, well, I don't have a blanket to snuggle under, and I finally remember *why*. There are so many people in my house that I had to loan my own blanket to one of them.

It doesn't help that I dreamt of a palomino chasing me all night long.

When I finally drag myself out of bed, it's six minutes before my alarm was set to go off, and my eyes are burning like I mixed up eyedrops with acid. I hop up and race to my shower, setting the water to cold to ensure I'm awake and kicking. After my disastrous start yesterday, I can't afford any more screw-ups. I need to hit all four meetings today, full force.

One's with a large European bank, which is perfect, because one of the things I'm hoping the IPO will do is get us some backers in Europe. Horse racing's even bigger there than it is in the US, and there aren't a lot of online gambling operations that are popular in Europe yet. I'd like to start sucking up some of the online marketshare as soon as possible.

Shockingly, by the time I emerge from my room, clean-shaven, dressed in my nicest tan suit, with my hair neatly combed, all seven of my uninvited guests are already awake.

"Where are we going first today?" Kris asks.

"Oh, no." I shake my head. "You're all staying here today. You can research what that lunatic running Russia is doing. You can sit in my massage chair. You can order takeout, and you can use my credit cards for any of that you want. What you cannot do is accompany me to the meetings I'll be conducting."

"But I've looked into Trifecta," Aleks says. "I quite like the idea of a totes company that also has a separate arm that handles online gambling. It's like you're internally hedging your own bets. The totes companies are worried that online bets will destroy their onsite revenue, but if you also handle online betting, no matter which side becomes more popular, you still win."

"Don't forget his racehorse ownership company," Kristiana says. "That's my favorite part of the three. Betting's so much more exciting when you own a horse, and now people who could never afford it have the ability to go in on a partial share of one—a great one. Then when they bet, they're betting on themselves."

I do think Trifecta's brilliant, but their flattery doesn't change my mind. "I'm glad you like my company," I say. "But I don't need your help making my presentation. Stay here, please."

"We're coming," Kristiana says. "Now that we're here. . ." She glances at Katerina. "There's no telling when Leonid will decide you're a priority and show up."

Katerina shakes her head. "I'm not here to draw him out.

He told me specifically that he wants nothing to do with Gustav, as long as he stays away from his magic."

"It's quite difficult to draw out magical ability," Grigoriy says.

"And that's for us," Alexei says. "For you, it might be even harder."

"He'd have to do something truly noble," Katerina says. "I already told him. Without a significant sacrifice, he won't be able to access any powers at all."

"See?" I say, "No worries, then."

Kris looks exactly the same as my mom used to when she's disappointed. The small sigh. The drooping chin. The sad eyes. It's *disturbingly* the same. I wonder whether she knows that. "You're the only hope we have of defeating him."

"You said Grigoriy and Aleksandr still have their powers," I say. "They're strong, right? Rocks and air or something?"

Kris doesn't try to hide her irritation this time. "You can't believe Katerina's assurances that you'll be safe. She's close to Leonid."

"Scared of him and close aren't the same thing," Katerina says.

"She's the one who told him about his powers, she was there when he started using them, she gave him the electrical power, and she went to visit with him recently." Adriana folds her arms and glares. "The bottom line is, we can't trust her. So go to your meetings, and we'll just wait outside."

"You think Leonid's going to leave Russia, where he's surrounded by his people and an army, and fly to the United States. . .to what?" I ask. "To assassinate me?"

"He might send someone," Kris says. "Katerina's brother Boris held Adriana in a shack for days on end in a tiny room, threatening her. He works for Leonid."

"It wasn't fun," Adriana says. "I can vouch."

"Ask her how she escaped," Mirdza says.

Adriana jabs her twin. "Keep your mouth shut."

"Fine," I say. "You can come if you bring something to read or do and you just sit in the lobby while I do each presentation." I have no idea who I'll tell the people they are or why they're there, but I'll think of something. "But under no circumstance are you allowed to come into the room or speak at all while I'm working."

"Deal," Kris says.

Of course, that lasts exactly one minute.

"Kristiana?" A tall blond man stands when we walk through the doors of the conference room for our first meeting.

"You know him?" I glance from the man in the navy suit with the British accent to Kris. "How?"

"I'm her ex-boyfriend," the blond man in the suit says. "I'm also the Vice President of operations for the AIB Group, Sean—"

"Sean bloody McDermott." Aleksandr looks ready to punch him.

Kristiana's smiling.

Sean rolls his eyes. "That's me. But what are *you* doing here?"

"Daniel Belmont," Kris says, "is my big brother."

Sean blinks. "You're kidding."

Kristiana shakes her head.

"Well, tell me this, since you owe me. Is he a good investment?"

Kris shrugs. "I mean, I hear there's a maniac who wants him dead."

Sean nods slowly. "That's true for most of the best businessmen in the world."

"If you're ready to begin the meeting," I say, "we can—"

Sean waves his hand. "I think I have something better. Sisters are always the best judge of character for their brothers." He narrows his eyes. "You tell me whether I should invest." He frowns. "Are you investing?"

"Gustav's a bad brother. He never returns my calls, he never visits, and he doesn't ever call me. But it's because he's always put work first," Kris says slowly.

That stings a little, but she's not lying.

She goes on. "If you want to invest in something that has a solid plan, that has been conservative in every aspect, and that's sure to turn a solid profit, then yes." Kris nods. "He's not a bad investment, which is why I'll definitely invest in it myself."

Sean stares at her for a moment. Then that moment stretches.

I can't help glancing at Aleksandr, who looks ready to rearrange Sean's not-too-bad-looking face. That would be very inconvenient for me.

"I've brought some materials you may want to peruse." I offer Sean a folder, stepping intentionally between Aleksandr and the VP of Operations for one of the fifty largest banks in Europe. "And my sister's glowing recommendation notwithstanding, I'd be happy to explain anything—"

Sean takes the folder, and looks me in the eye. "She gave you about the best recommendation you could have gotten." He nods. "Count us in for the maximum allowable shares at your suggested price." The corner of his mouth turns up. "And now I should go. I'm afraid if I stick around much longer, Kristiana's Russian thug will try to rough me up."

Aleksandr's face has flushed, and he looks ready to do it.

Sean reaches the door, his lackeys falling in behind him, when he turns around. "You know, it's a little depressing when you don't win the girl, but it's a lot more fun to be the one who's free to say whatever he wants."

He ducks out before Aleksandr has a chance to rearrange any of the various parts of his face.

I have a little extra time now, thanks to Kris, to prepare to meet with Ameritrade. In spite of that, the meeting does not go well. They ask about what happened with Black Rock, and they ask a lot of questions about how the company was founded, and why I moved to New York right before college. Frankly, they're asking questions I didn't think anyone would even know to ask.

While I should be anticipating what other questions they might come up with, I find myself thinking about that stupid palomino from my dream last night. When I'm not thinking of that, I keep imagining Katerina in the middle of the night, offering to buy some of my company herself.

Once, in college, I had a friend who was desperate to get published. She kept talking about selling her book—she meant to a publisher. But this little boy who overheard us talking told her he would buy her book.

She melted.

That's how I felt when that little lost Russian woman told me if she had money, she would buy part of my company. I don't actually need anyone to buy it. My company's doing great on its own. Most companies go public when they need money to expand, or when their employees need to be able to sell their shares, but for me, it's all about recognition. It's about showing my grandfather that I'm competent and capable and that I'll be the best person to take over when he retires.

When the Ameritrade meeting ends, I'm not sure whether they'll buy a decent chunk of shares or not. I'm reviewing some things with Jean and the team when someone who had just left comes back in the room. I recognize him, because I could hardly see his face thanks to the tall man in front of him. He was wearing a pinstriped suit and four thousand dollar shoes, so I tried to catch a glimpse, but it never happened.

Jean sees him coming, too. "Welcome back. Did you forget—"

The man looks up, and I realize that I know him.

It's my cousin, Prescott Belmont.

"I didn't forget anything, but you sure did." His smirk's very, very self-satisfied. "You know, I was worried about this whole last-minute IPO. It's very *Hail Mary* of you. Coming in with the public offering *just* before Grandfather's party." He shakes his head. "Sneaky. I didn't realize you had it in you." He steps closer, his grin deepening. "But then you botch Black Rock, which Grandfather practically gift-wrapped, and today you put on the worst presentation I've ever seen with Ameritrade." He snorts. "What's wrong? I'm honestly worried about you."

I step closer and jab a finger against his breastbone. "You've been worried about me for ten years. You should be more worried about your own resume. Whereas you barely graduated from Temple University, and you waltzed into a ready-made job at Grandfather's company, I earned my way."

"I'd hardly call a mediocre online gambling start-up 'earning your way,' and I wasn't sure what you were even doing at first, with a gambling company." He sighs. "But then I remembered that you do what you know, and you've known about gambling your whole life, haven't you?"

"I'm not sure we've met." Kristiana steps closer, having ducked into the room through the door our sweet cousin left open. "It seems like we may be related."

"I doubt it." Prescott arches one dark eyebrow.

"Kristiana Liepa." Kris holds out her hand. "I think, unfortunately, that we're cousins."

Prescott steps back as if someone from the street's trying to sell him knock-off Oakleys. "How lovely. More of my Latvian relations."

"Your father was nearly as nasty as you are," Kris says. "Mom told me some stories. But do tell me, I'm sure we all want to know. She also said you were still wetting the bed at age ten. Or was it eleven? Did you ever get that fixed? Was it a medical thing? Or were you just too lazy to get up and go pee pee in the potty at night?"

Our bully of a first cousin glares, pivots on the heel of his expensive shoe, and storms off. The second he's gone, Jean starts to laugh. "That was the best thing I've ever seen." Her face is bright red. "It had to be true, or he'd have shut you down."

"Aunt Pearl called Mom once," Kris says. "I wasn't supposed to be listening in. It was past my bedtime, but when Aunt Pearl mentioned that her ten-year-old kid was still wetting the bed, I was stuck with my cheek to the door for twenty minutes."

"Thanks," I say. "It's not like his opinion matters, but I do appreciate the support."

Not only does Kris help me with stupid Prescott, but she sits in on the next meeting with Fidelity, and she makes so many jokes about horses and betting, and talks about Sean's commitment so casually, that the guy in charge decides to match Sean's generous pledges this morning. It's nice to have a few purchasers lined up and in my back pocket on the first full day.

I still want her to leave—especially if Katerina's right and the maniac will leave me alone as long as I do nothing—but I didn't hate having Kris here when Prescott showed up, and when I'm not fighting with them, they don't seem to destroy everything. Maybe I'll be able to survive the next few weeks, even if Kris insists on staying.

"Coffee?" Jean asks, pointing at the pot that's been sitting on the warmer for at least an hour.

"I'll walk downstairs and grab one," I say. "Anyone else need something decent?"

"Do they sell coffee here at three in the afternoon?" Kristiana asks.

"This is New York City," Jean says. "They have coffee twenty-four hours a day."

Kris blinks.

I'm walking through the front doors of Chase Tower on

Madison Avenue, reviewing the details of our last pitch for the day as I walk, when out of the corner of my eye, I see her.

Katerina.

She's staring at something on a screen on the other side of the street, and she steps out into the street without looking first. There's a bus barreling toward her, and there's no way it can stop in time.

In the movies, this would be where I would leap toward her and shove her out of the way, only to be crushed myself. I have no idea why people do that. It makes no sense. I jog toward her and lean out, grabbing her arm and yanking her back to the safety of the sidewalk. The bus rolls on by, honking, but Katerina's safe. She's also pressed against my side like a dryer sheet on wool pants, fresh from the laundry basket.

"Gustav." Her whisper's breathy, her eyes wide, and her hands are splayed against my chest. "That was—" She freezes. "That was a selfless act."

I practically drop her back into the street.

Something like that couldn't have. . . My heart pounds in my chest, my pulse roaring in my ears. "All I did was snatch you out of the way. You're fine, and so am I."

A smile creeps across her face, and her cheeks flush. "But it's in you, you know. The goodness, I mean."

"Don't walk into roads without looking." I roll my eyes, order my coffee, and march back upstairs, not even taking the time to find out what had her so enthralled that she wasn't paying attention to her own safety.

Once I reach the boardroom again, I realize that I forgot to grab Grigoriy's coffee in my rush. So much for being selfless. I wind up having to give him mine and pretend I already drank my cup, even though I'd already had three sips. Now he's sucking down my saliva with his coffee.

Maybe I should, but I don't feel at all guilty about being the selfish, focused, driven beast that I am. After all, it's because of that greed that I won't be at risk for Leonid's insane wrath, and if all seven of these people are scared of him, I want nothing to do with it. He can wreak as much havoc as he wants on that side of the world. It just makes me more relieved than ever that I emigrated when I did.

It's not my problem, and if everything goes according to plan, it never will be.

Gustav's a different person today. He's smiling, albeit occasionally, and he's not yelling nearly as much. I can't tell what made the difference, but no one wants his company to succeed as much as I do. If he does well here, if he stays in the United States and never touches his magic, Leonid will leave him alone, and I won't have to feel guilty about trying to trade knowledge about him for Alexei's powers.

Not that my trade worked.

I shouldn't have blurted the offer out like that. As if someone as honorable as Alexei Romanov would call off his engagement just to get his powers back. He would never be so blatantly selfish. Sometimes I project my own actions and feelings on him, and it always leads me to make the wrong call.

Like how I've backed myself into a corner.

I framed Leonid's demand too heavily, and I can't modify it without confessing that Leonid doesn't care about Alexei having his powers as long as Leonid himself can also use them, which negates my involvement and therefore the credit. It would also compel me to admit that I went there with an offer—betraying Gustav for my own gain.

I'm stuck either failing in my goal or being outed as a villain.

As if that's not bad enough, I'm also forced to sit here and watch Alexei and Adriana flirt and coo and generally behave like teenagers in lust. I can't really roll my eyes and huff, because then I look even more juvenile, so I'm stuck looking away and pretending not to see or care.

Only, there's not anywhere decent to look in this lobby.

"Why do we need to sit out here?" I ask. "Kristiana might be helpful. She knows a lot about betting and horse racing, plus she's his sister, but what are the rest of us supposed to do?"

"You could protect him if it comes to it." Grigoriy's scowling. Of the three men, he's always despised me the most. "Unless that's too much to ask from someone like you."

"Leonid took my powers when I went to beg for Alexei's," I mutter. "So I won't be much help there."

"Wait, he did?" Adriana looks shocked. "I—I'm sorry."

The only thing worse than watching them flirting is having her pity me. "It's fine," I say. "I barely use mine anyway, and I can still shift."

"Clearly," Mirdza says. "That's how you freaked out everyone at customs."

"Not customs," Grigoriy says. "The Department of Homeland Security. Customs is for declaring plants."

"*Anyway*," I say. "My point is that the rest of us could be. . .I don't know. Doing something else. What's the reason for all of us just hovering out here while he has meetings?"

"I need to keep all of you safe," Aleksandr says, "and we need to protect Gustav, at least until he fully understands what's at stake and what his role in it may be."

"Do we even know that?" I ask. "I already told you that as

long as he doesn't try to use his powers, Leonid will leave him alone."

"As if we can believe anything that maniac says." Aleksandr scowls.

"So what's your plan, then?" I ask. "Are you hoping to force Gustav into doing something selfless, and then train him into some kind of weapon to aim at Leonid?"

Grigoriy shrugs.

Aleksandr looks at the floor.

Alexei swallows.

And I realize that's *exactly* what they mean to do. "You three act like Leonid's the devil," I say. "Which is ironic, because you're almost as bad as he is, manipulating someone's life like that."

Aleks scoffs. "How can you, of all people, say that?"

"How dare you accuse them of being bad?" Adriana asks. "None of them incinerate massive groups of people."

"What?" I ask.

"That was my introduction to Leonid," Adriana says. "He barbecued a dozen men in the open street."

"None of them have the power of flame," I say. "Or who knows what you'd have seen them do?"

Mirdza looks a little sick.

"The difference between you guys and Leonid is that you don't have any faith in his moral compass. If it was Alexei who had won the election, he might have done the same exact thing as Leonid, eliminating the leader of Belarus." I can't help my frustration. "And now you're here, planning to craft yourself a dangerous puppet you can use to take him down, as if that's better than him. At least he attacks people himself."

None of them say a word to me, but they murmur amongst themselves plenty. What's ironic is that I don't trust Leonid any more than they do, but at least I can see the hypocrisy in what they want to do with Gustav.

Which makes the next three hours of waiting while Gustav merrily conducts his meetings and presentations torturous. I'm pacing in the hallway outside yet another boardroom, waiting for the presentation there to start so we can finally be done and head back to Gustav's place when Alexei approaches.

Without his girlfriend, for once.

"Are you okay?" He actually looks concerned.

I should ignore him. They probably sent him out here to pump me for information. His expression's so earnest, and his concern so terribly real that I can't help myself.

"I—this—using Gustav like a loaded gun feels wrong. I think you should tell him what you want, and then tell him the risks he'd be facing if he agrees, but let him choose." No one ever gives anyone else any choices, and isn't that their biggest issue with Leonid?

But then it hits me.

I'm a hypocrite.

Maybe that's why I've been so agitated.

Because isn't that what I've been doing with Alexei? Isn't that why I went to Leonid in the first place? He chose Adriana, not me. He's known me for a long time, and *he doesn't want me*. He wants her. I've been refusing to accept that, which is the same thing as them refusing to accept that Gustav wants nothing to do with the powers we all covet. Above all else, I don't want to be like Leonid, or like the three of them, forcing things on people that they don't even want. Which means. . .

That I have to let go of my lifelong dream, or that's how it feels.

It hurts.

My insides feel raw.

Loving Alexei has been who I am. It's been what makes me *me*.

I've wanted it—for him to want me back—for so very,

very long. I've wrecked things in my life. I've hurt people. I've done it all so that Alexei would realize that he loves me, but what if he never did? What if he never, under any circumstance, ever will?

Have I been the *villain* this whole time without realizing it?

I went to Leonid and offered to trade Gustav's whereabouts for Alexei's powers, for heaven's sake. This poor man —whom I've now met—I was willing to exchange his whole life for a chance at winning Alexei back.

Someone who doesn't *want* to be won.

He prefers having her to having his powers restored.

"I'm sorry." Tears spring up in my eyes. "I'm really sorry."

"For having an opinion?" Alexei looks concerned. "You've always had an opinion, and you've never been sorry about that before."

"Leonid didn't say you had to marry me." I wince. "He said he'd give your powers back any time, because then, every time you use them, you'd think of him. And if you ever confronted him, he'd have the kill switch. He could always just shut down your abilities again, as he did with me. It's a reminder." I shake my head. "I asked him to let me make the stipulations, so I could use your own powers to get what I want."

Alexei looks disgusted. "You colluded with him?"

"Only about this," I say. "Only to try and win you back, but I've realized that's never going to happen."

"You can't win back what you never had," Alexei says.

Even though he's not trying to hurt me, it stings. But he's right. I never had him. I never will have him.

"I'll text him now and tell him to give you the powers back."

Alexei shakes his head. "I mean to see whether Gustav, once he has control, can restore me. I don't want powers that only come with a kill switch."

Of course he doesn't. He wasn't born to serve someone else, to bow to some other ruler. He was born to be a king.

"I, um, I need to get some air." I push past him, and he doesn't stop me. It takes me a moment, but I finally get down from this horribly tall building, through the elevator full of people I've never met, and escape into a street that's teeming with more strangers.

I have no idea why anyone would choose to live in this place.

The streets smell like human urine and feces. There's a smoky smell coming from all sides. It smells like tobacco sometimes, and like something else others, something I can't place. Cars and buses crowd the streets, and trash rolls and squishes through any gaps. Construction structures crowd one side of the road. There are huge signs everywhere you look, all screaming for attention. It's more annoying than the morass of peddlers in the town square in St. Petersburg when I was younger.

None of it helps me feel better. None of it helps me to process what just happened. I let go of something huge, and now the world's crowding in on top of me to flood the gap, and I want to curl up into a ball here in the street and disappear.

Then I see a familiar face on the screen up ahead.

It's Leonid.

The devil himself, in some ways, and a lost little boy in others. "—discovered some things about Aleksandr Lukashenko that were. . .disturbing. He certainly wasn't a leader who had his people's best interest in mind. Our first meeting did not go well, and when I pressed him about his plans for his people, he revealed an agenda I could not allow to come to pass."

"You're saying that you're the white knight in this situation?" the man in a suit asks. "You've saved the citizens of Belarus?"

Leonid smiles.

I'd forgotten how beautiful his smile is. How compelling. It makes him dangerous in a way that few men are.

Devilishly good looking. It's a phrase that takes on new meaning with him. "A leader's first priority should always be making decisions that provide the most good for the most people, don't you agree?"

The suit-guy frowns. "Well, I don't know. Some ethical questions aren't clear-cut. What if there was a train headed down a track, and if you didn't stop it, it would hit someone who had become stuck and kill him. But if you delayed the train to save the man, thousands of passengers would be late, some of them to their detriment? Businesses might fail. Families might fall apart. Should the man die so the train keeps to its schedule?"

"People who come up with these scenarios should be shot," Leonid says with a grin. "It would save us all a lot of time. The world isn't as grey as people want to believe it is." Leonid turns toward the screen. "I seek out the white and eliminate the black. That's how you craft a better world. If the man was a good man, the delay would be worth it. If he was a bad man, the train should carry on." He shrugs. "It's that simple."

"But how do you know whether people are good or bad?" the interviewer asks. "Aren't most people somewhere in between?"

This time, when Leonid smiles, it's beatific. "Oh, I can always tell, and they're rarely as mixed a bag as you might think."

I don't even realize that I'm moving closer to the screen until a hand yanks me back, and I collapse against the person who just saved me. A very loud, very large, very dangerous bus rumbles past the spot I was standing, and I realize I would have been splattered into goo.

When I look up, the face I'm staring into is Gustav's. I

whisper his name, shocked that he was anywhere near. Shocked further that he would care whether a bus flattened me. Gustav had absolutely no reason to save me. "That was—that was a selfless act."

He dumps me as fast as he grabbed me, and I sprawl forward, my right hand bracing against the concrete to prevent me from face-planting. "All I did was snatch you out of the way," he says. "You're fine, and so am I."

He's saying he sacrificed nothing, but I'm not so sure. He's supposed to be preparing for his last presentation of the day, but he's here, on the street, snatching me out of the path of a bus. In all the worry over Leonid and what he may or may not do, I hadn't given much thought to what kind of person Gustav is. But maybe I was right to defend him. Maybe, deep down, he's a good guy. "It's in you, you know. The goodness, I mean."

"Just don't walk into roads without looking." He stalks off to buy a coffee and then marches back upstairs without so much as looking at me. But it's pointed. He's looking every-where *but* where I'm standing. Which means he feels bad that he was so gruff. He feels bad that he saved me as a reflex.

It's exactly the kind of thing that shows me who he really is. He doesn't want credit. He doesn't want accolades, but when it comes down to it, he does the right thing.

Sitting through the last presentation in yet another antechamber for yet another board room is a little awkward, but it's better than before, because instead of watching Alexei and Adriana interact with eyes of denial, I watch with insight. They only look at each other, much as Kris and Aleks track one another with their eyes constantly. Grigoriy's strong, almost dour face is in a state of perma-scowl. . .unless he's looking at Mirdza.

Now that I've accepted the reality, it's so painfully obvi-ous. Those three couples are *stupid* in love with one another. I thought that letting go of Alexei would hurt, but after the first wave of misery passed, I feel remarkably free. It's almost like I was holding on to something that hurt me, and I've finally released it.

Why didn't I let go sooner?

I wonder how often in life we hang on to things, not because we need them, not because they help us in any way, but because we can't remember how to let go. Like a child who clung so tightly to their mum's hand that they can't release it. Like a rope pulled taut for so long, it's fused with the other fibers and can't be separated.

None of those things are better for the clinging.

And neither was I.

"Hey." Mirdza takes a few steps toward me and sits down, ruining the perfectly good buffer of three chairs that I've carefully maintained on either side of myself all day. "Is this okay?"

I shrug. "It's a free country—America, right?"

Mirdza laughs. "You sound remarkably modern. Grigoriy still sounds like a Tolstoy novel sometimes."

"Tolstoy?" I cringe. "He was ancient a hundred years ago."

"Forget it," Mirdza says. "You seem to have caught up quite well."

"I watched a lot of television while I first woke up, when Leonid stuck me in a room, and then I watched more in that room at Kristiana's house."

"Ah, television. The great educator of our time." Mirdza looks at her hands.

"Did you want something?" I should be nicer to her. She's the first person who has actually tried to talk to me, but I can't help it. I'm not good with chit chat when I know the person wants something. I'd rather know what it is.

Her face scrunches.

"You can just ask. I'm a pretty straightforward person."

"I actually don't want anything," Mirdza says. "But you look so miserable over here that it got me thinking." She sighs. "Maybe I should just butt out, but I'm the kind of person who worries when horses in a herd are being excluded."

She's different than Kristiana, and definitely different from her twin. Is it possible she really just wanted to check on me? If so, she should know who I am. I can't really make friends with her when I wanted to betray her sister. "Sometimes there's a reason the herd ostracizes one horse. I—I came here to try and break Adriana and Alexei up."

She giggles.

Honest-to-goodness *giggles*, like a little girl. "Duh."

I blink.

"I mean, we all knew that, but it's fine. You didn't have a hope of success."

I start to laugh too. I can't help it. She's acting like I was a child in a superhero suit, bent on stopping crime.

"Those two are meant for each other," Mirdza says. "Nothing on heaven or earth could have stopped them from being together." She shrugs. "You might have annoyed Adriana. Her self-esteem isn't what it should be, but none of the rest of us were worried."

That makes me feel pretty lousy. I was the only one too stupid to see what she's saying, but now that she says it, it's painfully clear. "We don't get to pick what our hearts want."

"But we do get to choose what we do about it." Mirdza's voice is soft, and from anyone else, it would have sounded like a reproof, but not from her. It sounds like she's been there, and she's made the wrong choice before, too. "And for what it's worth, you look happier now that you've given up. You should think about that."

"What do you think it means?"

"You never had a mother," Mirdza says. "Alexei mentioned that."

"I'm not a charity case," I say. "I made my own decisions."

"But as someone who never had much of a mother

herself," Mirdza says, "I wonder. Is it possible that you wanted a family as much as you wanted Alexei himself?"

I blink.

"I'm certainly no expert, but I wonder whether you loved the idea more than the person." She shrugs. "Maybe not. Just thinking out loud."

"What if we choose wrong?" I ask. "What then?"

"I chose wrong." She snorts. "I bet most women have."

"You did?" I have trouble believing that.

"I think it might have been harder on you."

"I don't need pity."

"But Katerina, you grew up in a time when you *had* to find a man—to keep you safe." Mirdza taps her lip. "I won't lie and say that it's not nice to have Grigoriy around, ready to scare away the bad guys for me. But I spent most of my life having to deal with things myself, and Adriana never wanted to date, much less get married. We were raised with a plan to protect ourselves, to keep *ourselves* safe. We were raised to believe it was a woman's job to make herself happy." She turns and stares right at me. "I think you should stop thinking about Alexei or any other man and start thinking about Katerina and what *she* wants. Then maybe you'll find a guy whom you can love in a healthy way."

The door from the conference room opens, as I answer her. "No one finds joy by thinking only about themselves."

"Are you two talking about me?" Gustav's standing in the doorway, and none of the people from the meeting are beside him.

"Where did everyone go?" Mirdza asks. "Is your presentation finished?"

"This conference room has two entrances." He tosses his head. "They went out the other one."

"I wasn't talking about you," I say. "I just mean that, in general, trying to make yourself happy is doomed to fail. You can only really be happy when you're helping someone else to reach their goals."

"That's tragic, if it's true," Gustav says. "Just tragic."

"I don't know," Mirdza says. "I kind of like it. It feels vaguely religious, honestly, but it still might be true. As humans, I do think we find joy in service."

"You only think that because you have no goals of your own." Gustav brushes past me and pushes onward. "I have some work to do before tomorrow's meetings, and it'll take me at least two hours. After that, I'll spend the rest of the night doing whatever you need me to do." He looks pointedly at Kristiana. "Unless it's saving someone selflessly."

Then he winks at me.

For some reason, that stupid wink makes my heart race.

It's the only exciting thing that happens all night, however. The rest of the evening consists of Alexei, Aleksandr, and Grigoriy, interrupted frequently by the women, reciting the story of how they woke up in modern day, how they recovered their powers, and then how Leonid took Alexei's, along with the throne of Russia.

"And that's not even all of it," Alexei says. "He's got an unquenchable thirst for more."

I'm not sure that's really true, but it's pointless to argue. At least they aren't trying to force Gustav's hand.

"You might be safe, if you stay here," Alexei admits. "Katerina knows Leonid better than the rest of us, and she thinks he'll leave you alone. But you need to consider what will happen to the rest of the world if—"

"I don't buy the premise that the fate of the entire world is my responsibility," Gustav says. "And I can't believe that all of you think I'm the key to anything. If that were true, since I have zero powers, why wouldn't Kristiana be able to do the exact same thing as me? Are you saying this magic is somehow sexist?"

"You're older, dummy," Kristiana says. "All the other

powers were for an entire family line, but ours is different, we think."

"Leonid's powers are different too," I finally say.

The entire table turns to me. "What do you know?" Alexei's eyes are practically desperate. "I was there when he saved you, and nothing happened. He didn't shock or flame anything. He didn't exhibit any other elemental power at all at first."

"Nothing you could see, anyway," I mutter.

And then I go ahead and betray Leonid's trust all the way.

12

KATERINA

My plan is far, far easier to implement with Leonid than I expected.

Alexei's definitely jealous.

I just can't tell whether he's jealous of *my attention*, or just jealous that there's finally someone who's better looking and also smart among us. Alexei's had the luxury of being the smartest, the best looking, and the most talented since birth, essentially. And for someone who's had none of life's advantages, Leonid still manages to be good at almost everything.

Everyone else is coming in the next day, so we decide to play a little tennis to kill the time. It's Czar Nicholas' favorite sport, so his son plays pretty often.

"I've never so much as held a racket," Leonid says. "This is going to be embarrassing."

I show him how to grip the handle, and then we have to explain all the rules, one by one.

"You two can play together against me," Alexei says, always the gentleman. "It should help give you a fighting chance." His relaxed and yet cocky smile, the one I love so well, is firmly in place.

But it's quickly apparent that Leonid has a natural

knack for this. His hand-eye coordination's stellar, and he picks up the basics quickly. "Ah, you didn't hit it hard enough, so it bounced twice, and that means we get the point," he says.

Alexei's face flushes bright red. "Yes, that's right."

"Thanks for demonstrating," I say.

"But I think I get it now," Leonid says. "No need to slow down quite so much for me."

Halfway through the set, I bow out and let them play one another. And when, at the end, it's neck and neck, an experienced player against a novice, I can tell that Alexei's hackles are up.

"The sun's close to setting," I call.

"Huh?" Leonid turns.

Alexei could serve then, when he's distracted, but he's too good of a sport to do that. Instead he lowers his head. "And?"

"Everyone's coming tomorrow," I say. "I thought tonight might be a good time to go to Vyborgsky."

Alexei drops the ball, which bounces a few times and rolls into the base of the net. "Why?"

"Why do we ever go there?" I shrug, and then I stare. "To see." Because if Leonid really *is* one of us, we may as well find out. And if he is. . .Alexei might really become nervous.

Nervous enough to be jealous.

Even when he finds out Leonid's just a servant.

Alexei's frowning when he tosses his racket to one of his attendants and starts walking toward the back of the palace. "I'm not sure that's a good idea."

Leonid's following, but at a suitable distance. Like he's a servant. I hiss and wave for him to catch up.

"What could happen to us?" I roll my eyes. "Between the two of us, we can stop anything bad, and it's a great place to find a selfless act, don't you think?"

"It's not selfless if he's doing it for the wrong reasons."

Don't I know it. "We'll find out," I say. "If he can find

something to do, then we'll know that he either doesn't have the capacity, or his heart's in the wrong place."

"I guess." Alexei's moody through all of dinner, but when we're done, once his parents dismiss us, he calls for a car.

"No need for that," Leonid says. "I can drive—I hate having to wait for other people to take me places."

"It's why we brought the car," I say, softening the implied criticism.

"Fine," Alexei says.

Within five minutes, we're *en route* to the roughest part of town. As Petrograd has industrialized over the past fifteen years, it has swelled to more than twice its former size. The housing quarters have not been able to keep up, so there are always little groups of vagrants who converge in the areas with the most factories.

When you put that many people together, there are always some who don't behave properly. But we must've chosen an off night to come. Everyone we see ducks their head and walks away. Even when we leave the key unattended in the car and meander the other direction, no one seems inclined to do anything nefarious.

Finally, close to midnight, we catch a break.

I hope.

Someone's screaming a block or so away. "It's fine," I say. "I'll watch the car, and you guys go check that out."

"Are you sure?" Alexei asks.

I hold out my hands and a bolt arcs from my right to my left. "I'm fine."

They're gone for a while. Quite a while, in fact. They're gone long enough that I get bored. I shoot lightning bolts from one hand to the next for a while, but then even that gets old. Bored might be bad, but what's worse is sleepy. I must not even realize it when I drift off.

The hand that wakes me up is not Alexei's, and it's not Leonid's either. It's someone much older, much rougher, and far more aggressive. "Hey. You came with the pretty boys, didn't you?"

I reach out to zap them.

"I was going to kill them both—knocked them out cold—but then I thought about it. What if pretty boys like that has rich parents who could pay for 'em?" When he smiles, I notice one of his front teeth is dark brown.

I shudder.

"Ghislain, the pretty girl don't like us." He stoops down closer, spit from his mouth spraying my face when he says, "I don't care. Now, tell me if you got someone who'll pay for 'em?"

If I shock him, what will happen to Leonid and Alexei? How did he knock them both out? Before I can answer or knock the men senseless, a third man comes running, his sides heaving as he stops beside us. He doubles over. "Wait."

"What?" the first man asks, yanking my head up and exposing my throat. "What's all the fuss?"

"One of them boys is the tsarevich."

The man's response is crude in the extreme, but he drops my head in his shock. One second later, he whips me back up again. "Is that true?"

I don't immediately answer, trying to decide what's smartest, but he's not someone who waits, apparently.

He kicks me.

All my patience gone, I reach out without thinking and shock them so hard, they curl up into fetal balls on the ground. I kick the big man right in the gut, and then I shock them both again. "Where are they?"

Their only answer is moaning, so I shock them again. "Where are they? If you don't tell me, I'll shock you every five seconds until you do."

The big man's foaming at the mouth in a very satisfactory way when he points and splutters out his directions. But by the time I get there, it's too late.

Leonid's awake, and he's really taking a beating when I arrive. Two men are holding him, and two more are striking him. Blood's streaming down his face, one of his arms is dislocated—maybe broken—and his left eye's swelled up so big that I can't see the eyeball at all.

Alexei, meanwhile, is tied up, both his hands and his feet, lying in the corner, apparently forgotten.

"Hey," I shout. "Over here—what are you doing?"

The man who just slammed his fist into Leonid's stomach smiles. "This is the tsarevich—he admitted it. Can you believe it? We have a chance to get a little of our own back." As if he's just now taking in my clothing, he frowns. "Wait. You're—are you with them?" Now his smile widens.

The two men holding Leonid drop him, and he slumps in a way that isn't very encouraging. I hope he's alright, but I have other things to worry about currently. "Why would you think he's related to the tsar in any way?" I laugh. "That's ridiculous."

"He dropped this." The man holds up Alexei's ring. It's the signet of the tsarevich, and whenever we go out, Alexei takes it off and puts it in his belt pouch. His father isn't very popular in this area right now, not with the high taxes, the lack of housing, and the backlash from the Potemkin mess.

Which means I'm stuck.

Things are about to get messy, and although we aren't really supposed to use our magic in a public place, I'm sure Alexei's father would prefer that I expose our powers to his son being brutalized by these goons and then ransomed while war's looming on the horizon. The royal coffers are already dangerously low from what I hear. He wouldn't appreciate forking over any of his diminishing funds to these idiots.

"Ooh, let me see it." I hold out my hand.

The man laughs. "I'm not stupid."

"Empirically disproven by your actions."

While the jerk furrows his brow, trying to work out the

meaning of my words, I strike. I can only split my power into two different streams at a time, which I'm supposed to be working on improving in the next few weeks here, but with just four men in the room, it's enough. I hit the two closest to me first, shocking them for much, much longer than I did the last two. And just before the other two reach me, I release the first guys and slam the others with full force. They fly backward, away from me and toward Leonid.

Before their bodies collide with his, I release them.

All four slump to the ground, and I'm confident they won't recover enough to harm us, but I still have to figure out how to get Leonid and an unconscious Alexei back to our waiting car.

If it's even still there. I stupidly didn't think to swing by and grab the key. I groan inwardly, and jog across to where Alexei's body is curled up and tied. I lean close enough to confirm that he's breathing—short, shallow breaths—and then I keep moving to check on Leonid.

Up close, he looks even worse than I thought at first. His leg's bent and looks broken. His nose is clearly broken, too. His eye's swollen up like a grapefruit, and I'm worried there's not much left under the damage. I can't bring myself to poke around and check.

I've always lamented that the electric and fire powers don't come with any healing abilities, but now it feels personal. I'm forced to watch as Alexei and Leonid suffer. I try to shift Leonid a bit—he slumped forward on his side. The only part of his face I can really see is the swollen eye, and I'd like to at least get him on his back. But when I try to shift him, the hand of his unbroken arm shoots out and grabs my wrist.

He's still got some fight in him, which is good.

"It's me," I say. "Katerina."

His hand loosens then. "You're alright."

"I am," I say. "Which is more than I can say for you. Why on earth did they think you were Alexei?"

"I told them I was." He groans. "I woke up—he didn't. They found his cursed ring on the ground between us, and they were arguing. They hated his father." He's wheezing as he talks, and then he coughs.

Blood sprays all over my boot.

"There's something wrong with my breathing." He coughs again, and this time, it's even worse.

I'm actually worried he won't be able to make it to the car, even if I drag him. "Leonid, I'm so sorry."

He shakes his head.

"Don't try to talk, okay? Don't do anything."

But he smiles, then. "I did something selfless." His smile becomes even wider, and I realize that one tooth isn't straight. "I took the beating for him."

Oh. My eyes widen. "And?"

He should have some kind of powers by now.

"Do you feel water calling to you? Or maybe the earth beneath you?"

He shakes his head.

"Okay, what, then? Anything?"

He coughs again and soaks the entire bottom hem of my dress in red.

"Maybe we should talk about this later."

He grabs my boot. "When I see people now, their faces look strange."

"Strange?" I crouch down near him again. "What does that mean?" Could it be water? Maybe it's not just their faces. Maybe it's everything—Alexei says he can see the water in all living things. "Do you mean—"

"Your face lights up." His eyes brighten. "It's beautiful."

I frown. "I'm not sure—"

"But the men who were beating me?" He shudders. "Their faces, it was like they were covered in tar. Like their faces were hidden behind a mask of evil. A mask of darkness." He shakes his head. "What does it mean?"

I stand, my hand shaking. "I—I'm not sure." I can't bring myself to tell him that it doesn't sound like *any* of our powers. It sounds. . .crazy. Useless and crazy. "Maybe don't talk about this to anyone else, alright?"

Leonid, through the oozing blood, the swollen eye, the crooked tooth, and the bruised jaw, looks truly broken for the first time.

"I'll get Alexei," I say. "If I can wake him up. . ."

"Don't," he says. "I think I can stand."

Watching him try and stand upright on a broken leg, with a broken and dislocated arm, with a face that's swollen like a pumpkin, is the most painful thing I've ever seen. "Leonid."

He shakes his head. "Maybe I haven't done enough yet." His speech is slurred. "Maybe it takes more." He stumbles his way over to Alexei and reaches underneath him.

"Wait," I say. "You can't do that. Your arm."

He straightens a bit, and then he turns to me. "I need some help." His one visible eye looks terrible, burning brightly.

"What?"

"Hold my arm up." He tosses his head. "Come over here, and hold my arm up."

"I don't think—"

"With all this noise, if he's not awake, there's a reason. The last thing you should do is try and wake him." He looks down at Alexei with concern. "Just do as I'm asking."

I shake my head. "If you can walk, I can—"

"Please," he says. "Maybe it takes more pain, more sacrifice, or more good. Whatever it is, I'll do it."

I can't argue, not with that. Not with his burning, desperate desire. I've seen the same look in his father's face, and I'm pretty sure it hollowed him from the inside out. "Fine."

The next forty-five seconds are *horrible* as he walks me through lifting his arm and rotating it—says he's seen a healer do it. After an awful ordeal, his shoulder finally pops into place with a strange sound and a shift. He doesn't even cry out or moan. He just shudders and exhales sharply.

And then he nods. "Alright."

He crouches down, putting very little weight on his left leg, and reaches under Alexei. Then he lifts him up, his good arm straining, and his teeth gritted, and he carries him. Not just a few yards. He carries him on and on, step by stumbling step. Blood runs down the side of his face and drips to the ground. The furrows in his brow deepen. The redness in his cheek and eye darken.

And still he trudges along.

Until finally, miracle of miracles, we reach the car, and it's still there, the key untouched. We load Alexei into the back, and I drive them both back to the palace. Just as we arrive, Alexei starts to moan. The sound's horrifying, but I take it as a good sign. It means he's still alive.

In the end, Alexei's father heals them both.

It's as miraculous to watch that day as it ever has been. Sure, in the moment it's painful, but all healing is. It's so fast, so complete, and so wondrous that I nearly start to cry.

Once he's done, Alexei's father asks me what happened. There's no way he would condone our trip, not without more evidence that Leonid might be able to use magic. And if we were doing it, we should have gotten permission.

So I lie.

I tell him that we were out looking at the area, because Alexei was worried about some reports he'd heard from friends that the people didn't have the best living conditions. Then I tell him that the men who attacked us saw Alexei's ring on the ground and that they became even angrier. It's not exactly comfortable, telling the leader of Russia that his citizens don't like him, but I'm pretty sure he already knows. I'm about to tell him about Leonid's bravery in protecting Alexei, but Leonid's eyes widen and his head shakes just a small amount, so I don't share that. I change course.

"I'm sorry I didn't recover the ring," I say. "I didn't think to get it—we were really struggling to get Alexei back to the car. He was too heavy for me to carry, and as you saw, Leonid was badly injured."

Alexei's father doesn't yell or rant. He places a hand on my head and bows his own. "I'm glad you're all safe, and I'm sorry things are in such a state of unrest." Then he walks away.

His calm, understated nature always stands out to me—it's there inside of Alexei, but his mother Alexandra's tempestuous temperament rises to the surface more often. Once I'm sure Alexei's fine, and once we've answered his questions about the men and how we got him away, we bid him good night.

"I'll see Leonid to his room," I say. "You rest."

Alexei's too tired to argue, so I manage to trot after a now-healed Leonid alone.

"That was *amazing*." Leonid's practically skipping. "I've never seen anything like it."

"You were in a lot of pain," I say. "For a really long time. I'm so sorry."

He spins around so fast that I stumble backward. "Who cares about the pain? Did you see the way the czar healed us? Did you see how, between one second and the next, what was broken, what was dying, was simply. . ." He snaps. "Restored?"

I nod slowly. "Yeah, that's the best thing about the water power. You can fix things with it. A lot of things."

"I need to figure out what I can do." He's nodding as he walks now, and I'm forced to jog to keep up. "We have to find out what all this means."

Except, even after several hours of questions, I'm no closer to guessing. He has no affinity to any of the things I know about. No ability to manipulate water. He burns easily from fire—proven by both a candle and his room's hearth. He's got no connection to the earth, the wind, or electricity.

His power appears to be limited to seeing what he believes to be the goodness in other people and possibly the evil, too.

"What a useless ability." He drops into the wooden chair in the corner of his room. "That can't be all of it."

"I'm not sure what more—"

He shoots to his feet again and starts pacing. "That *can't* be it."

"I've never heard of anything like this, so we'll need to ask the czar—"

His head whips toward mine. "No." He shakes his head vehemently. "That you must not do. There must be books or recordings we can search."

"Why not tell them what you did for Alexei and what you can see now, so that if they know something—"

"No." He sits again, staring at his hands. "The only thing worse than having no power is having a useless one that no one values. Believe me when I say that being different, being a freak?" He looks up at me, his eyes blazing. "That's the worst possibility of all. Promise me you'll keep quiet. Promise me you won't tell anyone about this."

I don't want to agree. I try to put him off, but in the end, I promise.

And I keep that promise.

Or at least, I did.

Until today.

When I betray it to all the people who want Leonid dead.

13

GUSTAV

Katerina looks haunted as she tells her story.

For the first time in a long time, I forget all about the IPO, my grandfather, and basically my entire life plan.

"I didn't know he told them he was me," Alexei says. "Why did you leave that out?"

"He didn't want you backing into the question of whether he had developed powers," Katerina says. "He was embarrassed. His entire life, he had been the strange, motherless child of a father who was usually drunk and always raving about his prominent ancestors—about the fact that he should've been the leader of Russia."

"Which means that Leonid was already mentally unstable then," Alexei says. "What I thought was a joke, he was deadly serious about. I wish I'd known at the time."

Katerina frowns. "He didn't have any plans to try and take the throne from you—not then."

"Oh, really?" Adriana asks. "So that all came way later, then?"

"I mean, yes," Katerina says. "It did."

"Alright," Alexei says. "Then when did you—"

Katerina stands. "I don't have a room to storm off to, but I think it's about time I found one." She grabs her bag and heads for the door.

"You don't have to talk to anyone." I stand up and follow her. "You can storm off to my room, and I promise no one will bother you in there."

She shakes her head. "It's alright. It's time for me to get some distance between me and them. We're clearly not on the same team."

"Speaking of teams." Alexei stands. "How were you planning to let Leonid know when he could restore my powers?" He lifts both eyebrows. "Do you have his phone number? Because the one Adriana used to call him before was disconnected a while ago."

"He gave me a phone." I shrug. "It has his number saved in it, and because it's a number he knows, he'll answer."

The room explodes as people who clearly understand modern technology better than Katerina lose their minds.

"He can track you with that," Kristiana says. "He could be waiting downstairs for us right now."

"I can't decide whether her ignorance is a good thing for us or very, very bad," Grigoriy says. "Although in this case, it's clearly bad."

"You might have led the wolves right to the door," Aleksandr says.

"I told you we should've kicked her out the second she arrived," Adriana says.

"I hardly think he's going to be flying out to the United States any time soon," Katerina finally says. "Turn on any news network. They're reporting on his whereabouts and actions constantly. He can't hop on the next United flight and stroll through the streets of New York City without everyone knowing about it."

"Maybe he'll come as a horse," Adriana says. "He could

escape customs without anyone knowing, the same way you did."

Katerina rolls her eyes like she doesn't know Adriana's kidding. "He can't shift into a horse. Everyone knows that."

"He could just get on a private jet. He's the leader of Russia," Adriana says.

"Wait, come back to the horse thing," I say. "Why can't this guy who has fire, electric, and water powers shift when the rest of you can? And Alexei and Katerina don't even have their powers, but they can still shift, right?"

I suddenly also find myself wondering what Katerina's horse looks like. Is it a palomino with a long, flowing whitish mane and tail?

"We have to master our powers before we can shift into a horse form," Alexei says softly. "Since Leonid has the capacity to master all the affinities, he won't be able to shift until. . ."

"He'd have to take Grigoriy and Aleksandr's powers first," Mirdza says. "Which means that once Leonid starts shifting, we're all doomed."

Katerina nods.

"But how did you discover what his powers were?" I ask. "I'm still confused. Katerina said they kept it a secret." Although, I did just tell Katerina she doesn't have to talk. I'm probably not being very helpful, with my irritating questions.

"Before we get into any of that, hand it over." Grigoriy prowls across the room and extends his hand toward her. "Now."

"Hand over—oh. The phone?" Katerina blinks.

"No, your makeup bag." Grigoriy rolls his eyes. "Yes, the phone he can use to track your location."

It takes her a moment, but Katerina rummages around in her bag and pulls out a slim silver phone. "Here."

After smashing it rather violently on my wooden floor, leaving several gouges that make me cringe, he fills the sink with water and drops the pieces in.

"Was that really necessary?" I sigh. "You know barely more than she does about technology, clearly."

"Leonid already knew Gustav's name—Daniel Belmont—and his location—New York City." Katerina shoots me an apologetic look. "I'm sorry that he knows all that, but I swear he seemed entirely serious about not having an interest in you. . .unless you start trying to. . ."

"Use the magic I'm supposed to have, I know. Here's what I don't get," I say. "Why would he care about me?" I shake my head. "I'm an adult who knew nothing about any of this, and I have no idea what you people think I can do."

"Baba Yaga said something about plumbing." Adriana says. "She said she had given magic to Rurik's line, and then later, when she thought it had died out, she gave the same magic to the new ruling class, only instead of giving everything to one person, she split it up. Fire. Water. Air. Electricity. Earth." Adriana inhales slowly. "But she didn't explain anything other than the fact that the power comes from the same place. In order to use his power, Leonid needs permission from the new magic users, but once he has it, only he can allow them to use it. Or more importantly, he can cut them off."

"And you think that I. . .?" I raise my eyebrows. "What? What do you think I can do about all that?"

"We think that Leonid has the original Rurikid power," Kristiana says from her spot on the sofa. "And we think that our family was the balancer in the new round."

"Which means?"

"We think you can do what Leonid can," Aleksandr says. "Or at least, we hope you can."

"And by that, you mean that you hope I can use all the powers?" I frown. "So you think I'm going to, like, what? Train my powers and then attack him head on?"

"It sounds a little silly when you put it that way," Kristiana says, "but yes. Something like that."

I stare at my little sister who thinks I'm the future Iron

Man. "That's never going to happen. It's not who I am, not even deep down. I'm the guy who ran after Mom died. I'm the guy who put as much distance as I could between myself and Dad's gambling problem. I'm not proud of it, but I'm not the guy who trains and fights the villains of the world. I'm the guy who turns and runs."

Kristiana doesn't even bother arguing with me.

Because better than anyone, she knows I'm right.

14

KATERINA

I didn't think I'd ever get away from everyone. They're all so angry at me, and there are lots of things they don't even know I'm not sharing. I wind up hiding in Gustav's room until they go to sleep, and then sneaking out to the couch. The next morning, while they're arguing with Gustav about whether he has what it takes to be a superhero, basically, I duck out.

Gustav has another full day of pitch meetings, and the fabulous six are planning to accompany him and sit outside again. I'm not sure why? But they're doggedly determined that he's the key to saving the world.

At first, I wondered whether someone would come after me. I looked over my shoulder a dozen times after exiting the elevator and waving goodbye to Norm. As I walked down Gustav's street, I practically developed a crick in my neck from checking for them. Maybe part of me wanted them to come chasing after me, which is sad if it's true. But once I'm two or three long, city blocks away, I breathe a prolonged sigh of relief. This is New York City. If they haven't followed me by now, their chances of coming after me have gone way down, right?

But as I walk, I realize that I'm confused.

I know Alexei's a good person. I've spent most of my life thinking I was in love with him. But now that I've accepted that he's with Adriana. . .I'm not even that upset. I feel numb. Like someone who's been zapped so many times, she's past feeling.

Maybe the misery and despair will come later, but I doubt it.

I wonder whether that means I've been holding on to some kind of childish image of what our life would be like together, but I had really long since given up on him. I'm like one of those dumb people that are on daytime talk shows, only, at least I figured this boringly obvious stuff out myself.

Why did it take me so long? Am I an idiot?

My bag isn't very heavy, but after I carry it for five minutes or so, my shoulder starts to complain anyway. I really need to find a hotel and check in. Only, the farther I get from Gustav's nice apartment, the more disgusting the city around me becomes. I scan the billboards, wondering what exactly people in this time care about.

Mirdza was right that in my time, women needed to find a man to protect them. Without one, you were vulnerable. I had my father, sort of, and my brother, almost. But I never really had anyone who was in my corner. I never had someone who listened to what I wanted or needed. I had hoped Alexei would be that person, and a large part of that desire might have had to do with the fact that, as the tsarina, no one could tell me no. Except Alexei, I suppose. But it would have put me in a protected position unlike any other.

That doesn't seem to be what women are looking for now.

As I scan the billboards, most of the women on them are wearing a lot of heavy makeup that reminds me of a raccoon that got into paint, and they're all so thin, they make jockeys look hefty. Is that what brings women joy, now? Emaciated frames and a lot of face paint?

If it is, why?

If not, why is that what we're stuck staring at?

As I try to work out how the world has changed and why, reviewing bits and pieces of movies I've seen in my mind, I decide to sit. There's a big, empty bench at the edge of a large park. The sign says, "Central Park."

I sit on the edge of a lacquered black bench.

Within a handful of moments—I've resolved nothing in my mind—a man approaches me. He's wearing dark pants, a dark shirt, and thick glasses with a heavy black frame. "This is going to sound strange." He holds up his hands. "But at least hear me out."

I frown, preparing to walk away.

"We have a photoshoot today, and it's for a seasonal product—a lovely silk scarf. We need someone with gorgeous hair and an effortless look. The client even said they want someone with beautiful strawberry blonde or auburn hair." He smiles and bites his lip.

"I'm sorry, but I have no idea what you're talking about." I stand.

"Our model has the chicken pox. I wish I was kidding, but she can't stop scratching. No amount of makeup is going to soothe all those splotches, and if we wanted to use CGI, we would've—"

"Oh." I shake my head. "You want to put me on one of those." I point at a billboard of a woman who's wearing what looks like underwear and sneakers and drinking water out of a blue bottle that glistens. I have no idea what they're trying to sell, if anything.

"Not a billboard." The man chuckles. "No, you'd be in an online ad and perhaps some marketing for the fall line in the store, maybe on the side of a bus."

"That's not what I do," I say.

"You're not a model?" He raises one eyebrow. "No way."

I shake my head.

"With that face—with your hair. You must be lying."

Now I'm a little flattered—not that the women on the billboards really look that attractive, but clearly someone thinks they do. "I don't look like those women." I point. "I'm not bony."

"No, you're not, but you're just the right kind of thin for this campaign."

"I'm sorry," I say, "but I just can't."

"We pay in cash on site."

I'm about to walk away, but I feel compelled to ask. "How much?" I have some money, thanks to Aleksandr's generosity, but it's shrinking by the day, and it would be nice to add to it.

The amount he states—it takes me a moment to put it in terms that make sense to me, but it's not bad. Not bad at all. "How long will this take?"

"All morning and part of the afternoon, but you'll be done by two. Three, tops."

It takes them an *hour* to add what appear to be dark smudges over my eyelids. They paint darkener on my eyelashes. Some person with a terribly pinched face snips at the ends of my hair, in spite of my objections. She keeps muttering, "Split ends. Split *ends*!"

But finally, they have me do a lot of walking back and forth with large fans blowing in my direction. At some points, they even have people throwing buckets of *leaves* in front of the fans that pelt me in the face and get stuck in my hair.

It's very, very odd.

The shoes they give me make one blister. Then two more. But finally, we're done, and they do pay me, as promised.

"I threw in my business card," blocky glasses says, "as well as a small tip. Please call me and leave your number. I can think of a half dozen other things you'd also be perfect for, and a fresh look in the New York scene is always appreciated. Heroin chic gets old fast."

"Uh-huh," I say. "Sure."

But as I wander down the streets once again, more makeup on my face, and more money in my pocket, I can't help thinking that the United States's biggest, baddest city isn't so bad. I'm not paying much attention to where I'm going, just meandering, and I keep coming back to the same question.

What am I doing here?

None of the people I came to help want me here. I've given up on Alexei. Gustav will be fine, as long as he sticks to his guns and shoves them all away. And clearly Adriana, Mirdza, and Kristiana do not need me around. I could return to Russia, but I'm still scared of Leonid.

Yes, I know more about him than most. I understand how he got started. But he's powerful, and he's amoral, and it's a dangerous combination. What I really should do is stay as far away from him as I possibly can. In that regard, my present company's nearly as bad as he is. The easiest way to get blown up is to hang out near a bomb.

In that moment, I decide to figure out where on the map is the farthest from both New York City and St. Petersburg, and then go there with the money I just earned. It'll be enough to buy a ticket there, assuming I can escape their customs as I did recently, and then I can figure out what to do to support myself once I'm there.

Maybe they'll need scarf models.

I've pulled out my phone and I'm peering at the tiny screen, trying to figure out the midpoint. There *is* something in between, and as I pinch at the screen, zooming in, I realize it's a small island called Iceland.

It sounds cold, but I'm sure I'd acclimate—it can't be much worse than St. Petersburg.

I wonder whether they have horses there, and whether Boris might join me. He has been working with Leonid for a while now, but I'm not sure he's happy. I've often wondered, if given an alternative, whether Boris would do the right thing. Would he walk away? Would he give it all up? I can at least ask—as long as I'm vague on where I'll be.

I'll probably need to throw this phone away, just to make sure no one can track me with it.

I'm distracted by details when I bump into someone. A rather large, rather smelly person. He smells of that smoke that's not the processed tobacco I've seen people using. It's the other thing—it's almost sweet, but not in a good way.

I'm not sure it was my fault, but I apologize anyway. "Sorry." I duck my head, and he turns back to what he was doing when I interrupted him.

Only, now that I'm paying attention, I can see what that is. He's pointing a gun at a woman who looks barely more than a few years older than me. She's shivering, and not only from the cool air. She's not wearing nearly enough clothing for the brisk fall weather, but her arms aren't pebbled with flesh. She does look like her skin is crawling, though.

"Walk along, witch," he says.

I'm not sure why he called me a witch when I haven't exhibited a single bit of magic, until I realize that's not the word he used. His word does rhyme with witch, however, so I refuse to feel too stupid. "Should you really be waving a gun around in broad daylight?" The words just pop out of my mouth. I swear, it's like I just keep *forgetting* that I have no magical powers right now. Picking fights is very stupid when he outweighs me, and he's clearly better armed.

Not that I'd know what to do with a gun even if I had one.

"I already said. Witch, move on before I shoot you."

I should listen to him. Being shot sounds. . .not fun at all. But the woman in front of me's trembling, and no one else around us has even seemed to notice. "Why do you have a gun pressed against that woman's head? Is that legal here?"

The man yanks the gun away from the woman, who scrambles away on all fours without so much as even glancing my way. Then he swings the gun around toward me.

I mean, I really should have expected that. He's clearly emotionally unstable. "Alright," I say. "But you don't even know me."

"You get to take Jazzy's place." He nods. "She ran because of you, so you can fix it."

"Oh, I really don't think so." I may not be able to shock the ever-loving daylights right out of him, but I can still shift into a much larger and much scarier being. Without stopping to think about it, I just do it. I shift into my horse form, and I strike at him with my front hoof, knocking the gun onto the ground. It makes a terribly loud sound as it strikes the pavement and skitters away.

It's gratifying, though, watching the look on his face. I can't be sure, of course, but it almost looks like he knows it's me. I can't help smiling a little, and then neighing, loudly.

Unfortunately, I failed to note that the jerk was not alone. A half dozen other men emerge, some from a nearby parked car, and at least two from the door a few steps behind us.

They're all holding guns.

I'm bigger and more powerful, but I don't have six hooves, sadly. And I'm pretty sure the element of surprise is now gone.

"What are you waiting for?" the man in front of me asks. "Shoot the devil."

Devil? I may have knocked his gun away, but even for someone who doesn't like horses, I'm stunningly beautiful in this form. I whinny again, this time louder, and to my utter shock, before any of the men can fire, Gustav steps out in front of me. I didn't even see him—I have no idea where he came from.

"You will *not* shoot my horse."

Oh, no.

He's even dumber than I am, because he's not armed, *and* he has no magic. Now instead of just me getting shot, we're both going down.

15

GUSTAV

The first time I came to Manhattan to visit my grandfather, I'd been at Yale for less than a month. He had a party for work, and he wanted to introduce me. I carefully prepared my clothing for the event from among things Grandfather's personal shopper had chosen.

I was going to make him proud.

But less than three blocks from his New York City office, I was mugged. They took my wallet, my watch, and my pride. When I limped up to the party, my shirt torn, my face dirty from being pressed against the filthy ground, I swore that would never happen again.

The only thing I studied harder for than econ classes was boxing.

Ivy League schools are known for having fine instructors. Yale has the best economics program in the country. Its political theory classes are unparalleled. But my boxing instructor at Yale was, perhaps, not the very best. He wasn't horrible, but I felt like he was preparing me to perform some kind of shadowboxing showcase.

I wanted to learn how to get out of a bad situation, and that meant I needed to learn street fighting.

Luckily, MMA had really gained a foothold in the United States at the time, and one of the top trainers was only a twenty-minute drive from New Haven. It took me three years to really become competitive, but that last year of school, I focused on multi-opponent fighting. The key is distraction and elimination.

They're principles I still use in my everyday life.

For instance, I escape my apartment with promises that I'll return with the best Italian food in New York City, but really I just wanted to get away from their incessant hounding for a moment. I'm still two blocks from Pistoia, my favorite Italian place, when I hear a strange sort of clattering sound. It's one I'll probably still recognize when I'm a hundred years old.

It's the distinct sound of hooves striking the pavement.

I turn around just in time to watch the gorgeous palomino from my dreams the past two nights *kick* a gun from some man's hand. I can hardly believe my eyes. What on earth is that horse doing in the middle of New York City? And what's more, why is it the one from my *dreams* for the past two nights? I'd actually started to worry that the palomino was *me*, and that my subconscious was telling me that my destiny was to master my powers and start shifting into some golden horse.

It's absurd.

Because horses aren't a superhero form. They aren't terrifying. But watching this horse strike at the shady character across the street, I rethink my position a little. Only, after disarming the aggressive man, more men pour out of the neighboring building and the parked car, and suddenly, there are six men pointing guns at the poor thing.

I don't think. I just move.

Before I know it, I've shot across the street, sprinting through a gap between a bus and a BMW. The edge of the BMW clips my arm, but the pain is brief. I manage to leap onto the curb in front of the man the horse just disarmed. He seems to be the one in charge, and I'm not about to let these criminals mow this gorgeous creature down.

"You will *not* shoot my horse."

The horse turns its head toward me, for all the world acting as if it understands exactly what I just said.

"Do you know what the penalty is in New York City for shooting a police horse?" I lift both eyebrows as if these guys care what the penalties for any laws are.

"This isn't a police horse," the large man facing the horse says. "Now get out of here, before you find out what happens when I shoot a man."

Distract. And eliminate.

I pull a pack of gum out of my pocket and toss it behind the horse, gum and wrappers flying in every direction in front of two of the men. At the same time, I kick the accumulated debris from the gutter at the two men closest to me, and then I slide under the horse's neck, kick one gun out of the farthest man's hand, and strike the other man's wrist, taking his gun for myself.

The horse hasn't been inactive—after I flung the gum, she kicked back with full force, knocking those men back into the windshield of the car behind us. Its alarm immediately starts to blare, woo, woo, woo, and I use the helpful distraction to drop the aggressive man into a headlock, the gun I nabbed pressed against his temple. "What was that you just said about what happens when I shoot a man?"

The man swallows, his eyes bulging.

"I wonder whether it matters," I say, "*where* I shoot him. Would the result be different if I shot his foot?" I point the gun downward. "Or is the head better?" I press it back against the side of his head.

"What?" The man's spluttering. "No."

"Put your weapons down," I say quietly to the men who are now covered with mud, trash, and bits of leaves. "Or I'll splatter his brains on the side of that building." I toss my head. "Now."

"Do it, idiots," the man says, spit flying from his mouth.

The horse snorts and paws at the ground. "Now, all of you will back away." I toss my head toward the building they emerged from. "I want you all to go inside that building and I want to hear the door close and lock."

The man I'm holding panics, his eyes widening, and he struggles against me.

"Careful." I tighten my headlock. "If you keep wiggling like that, my finger might catch." I sigh. "I'm not a big fan of guns. In fact, when I learned to shoot, my trainer said I should never use one. I have a bit of a trigger finger, apparently."

He whimpers—the massive nightmare of a man whimpers.

But his men move, and then I hear the turning of the lock on the front door.

"Alright," I say. "This is what we're about to do." I spin toward the horse. "You want to get out of here, right?"

The horse nods.

It's confirming my suspicion. "We've met before, right?"

Another nod.

"You're going to give me a ride out of here, got it?"

It nods again.

One quick check, and I've confirmed it really is a mare, and then I fling the man away, out into the street. He has to scramble to avoid slamming into a moving car.

Only in New York City would this entire thing happen in the open on the street without a single passerby doing anything to stop it, but I can hear the police sirens now, and I'd rather be out of here by the time they arrive. I doubt Grandfather will praise me for getting involved in some kind of drug-dealer altercation, even if no shots were fired.

I pat the horse's side. "I'm getting up now," I hiss. "Move toward that fire hydrant."

I'm not sure she knows that word in English, so I point. "That thing."

She sidles over, and I use it to boost up on her back.

I haven't been on a horse in at least ten years. Maybe twelve. I didn't miss it at all. The skin feels strange against my hand, all disconnected from its body, and without a saddle or bridle, I feel like I could go sailing off at any time. I grab a fistful of mane, and then I empty the gun of bullets, cringing a little as they clatter on the pavement, and throw the empty gun at the jerk who started all this.

The sirens are closer, closer, growing ever closer.

I kick the mare and grab her mane with my other fist as well. "Let's go before the cops get here."

She doesn't take off, though. She ducks her head down and snags a bag off the ground with her teeth, and then she leaps forward. No saddle, and I haven't ridden in ages, so when she starts to really move, I nearly slide off. I shift until I'm crouched a little lower, my legs coming forward to try and balance my upper body a bit. I'm sure she's hating the feeling of all my weight falling on her shoulders, but she's going to have to deal with it.

"Katerina, right?" I sigh.

She snorts, which is probably the best she can do, with a bag handle clamped between her teeth.

"How on earth did you wind up with six men holding guns on you?"

She tosses her head.

I deserve that. This isn't exactly the best way for us to talk. "Alright, here's our plan."

Before I can explain anything, a police car turns down this street and stops. He rolls his window down. "Hey!" the officer shouts. "What on earth are you doing, weirdo?"

"Door dash keeps raising its prices," I say. "I decided to grab my Italian food myself."

His jaw drops.

I salute him. And thankfully, Katerina continues to walk.

"Hey," the cop shouts again. "You can't just ride down the sidewalk."

Adrenaline starts to pump through my system. Is this story going to be even harder to explain than my interference with a bunch of criminals? Am I still going to make the news, but in an even stranger way?

"Oh?" I turn back and look at him over my shoulder, tugging on Katerina's mane so she'll stop. Thankfully, she does.

"You can only ride horses in the street, with the flow of traffic." The cop points. He doesn't comment on my lack of bridle or saddle. He doesn't comment on the fact that my horse is carrying a bag in her mouth, either. I seriously doubt there are laws about any of that, which is good.

I ask Katerina, with pressure from my right knee, to step into the street, into the barely-long-enough space between the two idling cars. Blessedly, she does. I wasn't sure she was trained to interpret signals from a rider.

Would she be, when the horse is actually a person? Ugh. This is so awkward.

"Be careful," the cop shouts, and then he turns his lights and siren back on and heads down the road toward the intersection we just left. I wonder what he'll think when the witnesses there tell him a golden horse was in the middle of the whole ruckus.

Luckily, two blocks down, we reach Central Park, and Katerina listens as I nudge her forward. The second we can, I send her into the center of a bush and slide off her back. "Phew," I say. "That was a really weird hour."

She *melts*, then. I'm not sure how else to describe it, when a sixteen hand mare sort of swirls down into a perfectly small woman, wearing camel slacks, a mahogany blouse, and a long, flowing scarf. She shakes off, for all the world, just like my mom's horses used to after rolling, and then picks up the bag she dropped. "Well. That was strange. I'd appreciate if you didn't tell anyone you saw me, because I'm on my way to Icel—no, wait. I'm not telling anyone. Forget you heard that."

Now I'm the one whose jaw is dropping. "You're kidding, right?"

Just then, a strange tingling sensation blankets my entire body. It's like my leg fell asleep, but instead of my leg, it's every part of me. I drop to the ground, pulling my knees up against my chin while my teeth chatter.

Then just as suddenly, the feeling's gone.

When I glance up at the motion beyond Katerina's head, it's a runner, and his face is bizarrely obscured by strange black splotches. A sick feeling forms in the pit of my stomach, like the sludge that accumulates on the rubber liner of the washing machine.

"Oh, no," Katerina says. "You saved me." Her eyes widen.

"But it was at no cost to me," I say. "So that can't—no way."

"What happened to your arm?" She's looking at my right shoulder, the one the BMW clipped, and I turn to look down at it.

Somehow, the bumper tore my jacket and gashed open the skin. It's not a huge cut, but it's bleeding pretty consistently. The swear words I use are a mixture of Latvian, English, and Russian. It's how my dad always swore, and I haven't done it in a very long time, but it feels fitting.

"I'm so sorry." Her voice is small. Her face looks utterly sincere.

"You, missy, aren't flying anywhere," I say. "Because now that this is going down, you're the only one I even partially trust."

Her face falls, and she shakes her head back and forth. "You should not trust me. I'm a bad person."

But her face says otherwise. Unlike the runner I just saw, it's clear, it's clean, and in fact, there are tiny golden sparkles I can see out of the corner of my eye when I shift the way I'm looking at her. "I don't mean to call you a liar, but my new superpower—and Leonid was right. This is kind of lame—says you're not."

She blinks. "You can—" She pivots. "Look at that guy." She points through the bushes at a man on his phone, yelling.

"Yeah, I see him for a split second, and then." A strange sort of film comes over his face, and suddenly, it's like he's been splattered with mud. I blink, but it's still there. "Not a great guy. I would not encourage you to go out with him on a blind date, for instance. Probably has a vial of date-rape-drug in his pocket."

Katerina looks ill. "This is terrible."

I realize what she means. Her big, bad evil ex-friend said he'd leave me alone. . .unless I did what I *just* did.

"So, Iceland's off, right? At least I've earned that much, right? This did happen to me while I was trying to save you."

She sighs and slings the strap for her bag over her shoulder. "I have even more reason to go now."

"But you're a good person. I can see it, so you're going to stay and help me. Right?"

She looks directly into my face. "I went to Leonid to trade your whereabouts to him for Alexei's powers."

"Ouch," I say. "But see? You're telling me that so you'll have a clear conscience, and you didn't even know me then."

"I know you now, and I'm not that impressed." She folds her arms. "I should get as far away from all this as I possibly can."

"You don't think the fate of the world rests in my hands?"

She shrugs. "It may, but I don't want anything to do with it."

"Which is exactly why I need your help. It's the heroes who don't want to be heroes who make the best ones."

"Isn't that advice more suited to you?" She smirks. "Super Gustav?"

I cringe. "That's the worst superhero name I've ever heard in my life. And if you're from the nineteen hundreds, why do you know about superheroes?"

"I'm *from* the nineteen hundreds, but I've spent a lot of time in the present sitting in locked rooms, and what better way to kill the time than watching Marvel movies?"

"Better than the DC ones, I guess." I can't help chuckling. "I think we'll be able to come up with some better things for you to do now, though."

"Like training you to be a superhero?"

I groan. "Anything but that."

16

KATERINA

The man I betrayed is asking me to stay. If it was *anyone* else, I'd say no. But he's the one person I owe. He's the one person I can't turn down. Still, maybe I can convince him to let me go.

"I'm not going back there," I say. "No one wants me there, either."

"I do," Gustav says. "And it's my apartment. That should count for something."

"You barely know me," I say. "You'll change your mind. Trust me."

"I barely know my sister, and I don't know any of them at all." Gustav leans down and snatches my bag out of my hands. "And so far, you're by far the least annoying."

"Really?" I tilt my head so I can see him a little better. He towers over me, and when we're walking side-by-side down the street, I can basically only see his shoulder. "Because I seem to recall almost getting you shot a few minutes ago."

"I could've stayed out of it." He shrugs.

"Why didn't you?" I almost trip over an uneven spot in the pavement. "You didn't even know it was me."

He clears his throat. "We're almost to the restaurant, and our order will be waiting, I think."

"Why are you picking up food for everyone?" I can't help thinking there must be someone better. "Don't rich people get delivery these days? I've seen ads for Door Dash. I think that's what they do."

"This place doesn't do deliveries, and I love their chicken parmesan. And their breadsticks." He shrugs. "It's one of the best things about New York."

"You can give my bag back," I say. "You won't be able to carry the food and the bag."

He clutches my bag against his chest. "I'm not letting go of this. You'll bolt for Iceland."

I roll my eyes. "Like I can't go without my bag."

"You can't." He frowns. "Women need their stuff."

"You know nothing about women."

"It seemed like most of the people in there knew nothing about you," he says. "Do you really think that now, Leonid will fly right out here and try to kill me?"

I wish I knew. "Leonid has never been someone that anyone understands." I sigh. "Sometimes he tells me what he'll do, like when he said he'll leave you alone unless you access your magic. But other times, I have no idea what to expect. This is one of those. I knew what he would do if you *didn't* access your powers, but now that you have?" I stop and look up at the signage on the brick storefront.

We're here.

"I'll wait outside," I say.

"Nice try." He points. "March."

I act annoyed, but it's actually kind of funny that he's treating me like I'm some kind of miscreant he has to keep an eye on. I could shift into a horse and bolt if I really wanted to, and there's no way he could stop me.

I'm officially sad that he came into his powers by commit-ting a selfless act, but it feels just a little nice that someone wants me to stick around. I can't even think of the last time someone actually *wanted* me.

Gustav leans in and murmurs something to the woman behind the front desk and she waves us over to the bar. A moment later, we're on our way, Gustav's free hand and one of mine laden with bags of food. It smells really, really good. "Let's hope none of the others have a garlic allergy," I say.

He chuckles.

"Actually, it would be fine if Adriana does."

"Do you really hate her?" His eyes look genuinely curious when I glance his way. "And do you still love him?"

I shrug. "I mean, I thought I did, but I'm way less upset than I thought I'd be. It's pretty clear that he's made his choice, and it's not me. I should've seen that before, I guess."

"He does look at her like she's the last cookie in New York."

The image of Alexei looking at Adriana like she's something to eat makes me smile. "Gives new meaning to that English phrase, 'have your cookie and eat it too.'"

"Cake," Gustav says.

"Huh?"

"Never mind." He sighs. "But tell me this, before you're standing in front of the firing squad. How did Leonid get his first ability? After he found out he could see people's good and bad like me, then what? Because now he has three powers, right?"

I sigh.

"You don't have to tell me, but I feel like it might become relevant."

I hold out my hand. "You may want to give me my bag, because this one's also my fault."

"Give you your—why? Oh. Because after this I'll want you to leave?" He snorts. "I'll take my chances."

"Things had been bad between the Romanovs and our family for a while." I start walking again, kicking at trash as we go. "Really, they were bad for both my family and the Kurakins. The Romanov family really liked Grigoriy and Aleksandr's families, and they did things together."

"Things?"

I shrug. "You know, they went in on projects, like building libraries. They co-hosted balls. The Romanovs would make sure their crops were watered and the Volkonsky family would bring them baskets full of gems. It was very. . .exclusive, and our families were always left out. But when they went to war, you better believe they called on us then."

"I imagine burning and zapping powers are pretty helpful in war."

"I don't think this came up before, but Alexei pretended to be my suitor for a little over three years, and my dad got pretty excited about the prospect of us marrying." I cringe. "So when I used Leonid to make Alexei jealous, it didn't go as I had hoped."

"What happened?"

"After that initial incident, Leonid and I told the others that we were recovering. We used that time to search the records in the library for any mentions of the magical powers that were possessed by Rurik, and we found quite a few. We knew that Rurik had all five powers, and the records were also clear that there was only one person who could master the powers in each generation—only the oldest child."

"Okay."

"That frustrated Leonid. He wasn't the oldest child—he was the *only* person, other than his dad, who seemed to have no interest and had certainly not ever done a selfless act to qualify himself. It seemed to both of us like Leonid didn't have any of the powers he was supposed to have because they'd been given to others, leaving him with nothing but the strange ability to tell what kind of person someone was deep down."

"Right."

"But on our fourth night there, Leonid read a passage that said that the Rurikid line had to accept the powers."

"Huh?" We're in front of his building now, and Gustav has stopped. "What does that even mean?"

"I wasn't sure, either. I thought maybe it was a transcription error. The journals were really old, and they had basically stolen them from the royal record chamber, after the Time of Troubles when the Romanovs took over. It had been hundreds of years since then, as well. But Leonid had this idea. He wondered whether he had to accept the abilities first in some way, but in order to accept something. . ."

"It has to be offered to you."

"I know it might sound reckless, but you have no idea how pathetic Leonid looked at the time. He was my servant. He'd done everything he could, and nothing had helped. He had been doing his best at dinners and training sessions to help me make Alexei jealous. It almost felt like it was working. Alexei hated him, at the very least, possibly because he felt guilty about how bad things got that first night. I felt like I owed him my best efforts, and so. . ."

"You gave him his first power."

"There was a big fight," I say. "On the last day of training, Alexei caught Leonid and me in the records room."

Gustav cringes.

"To cover up what we were doing. . ." I swallow. "I didn't know what else to do, so I kissed Leonid."

Gustav inhales sharply.

"It shocked Alexei, I think, and at the time, I thought he might confess that he liked me. Alexei knew, at that point, that Leonid worked for our family. But. . .instead of moving Alexei to action like I wanted, he shifted and we saw that his father was standing behind him." I still cringe at the memory.

"The czar."

"The thing is, Alexei and I knew our courtship was fake, and I knew he was kind of pulling away—he had said he was ready to end it—but his father thought it was real. Seeing me kissing Leonid inside the palace, well." I shake my head. "He broke off our understanding in a rather violent way, sending me home to my father immediately."

"I bet that didn't go over well."

"It did not," I say. "And actually." I hate even thinking about this. "My dad was so angry that he fired Leonid's father, and they both left. Leonid's dad got really, really drunk, and then he got into a fight, and when he struck his head on the stones outside the bar. . ." I sigh. "He died the night Dad fired him, and Leonid was beside himself. His dad was crazy, but he was the only person who had ever really loved him. He blamed himself for agreeing to help me, and he blamed my dad for firing them, and he blamed me a little bit, because he had gotten no powers, and he couldn't save his own dad."

"It sounds pretty tragic," Gustav agrees.

"The next morning, when I heard what happened, I went looking for him. I offered him my powers, and it worked." I sigh. "Suddenly, he could use my powers. . .and I couldn't."

"Whoops."

"To make matters worse, my father and my brother Boris couldn't use theirs either. I hadn't even thought of that—Leonid was angry with them for how things went down with his dad."

Gustav cringes.

"Leonid wasn't entirely unreasonable," I say. "Before Boris or my dad knew the cause of all of us losing our abilities, I convinced him to restore our powers to us, but it took him all of five minutes to realize that he could cut us off at any point."

"Okay."

"And when Alexei found out what had happened, that Leonid could use my powers, he was even more unhappy. His father was livid. My dad had just made a petition for the

Romanovs to help us, because we were in the middle of a drought."

"A drought?"

"People were already starving—it was a really terrible one. Our family and the Kurakins both begged Alexei to defy his father and direct rain to our villages, but the whole Romanov family refused. The czar was so angry about the Leonid thing, and about my supposed relationship with him, that he thought we deserved to fend for ourselves. He told us to use buckets and pipes to water our crops, like the rest of the world. The drought wasn't his problem, and he didn't have an obligation to fix it."

"I wonder what his face looked like," Gustav mumbles. "Not light and bright, I'm guessing."

"I don't know whether he was a villain, or just on the opposite side of things," I say. "But not knowing much about what happened with Leonid, the Kurakins saw the Romanov refusal to help as more preferential treatment for the magical families they liked—they were very angry. Not even a month later, when there was an uprising, the Kurakins took the chance to take their revenge on the Romanov-Volkonsky-Khilkov alliance. They sort of caused an uprising, and in the process, the Kurakins—Mikhail's parents—killed both of Grigoriy's parents, and it only got worse from there."

We've reached the apartment building, so I push my way through the door and nod at Norm. His big smile makes me feel better. One day, when I have a job and a purpose and a place of my own to live, I really want a doorman.

"Once the Romanovs were firmly aligned against our family and the Kurakins, Mikhail came to visit. Leonid wasn't living with us anymore, but he and I still talked. I would meet him in the town square a few times a week and give him food. He was practicing using his new powers, and I taught him things. I didn't think he was a villain, honestly, just a man who had been dealt a very lousy hand in life. If I'd had more control over my own life, I'd have helped him more. Mikhail followed me once, and he caught us. Instead of being angry, he asked Leonid what he could do if he had *two* powers. Mikhail wanted him to right wrongs and exact vengeance on the Romanovs in a way he and his father couldn't."

Gustav stares at me with wide eyes. "So you accidentally gave him your powers, giving him power over you and your family."

I nod.

"But this other guy, this Mikhail, he surrendered intentionally?"

"I begged Mikhail not to do it, and I begged Leonid not to listen, but they ignored me. Actually, I think my begging upset Leonid further. He couldn't believe that even after all that had happened, I would side with Alexei. I really just wanted everything to go back to how it was. I wanted to heal things, but they just kept getting angrier and angrier."

"That explains a lot about Grigoriy," Gustav says. "He lost his parents. That won't be an easy injury to recover from."

"But to make matters worse, Leonid followed through on his end of their bargain to attack the Romanovs," I say. "Although, not quite as Mikhail had imagined, I think."

The elevators open, and I don't have time to say anything else. We both step inside. It's time to tell everyone what happened—that Gustav has the powers they came to try and force on him. But before we can even step out of the elevator and into Gustav's apartment, we're wrapped in bands of air and floated into the family room.

"You accessed your power." Grigoriy's furiously pacing, his eyes flashing.

"You've been gone for almost an hour since you did it, too." Aleksandr stands up and joins Grigoriy. They're going to wear a thin spot in the rug at this rate.

"I brought dinner," Gustav says.

"We have a lot to do," Kristiana says.

"But how do you guys even know that I accessed them?" Gustav asks.

"We felt it," Grigoriy says.

"Like a static shock to our brains, pulsing where our power usually rests," Aleksandr says.

I look at Alexei to see whether he agrees.

"Don't look at me," he says. "I felt nothing."

That's not promising.

"We have a lot of work to do," Aleksandr says.

"But I have meetings for another ten days," Gustav says.

"Face it, brother," Kristiana says. "Your IPO's going to have to sink or float without you. Your days of pretending you're normal are over."

17

GUSTAV

This is ridiculous.

They want me to sacrifice my entire life, all my hopes and dreams, for a bag of parlor tricks, because of a threat that may never materialize.

"I'll give you the horse thing," I say. "You can shift into horses."

"And harness the power of air." When Grigoriy folds his arms, his already beefy arms get thicker, and I can't help but notice that his face is not entirely light and bright. There are definite flashes of darkness in him.

He did drag me across the room right before we met. I suppose that's not exactly a parlor trick, and his life hasn't really been a party. Hearing about how someone he knew killed his parents. . .that sounded rough.

"But this is my entire life," I say. "I left my home for this, gave up my name, my family, and my country—"

"So you could kiss up to Grandfather in the hopes that he'd give you all his money?" Kristiana's lip curls. Her face is, blessedly, entirely shiny. No more than flecks of occasional grey here and there.

"You can be disdainful all you want," I say. "But would you have liked Aleksandr if he was broke?" I shake my head. "Money is security, and money is power, and I have spent the last eleven and a half years convincing Grandfather that I'm just like he is—that I can safeguard his legacy. I'm not about to. . .I'm not even sure what you want me to do. In movies, this is when there's like, some kind of cheesy training montage. Swords flash and smash, and like, the hero struggles, and you can see sweat on his brow."

"What's he talking about?" Alexei's mostly strands of shining light, but there are a few ropy dark lines as well.

"You need to show him more movies." Kristiana looks smug. "I told you all that election crap took too much time."

"We don't want to drag you to Russia," Grigoriy says.

"What, then? Because whatever you want to do, I'll do it right here, around the meetings I have to attend to convince people to buy my shares. Cool?" I look around the room.

Other than Katerina, everyone's glaring.

"I'll just buy all the shares when they go live," Aleksandr says.

"No." I shake my head vehemently. "I'm not sure you know how much that would cost, but even if you were, like, a billionaire or something—"

"He is," Grigoriy says.

I blink.

"Actually, I am too." Alexei waves, and the disgustingly good-looking man whom I'm discovering I don't like very well lights up like a lantern.

I hate it.

"They're kidding about being loaded, right?" I glance at Kristiana.

She shakes her head. "Not really, no."

"But I can't have you guys do that," I say. "Because Grandfather needs to see this IPO as a huge success, and that means all the main banks and funds need to buy their portion of the shares at full price."

Alexei's sigh is very beleaguered, like I'm worse than a class full of kindergarteners who want to fingerpaint his beloved family palace.

"Just tell me," I say. "What do you even want me to do, exactly?"

"Leonid has mastered electrical powers, and the power of fire," Grigoriy says. "Those are very scary, very strong assault powers."

"And now he has water, too," Katerina says. "He's been working on combining them to blow things up."

"Of course that's the first thing he'd do," Aleksandr says. "Why does that not even surprise me? Everything's a weapon to him."

"We need to get you some powers too," Grigoriy says, "and we need to train you to use them together, in ways we can't."

"If you can't use them together, how can you train me?" I arch one eyebrow.

"We can teach you to do everything we can do," Aleksandr says. "And then help come up with ideas of what else you might be able to do."

I sigh. "Alright, let's say we actually do the training montage—"

"It's not a montage," Kristiana says. "Stop pretending this is a movie."

"If we do the training montage," I insist, because ignoring my little sister's objections is ingrained, "around my meetings, then I'll do it. But you guys have to help me, not just buy all my shares. My life's important too."

Grigoriy's face and body is strained like he just ran across hot coals or jogged through a crosswalk full of broken glass, but he doesn't argue.

"How do we do that?" Aleksandr asks.

"Do what?" I ask.

"How do we give you our powers?" My sister's apparently billionaire husband is eyeing me like I'm a skin suit he needs to step into. It's giving me the heebie jeebies.

"What did Leonid do?" Kristiana asks. "How did he take Alexei's power?"

"He just had me say that he could use my powers," Alexei says. "Pretty simple."

"I hereby grant the use of my powers to Gustav Liepa," Grigoriy says.

"Wait!" Katerina's grass-green eyes are wide. Her breathing's staccato.

I was already looking at her whenever I could sneak a glance—the flame-red hair, and her startling eyes call to me. I find myself looking at her too often already. But after that outcry, everyone else turns to look at her, too.

"What?" Grigoriy frowns.

She sighs and closes her eyes. "After he got a new power, Leonid was incapacitated, sometimes for as long as three days."

"Three days?" That cannot be true. I can't miss the next three days of meetings. "What does that mean, wiped out?"

"It didn't happen at the palace after that initial attack," Katerina says. "But when he got the electrical powers, it was like he had the flu."

"And the second time?" I ask. "When he took the fire powers?"

"It was worse," she says. "That's why he was in such a hurry to rush you guys out after Alexei surrendered."

Aleksandr's shaking his head.

Adriana looks sick—and I'm not shocked to notice that of the fireflies of light dancing around her, a good twenty percent of them are dark. She's always been a bit of a moral grey.

Alexei's scowling. "Whose side are you on?" He steps closer to her. "You could have told us that before."

Katerina shrugs. "No one's ever been on my side."

But she confessed that little secret when they started trying to give me their powers. I realize that, since she arrived, other than the whole incident with homeland security, which she started before meeting me, she's been the only one who is always seemingly on my side.

She was worried if they gave me their powers now, it would mess up my meetings.

Unlike the others, Katerina's trying to help in the way I want help.

"At least see whether it worked," Grigoriy says. "Can you do this?" The wind screams through my family room, ruffling everyone's hair and knocking over a bag of takeout. The smell of garlic fills the air.

And a splotch of red spreads across my white wool rug.

"Oh, man, G, why do you always do that?" Kristiana's bending over, using a handful of napkins to try and salvage my rug.

"I can't do a thing," I say. "Should I be able to feel something?"

"The second I told Leonid I'd be happy for him to have the same power as me, if only that was possible, he zapped me." Katerina shrugs. "It was an accident, but—"

"Yeah, right," Aleksandr says. "That guy's villainous."

"It was an accident," Katerina insists. "At the time, he was very apologetic."

"So why can't I use wind?" I frown. "I thought you said all you had to do was—"

"If it didn't work, maybe that means you won't get sick." Katerina's forced smile is cute.

"I, Aleksandr Volkonsky, hereby give all my powers, strength, and abilities to Gustav Liepa, or Daniel Belmont, or whoever you are. You will have and control them irrevocably."

"Geez," Kristiana says. "He just said he doesn't want to be wiped out for—"

"We can't wait two weeks," Aleks says. "We need to start training him now."

"But, still," Kris says. "He has some rights."

"And?" Katerina's staring at my face. "Can you feel anything?"

"What should I feel?"

"You should be able to sense that there's dust underneath your sofa," Aleks says. "In that potted plant, there's real soil." Aleks points. "And there's an accumulation of junk under your dishwasher, and in the bottom of that pipe." Aleks steps closer. "I can feel it, all of it, and the earth down below this building almost quivers. It would be hard, but I could force it upward if I tried, shearing through the layers of the building, or I could bring it up and around and through the windows." He's still watching me like a researcher in a lab, looking through a microscope. "Do you feel *any* of that?"

I shake my head.

"What about her ring?" Aleks points at Kristiana without turning his head. "Or the other women's jewels? Can you sense them?"

"*Sense* them?"

Aleks gestures with two fingers and the ring flies off Kristiana's finger and into his hand. "You can call the elements, the earth, and any of its parts, and you can bend them to your bidding."

I snort. "Nope. Nada."

"Why isn't it working?" Grigoriy's roar's a little unsettling, and then he starts pacing, seemingly not noticing that he's walking right through the center of the big red stain on my carpet. His boots are smearing it and tracking the sauce across the entire rug.

"Maybe it's different since he's not Rurikid?" Katerina asks.

Aleksandr's head tilts. "Or is he? Maybe he *is* Rurikid like Leonid, and because Leonid's older, he gets it all."

"I thought so at first," Katerina says. "But now I'm not sure." Her brow furrows. "I mean, Leonid just has to be given a power, and bam. He can use it." She shrugs. "That obviously doesn't work with him."

"But he has the same powers that Leonid had at first, right?" Kristiana asks. "You said he saw the good and bad in people."

"Speaking of that," Adriana asks. "What do you see when you look at me?"

"You don't want to know," Katerina mutters. "Trust me."

"What?" Adriana scowls. "But I do want to know."

"I asked Leonid once," Katerina says, "and trust me. Just don't."

"Your face is surrounded with susurrating light," I say. "Like little soft fireflies, darting and spinning."

"Oh," Adriana says. "That's nice."

I don't mention that a good twenty percent of them are dark, like horseflies. "But Katerina, why would Leonid say anything about yours?" My voice is flatter than I intended, and I would like to punch the Leonid guy.

"I asked him to tell me." Katerina has frozen in place, and her eyes are intent on mine.

I nod. "And? What did he say?"

"Nothing good," she says.

"Well, maybe you got better," Kristiana says.

"I doubt it." Katerina sighs. "But that still doesn't help us. Gustav's description for Adriana sounds just like Leonid's did."

I drop it, unwilling to keep being compared to him.

"He called Kris a null," Adriana says. "Right?"

Kristiana nods. "Yeah, but there isn't anything to tell us what that means, or how he knows. . ."

"It's in the journals," Katerina says. "We found some journals in the Romanov palace, and we were reading through them."

"It said something about a null?" I ask.

Katerina bangs on the side of her head. "They were in a really old dialect, and I had a lot of trouble reading them. They made my head hurt, so I was looking at newer ones while Leonid read those, but I remember him saying something about it."

"We need to see those," I say. "They could explain what's going on."

"We'll never get to them," Grigoriy says. "Leonid surely has them for himself, if they weren't destroyed long ago."

"But wait," Kristiana says. "My dad says we had journals— our family. Remember? He said they came to America with his great-uncle."

"We need to find those," Aleksandr says. "We were all assuming that if we could find your brother, we'd be able to prepare some kind of defense."

"Let me get this straight," I say. "The last time you saw Leonid, you went to try and defeat him, and you had three powers, while he had just two."

No one disagrees with me.

"And now, he has three, and he's the ruler of Russia—"

"He was already the leader of Russia then," Katerina says. "And they did manage to escape with me."

"You waltzed in and then back out on your own though, right?" I ask. "It doesn't sound like he was working very hard to keep you there. You said you—"

Katerina jumps toward me so fast that she stumbles on the edge of the coffee table and falls forward.

I have to drop to my knees to keep her from hitting her head on the tile. "Whoa there, tiger."

"I'm not a tiger." She's glaring at me.

That's when I realize she probably didn't tell anyone else that she offered to trade my safety for Alexei's powers. It doesn't make her look very good, but she told the person she put at risk.

And they already don't like her.

"Returning to my initial point," I say. "You had three powers to his two, and now you have two to his three. Yes?"

No one argues.

"But somehow you think that after finding me. . .what's the long-term plan?"

"We don't have one," Kris says.

"And we really should have one." Aleksandr's looking at his phone. "Because. . . Can you turn on the television?"

It takes a moment, but we toggle to the news app, and. . .

"We haven't had an envoy from Russia visit the United States in quite some time, but certainly not since the new leader took power. And lo and behold, he's about to leave his country, and the one he just seized, and visit America." The commentator shakes his head. "This man just has no fear."

"None at all, Ralph. I think the US President is just as shocked as you and I. I mean, look at her face when they handed her the missive."

The screen cuts to a clip of the President talking, not sure what about, and then she turns as someone walks toward her. He hands her a piece of paper, and as she reads it, her eyebrows draw together, and her mouth compresses hard and fast. She blinks three times in quick succession, and then she turns toward her Vice President.

"It must have been the news about the proposed visit, right? And you can't really tell the leader of one of the biggest, strongest, and most aggressive nations in the world that they can't come for a little chat, right? You can't say no?"

"Even if she *could* have said no, she didn't. President Kincaid is set to welcome this Ivanovich maniac to the United States with just under twenty-four hours' notice."

Aleksandr turns toward me. "Still worried about your IPO?"

"How rich did you say you were?" I cringe. "Maybe having you buy the shares once they go live would be better than nothing."

"We have got to find those journals," Kristiana says. "Unless you have any ideas for how to summon Baba Yaga?" She's looking at Adriana.

Adriana says, "None at all, sadly. She just showed up."

Kristiana swivels around to look at Mirdza. "What about you?"

Mirdza shrugs. "I saw her on that train, where she did nothing to help me or that poor woman, and then I saw her at the horse show. She didn't even warn me that anyone was coming for us." She shakes her head. "I have no idea how to get her attention, and I'm not sure she'd do anything to help us, even if I did."

Kristiana growl-screams. "This is so annoying. How can we have these connections, these powers, and know nothing? Baba Yaga, I hate you! Can you hear me? Why are you ruining my life? Why can't you help us defeat the monster *you* created?"

"Actually," Katerina says. "I was there when Leonid summoned her, and before you ask, I have no idea how he did it. Some recipe from some old journal he kept. But she didn't give him the powers—he already had lightning and fire at that point."

"You were *there*?" Kristiana asks. "What else are we going to find out? Were you the second gunman on the grassy knoll?"

"Huh?" Katerina asks.

"Never mind. It's one of the few things they made us learn about American history."

"It's one of the few things kids were fascinated enough with to remember," I say. "The mystery of whether one or two people helped assassinate a beloved US President."

"Regardless. . ." Katerina looks torn. "There isn't anything to tell. When she came, she actually told him the *only* way he could get the other powers was to have you all voluntarily offer them. Then she left."

"Why not?" Adriana asks. "Why can't she control her own magic?"

"She said she gave Rurik power," Katerina says, "but then later gave it to the Romanovs and the other families, split up that second time." She shrugs. "At first I thought Gustav was another Rurikid, but now I think he was part of the second pass."

"Why do you think that?" Mirdza asks.

Katerina shakes her head. "I don't really know. I'm just guessing, but Leonid can only access the power when we let him, because we're already using it. He has to wait for our permission. What if, when she gave the Romanovs and all our families our powers, she had someone else, another person who was *in charge* of us?"

"Like, checks and balances?" I raise one eyebrow. "You're saying, she appointed a supervisor the second time?"

She shrugs. "I have no idea, but if you're related to the second round of powers, your abilities won't work the same way as Leonid's, so. I think our best bet would be looking for those journals—the ones from your family. At least they might tell us whether you're Rurikid or something else."

"The last we heard about them," Kristiana says, "Dad says they were in the middle of absolutely nowhere." She taps through her phone, squinting.

"Please tell me you didn't have Dad text you the information," I say. "Because texts are so easy to monitor."

Kris rolls her eyes. "Of course not. He told me, and I entered it into this little note."

It's not much better, but at least she's not flinging the information around. "Alright, where was the last known location?"

Kristiana cringes a little. "Dad says he actually called the lady once—our, like, second cousin or something."

Oh, no. Dad calling someone is never good.

"At first she insisted that she wasn't even a Liepa. She said her name was *Saddler*, but I guess she finally relented and said her dad's name was Liepa."

"So where is she?" Kris has always known how to bury the lead.

"Some place called Manila, Utah," she says. "It's on the border of Utah and Wyoming in a town of like, four hundred people."

"How fabulous," Adriana says.

"Actually, it is good," I say. "I doubt Leonid would ever think to look for us there."

Aleksandr's money comes in handy again when we pay cash for a new Escalade and load all our stuff into it. Aleksandr heads for the driver's side, but I step in front of him.

"Whoa, you don't even have a license here."

"My license from Russia—"

"Is probably pretty expired, given that it's now two thousand and—"

"I got a new one." He scowls. "Move."

"Hand me the keys," I insist.

"Oh, just give him the keys," Kristiana says. "If we sit in the back, I can take a nap on your lap."

"I call the middle," Alexei says. "Come on." He's hopping into the middle seats before I've even taken the keys.

"No way." Mirdza huffs. "Why do we always get split up and you two always wind up sitting together?"

"We're trading seats at the first gas station." Grigoriy doesn't ask. He just climbs into the back, grumbling.

Which leaves Katerina and me to load all the luggage. "Go up there," I say. "It's fine."

But she doggedly stays back with me, hefting huge rolling bags into the trunk.

"Are you sure you're fine to drive?" Her voice is soft. "It's late, and you haven't been sleeping much."

"You'll stay awake and talk to me?"

She nods. "Sure, if you want me to."

I'm surprised, but after this long, bizarre, not encouraging day, I actually do want to talk to her. That may be the oddest thing that has happened yet.

18

KATERINA

Within half an hour, every single member of the happy couples club is asleep. Two of them are snoring, and I can't even tell which ones it is from the front seat.

"Everyone jumps on you a lot." Gustav's eyes are on the road, but his tone is light. Actually, it's not just light. It's something I haven't felt in a while.

It's kind.

"I deserve it." I keep my eyes trained on the road ahead, too.

"I'm not sure that's true," he says. "I wasn't lying about the white lights. I've seen a few people since that weird dark and light thing kicked in. Everyone has some darkness, but yours is very, very small."

"I wish that was true, but I've made some really dumb mistakes. I don't blame them for being a little leery of me."

He's quiet then, and I start counting the miles. He says nothing at all for thirty-one miles. That's when I find myself asking him something. "Why did you do it?"

"Do what?" He turns to look at me. We're finally out of

the New York congestion, and we're actually making decent time.

"You didn't even know it was me," I say. "You saw a horse, and six men were aiming guns at it, and you leapt right into the middle of it."

"Ah." He sighs, his hands shifting on the steering wheel and tightening a little. "The moronic move that has prompted the Russian maniac to visit the United States, presumably to kill me."

"Yeah," I say. "That."

"I'm not sure."

"Oh, come on."

"I'm really not." He shakes his head slowly. "I hate horses. And all my life, I've witnessed the misery that follows any kind of gambling. I hate taking risks. I hedge all my bets in life, and I always take the safe path."

"Except when someone wants to shoot a random horse on the streets of New York City."

"I guess." The corner of his mouth is turning up, though.

"If it's any consolation," I say, "every gamble I make always turns out badly for me."

"When people say 'if it's any consolation,' it never is."

"I suppose not," I say. "But at least you have a sister who loves you."

"Do you mean the sister with the deviated septum?"

"Huh?"

He's smiling. "It's a common cause of snoring."

I turn around and crane my neck, but with her head canted sideways on Aleksandr's chest, their noses are inches apart, and I can't tell which of them is making the wheezing-rattle that's coming from the back seat.

"Seriously, though." I lean the back of my head against the side window so I can kind of see Gustav's profile while I pretend to look straight ahead. "My brother Boris would hand me over to Leonid on a silver platter if he thought it would win him points."

"And yet, I haven't been much better than Boris." He frowns. "Kris has called me over and over, and every time, I've either ignored her call or told her I can't help."

"If you can't help, then—"

"I could've helped, though," he says. "I had plenty of money. It was just that, with people who gamble like my dad, no amount is ever enough. I knew that if I helped her at all, she'd just keep coming back to me over and over."

"But you said she did call over and over."

His sideways grin is back. "Even sticking to my guns didn't really work."

"I'm surprised you could do it." I sigh. "I think I'd have caved."

His voice is small. Barely audible. "I would have too, but I was afraid my grandfather would find out I had helped, and trust me. If he knew I was funneling money back there, he'd have cut me off on the spot."

"But your mother was his daughter."

"And he gave and gave and gave to her—but it was never enough. It's his keenest embarrassment," he says. "It took me a long time to figure that out, but he felt like his generosity with her, his repeated gifts, made him a chump. Even thinking about it made him angry."

"Is that why you hate horses?"

He doesn't answer, but a muscle in his jaw pops.

"You founded a company that makes all its revenue from horse-racing. Your parents both loved horses, right?"

"Why do you say that?" He glances at me.

When our eyes meet, for some reason, it makes my heart race. "I mean, just from what I've heard about how Aleks and Kristiana met."

He frowns. "How did they meet? She bought him thinking he was a horse, right?"

I fill him in on what I've worked out, which is basically just the broad strokes. She was gambling on her own horse winning—some horse named Five—and then he was going to lose. But then this big black stallion, who must have overheard how much she needed to win, *lets* her win. So when she sees him being abused, she spends the winnings buying him, instead of spending it to save the family farm.

Gustav shakes his head. "I swear, that's how my family always is. They can have the money in their hand, but if there's a horse thing calling them, they're categorically unable to make the right decision." He sighs. "And that's why I hate horses. I actually loved horses, right up until I saw one kill my mother. Her love for racing, her love of horses, it destroyed her. It destroyed my dad. And it'll destroy Kris, too, because she always puts them first."

"I don't blame you," I say. "Leaving all that behind sounds like the smart move."

"What?" His head snaps sideways.

"Horses are born looking for a way to injure themselves." I shrug. "I do like them a lot, but it's the simple truth."

"I'm pretty sure my mother thought that was part of their charm."

I can't help adding, "In horses' defense, humans kind of do the same thing."

"They do," Gustav agrees. "But at least we can articulate our reasons. For a horse, they're often injured because they saw a plastic bag."

"But not for horse-shifters," I say. "When we take our horse forms, we aren't stupid like they are. So you shouldn't push that dislike onto us." I'm not sure why I want him to like the idea of shifting into a horse. It doesn't really affect me, except in the sense that Leonid's coming, and he'll probably kill us all unless Gustav figures out how to stop him.

As if we're on the same wavelength, Gustav asks, "Do you really think he's coming to America to kill me?"

"I'm not sure," I say. "Every time I thought I understood Leonid, he surprised me."

"He was your servant," Gustav says. "People never pay attention to their servants."

"He was also my friend," I say. "Or at least, I thought he was for a while."

"What changed?"

"Once I gave him my magic, he wanted more." I fold my hands in my lap and look down at them. "He became obsessed with it, really."

"He stopped caring about helping you win over Alexei, I take it?"

That was what made me the angriest. "Not only that, he told me I was an idiot for loving him." He might have been right about that, in retrospect. "He told me no one ever starts loving someone who's as pathetically desperate for that love." It hurt when he said that.

"Sounds like he knew that from past experience," Gustav says. "Did he love you?"

"Leonid has no idea what love is. His father was the only family he had, and he was totally crazy. It made him unstable."

Gustav's quiet for at least twenty more miles. We almost miss our turn.

Once we're on the new road, one we'll be sticking with for a while, I try for a safer question, one about his company. "Why'd you start Trifecta?"

"What?" He seems genuinely surprised by the question.

"You hate horses," I remind him. "And Trifecta's a combination totes company—which handles on-track betting—and online gambling, and you said it allows people to buy a share in various racehorses, too."

"Right. It covers all the angles of betting, so as a businessman, it's a marketshare-spread, so to speak."

"But you hate gambling—"

"Because the house always wins," he says. "What better play than to *be* the house?"

"I guess."

"What?" He's scowling whenever he glances my way.

"I don't know. I guess I still find it strange that you hate horses, but you make your living off them."

"I make my living by taking money from people who contribute to the industry that took my mother away."

"There it is." I sigh. "Now it makes sense. It's both revenge *and* a stable income plan."

"Why do you care? Are you a therapist or something?"

"A what?"

"They're people who analyze other people and try to break them down so they can help the people work through their issues."

For a while now, I've felt lost. Alexei has been true north for me, my only goal, for a decade. Other people, like Gustav, have things they love, like his company. But all I've had was my obsession with Alexei. Now that I've let it go, I have nothing else to replace it with.

But in that moment, I know. If we can get the world under control, once the threat of Leonid's gone, that's what I want to do—I want to learn to be a therapist. "It's really hard to see your own problems, but it's easier to see other people's stuff."

"What?"

"Think about it. When someone's riding," I say, "they can't see what they're doing wrong on the horse. It's the reason that even the best riders still need trainers. They need someone to see what they're doing wrong and tell them how to fix it. People are like that, too. They cling to whatever dumb thing they think they need way longer than they should. That means these people—therapists—they're basically like trainers for horseback riding, but they help fix the broken stuff in humans' lives, right?"

"I guess so."

Nothing in my life has felt this right in a long time. "And they have schools to teach you how to do that?"

Gustav nods. "Lots of them."

"You're so lucky to be alive now. When I was born, women like me didn't have jobs. They didn't look for meaning or purpose. Their purpose was to get married and have children, but now everyone gets to do what they want."

"I'm not sure that's really true," Gustav says. "Plenty of people today still don't do what they want."

"Why not?"

"They don't have the money to go to school, the time to pursue it, or the intellectual capacity to succeed even if they try. They may get stuck in a job because of other responsibilities, or they might be afraid to lose what they already have in the pursuit of what they really want."

That only convinces me further. "It sounds like those people need a therapist to get them back on track."

He's smiling as he shakes his head, and I realize he's probably mocking me. I don't care. It doesn't feel malicious. It feels. . .fond. Like he's treating me as someone he thinks is amusing in an endearing way.

I find myself looking at his hands where they're gripping the steering wheel—they're large, but also refined. My eyes slide upward to his forearms, the muscles in them shifting infinitesimally as he adjusts the car to follow between the stripes on the road. I watch where his chest rises and falls with his breath, and his mouth, the curve of his lips, and then when I look upward again. . .

He's staring right at me.

And I feel like a total idiot. This is exactly what I am *not* going to do. After we defeat Leonid, I'm going to figure out how to make the time and find the money to go to school, and I'm going to help people make better decisions in their lives.

While also making better decisions in mine.

Starting with *not* looking longingly at Gustav and his muscular forearms.

"Why were you looking at me?"

I can feel my face heat, but it's dark enough, I doubt he can see it. "I wasn't. I was just looking at the speedometer."

"Can you even see it from where you're sitting?"

"Not very well," I say. "Which is why I had to stare."

"If you want to be a therapist," he says, "then finish analyzing me. Maybe I chose the company I chose because I wanted to stick it to people who gamble while staying safe. But why didn't I just go to work for my grandfather? That would've been easier and safer."

"You admire him," I say, "but I think you didn't really want to be around him very much. He probably makes you angry, even if you wish he didn't. He's upset that he enabled your mother, but your mom did what she did, at least in part, because he cut her off."

Luckily the road is straight and flat, because he glares at me for way too long. "You might be right." His head snaps back, and he says nothing else for quite some time.

I let him sit in his thoughts.

It's what I'm doing—reminding myself of *why* I'm not supposed to be gawking at Gustav. I have a goal now. A goal that's not just 'get some guy to like me.' I have a plan.

I mean, assuming we don't all get killed.

But for some reason, I don't think Leonid will kill me. He might kill Gustav, though, and that bothers me more than it should. I barely know the guy.

Whether I like it or not, though, I'm vested. I want him to at least survive, and more than that, I find that I want him to succeed. I want him to reach his goal—the one we basically just tried to derail entirely. "Will your grandfather really not choose you to be his successor if the IPO doesn't go perfectly?"

"Aleksandr, Grigoriy, and Alexei really do appear to have the funds to buy most of the shares," he says. "Grandfather won't like it, though. Having private Russian citizens prop up my company?" He sighs. "I'm pretty sure that driving back here with all of you ruined my chances to be his successor, yes." He looks. . .resigned.

Not depressed.

But not far from it.

"I'm really sorry," I say.

"It's not your fault." He huffs. "It's not really Kristiana's fault either. I do know that, but I can't help wishing things were different."

"Why do you want to take over his company? Yours seems to be doing well, and you said you have plenty of money."

"Part of it is that I hate losing, and my cousin's a total jerk." He's frowning. "But part of it is that having that kind of control, owning that company, would be the kind of security that's almost impossible to obtain."

"Security?"

"No matter what happens with the economy, no matter what someone tries to do or take, I would be safe."

"Would you though?"

He scowls.

"I'm not trying to be a jerk, but if you've learned anything in the past few days, isn't it that there really *is* no way to be safe? I mean, life isn't ever guaranteed."

"So that's it?" His hands are gripping the steering wheel so tightly, I worry he'll pop it off. "We should just *give up*? There's no way to be safe. We can all just float around life, letting what happens happen?"

I turn back and look over my shoulder. "Those six idiots are the safest people I know," I say. "They have each other, and they trust each other. That's rare."

"Wonderful," he says. "Well, they don't trust me, and I don't trust them, so I guess I'm still at square one."

"I'm not sure."

"What now?"

"You can look at people now and know what you're looking at. Bad people. Good people. Complicated people, whatever the case may be, now you know it."

"I guess."

"You know people better than they know themselves. You said I'm not entirely black, but what do you see when you look at the six of them?"

"Why do you think I agreed to come?" He huffs. "They're mostly sparkly and shiny and bright. Disgustingly so."

"And other people? The guys at the rental car place, for instance? People on the streets?"

"Various levels of dark," he says. "A few bright lights here and there, but most of the people I meet are pretty mixed."

"That's depressing."

"It is."

"But think," I say. "Now you have that ability. You can sort people out and know whether to believe what they're saying. That'll keep you safe, to a certain extent, or safer than before."

"It's the lamest power ever," he says. "I can't even tell whether they're telling the truth when they talk to me. I can just tell whether they're light or dark people."

"Leonid said almost the exact same thing to me when he found out."

"I get why he was bummed."

"He was so upset, so disappointed, that I didn't try to stop him when he summoned Baba Yaga."

The car swerves, and the people in the back wake up. We stop for gas. Everyone gets snacks. Grigoriy and Aleksandr both try to take over for Gustav.

Aleksandr's the most adamant. "You should get some sleep."

Gustav shakes his head. "I'm fine, I swear. I'll take a break in a few more hours."

It takes almost forty minutes for everyone to fall asleep again once we're back on the road, but Gustav has not been distracted. "Tell me."

"What?" I try to avoid the question.

"Tell me how you summoned her, and what happened when you did."

"You didn't ask when everyone was awake."

"I think there's a reason why you haven't told everyone this story, and I want to hear it. I think I deserve to hear it." He's not angry, but he's not going to let this go, either.

He's probably right.

＃ 19 ＃

KATERINA

A HUNDRED YEARS BEFORE

I understand why my dad's mad at the czar. I really do.
They should've helped our families when there was a
drought. Punishing us is one thing, but watching our
people starve over a personal grudge, well, it's maddening. I
alternate between hating myself and hating the Romanovs,
but it's harder to hate yourself.

But Alexei's just doing as his father orders. It's not his
fault.

"You can't be serious," Leonid says. "You're really not
upset at him?"

"Being angry only makes things worse for everyone," I say.
"I'm trying to protect you, too. Going up against Alexei and
his father would be very bad, but trying to fight all three of
the families?" I shake my head. "It's suicide."

Leonid looks hurt. "Mikhail says—"

"Mikhail's an idiot, and he doesn't care what happens to
you. Don't you see that? He's angry, so he just nocked an arrow
and he's firing it. He doesn't care what happens to the arrow."

Leonid frowns.

"It's so true—I can't believe you don't see that. He and Boris aren't partnering up to go attack them. They want *you* to do it. Our families have cut ties with you, so they'll be blameless if it goes badly." I huff. "*When* it goes badly."

"You've seen me," he says. "I can do things that you can't do, things neither of you can do, using both powers at the same time."

"I know," I say. "And it's amazing, but Leonid, it's a still a bad call. You can't fight them all."

"Unless I could get their powers, too."

"We read all the documents," I say. "They're not about to offer them to you, and that's the only way."

"There's one thing I didn't show you." His broad shoulders droop a bit. "I—I knew you'd be upset."

After Mikhail followed me to the clearing at the edge of our property where I'd been meeting him, we had to change locations. The abandoned hut Leonid's been living in is pretty depressing, but I wasn't sure where else to meet him. Leonid's managed to scavenge some things—mismatched chairs. A scarred and pitted, rough-hewn table. A pitcher and some matching clay cups made by a somewhat skilled artisan, but chipped and worn down by time. The hut isn't welcoming, but it's at least got a lived-in feeling. I brought him a pile of blankets when I came this time.

Leonid rummages around underneath the chair I piled the blankets on, and then he stands.

He's holding an old book.

A *very* old book.

"What is that?" I'm nervous, because it looks an awful lot like the journals we were studying in secret at the palace. "Please tell me you didn't steal that."

"It belonged to *my* ancestors," Leonid says. "They stole it from us first."

I close my eyes and sigh. "Leonid, that all happened hundreds of years ago. You have to let it go."

"But we're still dealing with the aftermath now," he says, his eyes bright. "Your family's being punished *right now* by the people who stole it. They're ignoring you and your people, and they're not doing what they were tasked to do, which is serving the people of Russia, keeping them safe and healthy."

"Right, and I plan to keep telling them—"

"They ignore you." He balls his free hand into a fist. "They mock you. They don't respect you."

"I know they aren't perfect, but they had reasons for—"

"Stop defending them!" Leonid's beautiful face is smudged with dirt. His hair, pulled back with a leather strap, has come undone, and now it streams around his face like sunlight surrounding a work of art. How he can be so ungodly beautiful in the midst of such squalor, I don't know.

But it makes him look even more unhinged.

No one that gorgeous should be living in a hut like this, shouting. No one like him should be raging about the injustices of the world. He should be ruling it. It's plain when you see his face. He's the kind of person who was created for others to bow down to.

And judging from his face, he means to try to take his rightful place.

I have to at least *try* to stop him, because no matter what his bloodlines said, he is where he is, and he's going to smash himself against the cliffs, trying to fix the injustices he's fixated on.

"Mikhail's using you," I say. "They won't notice the book is gone, so if you just make sure—"

"Katerina," he says. "I kept this particular book for a reason." He kicks the chair toward the table, and then he straddles it, slamming the old book down on the pitted surface. "Look."

The writing's ancient. I'm not sure how he can even read it. I squint.

"Here." He points. "Read this part."

"*To summon the all-mother?*" I look up at him. "What does this even mean?"

"I think it's her. You know the journals make it seem like she chose Rurik for a reason? This is how we find out what that reason was. We can summon her!"

"The All-Mother?" I shake my head. "That sounds very, very inadvisable. I think it's a bad plan. It's either complete nonsense, or it works and we're even worse off."

"I think it's talking about the witch known as Baba Yaga."

"So what?" I ask. "You know what the stories say about her."

He rolls his eyes. "I hardly think she travels around in a house with chicken feet and eats small children."

"But maybe she does." I shudder. "This is a bad idea, Leonid."

"Well, if it is, you'll be able to tell everyone just how bad." He closes the book. "Because I've already done it."

He stands and grabs a bowl from a shelf in the top corner of the small room, and he pours the contents into the fireplace. The flames crackle as he does, and I can feel it—the injection of our magic into the dark, sticky-looking liquid. "I followed all the horrible, bizarre instructions. Dig up earth of loam, of sand, of clay, and of peat. Add water of stream, ocean, lake, and snow. Mix it with the wind from the steppe, and the air from the ocean." He smiles. "Slaughter a crowing rooster and mix his blood, laced with the sparking power of the earth."

Fire blooms in the hearth.

"And burn it all to ash."

I'm shaking my head. "No. This is a terrible idea. Stop now, before—"

But it's too late.

Thunder roars above us. The earth shakes beneath our feet, and the roof of the miserable hut trembles, chunks of sod crumbling down on our heads. The sound that follows, like the lowing of cattle, the groaning of the earth beneath, and the rumbling of thunder above, fills the air around us, somehow combining in an unholy and unnatural way.

"Who dares to summon me?" The voice pounds against my skull. I drop to my knees and wrap my arms around my legs, closing my eyes and pressing them against the tops of my thighs.

"Who summoned me here?" The voice is louder, somehow, rattling my very brain inside my skull. "Present yourself."

"It was I, Leonid Ivanovich." I look up, and moonlight streams through the ravaged roof, lighting up Leonid's proud, but filthy face. "I called you, because *I'm* the rightful heir to your power. Others have usurped it, but I call on you to make it right."

The cacophony, the wind, the trembling, it all stops.

The moonlight on Leonid's face is all that remains. I uncurl myself, wondering whether it's good or bad that the noise and pressure and battering of the unnatural wind has abated.

And then a woman steps through the front of the hut.

"Leonid Ivanovich." The woman's ancient—a hunched crone. Then I blink, and she's middle-aged, her hair just beginning to grey at the temples. Small creases on the edges of her eyes are there, but only just. Not a second later, she's a maiden, fair and lovely to behold, with streaming blonde hair and eyes just like Leonid's.

She smiles. "My child."

Her *child?*

"I called for your help," Leonid says. "The Romanov

family, as well as two others, possess the powers that were meant for me."

The woman extends her arm, and her hand presses against the side of his face. "You're as beautiful as your ancestor." Her smile's soft and kind. Her face is as gentle as the summer rain. Her eyes are still every bit as bright and startling as Leonid's— the most vibrant green of grass growing in the middle of summer.

"Help me," he says.

"No one's entitled to powers, child," she says. "Not you, and not the Romanovs."

He frowns. "But—"

"I thought your line had gone." She shakes her head. "Had I known you yet lived—I couldn't sense you." She peers at him. "How did I miss. . ."

"Father says our ancestors fled. They traveled far, into old England, until when I was a young child, he and his father finally returned."

She closes her eyes. "They left my realm, beyond my reach." She shakes her head. "What's done cannot be undone." When she opens her eyes again, they're no longer bright green. They're the deep brown of loamy earth. "I cannot help you. The only way you can regain your power is if they're given back to you by the others. Those I bestowed them upon must relinquish them to you."

"But—"

She presses her index finger against his mouth, and in that moment, she ages what looks like a hundred years. Her back is hunched. Her eyes are rheumy, and her fingers are crooked and covered with blotches. "You must not attempt to force them, my child. Promise."

Leonid's nostrils flare. "You say there's no way, but—"

"My calling is to provide balance to the world. It always has been. I'm not the only force in this world, and nature seeks balance, always. Light begets dark. Life begets death.

High requires low. Sky cries out to earth, and fire calls for dousing moisture."

"But—"

"You're very keen on talking," she says. "But you need to learn to listen."

Leonid's eyes flash. He's not happy.

"Heed my warning." She's middle-aged again, and she's grown at least four or five feet in height. She towers over him. "If you attempt to force my powers under your control, you'll harm yourself, and you'll harm those you're trying to force as well. You must not attempt it. The only way you may regain strength is through surrender. Do you understand? Are you listening?"

"But why?" Leonid's pleading again. "You can't be strong if you surrender."

"When I gave your ancestors their powers, I broke several rules." She sighs, shrinking back down. "I punched into my abilities and drilled them out, forcing a conduit."

"Tell me how," Leonid says.

She shakes her head. "When the Romanovs and the other families approached me, it wasn't because they wanted power. The loss of the Rurikid line left a gaping hole, you see. No one could claim the throne. My mistake continued to cost all the people of the earth. I had to try and fix it. But this time, instead of carving out the power, I found a weak spot, and I teased it out. As I did it, my power split. I realized that the largest part of my problem was that I offered too much—I had thrown off the balance in the land. One human should never have had access to all that magic. Splitting the elements of my strength creates a web of balance, a net of control. But by sharing my abilities through both force and release, my power flows outward and inward. I didn't worry at the time, as the inward flow was sealed." She frowns. "Until you reclaimed it."

"And now the powers are at odds?" I ask.

Her head whips around like a snake's, both verdant green eyes intent on my face. "Who are you?"

"I'm a daughter of your second attempt," I say. "I have the power of lightning."

She nods. "You surrendered already to my child."

"I—well. I guess I did."

"Ask this girl for help," Baba Yaga says. "Perhaps she can help you convince the others."

"That's why we called you," Leonid says. "They won't listen."

"Then you suffer from the same affliction." Her eyes sparkle. "I can do no more. I wish you luck in restoring balance, child." She inclines her head, and then she simply *disappears*. Where she once was, there's nothing. No smoke, no sparkles.

Nothing at all.

I sink back on my haunches, both relieved and overwhelmed at the same time.

"She was worse than useless," Leonid says.

"I'm not sure," I say. "At least we understand *why* you have to obtain the surrender."

"Because she screwed up," he says. "Because my ancestors were dumb and left." He sighs. "This whole thing—" He freezes. "Why do you think she told me *not* to try and force the powers so many times?"

I blink. "What?"

"She said it more than once. She was really worried that I'd do that." A slow smile creeps across his face. "I think she warned me off of it, because it's *possible*."

"Leonid, no." I scramble to my feet. "She was so adamant—"

"And if I was worried about someone taking over, if I had split my powers out for a reason, wouldn't I be just as adamant in my warnings?" He's delighted. He thinks he's found a solution.

But I know he hasn't. "This is a bad plan."

"Why?" He shrugs. "I'll gather the players. I'll ask them again, as she told me I should, and if they still refuse?" He nods slowly. "Then I'll do exactly what she made me promise never to do." He grins his devilish grin. "I'll *take* what I'm due, consequences bedamned."

$\clubsuit$ 20 $\clubsuit$

GUSTAV

Her face shines so brightly that it's hard to see the road. It is, however, easy to see how guilty she feels. I may have chosen not to work with my grandfather because I dislike him, deep down, or even because I blame him. But if that's the case, I think she loves Leonid almost as much as she hates him.

She may feel guilty about going to him before coming here, but I'm not sure she could have done any differently. She has as much family trauma as I do.

"He was a bad guy," I say. "In case you've been beating yourself up about leaving him."

"I'm not sure," Katerina says. "I want to believe that. I really do. It absolves me of my role in everything."

"No one good tries to rape-steal someone else's powers."

"But he did think they were making bad decisions." Her shoulders slump, and she leans against the side window. "They did refuse to help us, and a lot of our people died in that famine."

"He used that to justify his decision to do what he wanted, deep down."

"Maybe."

"What happened when he tried to force the powers?"

"I'm not entirely sure," Katerina says. "I remember the guys laughing at him. They told him to do his best. They were ready to fight. But then, once they said they were absolutely unwilling to return his power to him, when they said he had no right and that being Rurikid was irrelevant, he set his feet, closed his eyes, and. . ." She shrugs. "I'm not sure what he did, but it felt like. . .like the ceiling was caving in. Like the air was all gone. Like my insides were being forced outside. I don't know how else to describe it."

I shudder.

"Whatever he did forced me to shift into my equine form. That's really the last thing I remember. It had never happened before, a forced shift. Nothing like that."

"And when you woke up?"

"Leonid woke me up," she says. "He was patting my cheek and saying my name."

"You were in your human form?"

Katerina nods. "I know the guys woke stuck in their horse form, but I woke as a human and I could only shift when he specifically ordered it. I think maybe it has to do with my having surrendered to him. I'm not sure."

"Do you really think we might find the answers in the middle of nowhere?" I want to believe there might be old family journals that explain everything, but it feels highly unlikely.

"I don't know." She shakes her head. "At first, I thought you were like Leonid—maybe from another branch of his family. I thought you were Rurikid. But if they offer you their powers and you don't get them?" She frowns. "It must be something different. Like Leonid, I think your best bet at finding the truth is going to be searching whatever was written by your family."

"Or summoning Baba Yaga." I can't help my smirk.

"I strongly advise against that," she says. "Though the girls have apparently seen her from time to time."

"She scared you?"

"Deeply," Katerina says.

I yawn.

"I saw that," she says. "You need to sleep." Before I can stop her, she's shaking Grigoriy awake by grabbing his knee. "Your turn to drive."

I want to argue—I'm learning more from her on this drive than I have from all the chats with the others over the course of days—but she's probably right. No matter what the guys may be hoping I'll become, I'm far from superhuman now. If I don't sleep, at least a little bit, I'll eventually crash this car and kill us all.

The sun's about to rise, the first rays brightening the horizon as I finally lean my head against the window and go to sleep. At some point, we stop. People are talking and some are getting out, presumably to eat or go to the restroom. I shrug out of my jacket, ball it up, and go right back to sleep.

I'm not sure how long I've slept when I finally wake up, but the sight I wake up to is breathtaking. There's a gorge—tall, flat-topped but surrounded by sloping mountains with a winding river that threads through them. Maybe the river created the pass. I'm no geologist.

But what's most breathtaking about them is the color.

The river water is the brightest blue, almost like a blue highlighter. The rocks that form the mountain sides are streaked with bright, flaming reds and oranges. The sky behind it is a light blue, and there's both scattered greenery along the edges and patches of bright, golden sandstone, leaving the whole thing an almost unbelievable rainbow cascade of colors.

I'm not really one for faith or God, but this could almost change my mind.

I rub my eyes and yawn. "Where are we?" My voice cracks in the middle of we, and I cough to clear it.

"Good morning, sunshine," Aleksandr says from the driver's seat. "You've been asleep for almost fourteen hours, and we're almost there."

"That's the Flaming Gorge," Kristiana says. "Isn't it beautiful? It's the landmark this entire area's known for."

I don't really want to agree with her, and I don't want to think about why, so I just grunt.

"It's absolutely stunning," Katerina says with a sigh. She's sitting directly behind me, and something about the way she says it, as if she's barely ever seen beauty in her life, has me smiling but ducking my head so no one else notices.

"Your assistant called about a hundred times." Kris chucks my phone at my head.

I barely throw my hand up in time to keep from being clocked in the nose. "Why didn't you wake me up, then?"

"We did try," Kris says. "But I think you were operating on a pretty big sleep deficit."

I finally call Jean back. She answers before the phone has even rung a single time. "The SEC put the IPO on hold."

"I'm sorry, *what*?" I can barely formulate words. "They can't do that. They already approved the filing."

"They have, though," Jean says. "Something about chatter that a bunch of Russian nationals and the Russian government are all planning to purchase the shares at a higher than market rate. They said it's a national security issue."

Aleks, Grigoriy, Alexei, and apparently, possibly Leonid.

Before they showed up, I would have said that nothing could stop me—my company would go public, and Grandfather would choose me. There's no way I don't beat Prescott, right?

Then the harbingers of doom arrived.

They've embarrassed me, caused me legal trouble, ruined meetings, and now, it seems they've completely torched my

IPO, and consequently my shot with taking over Grandfather's company. I should be full-on livid. I should be calling the SEC. I should be frothing at the mouth. I should be strangling Aleksandr.

The whole situation, or rather, my reaction to it, reminds me of something. When I was a kid, I watched my mother sail over jumps every day. I rode daily as well, but I didn't jump. Mother was very severe about our form before she ever let us turn the horse toward any kind of poles.

She didn't even let me ride the kind of horse that had the capacity to jump over more than a few boring crossrails. I mostly rode retired horses, the ones who were a little slower, a little more patient, and a little more arthritic. Big jumps were out of the question. But once, she was busy talking to the trainer, and her horse was all tacked up and ready to go. Instead of waiting on the groom to check my tack, I went and slid the halter off her massive jumper. He dropped his head so I could reach to bridle him.

I took it as a sign.

Two minutes later, I had the stirrups moved to the shortest setting, and I scrambled on top of Kettegast's shiny black saddle. He threw his head a few times and danced sideways, but I shortened my reins as Mother had taught, and I yanked until he knew I was the boss, and then I urged him forward, and we were off.

At first, everything seemed great.

He was fast—just like I wanted. He was eager, practically diving toward the jumps that were set up in the arena. And he could jump—I knew that. I'd seen him sail over four and a half feet in height just the day before. So I aimed him at the large wooden rail like Mom always did, and I clicked to encourage him, and when we drew near, I leaned forward too.

I knew that when he started to jump, I was supposed to lean forward. I knew that was called "jump position." I wasn't quite sure what to do with my hands, so I pulled them back, bringing them close to the saddle so I could grab it as necessary.

Unfortunately, Kettegast didn't appreciate me popping him in the mouth, and he stopped abruptly just before the jump. That sent me sailing over his shoulders.

There was a split second between his halt and my impact when I realized what was happening and panicked, but then in that next split second, I just *let go*. There was nothing I could do. I had already done the moronic thing, and now I just had to face the consequences.

That's how I feel in this moment.

My life was set on this path many years before when I was born to Mom and Dad. I didn't make them who they were, and I didn't make Grandfather who he was, either. I can't control who I am, and I can't change what the people outside of me are doing. I see the catastrophic crash into the large wooden jump standard coming, but I can't stop it.

No amount of frothing or screaming or ranting will change the inevitable—I should have worn a helmet, but here we are.

"Daniel?" Jean says. "Where are you? Why aren't you here? We've spent more than six years on this, and it's falling apart."

"I'm working on it," I say. "Believe me, I am, and it's work I can't do in New York. Hold tight, keep running Trifecta, and I'll be back as soon as I can."

Or, you know, I'll be dead.

I don't mention that part.

"But your grandfather's calling about every five minutes, and he said if you can't—"

"Jean." I pause to make sure she heard me.

"What?"

"You're going to have to trust me. What I'm doing? It's our only play."

"I'm pregnant," she whispers. "I just told Javi about the baby, and we're really excited. I need things not to fall apart."

"Jean," I say again. "No matter what happens with Trifecta, you will be just fine. Don't work more than ten-hour days. Do what you can, celebrate your baby with your husband, and I'll be back as soon as possible." I hang up.

"We really need to find these journals," Kris says.

The understatement of the year for me.

"We don't have an address," Kris says, "but in a town of four hundred, I bet someone can tell us where she lives."

Only, predictably, when we park in front of the local grocery store, which appears to also be a hardware store, and walk inside, the people are a little less than forthcoming.

"No," Kristiana's saying. "We're not mobsters. A few of us are from Russia, yes, but I went to school at Oxford, which is a prestigious university in a town about an hour outside of London. Trust me, we don't mean anyone here harm."

The woman behind the counter folds her arms and scowls. In spite of her irritated demeanor, I know she's trying to do the right thing, because in front of her face, there's a mask of swirling little golden lights. "Amanda's tough, no doubt, and I'm not sure she'd be scared of you folk, but I'll tell you this." She plants her hands on the top of the counter and leans forward. "If you want some snacks or maybe a frozen pizza, I'm happy to help. But if you want personal information about one of my friends, I ain't playing."

"We just need to ask her—"

The woman sighs and straightens. "I'm more afraid of her than I am of you, so I'm not about to send you out there."

"Out where?" Kris asks. "As in, outside of town?"

I'll give my sister this much—she's determined.

Aleksandr plonks a stack of cash on the counter. "We mean her no harm, but it's urgent that we speak with her."

The woman knocks the money off the counter without even looking at it first. Bills flutter down and all around, coming to rest in little piles all over the floor. "Offering me cash just confirms that you folks aren't savory." She glares.

The door jingles as someone walks in. "Well, Venetia, I reckon you did the right thing by calling me over." An older man with grey-streaked but otherwise dark brown hair saunters into the already crowded entry. His right hand's resting on a gun where it sits in a holster. "I'm the sheriff in this tiny town, and think I speak for everyone when I say we don't want no trouble."

"We don't either," I say, stepping around Kristiana. "My name's Daniel Belmont, and I'm actually a business owner back in New York City, and—"

"I watch the news, boy, and I know your city's a mess." His face is mostly light, with just small streaks of dark appearing now and again.

"It's not my city." I frown. "I'm in the middle of an IPO for my company, and I'm not even supposed to be here right now. Believe me when I tell you that this is a very bad time for all of us, but we need to talk to Amanda Saddler urgently. Once we've spoken to her, we'll leave peacefully and amicably."

The man scowls, the darker patches flaring a little more often here and there.

"You could come with us," I say. "To watch and make sure we honor our word."

"I'm not ashamed to say that I've gone my entire career without shooting a single human being." He sighs. "I'd rather not change that today."

"We're on the same page," I say.

He's thinking, but he hasn't made up his mind.

I whip out my wallet and drop it on the counter. "Look here." I pull out my driver's license. "Daniel Belmont, just like I said. The address listed is for my apartment in New York. I own it outright—I'm an upstanding citizen. You can run my

license and see that I don't have so much as a parking viola-
tion outstanding."

Kris chokes, and I realize that someone in law enforce-
ment running my ID would lead Leonid right to us, assuming
he's looking, which I think is a fair assumption. I hold my
breath, wishing I could kick myself for my own idiocy.

But the old man just bobs his head and says, "Alright. Let's
mosey."

Mosey?

It apparently means that we'll go see Amanda. He loads up in
his car and waits, a bit impatiently, spitting out the window twice
while he waits for all of us to climb into our clown-car of an SUV,
and then takes off the same direction we just drove to get here.

We literally drive down the road eight miles or so, and
then pull up a drive we blew right past. There's a big, old,
rusting truck at the front of the driveway, which is why I
remember it, and the bed of the truck's full of profusely
blooming mums. This woman turned an old vehicle into a
planter? What kind of person does that?

As we round a corner and stop in front of the farmhouse,
I scan the area, trying to get a feel for what we're driving into.
The long white house is pretty welcoming, with a circular
gravel drive, a large open porch with a swing, and big potted
mums on either side of the navy blue front door.

The sheriff pulls up and cuts the engine, swinging out and
gesturing for us to exit the car, too. He waits until we're all
out before walking toward the front porch. Before he can
even knock, the door springs open.

The woman's voice precedes her. "Archer, what on earth
are you doing and who are all those people following you like
you're their mama duck?" The woman's small, and her white
hair's knotted into a bun on top of her head, wisps escaping
on all sides. Her eyes are scanning us with an intense and
almost aggressive intelligence I rarely see in women her age.

Her whole face burns like a lighthouse.

"I'm Kristiana—"

The sheriff cuts my sister off. "They were at the True Value downtown, trying to browbeat everyone in town into giving them your address." He shakes his head. "I don't know what they want, but I'm here to help see them off if you're not interested in buying it."

Amanda's eyes shift to Kristiana. "Alright, girl. Out with it. Why'd you come?"

"My name's Kristiana Liepa," she says.

Amanda's laugh reminds me of the braying of a donkey. "Oh my, you came a long way just to ask me for money, didn't you? Latvia, isn't it? It must be a great deal of money you need this time."

"Excuse me?" Kristiana's eyes are round as coasters.

"Your daddy or someone called me a few years back, begging me to buy a share in his farm, as if I'd have any interest in some horse farm in Europe." She sighs. "Let's hear it, then? What are you offering me, and how much do you want for it?"

"We aren't offering you anything," Kristiana says. "We're actually only here because—"

"You missed your long-lost family that much?" Amanda's frowning. "You think I'll believe that?"

"No," Kristiana says. "Well, I mean, sure, we're happy to finally meet you, but the thing is—"

"Your daddy called me so many times after I turned him down that I had to change my number. So, the thing is, you heard that I'm loaded, and you want to be friends now that you hear I'm childless." She shakes her head. "You're wasting your time. I may not have popped children out myself, but I've got family that I love more than any other granny I know. We clear?" She turns to the sheriff. "I'm done here, Archer. Please see them off."

Aleksandr looks ready to bury the old sheriff under a ton

of dirt, but I wave them back. "Let's not do anything that might make the local news," I hiss. "We'll just grab some food and a hotel room, and—"

But before I can illuminate our plans in a nonthreatening way, Amanda slams the door with a bang.

"At least we know where she lives now," Kristiana says.

That earns us a pointed scowl from the old Archer guy.

Before anyone can say something that ends with the FBI being called as backup, I wave them back into the SUV. "Food," I shout. "I'm starving."

We wind up at some place called Brownings, which also boasts a hotel apparently, and we argue for a bit about our next move. We haven't really made any decisions when Katerina leans in close and whispers, "The people at the table next to us are talking about some kind of rodeo that's happening tomorrow, and they said the whole town's going."

"So what?" I ask. "Do you like rodeos?"

Katerina glares. "Of course not, but it's sponsored by Saddler Industries, and I feel like that's not a coincidence. Maybe we could approach her in a less hostile environment."

It takes us almost two hours to sort out the details, but by the end of the night, we've confirmed that Amanda Saddler's development company and resort are major sponsors of the rodeo, and she's likely to be there. As the only US citizen among us, I sign up to do one of the only open events on the roster—something I never in a million years thought I'd ever do.

A barrel race.

"You have a horse?" The woman signing us up eyes me strangely, possibly because I'm wearing six hundred dollar slacks, two thousand dollar shoes, and a button-down french-cuffed dress shirt.

"Of course he does." Katerina's beaming. "The prettiest palomino you've ever seen."

"Not a stallion, right?" The woman glares. "They're not allowed."

I can't help wondering whether they're really not allowed, or whether she's worried about the greenhorn trying to ride a totally unsuitable horse. "It's a very nice mare." I force what I hope is a friendly smile.

The woman isn't impressed, but she takes my money and writes down my name. I'm pleased it all appears to be done by hand, because that's less of a record that we're here.

"This is a mistake," Aleksandr says. "When's the last time you even rode a horse?"

"I was on a horse just two days ago." I can't help glancing at Katerina.

"You guys worry about talking to Amanda Saddler," she says, "and we'll worry about winning that barrel race."

"Winning?" I raise both eyebrows. "I'm just hoping I don't fall off."

"That too." Katerina's smile's a little too bright, given the circumstances.

"Why are you in such a good mood?"

"Leonid has no idea where we are, we actually found Amanda Saddler, and she's not dead," she says. "So far, this plan isn't that far off course."

When we're celebrating the person we were seeking *being alive*, I feel like our plan is doomed to failure, but I keep my mouth shut. A little hope never hurt anyone.

Or at least, I really hope it didn't.

KATERINA

"I'm so sorry," the woman at the front desk says. "Because of the rodeo, we only have two rooms."

"We'll take them," Aleksandr says. "How much?"

Almost as soon as she names an amount, he plonks the cash down on the counter. He's not keen on using any plastic with Leonid following us, and I don't blame him. But when he turns around, it's not pretty. He extends his hand. . .to Gustav.

"Whoa," I say. "I think I should get a room, obviously."

"Obviously?" Gustav frowns.

"You can stay with your sister," I say. "But I need my own room." For once. I've been sleeping in a van for thirty plus hours, and before that, I was traveling, stuck in a cubicle, and then on a couch. I don't point that out, but they all know.

"We're newlyweds who have been traveling in a pack for a week," Kristiana says. "We figured you two could share."

"What about the Hideout?" I look at Gustav. "Didn't that Flaming Gorge Hideout place have some rooms too?"

"Only two rooms as well," he says. "And Grigoriy and Alexei snatched them so fast I almost lost a finger."

"What is this?" I ask. "Are we characters in some kind of

corny romance novel, and the writer's panicking because she's writing chapter twenty-one and she hasn't even written a single kiss scene yet?"

No one laughs. Gustav kicks at a weird blotch on the carpet.

"Oh, come on," Aleksandr says. "We're adults, and you'll be fine sharing for one night. You don't even like one another. It's not like you close the door to the outside and suddenly you fall madly in love."

I huff, and I grumble, but he's right. There's not much I can do, if Gustav doesn't offer to sleep on the floor in his estranged sister's room. It's not like I'd want to share a room with Boris if the roles were reversed.

"Fine." I reach for my bag, but Gustav has already grabbed it. "If you think that carrying my bag is going to make me less crabby. . ." I snort. "Well, I guess you'd be right."

We're laughing as we circle the bend outside and walk right into room number eleven. "This is us." Gustav dangles the key in front of the lock. "Come on, double beds."

I suppress my laugh.

But when the door opens, there's just the one big king size bed staring at us.

"This is ridiculous," I say. "Really."

"I'll sleep on the floor." Gustav breezes inside, sets our bags on the floor of the window-wall and shrugs out of his jacket.

For some reason, watching him taking clothing off sends a shiver up my spine, proving that I'm just as ridiculous as this situation. I turn to face the door, focusing an inordinate amount of attention on closing it and turning the deadbolt. For some reason, the simple act of turning the deadbolt makes heat rise in my face.

It's a normal thing to do in a hotel, locking the door, but it feels. . .like I'm closing out the world so it'll just be the two of us.

I shake my head and turn back, ready to just get it out there that we are clearly just roommates with a shared space, but instead of being halfway across the small room, Gustav's standing right in front of me, his shirt half unbuttoned. He's big—something I had never noticed before. The last time we were standing this close together, I was a horse.

"Oh." I look up at his face, struck stupid by the curve of his brow, the strong, square shape of his jaw, and the deep golden stubble that has grown in on it. My stomach flutters. My mouth goes dry.

And he reaches past me and smashes some kind of bug on the wall.

I blink.

"Thank goodness you're not the kind of girl who screeches for an hour because she saw a beetle."

Except, I totally am.

I am one hundred percent that girl, when I'm not all choked up on hormones and, like, buzzing because for the first time since the early nineteen hundreds, I'm getting all hot and bothered over someone who *isn't* the future czar of Russia. Someone who might one day like me back.

"You want to shower first?" He lifts his eyebrows.

"Uh, you can go first."

He cringes a little. "That's probably not wise. I need to use the toilet, too, if you know what I mean."

I'm absolutely not sure whether to laugh or cry. I'm thinking about how hot he is, and how into him I am, and he's thinking about how he needs to poop. I grab my bag and practically run into the bathroom.

The shower's small and the tile badly needs to be redone, but the water's hot, and it's *heavenly* to finally feel clean. The single best thing about the twenty-first century is razors. I have never liked armpit or leg hair, but everyone I knew, every woman I'd ever met, always had both. Razors were not easy or cheap to find.

The first movie I saw after waking up was called *How to Lose a Guy in Ten Days*, and I immediately noticed the blonde woman had smooth legs. When, a week later, I saw an advertisement for a Venus razor, I sent Boris to the store with threats if he didn't come back with a whole handful of them.

They've changed my life.

I no longer feel clean if my legs are hairy, and for the first time in days, I feel both clean and moderately attractive. I've almost forgotten about my embarrassing moment of weakness earlier, swooning right before Gustav smashed a bug. I throw on my clothes, towel dry my hair, and shoot out of the bathroom, leaving the door open so some of the steamy air the fan couldn't keep up with can escape.

"Your turn."

But Gustav isn't there.

I'm about three seconds from a meltdown—visions of Leonid hauling him out and dicing him into a million pieces or torching him into a pile of ash crowding my mind—when he waltzes through the door, not a care in the world.

"Where did you go?"

"I remembered there was a bathroom in the lobby," he says.

He doesn't even look embarrassed. Is poo not embarrassing to men? "Oh."

"Is it fine if I shower now?" He points.

I nod, dumbly.

It must not be. He flashes me a half smile as he breezes past me, bag in hand, ready to get totally naked and stand under running water three feet from where I'm standing. I'm staring at him when he turns to close the door.

He tilts his head, winks at me, and shuts the door.

He winks.

I want to huddle under the covers and cry. Only, would he see that as some kind of invitation? I feel like Gustav is some kind of game I did not get the rules to interpret. Also, in movies that I've seen, men and women in the same room do sometimes just tear clothing off one another after a long glance, and. . .

I shake my head.

That's not what is going on. I've gotten confused. He's a wealthy, smart, professional man who knows we're just stuck here for a night, and he respects me enough—but wait. Does he respect me?

He should at least be afraid of me.

I can turn into a horse.

Yes, I'll be fine. What's wrong with me?

He's out of the bathroom shockingly fast—men must not do half the things we do in the shower—and I still haven't even claimed a side of the bed. Although his pajama pants are dark and perfectly respectable. . .he's not wearing a shirt. I mean, he's *holding* a shirt, and he's in the process of putting it on, but it's not on yet. There's so much perfect, smooth, almost shining skin on display that my brain just quits working. While he stretches the grey t-shirt out, shifting it to slide his arms inside, I stare, transfixed. His skin isn't totally dry yet—tiny droplets of water cling to the side of his left chest muscle, his neck, and his shoulder. One droplet on his stomach slides, slowly, down his abdominal muscles.

Which are *glorious*.

I can't help swallowing.

Not that he can see me. He's pulling the shirt over his head, and the muscles in his stomach all seem to be involved in that one movement. They're rippling, and instead of focusing on the six defined muscles right there in the center of his stomach, I'm stuck looking at all the things at once. I suppress a shiver and blink repeatedly before he pulls his shirt all the way down to make sure he doesn't notice how shamelessly I'm gawking.

I need to get it together. He's putting the shirt on, not taking it off.

My plan was to just ask him which side of the bed he wants, but there's no way I can even say the word *bed* right now. He didn't even seem to notice that I've been staring at him. No, he goes right along his merry way, whipping a clean towel outward, and laying it down on the floor near the bathroom.

Wait. He's doing what? "What—uh—whatcha doing with that towel?"

He freezes. "Did you want this one for the morning? I figured if we each reused our towels, I could spread this extra one out so I'm not just lying on the carpet. It doesn't look the cleanest."

"You can sleep in the bed," I say.

"I'm certainly not watching you sleep on the floor." He picks the towel up and folds his arms, the little white towel clearly inadequate as any sort of bedroll for someone his size.

"We can share the bed," I say. "It's not like I'm going to attack you or something."

"Oh." He frowns. "But wouldn't that make you uncomfortable?"

I shake my head.

"So you've slept with a guy before?"

My heart races.

"I mean, have you shared a bed before?" Now even Gustav looks uncomfortable.

"No."

"I'm a bit heavier than you," he says. "So when the mattress looks like that." He points.

It doesn't look very thick.

"You may roll toward me." He brings his hands together, palms flat, and I can't help wondering what it would feel like to be between them.

Suddenly, sharing the bed with him seems like a monumentally bad plan. I can't even look at his hands without wanting to slide in between them. I'm clearly *cracked*. "All that sliding around sounds like it would be annoying. I don't mind sleeping on the floor. I'd fit on the towel better than you would, anyway."

He sighs. "Alright, let's just try it and we'll see."

"What will we see?" What's wrong with my heart? It thinks we're about to be in a footrace or something.

"How bad the mattress is?" He arches one eyebrow. "Or, not? Are we back to the towel?"

I can't help smiling at his nervous question-statement. At least it's not only me who's struggling. "Let's just try sharing the bed. If it causes any problems, I'll take the towel."

I shoot forward, claiming the side closest to the bathroom. If I have to wake up in the middle of the night to pee, I'm always really bleary and tired. I'd hate to trip and fall flat on my face, or worse, stumble over him and wake him up.

Gustav quietly circles around, sitting down on the edge of the bed near the window. The mattress creaks, predictably, because his frame is not small, but it doesn't appear to be collapsing down on his side or anything concerning.

I keep my eyes trained on my side of the bed, notably not looking at him or any part of his delicious body, and then I slowly lower myself toward the edge. And then we're both sitting on the bed at the same time, which feels like a coup. Gustav snags one of the pillows from the pile behind us—of which there appear to be four—and repositions it a little bit so it's in between us. "Look. There's a little barrier. I'll stay here on my side, and if you feel like you're rolling, you can lean on that." His easy smile's reassuring. That's not the face of someone who would do anything nefarious.

More's the pity.

I nod a bit, and without meaning to, I lean back at the same time he does. Now we're both lying down, but I realize that we never turned the lights off. The lamps on either side of us are both blazing. I sigh a little and sit back up.

"What's wrong?" Is it me, or does he sound nervous?

"Lamp." I shift over and shut mine off.

"Right." He's sitting up to turn his off as I lie back down.

And then we're lying beside one another, in the dark, on the same bed. The world isn't ending, and it looks like everything's going to be just fine. "No rolling at all."

"What?" His voice sounds deeper and even more unnerving in the dark.

"I just mean that the mattress is fine." I cringe a little, hearing myself.

"Yeah, it appears my worries were for nothing." His chuckle relaxes me a little, thankfully.

"Let's hope lots of things we're fretting about turn out like that," I say.

"Do you mean Leonid?"

I wish. "No, I think he's coming, and I doubt it'll be no big deal when he finds us."

"Do you care about him?"

"That's a complicated question," I say. Though it's easier to think about it in the dark. "I've known him for a long time, but he's made some really bad decisions."

"Like what?" he asks. "What's the worst thing he's done?"

"Other than stealing Alexei's powers?" I ask. "He's held bizarre trials and executed people? He stole the throne from Alexei, twice."

"And didn't he kill the Romanov family?"

"I'm not sure," I say. "The thing is, there were a lot of complicated things happening at the same time. The world was weird—famine and unrest caused by some bad moves on his father's part. The world war. Russia was in a weird spot—it hadn't modernized like most countries had. People were angry. The Kurakins and my family were all angry, too."

"But—"

"I asked Leonid when I woke up—he was the first person I saw—what he had done. He said he had broken the rules.

He had tried to force the powers like Baba Yaga told him never to do, and he said we'd all paid the price."

"So maybe he didn't kill the Romanovs."

"I think something about what he did killed them," I say. "I'm just not sure what or how much of it was his fault."

"But from his perspective, they stole the Rurikid powers —you all did—from him."

Not much of an excuse. "And, he's killing people now, in the present."

"Good people or bad people?" Coming from Gustav, who shares the same power with him, the question's a strange one.

"Good people don't kill people," I say. "It's a basic super-hero tenet, isn't it?"

He sighs. "Maybe."

"He's murdering dictators, but only so he can steal their countries. That's sort of his MO. He justifies the bad things he does by doing them to bad people."

"So he is a bad man," Gustav says. "I'm just wondering how bad he really is."

"Don't wonder," I say. "If you do, you might hesitate when it matters. He's bad. Really, really bad."

"But if stopping him makes you hate me, is it worth it?" Gustav's last words haunt me. It must be the reason I toss and turn with disturbing dreams all night.

❧ 22 ❧

GUSTAV

I remember almost nothing from the night I spend sharing a bed with Katerina. Her whimpers did wake me up at one point, and I recall running my hand over the back of her head in what I hoped was a comforting manner. "It's alright," I whispered. "Everything's okay."

I wasn't at all sure it was true, but I hoped.

The next morning, when I wake up, I'm wrapped around her body like a pipe cleaner antenna twisted around a paper mâché butterfly. I want to spring away and claim I had nothing to do with it. The mattress—it must have sloped after all.

Instead, though, I flex a little bit in an attempt to stretch without waking her, because holding her feels *so* good. It feels better than beating my cousin in chess. It feels better than graduating summa cum laude. It feels better than counting stacks of cash—better even than depositing them in the bank.

It feels like I'm home again.

I haven't felt like that since my mom died.

She's warm, and she's small and soft and pliant, all at the same time. I never want to let her go. Which is insane. She's a woman who was born in the early nineteen hundreds and can turn into a *horse*, and if she ever gets her powers back, she could shock the ever-loving tar out of me for touching her at all, from what they say.

But in this moment, her face looks so delicate and so vulnerable, with tiny, almost translucent circles under her eyes. I can't help seeing her eyes, alive and sparkling in bright, eye-catching green with tiny golden flecks. Her russet lashes rest on her pale cheek, dusted with just a handful of freckles.

I want to shift my arm and brush the edges of them with my fingers, but that would end this moment, so I don't risk it. I simply exhale, my breath washing over her face like I'm claiming her, which is ridiculous.

She's been in love with Alexei her entire life.

It's not like she wants anything to do with me. I'm not regal, I'm not commanding, and I have no idea how to use any of these powers they're all obsessed with me gaining control of. For all I know, even if we do find these journals, they'll say absolutely nothing of value. With a maniac coming our way, probably bent on destroying me, I should steer very clear of Katerina. I should send her to Iceland.

Instead, I kept her here.

And depending on who I talk to, that maniac may be in love with her.

I think that's my biggest motivator, honestly.

As I look at her, so innocent, lost in sleep, I can't help wanting to protect her. No one ever has. Not her father, who should have, not the mother she never knew, and certainly not the great and vaunted Alexei, who used her like a social shield and cast her aside when it was no longer convenient. Not Leonid, who was her servant and then stole her powers and then quickly became her master, forcing her to do anything he wanted.

As much as I've worked to regain, she's lost. Her home, her sense of belonging, and any ability to protect herself.

She's had to rely on the whims of others and her ability to please them to stay safe.

I hated trying to please others more than anything.

Trying to please Grandfather with every word and action, in the hopes that he would give me the keys to the kingdom. Even the company I built from the ground up is only really a success if he declares it to be. I've hated how every part of my life has been wrapped around gaining his admiration, his acceptance, and his approval.

I wish I was strong enough to protect Katerina as she deserves, but I can't even keep myself safe. In disgust, I pull my arms back, retreating to my side of the bed.

Katerina's eyes open almost immediately. "What time is it?"

I slide off the bed and stand, glancing at my phone on the nightstand. "Nearly seven a.m."

"Oh, no," she says. "We need to practice."

"The rodeo isn't until this afternoon," I remind her.

"Right, but how long has it been since you've ridden a horse?" She arches one eyebrow.

"A while."

"I doubt Amanda Saddler will be impressed with you falling off and breaking your wrist."

She's probably right.

"And we need to buy a saddle."

"Right."

"And unless you're planning on wearing a suit to the barrel race?" Her eyebrows shoot up. "You might need some new clothes."

Today is going to suck.

Especially since, as it turns out, Manila, UT has exactly one place that sells clothing.

The True Value Hardware store, which also doubles as a grocery store. Their selection is not good. "And if you want a saddle," the woman from yesterday says with a half-smile, "you're going to have to drive into Green River." Her face, like yesterday, still swirls, surrounded with what look like tiny golden fireflies. She's a good person, but that doesn't mean she can help us. In fact, that's probably why she refused to help us.

Which is just great.

"Can I ask you something?" The woman's face is scrunched up. "I saw you folks drive in yesterday, all piling out of an SUV. Where exactly are you getting a horse from?"

It's a good question.

"A friend of mine is keeping her for us," Kristiana says without missing a beat. "We're about to go pick her up."

The woman nods. "Most everybody around here has a saddle. Maybe you could borrow one from your friend."

Kris smiles slowly. "My friend doesn't have one—she already told me. But. . ." She steps closer. "Any chance we could rent one from you?"

The woman shakes her head. "No way."

Kristiana's shoulders slump.

"You could borrow one, though." The checkout woman's eyes crinkle up when she smiles. "Anyone who's willing to sign up for a rodeo just to talk to Amanda Saddler?" She's full-on beaming now. "I've gotta see it. That's all."

I'm not sure whether she's looking forward to my crashing and burning in the rodeo, or whether she's referring to watching me trying to talk to Amanda. Either way, I suppose my outlook isn't great.

Venetia, that turns out to be the woman's name, gives us her address—which was easier to get than Amanda Saddler's —and then agrees to meet us in an hour. We have to go and get our horse, *of course*. So that's a little tricky. When I suggested that she just let us pick up the saddle, she told us she has a dozen, and we'll want to find one that fits our horse.

It was hard to argue with that.

"See you then," I say.

And now we just have to show up at her house, down one person, and up one horse for which we do not have so much as a halter, bridle, or saddle pad. Then we need to get that horse to the rodeo without anyone noticing our lack of a trailer. And then I have to ride in a barrel race, not die, and get Amanda Saddler's attention.

This is a stupid plan.

"It would be easier to just bash that old lady over the head and drag her into some empty field," Grigoriy says.

Mirdza hits his shoulder, but it's half-hearted.

"This does feel like it has a high likelihood of failure," Katerina says. "I didn't think about how complicated it would be to enter a horse race without any of the things you need to properly ride a horse." She doesn't mention that I'm the worst rider in the group, but I'm pretty sure it's true.

It's going to be a heck of a lot harder than riding bareback through the streets of New York City for a few city blocks, that's for sure. Even that was weird, though. "You people must find yourselves in strange situations all the time," I say.

The ride to the woman's house, which we're making early to hopefully avoid her noticing that we don't have any of the proper equipment, is filled with laugh-laden accounts of the mishaps they've all worked through as a part of the horse-shifter relationship.

"—and Sean, whom you met in that meeting, *hated* Obsidian Devil," Kris says.

"And me," Aleks says. "He thought I was a penniless Russian horse trainer."

"Which you were," Kris says.

"Even though this sounds bad," Mirdza says. "I really do think you'll be fine. If Kris and Aleks could win the Grand National—"

"Wait," I say. "You were riding on your husband in that race?" I can hardly believe it. "Is that legal?"

"You know," Kristiana says, "I didn't actually stop to ask

the racing commission if they were alright with horses who could also shift into humans racing alongside real horses."

I guess not.

By the time we've arrived, pulling up a hundred yards from Venetia's house, our SUV partially obscured behind the only patch of pine trees we could find, Kris hands me a rope.

"Where'd you get this?" I take it—it's blue, and it's all knotted.

"I bought the rope," she says. "And then I made it into a halter."

"How could you—"

She yanks it back. "Watch." She twists it around and shifts it, and voila. I see the part that hooks over the nose, the part that wraps around behind the ears. . .she's amazing.

"Well I'll be darned—"

Without any kind of warning, Katerina shifts from a human, standing right in front of me, into a tall, shining palomino mare. She tosses her head, and her white-blonde mane billows out, like we're shooting a commercial for some kind of mane and tail product.

Kris looks at me and tosses her head, like I'm a dolt.

"Right." Because I am just standing, staring, stupidly. "I should put it on her." I hold out my hands, and Katerina slides her face right into the nose hole, leaving me to fumble around trying to work out how to tie the end.

"Like this," Kristiana says, but from her tone, what she means is, 'you big idiot.' I remember that much about girl-speak from when I lived at home.

"Before the lady arrives, you should try getting on her and riding in that loopy pattern," Adriana says. "It might help you look less half-witted later today."

Doubtful.

I'm wearing the most casual clothing I have—khaki slacks and brown Ferragamo dress shoes. It's still about as inappropriate for riding a horse as I can imagine. "I need to get some clothing first."

"Kris rode me bareback more than she rode in a saddle, and once, she was wearing an evening gown," Aleksandr says.

"I'm clearly not Kris." I do, however, want to punch her husband.

"It wasn't an evening gown," Kris says. "It was—"

"Just get on and let's see whether this is going to be a comedy or a tragedy," Adriana says.

"Maybe a little of both," Grigoriy says.

It takes a boost from Aleksandr, which is a little embarrassing, but at least Katerina's not dirty when I slide onto her back. I didn't see a dry cleaner for at least fifty miles.

I'm nervous.

Of course I'm nervous.

Other than the walk down eighty-first street, I haven't been on a horse in more than a decade. With the parents I had, I was pretty much on a horse every day of my life before then, but you never know how much you'll retain.

My legs aren't used to gripping the side of a horse.

My hands are no longer accustomed to holding the—well, in this case, Kristiana's in the process of wrapping the end of the rope around to the other side of Katerina's mouth to form a sort of rope-halter-bridle. But I haven't held reins in so long I've nearly forgotten how to thread the rope through my pinkie and ring finger and then up between my thumb and index finger.

The extra rope at the top slides to the right side as my mother taught, and the second Kris finishes, I squeeze my legs at the thigh to urge my mare forward. Katerina walks off immediately, pushing past Adriana and Grigoriy as if she's as eager as I am to put them all behind us. And if her tail swishes and smacks Adriana in the face, well, I'm sure it was an accident.

A moment later, without any urging from me, Katerina

takes off at a very brisk canter, jogging through the woods in a bounding, ground-eating pace that I'm hard-pressed to keep my seat through. "Whoa," I say. "Why are you running?"

Katerina just neighs and ducks her head, picking up even more speed.

The wind whips through her mane and my hair alike.

My thighs grip her more tightly. I crouch low over her neck, remembering the feeling better than I expected. And something inside my heart cracks wide open.

I had forgotten how much I liked to ride.

Buried under bad memories, suppressed by a mountain of resentment and anger, I had almost erased my joy at being near a horse. They may have ruined my life, and they may be responsible for the death of my mother, but there's still something freeing, something energizing about moving in tandem with such a large, magnificent creature. The world falls away. The dangers chasing us feel a little less terrifying, and my heart forgets all its terror as we move.

It almost feels like my small heart syncs with the horse's large one.

Or, Katerina's, in this case.

Movement like this is good for the soul. Or at least, I think it is.

Movement in general isn't valued like it should be. It clears your mind, it cleanses your soul, I'm sure of it. By the time Katerina finally swings back around and heads for the car we abandoned, which is now so far back I can barely see it, I feel more grounded. I feel less panicky.

And my inner thighs are *shaking*.

I'm so painfully out of shape.

Just as we draw up alongside the SUV again, I see a blue truck turn down the drive up ahead. "We'll head for the house," I say loudly.

Katerina doesn't slow down as we approach, and in fact, as we pass Alexei, she bolts, spraying loamy soil all over Alexei's blue shirt and pristine slacks. That time, it definitely wasn't an accident.

I don't have the bandwidth to turn around and see how he takes it. I'm barely clinging on as it is. When we draw near the house and turn to head down the drive, Katerina slows to a trot, and other than having my teeth rattled out and smashing my man-parts once, I'm surprised at how well I handle it all.

"You—well." Venetia climbs out of her truck, leaning on the door frame. "You do have a horse." Her brow furrows. "But please tell me you don't plan on wearing that."

I snort. "It's the best I have right now, but believe me. Once we get the saddle worked out, that's our next stop."

"And do you have a place to leave your horse while you go shopping?" She tilts her head. "Because I didn't even see a trailer."

"We're borrowing one," I say. "And our friend just dropped her off, but she'll be back by to pick her up in a minute, after running an errand." I'm proud of myself for making that up on the fly.

Venetia frowns, but she doesn't argue. "Well, follow me to the barn, then. We'll take a look at what we have. You should really borrow a bridle, too, though. That mare's just pulling you around with that rope."

"Right," I say. "That would be amazing, if I could."

Katerina's head whips around, and her eye flashes. I'm pretty sure she likes dragging me around. I can't say I blame her. I wouldn't be keen to arm a lousy rider with a bar of iron with which to yank on her face, but I'm going to look crazy enough without trying to compete with a halter as a bridle.

When we trot past Venetia's pasture, at least a dozen horses race toward the fence, tails streaming behind them, nostrils flared, several of them calling out.

Venetia watches my mare carefully. "She's not spooky, and

she's not reactive. You're either a much better rider than I thought, or she's a much better horse."

"A little from column a," I say. "A little from column b."

Her grin is like a piece of buttered toast—warm, comforting, and a little salty. "Amanda should really talk to you folks." She nods. "I can't figure out what you might want with her, and I have no idea where you found this horse, but in a small town, stuff like this has a way of coming out."

I really doubt that. But if Venetia likes us now. . . "You could give her a call and—"

"Miss out on watching you try to do the barrel pattern?" She chuckles. "Not a chance."

We spend the next few moments running through saddle options, and while she has quite a few saddles, most of them are fitted for a woman her size, which I most definitely am not. The two saddles she has that will accommodate someone my size are both heavy trail saddles. Shockingly, the super-annoying Russians and their Latvian lovers stay near the SUV, letting Katerina and me handle this alone.

They're probably just avoiding an awkward situation, but it's helpful.

"I'm not sure whether you'd be better off squeezing into a barrel saddle with an uncomfortably small seat," Venetia says, "or a heavy trail saddle that actually fits."

"To be perfectly honest," I say, "I'm not sure it really matters." I can't help my smile. "We're going to get dead last either way."

"You never know," Venetia says. "But I do wonder how you're going to find clothing in time when you have to report to the fairground in less than an hour."

"The races aren't until one o'clock," I say.

"Right." She pauses. "But there's check-in, and then there's the warm-up, so you only have about an hour or so before all that starts."

Katerina bumps the trail saddle with her nose and tosses her head toward the exit.

"Is your horse. . ." Venetia blinks and then shakes her head. "Never mind."

I kick Katerina. "I think the trail saddle will be best."

"You could probably borrow some of my husband's clothing." Venetia cringes. "It won't fit you perfectly, but it would be better than. . ."

She doesn't insult my clothes, but she doesn't need to. It's obvious. "Um, that would be amazing."

I almost take it back when she comes out with jeans that are at least two sizes too big and the ugliest western shirt I've ever seen. It has different fabric on the cuff, like I'm auditioning for some kind of line-dancing team. "Oh."

"Trust me," she says. "You want to look very western when you compete."

I don't want to trust her, not on this, but I don't have much choice. Luckily, her husband Doug and I wear the same size shoe, and the shiny, dark brown boots she brings out look way better than the ridiculous navy and bright green shirt with shiny metal snaps. Katerina stands tied nicely while I change—I can see her through the window of the bathroom —but when I emerge, she starts craning her neck for a peek, which is about the least horse-like behavior I can imagine.

Reaching for some grass? Sure. Trying to catch a glimpse of her rider in his newly borrowed western wear?

Ha.

"You look much better." At least Venetia hasn't noticed Katerina's odd behavior. Or if she has, she hasn't commented on it. A moment later, I'm riding off on Katerina's back. The western saddle feels strange—I always rode English back home—but it's a far cry easier to ride in than bareback was, and I probably overdo it with my waving and professions of gratitude as we leave.

Katerina picks up the pace, trotting toward the team, as

we draw closer. The pile of my clothes and shoes that have been clutched on my lap with my elbow since we left Venetia's barn finally breaks free of my hold just as we reach them, tilting forward and billowing out into the dirt.

One of my shoes spins and rolls, stopping in front of Grigoriy. He looks from the shoe, upward, his eyes stopping on the cuffs of my shirt.

As if his laughter is the impetus for the others, pretty soon they're all howling. I've barely started to swing off her back when Katerina changes—wearing totally different clothing than she had before—and starts to yell.

"Three actual horses in this bunch, and three much more proficient riders. You should be ashamed of yourselves, laughing at him. He's sacrificed more than any of you. His company's IPO, his grandfather's long-sought favor, and now his pride, just to try and help you find the journals you want so that he can keep your ungrateful hides safe. He doesn't live in Russia, and he doesn't care about Leonid. Or, you know, he didn't, before you lot showed up and wrecked his life, and now you're laughing at him."

It appears they've struck a nerve.

"I'm sorry," Grigoriy says. But his lip is twitching and he doesn't really look very sorry.

"Me too," Kris says. Only, she actually looks penitent. "The shirt was. . .unexpected, but—"

"We have to get to the fairground in the next hour," Katerina says. "That's why he borrowed clothes from that nice woman's husband, who's clearly much larger, and who also has no sense of style."

"Hey," I say. "The boots aren't bad." I lean over and pick up my poor clothing, now soiled beyond recognition. "Either way, we ought to go. Once we're there, Katerina and I will do our best to get her attention, but you need to find a time to talk to that Saddler woman, or this was a total waste of time."

"At least it was entertaining." Adriana holds up her phone and snaps a photo.

"Everyone still has their devices on airplane mode, right?" Aleksandr asks. "No signals whatsoever?"

"Yeah, yeah," Alexei says. "We heard you the first twenty times."

A few moments later, we're loading into the SUV again, my dirty clothing in the back, and Katerina's staring out the window, her expression strange. Before we've even begun down the road, she turns toward me, her voice soft. "Do you think your dad really called a cousin he'd never met in America and asked for money?"

"I'm guessing *hounded* is a better word for what he did," I say. "My dad was very good at one thing—manipulating people into giving him money so he could get out of all the tight spots he backed himself into."

"That's not entirely fair," Kris says. "Sometimes—"

"No." I shake my head. "It's more than fair. You love him, and I try to understand that, but in my life, he's done nothing but wreck everything I care about."

Kris's face crumples, but she doesn't argue.

Which makes me feel like the villain. In some ways, maybe I am. My mom would certainly have expected me to forgive him if she were here. The only thing in the world she loved more than horses was him. I'll never understand it, but I'm sure she'd tell me that I don't have to understand. Love is just love.

Their inexplicable love ruined the whole concept for me.

It always looked like another way to be duped.

"We're here."

I don't see a fairground anywhere close. "Are we?"

"It's a mile that way." Aleks points. "But if we drive up and unload there, I'm guessing people might have some questions."

"I checked out the map." Kristiana brandishes a map book that looks like it sat inside the gas station for twenty-six years before someone without a phone finally bought it. "The only thing along this stretch for maybe half a mile is a tiny farm—and I saw some scrub brush back there that should block your view of the road. You can change and just ride her back down this path until it dead-ends into the fairground."

"We'll head along to the rodeo and find a parking spot and seats," Mirdza says.

I keep forgetting how insane all this is. I'm going to be riding in a barrel race—which is already ridiculous enough—and I'll be riding *a person* who's turning into a horse for it. Only Katerina and I need to get out, which seems obvious now that we're doing it, but I wasn't thinking about it until now. Although we don't have a lot of gear, it falls to me to lug the saddle, saddle pad, and bridle, because I'm not about to fob it off on Katerina.

"I can at least take that." She reaches for the saddle pad at the same time that I swing the saddle over my shoulder, and I nearly clock her in the face with the pommel.

"Oh." I drop the saddle on the ground and reach for her, wanting to make sure she's alright. The motion takes her off guard, and she falls back, losing her balance and nearly stumbling. I grab her wrist and yank her forward, and suddenly she's leaning against my chest, both hands braced against my pecs. Her eyes are wide, and her breathing's shallow.

"Sorry." I shake my head. "That was clumsy."

But she's not moving, and I don't really want her to move, either. I stare at her, entranced by the contrast of her flame-red hair and golden-green eyes. It's a disturbingly beautiful combination.

"Wow, you're the definition of a one-trick pony," someone mutters behind us. It's a girl's voice. "Not that it'll work any better for her this time."

Katerina stiffens and shoves away from me. She's fast, but I can see her cheeks flush before she turns.

I turn and scowl at everyone in the car, directing most of my heat at Adriana. It might not be based on any evidence, but I'm guessing she's the one who made the snarky remark. By the time I grab the saddle and sling it over my shoulder, I have to jog to catch up with Katerina.

"What was that about?" I ask. "One trick?"

She walks faster.

I throw the bridle over my shoulder and use my free hand to grab her shoulder. "Hey."

When she does turn around, she's crying.

"What's going on?"

She shakes her head and wipes her cheeks. "Nothing."

"Something."

"It's just—now that I've actually given up on Alexei, they won't let me."

Oh.

They're saying she's trying to do the same thing with me as she did with Leonid—trying to make Alexei jealous. By flirting with me. That makes me feel. . .strange. I'm not sure why. "They think—but you and I aren't. . ."

She rolls her eyes. "I know. Believe me."

"I mean, not that I wouldn't want to, but—" I cough. "We certainly aren't faking anything."

When she looks up at me, it's slow. Her eyes look skittish, like a green horse I'm approaching with a saddle. "No. We aren't."

"If they think they see something between us, well." I shrug. "Whatever's there is real."

And this time, she smiles.

"We probably ought to get ready." Her eyes are soft, though, and it makes me happy. This is how she should look. I hated seeing her with that hunted look on her face. Even worse than the look she wore when we first met was the expression of despair I saw when the only people she knows in this century are mocking her. The girl who just fiercely defended me when they laughed.

In her century, the mocking of the other nobles was pretty devastating. She probably cares about earning their good opinion far more than I do.

A desire to gather her up in my arms and fight anyone who harms her rolls over me, and not for the first time. It is a foreign desire for me, however. Until now, the only person I've routinely wanted to protect was myself.

Not that I can really protect anyone right now.

I'm as powerless as Leonid ever was—and that's who's coming for us, thanks to my idiocy.

"Hey," a voice shouts from not too far away.

A dog shoots past us then, tail wagging, tongue lolling out.

"Peanuts," the same voice shouts. It sounds like a teenager, maybe. "Peeeeanuts!" The kid comes into view then, running, someone slightly shorter running along next to him.

They're chasing their dog, which likely means they live around here. They have reason to be here.

We do not.

"Are those people up ahead?" a girl asks.

"What are they doing here?" the boy says. "Maybe that's who Peanuts took off after."

Hardly. He shot past us like a socialite who spied a sample sale. I doubt they'll be keen to hear our explanations. And now that I think about it, I don't really have an explanation for why we're wandering along this road, lugging a saddle and a bridle with us. I can't really say, "We hiked out here so she could turn into a horse without anyone noticing."

In that moment, I'm not sure whether it's my own desires taking over or whether it's really the most expedient move to keep us from having to make up yet another lie. But I do what I've been dying to do all day—maybe longer if I'm being honest.

I grab sweet, gorgeous, svelte Katerina by her shoulders, and I duck down and press my mouth against hers.

I've never been kissed.

With Alexei, we both knew we were faking. It wasn't common to kiss back then anyway, and the last thing I was going to do was kiss someone who wanted to dump me. With Leonid, we were also faking, so the one time our mouths touched, it's because I shoved my face against his to hide another misstep.

My only kiss, up until now, was a total lie. Everything in my life has been a lie.

Dating Alexei.

Fake-dating Leonid.

It was all nonsense.

But in the past few hours, I've realized that I *like* Gustav.

It's boring of me, to be honest. I mean, of course I like the tall, handsome, smart, accomplished man with the beautiful abs and the magical powers. The one man who could conceivably take all the powers we know about and defeat Leonid. The one man who might actually be able to keep me safe from anyone who threatens me, if only we can get his magic working.

Of course I like him.

I'm so predictable, like a monkey always chasing the higher branch.

The others have reason to mock me.

But when he kisses me, my heart *soars*. When I've seen people kiss in movies, it always sends a little thrill through my whole body. They press their *mouths* together, of all things. It makes no sense, if you're thinking about it objectively. I mean, that's where we put food. We speak from our lips and with our tongue. Why would we want to press them against someone else's?

Madness.

But when Gustav shifts to fill the space right in front of me, drops the saddle to the ground, and his hands grab my upper arms. . . When his head lowers over mine. . .

My breath catches.

My eyes close.

And his mouth *finally* closes over mine. Every single nerve ending in my body sets fire. My knees stop working, and I nearly collapse, but his arms tighten around me, bringing me closer. His mouth *moves* over mine, and then his tongue *darts into my mouth*, like a tiny conqueror.

It's the most electric thing I've ever experienced, and I harness the power of lightning, until the voices we heard come closer, and Gustav freezes. I'm terrified that he'll pull away until he kisses me with even more fervor.

That's when I realize that *it's fake*.

For once in my life, I thought someone actually liked me. He said it was real. But just like the others, he's kissing me to avoid having to explain our reasons for being here to some errant teenagers chasing their dog.

The boy makes a sort of snorting sound, and the girl giggles, and then they rush past us.

Once they're gone, I shove away.

"Well, that worked." I wipe my mouth on the back of my hand. "I can't say it was exactly sanitary, though."

Gustav's face falls.

Was I too blasé? Is there a chance he kissed me, at least in part, because he wanted to?

"You better shift fast, or I may have to kiss you again." Whatever I imagined, there's no trace of it. His face is one hundred percent mocking.

I nod, and I turn away so he can't see how gutted I am. And then I shift into the good little horse he needs me to be. I can't look at him while he saddles me. I force myself to act like what I am—a means to an end. A horse he'll ride to get the attention of the woman who hopefully has the journals we need so he can learn how to defeat Leonid.

The man I alerted to his whereabouts.

Or, you know, the man I tried to rat out.

At least the weather's brisk as we head for the Daggett County Fairgrounds. The wind keeps me from being too hot, and now that he's got a saddle, Gustav feels remarkably balanced on my back. Riding a horse isn't quite like riding a bike, but a lot of it does come back when you restart. Hopefully he'll manage to do reasonably well as we add speed to the mix. We walk for a bit, then we trot a while, and eventually, he asks me to speed up, so I canter a ways down the side of the road.

A few passengers in cars and trucks gawk at us, but not too many. I doubt trail riders are rare in this area. It's probably just strange that we're out alone, or perhaps that no one knows us.

When we reach the fairgrounds, already warmed up, Aleks has checked us in, and we stand and watch as the other barrel racers run the pattern a time or two. Other than Gustav, there don't appear to be any boys riding. I'm not sure how to ask about that, but another thing I've noticed is that the girls don't seem to be very consistent on which direction they go around the first barrel.

Some take the left one first.

Some take the right.

I turn to catch Gustav's eye, and then I toss my head to the left. Then to the right. I'm worried he'll have no idea what I'm saying, but he nods.

"Hey." He catches the eye of one of the riders who's leaving through a narrow alleyway. "Does it matter which direction you take that first barrel?"

The rider's smile is disbelieving. "Hasn't anyone taught you to ride the pattern?"

"Um," Gustav says. "Not exactly."

She looks heavenward and mutters something I can't quite catch under her breath. "Come with me." She tosses her head, and Gustav spins me around to follow.

I'm a little worried she's going to report us to someone. She's a tiny little girl. She doesn't look like she's even twenty yet, and she looks like she weighs less than fifty kilos. Her light blonde hair's pulled into a ponytail that streams down behind a blue cowboy hat. (Or is it a cowgirl hat, with a girl wearing it?) Her horse's tiny, too, a sorrel mare with a floofy white-blonde mane that looks fully twice as thick as any other horse's mane I've seen in my life.

"I'm Emery," she says. "And that's my cousin." She points with her free hand. "Whitney's the best barrel racer here, and she always wins. But the great thing about barrels is that they have different brackets. So even if you don't make 1D, you can still win money in 2D or even 3D."

"But how?" Gustav asks.

Whitney has walked up, atop a big, brassy chestnut gelding with a gorgeous face blaze. She doesn't look much bigger than Emery, but on her horse, she towers over her cousin. "What's going on?"

"This poor guy's never barrel raced. He was asking me if it matters which barrel they take first." Emery purses her lips.

I expect Whitney to laugh.

She smiles. "Ah, your first barrel race is the most fun."

When she starts talking, she looks way less fierce than I expected. "You should definitely run a round or two before we go, though. The idea is to rate around the barrels."

"Rate?" Gustav must be frowning, because both Whitney and Emery laugh.

Emery takes over again. "It means slowing the horse down a little. You have to make them a pocket on the far side, too, so they don't just crash right into the barrel when you go to turn."

"Okay," Gustav says.

"What made you want to run in the race if you've never done it?" Whitney asks.

Gustav sighs. "There's this woman in town, and my dad managed to really make her mad, but I need to ask her a favor."

Both girls' eyes widen.

"It's not about money," he's quick to say. "I just need to see if she has some old family stuff I think she may have held on to, and I don't even want to take it. I just need to look at it."

"Who is it?" Emery asks.

"Her name's Amanda Saddler," Gustav says, speaking quickly. "I think she's a sponsor for the rodeo, and I'm hoping she'll be here and we can try to talk to her again."

"You already tried once?" Whitney asks.

Gustav nods. He shifts in the saddle, and I can tell he's uncomfortable by the whole thing, but he's doing things right. These girls clearly know Amanda, and they seem inclined to like Gustav. I'm not surprised. What's not to like? He may be too old for them, but he's good looking, and he's nice.

"After you're done racing, we might be able to get her attention," Emery says.

"Do you know her?" he asks.

Both girls giggle. I'm taking that as a yes.

"You do?" Gustav sounds so clueless.

I stomp my foot.

"She's our grandma," Whitney says. "I'd say we know her, yes."

"Oh." Gustav nods, a little embarrassed. And then it's our turn, apparently. Based on our draw number, we have a certain warm-up time. Gustav guides me with his feet, mostly, and a little with the reins, but I do appreciate how careful he is not to pop me in the mouth.

Before I know it, we're just outside the small dirt arena. Another horse—a large grey, is lining up, and then he's shooting through the alleyway, almost rearing back in his glee, it appears.

"A lot of horses get hot in the alley," Whitney says. "It's pretty common for the ones who love to race, but if you're not careful, they can get so excited it's hard to get them to go in. You'll want to do everything you can to keep your girl calm."

Gustav pats my neck. "I think I can handle that part."

The feel of his hand on my neck isn't very reassuring, however. It reminds me about how he kissed me not long ago, and I thought it was because he liked me, but really it was to cover for some people walking by. It makes me angry. And confused. I prance around just a little, to get my irritation out.

But then the grey's shooting back down the narrow passage, and we're up. Gustav kicks me sharply, and I pin my ears. *Unnecessary*, I want to tell him. *I know what we're doing, idiot.*

He seems to have realized that he isn't entirely a driver, and he eases up, letting me choose our speed going into the first barrel. He chose to go right first, which is fine, and I nearly stop once I'm even with the barrel, churning up dirt as I pivot and round the barrel, bee-lining for the second one.

Once we clear that one, it feels like it takes longer to

reach the third, and then we dead sprint back out toward the alley that apparently riles up the other horses. I thought it was a respectable showing, all in all, but when I glance up at our time—nineteen and a half seconds is not great.

It's a full three seconds longer than the grey ahead of us got.

Emery and Whitney, however, are not laughing.

"That looked surprisingly great," Whitney says. "I think I took twenty-two seconds my first time around, and that was at a race."

"Mine was twenty-five." Emery moans.

We wait with them for the racing to begin, and luckily, we don't have to wait very long. But once it starts, and my heart is pounding, I realize that we have a lot of horses to wait through.

At least we know two of them, now.

The others are all in the stands, and I can tell they sat about as close as they possibly could to Amanda Saddler, who's perched near the officials at the top, in the back of the bleachers.

I crane my neck as Whitney does her run, the hooves of her tall, leggy sorrel nearly impossible to track as they whirl and spin their way through the pattern. She hunches over the pommel at the end and they fly down the path and out, her hand flung straight out in front of her, and her ponytail straight back, just like her gelding's tail.

"Fifteen point eight six seconds," the announcer blares. "A new record here, at the Daggett County Fairgrounds, set by Whitney Brooks."

I forget for a moment that I'm in my horse form, and I scream my approval. Two horses behind us whinny in response.

Gustav frowns.

But Emery does her run about four horses later, and I can't help it. She's just so nice, and her horse is just so tiny, I lean forward, my nostrils flaring and my sides heaving as I crane my neck to watch.

"Hey," Gustav hisses. "You look really strange. None of the other horses are watching."

I don't care. It's not like someone's going to suspect me of really being a human. I pin my ears and keep right on watching.

"Mares, am I right?" Whitney laughs.

Gustav does, too, but it's forced.

When Emery breezes through, and they announce her time—sixteen point one three seconds—she looks disappointed. I feel like if they graded her tiny mare on a curve for her leg length, she'd have won.

"She looked amazing," Gustav says.

I can't help thinking that we got nineteen seconds on our practice run, and I thought it went pretty well. These little girls are smoking us. But then it's our turn, and we're lining up.

"Grandma's sitting up in the judging stand," Whitney hisses. "Maybe throw her a smile if you can."

As if I hadn't already noticed her.

Hopefully Gustav will listen to their advice. If I smile at someone, it'll only serve to freak everyone out.

At least he doesn't kick me as we trot into the alley. I start to canter on our way in, and then as we burst through the opening into the arena, I put on a little more speed. I aim for the space beside the barrel, and I don't fully stop to pivot and turn this time, still moving just a little as I spin.

As we reach the second barrel, I try to turn a little earlier. My butt kind of clips the side of the barrel, but I turn and look back as I race away—it's still standing upright. By the time I swing around the third barrel and start racing home, I feel pretty good about my run.

When the announcer blasts our time, "eighteen point two

four seconds," I'm a little depressed. I'm not going to lie. I really thought we'd have improved more than that.

"You cut a whole second off your time!" Emery's practically bouncing up and down in her saddle. "That was *amazing*!"

It makes me feel a little better.

"Who are you talking to, exactly?" Amanda Saddler somehow magically beamed herself down from the judging booth to the side of the bleachers we all just walked past.

I spook a little and step backward. The girls both laugh. "Horses," Whitney says.

"I'm Gustav," he says. "We tried to talk to you yesterday—my father's pretty much a constant source of embarrassment, but I swear, we do not need money."

Amanda narrows her eyes. "What do you want, then?"

"Journals," he says. "Not to have them—but Dad told my sister Kristiana that our family had some old journals that might've talked about horses, actually. We were hoping to take a look at them."

Amanda frowns. "I did have some—kept them for far too long, probably. But a few years ago, there was a fire. Everything that I'd been storing in my barn burned to the ground."

My heart sinks.

Whitney's frowning. "But didn't Gabe—"

Amanda shakes her head. "I'm sorry you came all this way for nothing, but I can't help you." She pivots on the heel of her cowboy boot and marches away.

I kind of want to stick around and see whether Whitney and Emery win any prizes or money once all is said and done, but seeing as I can't talk, and with as depressed as Gustav looks, I don't even bother trying to argue when he points me back out the way we came. He's clearly keen on shifting me back and getting out of here.

I can't blame him.

We just wasted a lot of time on something that doesn't even exist, and Leonid's coming—probably closer to us with every passing hour—and we're no closer to having any idea how to save Gustav's life, much less how to vanquish the threat Leonid poses with his insane trials and massacres of perceived villains.

It hits me then.

I'm not sure why I didn't realize it before. His insane and undisclosed trials must be him simply *looking* at people, deciding if they're evil, and then ordering them to be eliminated. He's executing all the villains he finds in Russia before he's even found evidence that they've done something concrete wrong.

It's probably the most Leonid thing I've ever heard.

In his mind, he's making the world a better place, one murder at a time.

Gustav has slid off my back, and I notice a bare stall on the far corner—no tack, no chairs, nothing at all in front of it, and there's no one standing around within a hundred feet. I duck inside and shift, too eager to share what I just figured out to wait.

"Holy smoking goat meatballs," a male voice says.

I spit out the bit and yank the bridle off my face.

Gustav swears under his breath, and he doesn't use the word meatballs at all. When I turn, I realize there was a kid in the stall I ducked into, mucking it. He looks like a high school kid. He's staring at me like I'm—well, like I'm a horse who just turned into a person.

His jaw's dangling. His eyes are wide. And then he says, "I can't believe it was true. All of it was true!"

24

GUSTAV

T rue? What was true? What's this kid saying?

"I have got to find my grandma," he says. "Can you guys wait here for a second? She is *never* going to believe this."

I grab his wrist and drag him back.

The muck rake drops to the ground with a clatter.

"Not so fast, kid."

"I'm not a kid." The boy scowls. "I'm seventeen years old."

"That's still a kid," I say.

"You—are you Liepas?" He glances between Katerina and me. "Or from one of the other families?"

Now it's our turn to be shocked. "Who are you?" I release his wrist.

"I'm Gabriel Brooks," he says. "And I've known about you for a really long time." He shakes his head. "No one ever believes they're anything but stupid fantasy, but I've actually turned them into a comic book." He's beaming. "But to really see you, with my own two eyes." He whistles. "Grandma Mandy's *finally* going to have to read them."

"Wait, *them?*" I ask. "Do you have the journals?"

Gabe nods. "When I was like, ten, I was obsessed with them. After I translated the Russian parts with Google Translate, I pored over them."

This can't be happening. "So they didn't get burned up in a fire?"

"Oh, I stole them way before Grandma Mandy pretended to die."

"She. . .what?" I'm so confused.

"It's a long story, but when I bring the journals up, everyone just rolls their eyes. I gave up on talking about them a few years ago." Gabe's eyes are bright, and he grabs my wrist this time. "Let's go."

"But the stall?" Katerina points. "Did you need to. . .?"

Gabe shrugs. "Someone else'll get it. Who cares about fifteen bucks an hour when I'm talking to real horse-shifters." His eyes light up then. "What's your other power?"

"Lightning," Katerina says before I can wave her off.

"We should find my sister, too," I say. "Then we can all go over together."

"Oh, good idea," Gabe says. "The more the merrier." His eyes light up. "Wait, can your sister turn into a horse, too?"

"Not exactly," I say. "But we do have three more horse-shifters in the group."

Gabe's bouncing on his feet as he walks.

"Should we meet with this Amanda without everyone else first?" Katerina whispers. "She seemed pretty adamant earlier."

"Meet with her?" Gabe freezes. "Did you already talk to her?"

I nod slowly. "We came here looking for her, hoping to find the journals. But when we found her, she said they were destroyed."

Gabe balls his hands into fists and growl-shouts. "I swear, it's like they don't listen to me at all."

Seems like we've hit on a sore topic.

He inhales a time or two, and then he nods. "Well, they're going to have to listen now."

"Actually, the fewer people who know about all this, the better," Katerina says.

"Sure, sure," Gabe says. "But obviously Grandma Mandy can know, because, like, she can probably turn into a horse too, right?"

Katerina's frowning. "Gustav can't even—"

"She should know any part of it she wants," I say, before Katerina can bum the kid out. "But we have a few questions we're hoping to find answers to as well, and there's a dangerous man following us, so the quicker we can find them, the better."

"There you are." Aleksandr, Kristiana right behind him, barrels around the corner. He breathes a heavy sigh of relief.

"Over here," Kris says.

Grigoriy, Mirdza, Alexei, and Adriana round the bend, all of them showing signs of relief at finally finding us.

"Whoa," Mirdza says. "You already went all the way out and changed—" She freezes when she sees Gabe, her mouth clicking shut.

"They didn't go anywhere," the boy says with a grin that cannot be repressed. "She just ducked into that stall right there." He points. "And then *bam*, she turned into a human!"

Aleksandr turns toward us slowly, like he's trying to figure out how to bury us without anyone finding out.

"It's fine, though," Katerina says. "We spoke to Amanda and she told us the journals had been destroyed."

Grigoriy's massive shoulders droop. "How is that fine?"

"But when Gabe here saw me shift," Katerina says, "he told us he has the journals. He knew just what and who I was."

"Actually," Gabe says, "you didn't answer before." His brow furrows. "But you did say lightning. Does that mean you're a Kurakin? Or no, wait, they're the flame ones. You must be a Yurovsky. Right?" He spins around, meeting each person's eye in turn. "Am I right?"

Aleks, Grigoriy, and Alexei eye him strangely, like he's a bug they're contemplating the advisability of squashing.

"It's fine," I say. "He knows because of the journals. Apparently as a young child, he found them and took them." I clear my throat, specifically not saying he stole them. "And he's had them translated."

"Well, kind of." He shrugs. "I mean, Google Translate isn't amazing. Once, when I was using it for my homework, it translated sister as camera."

"It—what?" Adriana's having trouble following his rapid-fire English, I think.

"He's offered to take us to see them," I say. "I thought we should follow his lead."

We're nearly to the parking lot of the fairground when Gabe stops. "Dangit. I wonder if Whitney's done with her stupid barrel crap."

"Wait, you know Whitney?" It makes sense, I guess. She did say Amanda was her grandmother as well. "Is she your sister?"

"You met her too?" Gabe looks bummed. "Man, they always do things before me."

He's jealous—like we're his new toy. Teenage boys are the worst. And their focus is ridiculously bad. "Your sister— what's bad about her not being done with barrels?"

"Oh, right." He sighs. "When she went off to college, I got my own room—I'd had to share with my baby brother Nate—but now she's back for the summer, so she's *stolen* her room back, and the journals are in there, under my bed."

"We should hurry, then," I say.

"Or, at a thought," Kristiana says, "if she's home, we can just explain that we need to get in the room to grab something."

Gabe and I exchange a glance, and the kid laughs. "She clearly doesn't have a sister."

I laugh. "No, she doesn't."

But it's irrelevant. When we reach his house—we follow his beat-up old truck home—no one else is even there.

"We'll stay out here," I insist. There's no way we're going to follow a teenage boy inside his house. Part of me wants to drag him back to the fairground and insist that we meet his parents and clear this with his grandma first, but access to the journals is too important. Lately, it has felt like anything that could interfere with us does.

When he walks out, he hands us a stack of paper held together with black binder clips.

"What's this?" Kristiana looks annoyed. If she were a horse, she'd have her ears back.

"Oh, that's my translations." He nods. "And the parts that didn't make sense, I just kind of changed a little so the whole thing reads easier."

I might strangle him. "It's not an English project," I say. "It's journals, right? Why would you change it?"

"Some of it didn't make any sense after I plugged it into Google," he says. "Actually, a lot of it didn't."

Kris is gritting her teeth. "So you don't speak or read Russian?"

He shakes his head. "Took me a little bit of poking to realize it was Russian. I thought it'd be Latvian. I guess some of it was, but most is Russian for sure."

A vein in Aleksandr's head is throbbing. "Where are the original texts?"

"Hm." He scratches his chin. "I'm not totally sure. Did you want those instead?"

"It would be helpful," Kris says.

Unfortunately, while he's inside looking, three more cars pull into the drive. One of them was the same red truck that was parked outside Amanda Saddler's yesterday.

"What on earth is wrong with you people?" Amanda's wagging her finger at us, and if it was a light saber, I think we'd all be dead.

"The thing is," I say.

But before I can say anything else, Aleksandr shifts.

One second he's a tall, arrogant Russian man with dark hair and designer clothing. The next, he's a massive black stallion, his perfectly groomed hair blowing artfully in the breeze.

Doors pop open on all three of the new vehicles. Everyone's talking at once, so I can't keep anything straight.

"I'm Kristiana Liepa," my sister says. She points at me. "This is my brother Gustav."

Everyone falls silent.

"Amanda Saddler's our cousin, and her father took my grandfather's journals with him when he fled Latvia years ago."

"They belonged to my father," Amanda says with a huff. "Crazy old man."

Gabe shoots through the front door. "Whoa. Is this the big tall, scowly guy?" He's staring at Obsidian Devil, my sister's husband's horse name.

That is such a weird phrase to think.

"He is," I say. "His name's Aleksander Volkonsky. He's a very wealthy Russian nobleman who's currently fleeing because the lunatic who just took over the Russian government wants us all dead." I scan the circle.

There's a man and woman who look like they could be the boy's parents. The woman has light brown, blonde-streaked hair and a commanding air. The man's in pretty good shape for an old guy, and he's positioned himself slightly in front of her, as if he'll shield her from all the madness any way he can, even if it's with his body. Next to Amanda there's an older man with broad shoulders and bright eyes. He looks the most irritated with us.

When Whitney pops out of the back seat, though, she looks even more excited than Gabe. "Did that man just turn into a horse?" She steps forward. "I'm *so* not staying in there with Nate anymore."

Some kid, maybe Nate, is banging on the window.

A moment later, he bursts through the other door. "Wow, what a cool horse." He jogs toward Aleksandr, and everyone springs into action at once.

Kristiana reaches for the boy, as do four other hands, but the kid's quick. His little blond head shoots through all the hands as he walks right up to Obsidian Devil.

The massive stallion lowers his head and presses his nose into the boy's hand.

"It's fine," Kristiana says. "Because he's not really a huge stallion."

The boy turns back toward us, confused.

"I mean, he is," Kris says. "But he's also my husband."

A split second later, Aleksandr shifts again, and now he's back to being the same, arrogant force of nature I'm used to seeing.

"What's your power?" Gabe asks. "Please let it be flame."

"Mikhail Kurakin's a nightmare," Katerina snaps. "You should be glad he's not here."

Gabe smacks his own forehead. "He said Volkonsky. I should have known it's earth, but I'm just so excited that I can't think straight."

"I can't believe that my grandfather's claims weren't totally insane." Amanda Saddler's shaking her head. "We should probably go inside."

She's not wrong. Standing on the street is just inviting more madness, and that's the very last thing we need.

Gabe's house is largeish, but with this many people in it, three of them quite young, it feels very, very full.

"I can't believe you stole those journals," Amanda says.

"I told you like four times," Gabe says. "You told me to quit speaking nonsense."

"You told me that you thought our family had horse-shifters in it." Amanda's shaking her head. "Even my dad never said anything as crazy as that."

"He probably thought that one day, you'd read them," Gabe says.

"He probably didn't believe it himself," she says, still eyeing Aleksandr sideways.

But Gabe doesn't let us down. A few moments later, he emerges triumphant with a box, and in the bottom of it, there are four crumbling journals. He was right about the languages, too. Three were in Russian, and one's mostly Latvian.

"I'll take this one," Mirdza offers. "Since it's Latvian, it's probably the newest, and therefore the least helpful."

"I'll take a Russian one," Aleksandr says.

"And me," Alexei says.

"I'll take the third," Grigoriy says.

They're undeniably correct that their Russian is the best, so I'm left standing around like an idiot while my sister's husband and his friends pore over our family journals looking for any sort of clue we can use.

At least we don't have to wait for very long.

"This first entry. . ." Aleksandr whistles.

"What?" Kris is leaning over his shoulder, but the rest of us are stuck waiting.

"I think it has our answer, right here." Aleksandr's head never lifts from the journal, his hands as gentle as I've ever seen them where he's touching the edge. "For it to make sense, you need to know who the Seven Boyars were."

Alexei straightens. "They were the self-appointed leaders in Russia's provisional government during the Time of Troubles. They brought the misery to an end when they made my ancestor the new monarch. They chose the Romanovs to rule, basically."

Aleksandr finally looks up. "And Gustav and Kristiana's relative was Fyodor Sheremetev."

That name means something to them, I can tell.

"Why is everyone reacting like that?" Amanda asks. "Was he a villain?"

Alexei shakes his head. "He was the most powerful of the boyars. He set my family on the throne."

"The opening passage reads," Aleksandr says, "*I had no idea what I was agreeing to. When first we saw her, Baba Yaga appeared as a maiden. She had such an open air. She had such a lovely countenance. We were all inclined to listen to her, and to believe anything she promised.*"

"So it was them," Grigoriy says. "She did meet with our ancestors."

"We already knew all this," Alexei says.

"But we didn't know this," Aleksandr says. "*Had I known she intended to make me the individual responsible for commanding this group, I would have refused. Not a day goes by that one of the others does not come to me, complaining about some thing or other that Misha has done.*" Aleksandr looks up, like that should mean something.

"Who's Misha?" I ask.

"Short for Michael," Alexei says. "The first Romanov to rule."

"But why does that matter?" I ask.

"Because Fyodor's commanding the group," Aleksandr says, "not the Romanovs."

This is tedious and we're only five minutes into the search. "But you already said—"

"It goes on," Aleksandr says. "*At first, I resisted taking on all their powers. Baba Yaga said I didn't have to command them, but someone has to intervene, or these poor pups will destroy one another before this new government has a chance.*"

"Gustav has to *take* our powers," Grigoriy says. "So it is different than with Leonid. We can't just surrender them."

They all turn to look at me like that explains everything. "But how?" I ask. "How am I supposed to do that?"

The only answer they give is to turn their faces back into the books.

Fabulous.

25

KATERINA

Within an hour or two, all three journals have been read by the guys, and while they found another tidbit or two, none of it is very helpful. Kristiana has been busy snapping photos of nearly every page.

"You can take the journals," Amanda says. "You don't have to photograph them."

"You're just going to hand them over?" the middle-aged woman, whose name is Abigail, I discovered, asks.

"I'm aged fairly well," Amanda says. "So far, I've never once turned into a horse." She smirks. "I think we can safely assume it's not going to happen to me. They might need them more."

"To be fair," Gustav says, "I have also never turned into a horse."

"So what's the real problem, then?" Gabe asks. "Why did you come here?"

Gustav explains the basics about how Leonid was Rurikid, how they sort of lost track during the Time of Troubles, and his family wasn't in Russia. And then when they returned, and he managed to tap into his powers. . .things went a little haywire.

"You're from *the nineteen hundreds?*" Gabe asks.

I love that no one even questions anything we say now, after having witnessed the horse to human transformation.

"I'm not," Gustav says. "These four are." He points at the guys and me. "They brought their feud forward inadvertently. They thought they were cursed for refusing to help two of the families when there was a famine, but it turns out, Leonid sort of cursed all of them accidentally when he tried to force them to share their powers."

"Which is exactly what you have to do," I say. "I think that's how he got confused. Some of what was in the Romanov records mirrors what we're reading here, which was different than the method for the Rurikid line, because that first time, Baba Yaga gave all the power to just one person."

"And you're like the magical supervisor?" Abigail asks, catching on quickly. "So you can only really use your power when you force it?"

"Something like that," Gustav says. "For what it's worth, we're really sorry for dragging you nice people into this."

"You think the new ruler of Russia is coming here?" Amanda asks.

"We do," Gustav says. "Or at least, we think he'll be following us, and since we're here. . ." He spreads his hands. "Now that we've gotten the information from the journals, we should move along."

"If he finds out I'm a Liepa," Amanda says, "I'll be in danger either way."

"I doubt even Leonid would suddenly attack an—" I cut off, not wanting to call her an old woman.

"It's okay," Amanda says. "I'm more than ninety years old." She laughs. "You can always tell the truth around me. I'm not one for telling myself lies, at least, not anymore." She slams a hand against her heart. "I've got a pacemaker now, just in case I didn't feel ancient before."

Alexei stands up, and I realize he means to offer to heal the lady. I can tell the exact moment he remembers that he can't. My heart goes out to him. I may not love him anymore, but he's a good man. There's a reason I cared about him for so long.

"You don't have to run away." The man who has spent most of the night quietly sitting beside Abigail and watching over Gabe and Whitney finally speaks.

"We don't want to put your lovely family at risk," Gustav says. "We really do appreciate your help, but—"

"But you're our family now," Amanda says. "And we protect our family here in Birch Creek."

I start to laugh, assuming it's a joke, but then I realize they're not laughing. In fact, they're not even smiling.

"If there's some Russian dictator coming out here to attack you," Steve says, "it might be nice to have some people you know to back you up."

I can't believe these people are even saying this. "We could never ask—"

"Of course not." Amanda takes two steps over and sets a mug with tea in it at my shoulder. "But with family, you don't have to ask."

For some inexplicable reason, I burst into tears.

Abgail, Amanda, Amanda's old-man husband whose name I keep forgetting, and Whitney all stare at me, kindly. Gabe skips over and wraps his arms around my body, crumpling me against him. "It's fine, though. You can cry here, I promise."

Which only makes me cry harder.

A moment later, Whitney has also wrapped her arms around me from behind. The third person to join the group hug shocks me.

It's Gustav.

His big, warm arms wrap around both kids and me. When he finally lets go, I actually feel much better.

"I appreciate your offer more than you know," Gustav says. "I'm sure we all do. But we couldn't possibly endanger your family for the very same reason that you're willing to help. Once we have found a place to spend the night, we'll gather our things and go, and we'll head for good in the morning. Our best way to keep safe will be to continuously move."

"Or you could stay in a town that no one cares about with people who are watching your back." Steve crosses his arms. "Think about it overnight. You might decide to stick around for a few more days at least." He stands up. "But for now, you have to stay with us tonight. We insist."

There's a rather large scafuffle when they start assigning rooms and making sleeping arrangements, but in the end, Gabe and Whitney take sleeping bags in to join Nate in their parents' room, and the three couples disperse into the bedrooms, leaving me and Gustav on the sofas in the family room.

I'm surprised no one presses for Gustav to try and do anything that night, but we're all pretty tired, and if we want to be ready to leave in the morning, we should all catch up on some lost sleep. I won't lie and say it doesn't feel nice to sleep in a place that's mostly safe, but I almost miss the room with just the one bed. I'm about to drift off to sleep when I hear him.

"Do you think I can do it?" Gustav sounds more like Gabe than he does like himself.

"Do what?"

"You know—forcibly take someone's power?"

I'm not sure he wants to believe he can do it. It sounds like he might not want to be able to do any magic at all, with the way he phrased that question. I flip onto my back. "I'm not sure. I never had to take my power. After I earned it, so to speak, it just sort of showed up, whether I wanted it or not."

"How?"

I shrug, but then I realize he can't see me. "I zapped things, at first. Without meaning to, I'd just shock stuff. People and animals, mostly."

"That sounds really annoying."

I chuckle. "I mean, for me it wasn't."

"Still, if you didn't think you could control it."

"I guess, but I had Boris and Dad, who weren't generally super helpful or kind. But about that, they were at least telling me what to do and what was a bad idea."

"Like what?" Gustav asks. "Like, don't go outside in the rain, or you'll short circuit your brain?"

I can't help laughing at that notion. "Not so much, no. One nice side-effect of our ability is that electricity, specifically lightning or any other electric current, won't harm me. It would be like. . .if you had a catcher's mitt on and someone lobbed you a baseball. You'd catch it and be able to do what you wanted with it without hurting your hand."

"Even with a mitt, sometimes catching a ball hurts," Gustav says.

"That's not a very manly thing to say." I'm smiling in the dark, but again, he can't see it. "But it's honest, I suppose." I snort. "And sure, I mean, I suppose if I really was struck by lightning, it might be uncomfortable, but I could absorb and redirect it, so I'd be fine."

"I wonder what it's supposed to feel like for me. I mean, I have no idea where to even start in trying to force a power."

That's an interesting question. "It may not be the same for you, but I can feel the magic sort of pulsing in my head." I tap my forehead, and then I realize he can't see that either. We do a lot of things every day that rely on sight. It's strange for me to function without it. "My power usually kind of hovers right behind my forehead, just above my eyes. I can *feel* the power, sort of *waiting* there." It's weird because I can almost feel it right now, even though I know it's not there. "When I need it, I can kind of squint up my eyes and focus, and, bam."

I zap Gustav.

"Ow." He bolts upright on the sofa. "What just happened? That hurt!"

"I'm so sorry," I say. "I haven't had my power in so long that I didn't realize—" My powers. When did Leonid give them back? And more importantly, *why*?

"You—you have them?"

"I'm as shocked as you," I say. "What could it mean?"

Gustav's quiet. "Maybe it's his way of trying to get you to call him."

Of course it is.

Gustav's a genius.

I talked to Leonid. I offered him a deal, and he even gave me a phone. Then I never called, and now he can't so much as track it. I never asked him to restore Alexei's powers, and he has no idea where we are. . . But clearly he wants to find us.

So he's summoning me with a treat, like he would a dog.

"I don't want to use it now." My voice is small, and I remember my epiphany from earlier, the one that made me change without thinking. The one that led us here. "I think Leonid's been holding those weird trials. . .and just killing anyone he finds who's dark." I don't explain my guess very well, but Gustav's silence tells me that he gets it.

"Would he really do that?"

"You tell me," I whisper. "Would you feel confident doing that?"

"Not at all," he says. "But I've only had this ability for a few days. I wonder what having it for years and years would do to me? Would I become more sure of my ability? Would I be confident of what the light or dark means?"

"He can't just go around killing people," I say. "It's wrong."

"But it's okay for the government to execute people, even though they really have no way of knowing whether the criminals did what they're charged with doing?"

"I don't know, but—"

"He *is* the government," Gustav says. "The people elected him, and this is how he's chosen to keep people safe. There's a disturbing kind of simplicity in his version of justice."

"He's like a villain in a television show or a movie."

"He's literally out there, a wannabe Batman or something, eliminating anyone who's *bad*."

"And he has a bad-o-meter," I say. "Or at least, he thinks he does."

"What if he's right?" Gustav asks. "What if he's uniquely situated, better even than any impartial judge, to know what people will do and rid the world of all the darkness that threatens it?"

"You can't kill someone for what they might do," I say. "You can't kill them for 'badness' either. Unless he has a real reason—evidence of something they've done wrong—he should not, he *cannot* just kill people. These powers. . .you may not have them yet, but when you do, you have to remember that it's wrong to use them that way."

"I think maybe I do feel it," Gustav whispers. "I feel *something* up behind my forehead, kind of pressing on me."

I sit straight up on the sofa. "You do?" When I'm looking directly at him, I can make out his general shape and size, even in the dark.

He grunts. "I'm not sure. I thought it was just a headache before, but now that you've mentioned it, I think maybe it's not. It's been there since, well, since the day I leapt in front of the men to save you. Looking back, that sounds kind of stupid, but people get headaches."

I slide down to the end of the sofa that's closest to him. "When I want to use my power, I focus on that spot, and then I push."

"But what if I use one Leonid has?" he asks. "Would that pull him here?"

I wish I knew. "Do you think he felt me zap you?"

Even in the low light, I see his silhouette shrug.

"I hate just waiting here, helpless, hoping he won't find us," Gustav says. "I want to *do* something."

"Then do it," I say. "Just try."

"Try what, though?" He sighs. "I haven't even seen what any of you can do, not really."

"Aleks can find and feel the earth or rocks or minerals that are close, no matter where he is. He can summon diamonds from deep in the earth. He can create a swirling tornado of dirt. It sounds kind of weird, but it's actually pretty cool."

Gustav grunts, and then. . .something in the corner crashes.

A dog starts barking. Lights turn on. Bootsteps and the dog-barking come closer, and then Steve's staring down at a zebra plant that Gustav killed. Its dirt is spilled all over the floor.

"What happened?" Steve asks. His dog's spinning round and round in circles, whining.

I'm not sure Gustav knows what to say. We're both sitting, stock still, on our respective sofas, wide-eyed.

A door at the end of the hall whips open and Aleks shoots around the corner of the hallway. "You did it." He blinks quickly. "I felt it."

"I guess that answers the question of whether Leonid would know," I say.

"How did you do it?" Aleks asks.

"What are you people saying?" Steve asks in English. "Is everything alright?"

"It's better than alright," Aleks says in English. "We just found our weapon."

"Weapon?" Steve looks around the room intently. "What is it? *Where* is it?"

Gustav stands. "I guess it's me." But for all his talk earlier about not wanting to sit around helpless, he doesn't look very pleased. And when Aleks takes him outside and forces him to spend the next two hours trying to shove dirt piles around, he looks downright disheartened. Kristiana spends the whole time in with me, wringing her hands and watching out the window. I haven't given her much credit for being a very good sister, but she clearly does love him.

After Gustav comes back inside, dirt-coated and weary, trudging his way to the shower, I take the chance to ask Aleks what he thinks. Unlike Gustav, he's spotless.

"He's. . ." Aleks shrugs. "He's not very good at it, but that's hardly a shock. He's never done anything like this at all, and we're asking him to jog on day one. All of us learned by shifting a handful of dirt at a time." He sighs. "He's so dirty because, at the end, in addition to deflecting my little dirt tornadoes, he made one of his own."

I didn't expect Aleks to take it easy on him, but that sounds rough. "You know, Leonid crashed after he got a new power."

"He seems fine," Aleks says.

"What does that mean?" Kris asks. "He looked pretty tired to me."

"He was using a new power," Aleks says. "He should be tired."

A moment later, there's a loud wham in the bathroom. I very nearly rush in.

"Naked man," Aleks says, blocking me with his arm. "I'll go."

I can't help at least peeking around the corner of the open doorway, and what I see isn't encouraging. Poor Gustav, hair still sudsy, has passed out in the shower.

"Maybe he would have done better in his training," Kris says, "but he was worn out from accessing a new ability."

When he sleeps for the next twenty hours straight, we all

agree that might have been the issue. It does help us make up our minds about something.

We decide to stay in Birch Creek, at least for now. The nice thing about a tiny town is, if Leonid does turn up here, we'll know it right away. Amanda, Abigail, and Steve make up a lie about how we're on the run from the Russian mob, and their new leader's after us.

The entire town appears resolved to help keep us safe.

Which is really cute.

And it makes me very nervous for all of them, right down to sweet little teenage Gabe. He tears into his workouts on his Smith Machine in the garage like gaining more muscle mass will keep him safe from Leonid the Executioner.

I wish anything we were doing would be sure to keep us safe. I'm beginning to worry that nothing we do will make any difference when Leonid does find us.

GUSTAV

The longest I've ever slept in my life was fourteen hours after my first semester of exams at Yale. Or at least, that *was* the longest, until I managed to use the earth power for the first time.

When I finally wake up, my head's *pounding*.

Not that Aleksandr cares.

He doesn't let me eat, drink, or rest in any way until I can reproduce the tiny twister I made before I passed out.

"Now we know that you'll be tired right after," he says. "We can act accordingly."

He's acting like the fate of the world rests on my abilities, which I'm beginning to think is a little crazy. I mean, sure, Leonid's concerning, and he's here, but it's not like I'm the only person in the world who poses a threat. He's keeping his magic hidden, which means he's at least scared of people finding out what he can do.

We've been following Leonid's trip to America on the television, and so far, he's been meeting with lots of different groups. The most horrifying part is that, as he does, the public opinion on him and on Russia. . .shifts.

He was once the most hated dictator on earth, probably.

And now, all because he's a good-looking English speaker, most of the American media, at least, is eating out of his hand.

"I really didn't expect you to be quite so personable," Oprah says. "You're quite charming."

I shut the television off.

"The good news is, it doesn't seem like he knows where we are," Katerina says. "That means we still have some time."

"Maybe he didn't even come here to find us," I say.

Everyone laughs.

The timing is suspect. He did announce his travel plans immediately after I saved Katerina and gained the ability to use powers at all. And then, not long ago, he returned her powers. It's probably just what she suspects—a shameless bid to get her to call him.

She's been refusing to use them entirely on the outside chance that using them would draw him to us. Clearly the one time she shocked me wasn't enough.

Or, he's biding his time. Waiting for. . .we're not sure what.

It would be nice if super villains in real life provided monologues to tell us their plans. A memo or some kind of declaration would be equally helpful. As it is, we're left guessing.

And practicing making mini earth tornadoes, apparently.

"Today, we're going to learn how to bury someone in dirt," Aleksandr says. "And if that's easy to master, we'll work on defending against lightning strikes and fire attacks using earth. It's surprisingly effective, even with small amounts of soil or other debris."

"But—"

Katerina has been watching us—they all have. But she has spent at least half her time in her horse form, as if she's been denied it too long. Whatever else Birch Creek may not have, like great food, or anything at all interesting to do, it's flush with big, spacious pastures and rolling hills.

"I'm going for a run," she says. Again.

"Don't get caught," I say.

I've said that same thing every single day, like an idiot.

I have not mentioned our kiss. She hasn't either. But I catch her staring at me sometimes. It's enough to make me want to force myself to be able to use the lightning power, just so she can teach me instead of Aleksandr. I'm really sick of his high-handed superciliousness. I swear, I might knock him in the head with a tiny tornado of mud and claim it's an accident.

My one hesitation is that I'm not sure he'll buy it twice.

It might be worth the risk. Watching him race inside to change clothes was hilarious. An hour and a half later, I've managed to bury lots of things with piles of dirt, but I'm not doing as well at defending against fire.

It might be easier if Alexei wasn't using a flame thrower. It pretty much creates flame with a permanent power source, so defending against it requires an ongoing churn of additional dirt.

"Wow." Abigail's standing on her back porch. "You weren't kidding about wreaking havoc on our arena."

"I'm so sorry." I drop the earth immediately.

Aleksandr's smile is smug. "Don't worry. It's very easy to repair." With a few waves of his hands, the dirt flattens out and everything's even again.

Abigail blinks.

Motion from behind her, near the road, catches my eye. Something gold flashes—and I realize it's Katerina, running. Then I'm stuck watching. I can't seem to take my eyes off her, no matter what form she takes. It's strange that her horse form is the exact one I kept dreaming about, but also, it feels.
. .right. Like *of course* it was her.

I felt like maybe we were both interested in each other,

but then after I managed to use my earth powers the first time, she backed off.

Big time.

Aleksandr doesn't make any of it easier. So if I spend a little too long staring at her as she runs alongside the road toward us, well. I refuse to regret that.

In the fall weather, wind gusting down from the mountains, her mane billows out behind her like a gorgeous white-gold flag. Her nostrils are flaring—she's clearly been running hard—and her legs move like water running through a riverbank, fluid and tumultuous.

Her head turns then, and she sees me staring.

Our eyes meet, and I smile. I shouldn't be so obvious, not when I don't know what she thinks about me, but I can't seem to help myself. She tosses her head and whinnies, and that's when I see it.

A tractor coming around the bend where it's harvesting a large field. She, clearly, doesn't see it. I wave, and she tosses her head again. She has no idea what I'm trying to tell her.

They're about to collide.

I don't think about it.

I simply *push*, wrapping her up in the only way I can, and then I drag her toward me. She flies through the air like a wingless, airborne Pegasus, her legs still moving, her hooves flashing in the sunlight, and I set her gently down in the center of the arena.

"What on earth was that?" Abigail asks. "What just happened?"

Grigoriy whoops from behind her on the porch. "Our boy just forced his second power."

This time, I make it exactly one hour before I pass out mid-practice session. When I wake up, I'm lying on someone's bed. I rub my eyes and cast around for my phone. It's on perpetual airplane mode, and I have no idea how my own IPO's even going.

I can't risk Jean telling anyone where I am.

Not even Grandfather.

I expect them to file a missing person's report since I'm staying off the radar, but there's still nothing I can do about it. When I clear my vision enough to read the phone display, I realize that I was out more than two days this time. Ugh.

"Two days," I groan as I sit up.

"Gustav?" Katarina's sitting on a chair in the corner. Her legs are crossed, and as she uncrosses them, she stretches her hands up in the air over her head and yawns. "Thank goodness."

"It's been *two days*?" I ask. "That's not good."

"At least it was air," she says. "If you had tried to save me with water, it might have alerted Leonid to our whereabouts."

I can't help smiling. "What would that have looked like?" I'm sure I'm smirking now. "A tidal wave to shove you out of the way of that tractor?"

She rolls her eyes. "So glad you're awake. Did I mention that?"

I clear my throat, but before I can tell her that I'm glad she was there when those kids and that dog came along on that street, she looks down at her feet.

What does that mean? Is she annoyed with me? Does it make her uncomfortable that I saved her?

"Gustav." She looks right at me. "I think—"

I can't hear it. Whatever she's about to tell me, I'm not ready to hear it. I can't lie here in bed while she tells me that she's not into me. I haven't even *tried* to convince her that I'm not that bad yet.

"No, Katerina, I have to say something first." I shove upward until I'm sitting. "Okay?"

She nods, her mouth closing with an audible snap.

Now that I have her attention, though, I'm not sure quite what to say. "Um, so." I swallow. "The reason I saved you earlier—"

"Fifty hours ago, you mean?" She's smirking now.

I break into a smile. "Yes. I guess that's what I mean."

"And?"

"I can't take my eyes off you," I whisper. "I know you came here to try and win Alexei back, and I know that I'm this pathetic guy who only cared about his company, and who now can barely even shift a pile of dirt, and I know that Leonid's coming for us or whatever, and it's not a good time, but—"

Katerina stands up, and when she starts walking, I worry she's about to storm out.

I bite my lip, but she hangs a left around the side of the bed and grabs the collar of my strange, probably-borrowed nightshirt, and she pulls my head toward her. "I thought you were never going to say anything, you idiot."

Then she presses her mouth against mine.

I've been sleeping for more than two days, so I'm sure I'm not at my best. I have no idea what my hair looks like, for instance, and I'm not sure what I smell like. Hopefully nothing too bad.

But I forget about all of it.

Her hands on my lapels loosen, and her palms flatten against my chest, and I roar, my arms going around her backside and dragging her up and onto my lap. Her legs straddle my middle, and I turn my head so my mouth can slant down over hers.

The door to the bedroom opens, and a familiar voice asks, "You guys alright?"

We freeze, and I slowly shift to look around Katerina's messy bun.

It's Gabe.

Sweet, eager, adorable little teenage ball of energy, Gabe. The one who's been turning us into cartoon comic book characters for the past decade. I'm in his room, I think, and Katerina's basically straddling me on what's probably his bed.

She scrambles off my lap, her hands smoothing down her shirt and hair frantically.

His laughter's like the report of a cannon—high, clear, and sharp. "Mom heard something, and she wanted me to see if you were awake." He nods slowly. "I'm gonna tell her you're still sleeping." He winks and closes the door.

I love that kid.

I reach for Katerina, but she slaps my hand away. She *is* smiling, though, so I'm thinking it's not really bad.

"What?" I shrug. "He said he'd tell her that—"

She rolls her eyes. "Guys are all the same."

"Hardly." I fold my arms over my chest and flex a little. "I'm way better looking and more competent than that stupid czar baby."

"You can't call him a baby. He's a hundred years older than you."

I pull a face. "Don't tell me that's what you're into, because if so, I should warn Amanda Saddler to watch out. Her husband's almost that old."

She slaps my shoulder.

But Gabe's plan must have gone awry, because the door flings open and Kristiana runs through. "You're awake." Her eyes widen when she takes in the fact that Katerina's sitting next to me on the bed.

"We're dating," I say.

Not that we can really date here, in Birch Creek, while we wait for a maniac to discover us and I practice flinging dirt at people.

I brace myself for Katerina to play it off as a joke, but she scoots closer and drops her hand on top of mine with a shy smile that may be the cutest thing I've ever seen. "It's true."

Kristiana opens her mouth and closes it again without saying a word.

My sister's speechless.

I would've put money on that not even being possible a day ago.

It *must* be a first.

"I know it's not a great time." I lift my chin. "But that's why I won't wait. We have no idea what's coming, so I should get the one thing that makes me happy."

"I'm the one thing that makes you happy?" Katerina's looking up at me like I'm Christmas morning, her eyes bright. Her hand twists so that our fingers entwine.

Kristiana smiles then, and it's at least as big a shock as Gabe's wink. "That's one thing I actually understand, brother." She backs up and grabs the door handle. "I'll tell everyone you'll be out in a few."

A few. It's not enough time to do much, but. . .

I wrap both my arms around Katerina and hug her tightly against me. "I—this makes me really happy. I wasn't exaggerating."

She shivers, then.

"Are you alright?" I release her enough that I can look down at her face.

She nods, grinning. "Fine."

"You're not cold?"

"Sometimes I shiver when I'm happy." She shrugs. "Always have."

"I like it." I run one finger down the side of her face, and she shivers *for me*. That makes me beam.

"I like you," she whispers.

And that makes me smile even more broadly. "So about the other things you like to do—"

But the door bangs open, this time, without anyone in the doorway. At least, not for a good five seconds. When Grigoriy does appear, he's not grinning. "I hear you're twitterpated."

I frown. "What?"

"Well, too bad. We've been bored for days, waiting for you

wake up, Sleeping Beauty," he says. "And Mirdza's been on a *Disney cartoon kick*." His frown deepens. "But now that you're awake, we have work to do." He doesn't even have the decency to reach over and grab my arm.

No, he literally *whisks* me off the bed with phantom wind tendrils, just like he did that very first day in the lobby. Only, this time, I'm not a helpless little kitten. I don't just flail about as he drags me across the room.

I focus on him and push from my forehead out, just like I've been doing when working with earth. Only, nothing happens.

"Was that tiny little puff I barely felt you?" Grigoriy throws his entire head back and bellows. "That was hilarious. Let's go, *Moana*."

"Who's Moana?" I ask.

I barely see Katerina shrug before I'm floated through the hall and out the front door. I've had about enough of Grigoriy's high-handedness when he drops me on the soft ground of the arena. Or, at least, I thought I had.

When he starts attacking me with gusts of wind, buffeting me from the right and the left, I'm really torqued off. I was having the first nice moment I've had since they found me back in New York City, and he had to barge in and ruin it?

He wraps me around on both sides with air, lifts me into the air, and then drops me.

Before I can slam into the ground, two pillars of earth swirl up to brace underneath my feet, and I lift both hands, directing two more at the jerk.

They *almost* reach his face when he flings both hands out and sends them flying away. He's smiling like it's all some big joke when he says, "Is that all you've got, Ariel?"

"At least I'm not obsessed with little girl cartoons." I've never wanted to punch anyone so badly in my life.

"That's because you *are* a little cartoon girl." Grigoriy

comes at me himself this time, a knife in each hand. "Cry for me, Snow White."

I stop fuming, because he seems to be trying to kill me *for real*. I drop back into my combat training, which was *not* focused on weapons, and I match him, blow for blow. When his blades nearly slip past my guard, I fling dirt up to block, blowing it into his face afterward.

"Whoa," Aleks says. "He used both."

"Shut up," Grigoriy hisses.

But it's too late. I realized that Grigoriy was being that annoying on purpose. He's baiting me. "What's going on?"

"You overthink things." Grigoriy's bouncing back and forth from one foot to the other. "But when you get out of your own way, like when you see a tractor coming for your girlfriend. . ."

"You aren't a total dolt," Aleksandr says.

This time, they both come at me at the same time.

Two hours later, Grigoriy has had to heal a broken arm, a dislocated shoulder, and a gash on my face, but I'm actually using both wind and earth together moderately well. I'm not sure they'd agree with my assessment, but it feels like monumental progress to me.

It almost makes up for the fact that they're trying to end my life.

"If it takes you longer to recover each time," Aleksandr says, "then when you absorb another power, we won't have much time to work with it."

"Before Leonid finds us, you mean?" I ask.

"I think he should try to use all three of the remaining ones at once," Grigoriy says. "We can drive him around while he sleeps. That'll keep Leonid from finding us."

"I'm not sure," Aleks says. "It's a big risk. What if pushing him that hard kills him?"

"That's your fear?" I ask. "That they might kill me?"

"It's my fear too." Katerina's watching from the back porch. They all are, pretty much.

"Do you not have jobs?" I glare at Amanda Saddler, her husband Tom, and the Archer/Brooks crew. They're all just staring at me.

"It could be worse," Abby says. "We haven't told Ethan or Izzy, but if we did, they'd come over to watch too, for sure."

"Who?" I blink.

"My oldest two kids," she elaborates. "And I haven't told Amanda or her kids, either."

"Amanda's right there." I point.

"I'm Grandma Mandy," she says. "Trust me, the real Amanda is a lot to handle." She must be talking about Emery's mother, but coming from Amanda Saddler, saying someone is a lot to handle has meaning. She's already a plucky old broad.

"If she finds out what we've been hiding, Emery's going to *kill* me," Whitney says. "You have no idea."

"I just can't believe you don't have better things to do," I say.

"Better things than watching three superheroes beat on each other?" Gabe's grin is so contagious that I feel my irritation melting away.

"More like watching me get destroyed," I mutter.

"No way," Gabe says. "If I could pick to be one superhero, I'd have picked Iron Man for sure—until I met you. Now I'd pick you."

Grigoriy's laugh strikes again, even louder this time. "The guy who keeps getting his butt handed to him?"

Gabe rolls his eyes. "The best ones always do at first. It's the growth montage, duh."

"Duh," I say.

"I don't remember them having to be healed three times in an hour like little bit—"

"Language," Abigail says.

Grigoriy snaps his mouth shut.

Kristiana laughs. "I kind of like being in the audience. It's nice to watch my sweetheart in action."

"You mean Dirt Dude?" I ask.

"I am *not* Dirt Dude," Aleks says with a snarl.

"You prefer Mud Man?" I shrug. "I mean, I guess it's your call."

Gabe and Whitney are laughing so hard that I actually feel kind of bad for mocking Aleks.

"What should we call him?" Nate points at Grigoriy.

"Meathead?" I suggest.

"How about Wind Whipper?" Katerina says.

"Breeze Boy," I say. "Hands down."

"I like it," Aleksandr says.

"Do you like it, *Mud Man*?" Grigoriy slugs him on the shoulder. "You would."

"It's Mister Mud Man to you." Aleks is smiling, shockingly.

When Alexei and Adriana wander through the back door, they're tossed into the mix as well.

"Water Wuss," Grigoriy says. "Because he can't even use his power."

"Aquaman," Adriana says. "Obviously."

"But there's already an aqua man," Nate objects. "I don't think you can take a name that's already been taken."

"H2O Hombre," Steve says. "Or Lake Lad."

Gabe's chuckling. "You're all horrible at this."

"I think that's the point." Katerina's smiling.

I sling an arm around her, and for just a beat, I wish we could freeze time. I know Leonid's coming, and I know that when he gets here, things will be complicated. Probably even dangerous.

That means we'll need to leave here soon. We can't lead him to these nice people. It would be the worst way to repay their generosity. But I realize that, in this moment, I'm happy.

That hasn't happened for me much.

Ever, maybe.

For the next few days, I practice all day each day. And by practice, I mean Grigoriy and Aleksandr work harder and harder to try to kill me, and I improve at stopping them. We start at daybreak, and we stop well after the sun has gone down.

But for at least an hour after I shower and before I sleep, I sneak away with Katerina for a walk. Sometimes we literally just walk and talk. Other times, well. Holding her hand is magical. Kissing her neck is nirvana.

On the fifth day, just after lunch, I realize something has changed. Instead of hanging on for dear life as they pummel me, I'm going after them. And, alone, I'm beating them back. We still have an audience, but since people *do* have lives, it's often smaller and it varies. Right now, the only person watching us is my sister.

"It's time," Aleks says when we finally break from training.

"Time for what?" I'm panting, but this time, they're dirty and sweaty, and I look pretty clean.

"It's time for you to take water."

"Won't that maybe let Leonid know where we are?"

"We have one advantage," Aleks says. "He's being watched, so if he's coming for us, we'll see it. The media that so loves him follows him like a hawk."

I suppose he's right.

"If I'm about to summon the devil, I want something first."

"What?" Aleks and Grigoriy ask at the same time.

"A proper date."

"Here?" Grigoriy asks. "Where would you even go?"

"Who cares?" I ask. "Brownings. Or the Grill. Either way,

I'm going to take Katerina out for once—some place with just the two of us."

"It's unnecessary," Grigoriy says.

But Kristiana shakes her head. "I disagree. I think it's vital." She smiles. "Go shower and get changed. I'll find your date."

27

KATERINA

At first it was kind of fun watching Gustav master his magic. I remember learning myself, at a much younger age, but no one pushed me. I was allowed to discover what I could do at my own pace.

Part of that was that I'm a girl.

But a lot was that I wasn't very old.

And even more was because there wasn't a maniac coming for us when I was being taught.

Watching Grigoriy and Aleksandr attack him in earnest is the opposite of fun. When he breaks his arm the second time, I just can't do it anymore. I spend more and more time in my horse form, grazing. Or going for jogs—human or horse—and even learning to bake.

Abigail makes amazing cookies, especially her 'cowboy' ones.

But by far the most fun I have is when the guys aren't using the arena and Whitney suggests we practice running the barrel pattern. "I should've known something was wrong that day at the fairgrounds." She's shaking her head and smiling. "No riders as bad as Daniel improve that fast."

"He's not so bad."

"His heels stay down," she says. "It's clear he used to ride pretty well—I'll give him that. But he was bouncing around on your back like a sack of potatoes. He's lost his seat."

I can't argue with her assessment.

"Does it upset you to be ridden?" I should've seen it right away in the twinkle in her eyes.

I shrug. "Other than Daniel, I've never really *been* ridden."

"How'd you like to try it again?" Whitney inhales and doesn't let it out. She cares about my answer.

"Sure," I say. "Why not?"

An hour later, we've really improved my turning. When Whitney finally slides off, she's never looked so happy. "Holy catnip, you're fast."

I can't speak in this form, so I just toss my head.

"It's so cool, having a horse who knows what I'm saying. A real partner." She shakes her head. "You might have ruined me for regular horses forever."

I've barely shifted—I'm super sweaty—when Kristiana calls for me.

"What?" I might sound a little terse, but sometimes it feels like one of them is always looking for me, watching me, ready to find fault with some new flaw.

"Sorry." Kristiana's eyes are a little hurt when she reaches us. "Gustav was looking for you."

"Why do you guys call him both Gustav and Daniel?" Whitney asks. "It took me two days to realize they were the same guy."

"His real name," Kris says, "is Gustav."

"Unless you think his real name is the one he chose," I say, always unable to stop myself from playing the devil's advocate, even though I mostly call him Gustav.

"He didn't choose Daniel," Kris says.

And I realize she's right. His parents chose Gustav, and his grandfather forced Daniel Belmont on him. The poor guy has never been able to pick anything for himself. He was always being shoved one way or another by everyone who supposedly loved him.

I know how that feels better than most anyone.

"Do you know why he's looking for me?" I ask.

"What?" Kris frowns.

"Well." I gesture at myself. "I just shifted back to human, and I need a shower. But if there's something wrong, I should run straight to him."

"I think he's showering right now." Kris's eyes are twinkling. Does she mean. . .

I feel my cheeks flush. "Wait."

"You better hurry," she says.

I glance between poor, shocked Whitney and devilishly smiling Kristiana, and then I turn and run toward the house. What did Gustav say to her that made her. . . I can't even think about it.

But when I reach the house, there *is* water running in the guest bathroom—the one that opens onto the hallway. Did Gustav tell his *sister* that he wanted me to join him in the shower? Because that's a really disturbing way for him to. . .

No. That can't be right.

But what if it is? Will he be upset that I ignored him? The thought of seeing him in the shower. . . A shiver runs up my entire body. My hand hovers over the knob for a few seconds, and then for a few more. The water cuts off, like he's just getting out of the shower. My window's closing rapidly. I'm about to walk away when I remember what he said a few days ago.

I should get the one thing that makes me happy.

Me.

I'm what makes him happy.

Any doubts I had dissolve, and my hand grips the doorknob, yanking the door open and slipping inside.

Gustav makes a strangled sound and tightens the towel he

was tying around his waist. "Katerina." His brow's furrowed, and his eyes are full to the brim with shock.

"Kris said. . ." I realize she was messing with me at the exact same time he does, I think.

His outrage melts into a smile with a free eye roll. "I'm going to kill Kristiana."

"What did you really tell her?" I'm looking at the ground now, my cheeks bright red, I'm sure.

He steps out of the tub area, and I step back. He steps toward me again, and then, when my back hits the wall, he braces one hand against the mirror, just an inch from my face, forcing me to look up at him. "Katerina." Somehow, even in this steam-filled room, his breath warms my face. "I'm going to walk out of here right now, even though I don't really want to, because *this*—" He wags his finger between us. "It's not about raw heat. Or at least." His finger runs down the side of my face, and a shiver claws its way up my back again. "It's not *only* about that. Tonight, we're starting with something more substantial than heat."

He presses a quick kiss to my mouth, and then he steps even closer, pressing his still damp, very defined chest against mine.

His breath covers my face again when he says, "We're going on a proper date, you and me, and if we wind up back here again at the end, I won't be upset."

I look up at him then, our eyes locking. "A date? Why?"

"Because I like you, woman," he says. "And because the world's a mess, so I need this—something good—more than ever." He kisses me again, but this time, he takes his time. His mouth is so warm, so strong, and so generous that I practically dissolve against him.

That makes him stiffen and pull away. "There are a *lot* of people in this house, some of them children." He squares his shoulders. "But you should know that if we weren't in some kind of group home setup, I'd probably be carrying you into the bedroom right now." He kisses my cheek and disappears through the door.

When I'm through with my shower, there's a pile of clothing waiting on me just inside the door. He must have tucked it in while I was shampooing my hair. It's not my dress, so that means it's probably his sister's, which is really pretty cute of him.

The black heels he included are *not* cute, but they both make me smile for different reasons. And once I'm dressed and I step out, Gustav's waiting for me.

He's holding flowers.

I don't shiver, but something inside my heart contracts. "Hi."

He looks nearly as shy as I do, but he thrusts the flowers toward me. They're clearly something he stole from Abigail's little flowerbeds, a fistful of brightly colored pink and orange mums. I hope he asked her permission. "I—it's cheesy, right?"

I shake my head.

"Do you want to take them? Or leave them here?"

"Will Abigail speak to us again if she sees them?"

He laughs. "It was her idea."

That tracks.

And after we rummage around a bit, the kitchen and family area suspiciously devoid of people, we find a vase. I fill it with water and pop the flowers in, and then Gustav walks me out to the SUV we're all sharing. There's still no one around, which is really kind of strange.

Sure, it's a random Wednesday in early October, but this place is always hopping with people. Where did they all go? As I buckle, out of the corner of my eye, I see them. They're all on the side of the house, their heads peering out.

That's more like it.

As we pull down the drive, I wave, and they all hop back.

"I told them I wanted a date," Gustav says. "I didn't tell them they had to hide."

"They can't help themselves," I say. "I think it's kind of cute."

"I guess."

I've seen enough movies to know that your first official date when you've spent a lot of time together already is always awkward. I expect us to be out of sync, a little offbeat in our conversation and movements, and a little bit nervous.

But none of that happens.

When Gustav pulls into a parking space at the Grill, he does it like a pro. He even hops out and races around the car to open my door for me. He doesn't close my dress in the door. We don't bonk heads. And we don't start trying to talk at the same time repeatedly.

In fact, when Gustav reaches for my hand, his fingers slide effortlessly in between mine, and we move in tandem toward the restaurant like it's our fifteenth date, not our first. The woman who welcomes us in waves us toward the back. "Any table you want."

A moment later, a young girl dances her way over to the one we chose to take our order, and when I say dances, I really mean *dances*. She's walking like she's listening to music, but I don't see any of the little white stick things poking out of her ears. She just moves like she's happy.

I'm shocked when I actually recognize her, though in a small town, maybe it's not really that unusual. "Emery, right?"

She blinks, frowning in confusion, and then turning to look at Daniel. "Oh, wait. Daniel the newbie barrel racer, right? Don't take this the wrong way, but you look way better in these clothes." She's smirking, but then she turns back toward me and tilts her head. "I'm sorry, but did we meet too? I'm usually really good with names and faces."

I was a horse when we met, and Abigail and Amanda haven't told anyone else about our secret. I cringe a little at my *faux pas*.

"I told Katerina about you," Gustav says. "She has a

great mind for names, and there can't be very many waif-like girls who have light blonde hair like yours." He forces a smile.

"Oh." She nods. "I guess so." She lifts her pen and holds it over her notepad. "Well, did you get a chance to check out the menu yet?"

After we order, she skips away, like she has not a single care in the world. I really hope that her life can stay that way for quite some time. "We need to leave here," I say.

"They want me to use water," Gustav says.

I drop my fork and it clatters against the table and falls to the ground.

Gustav picks it up, wiping it on his napkin and handing me his.

"It's fine. I'll take that one." I reach for the one I dropped.

He sets it down and insists on pushing his into my hand. "We will need to leave soon, once I do that."

"Is it bad that I don't want to?" I look down at my water glass, as if focusing on something innocuous will somehow eliminate anything scary from my life.

"Do you think he'll try to kill me right away?" Gustav doesn't sound worried. He sounds. . .matter-of-fact.

"Yes." My mouth is so dry. "And I don't even think he's the devil. I just think he's misguided, but I do think he'll kill you." I pick up my water glass and take a sip. "You're too big of a risk to him."

"Not try?" He lifts his eyebrows. "You think he'll succeed?"

I choke, spitting water out everywhere.

The fastest waitress ever brings our food out with a perky smile. "If you need anything for that—more ketchup, mayo for the fries, you let me know." She bounces off before I can ask who eats mayo on their fries.

"I'm doing better," Gustav says.

"You're still not Leonid," I say. "And his powers are literally strike powers. Fire and lightning."

"I have Aleks and Grigoriy," he says.

"He has Mikhail and Boris." I shake my head. "Look, I hope you can beat him. I honestly do. And maybe you will, but I'm afraid." I look down at my hands. "Probably because I care too much."

"You want him dead?"

"More than I want you dead." I force myself to look up again.

He smiles slowly. "I should hope so."

"That came out wrong," I say.

"You don't want your boyfriend dead." He nods. "It's a weird start, but it's a start, and I'll take anything I can get."

My boyfriend. That makes my heart flip-flop. Is that what he is? My boyfriend? "Look, if I had what I wanted, Leonid would just go back to Russia. You could return to New York and smooth things over with your company and your grandfather, and then you and I could. . ." I pick up a french fry, wondering idly whether it *would* be good with mayonnaise.

"Could what?" His eyes are fixed on my face.

Why am I such a coward?

"Could. . .go our separate ways?" He hasn't touched his burger at all. He's too busy looking at me.

"No," I say. "Could see what we're like together. Could focus just on us."

Gustav leans back in his chair. "When I was young, my sister Kris begged and begged to watch this old movie. It was called *Speed.* Did you ever happen to see it?"

I shake my head.

"It's about this couple that get stuck on a bus that can't go below fifty miles per hour or something. It's weird. But they survive the whole ordeal, and they fall in love. Only, the guy has this line where he says that relationships based on trauma like theirs is never last, and then they're not together in the next movie."

I drop my fry. "What does that mean?"

"I always thought his statement was wrong." Gustav leans back in his chair. "Then when I was in school, I thought I liked this girl. She was pretty. She always had her hair pulled back with this little flower barrette, and she had this really pretty, high, bell-like laugh."

"I suddenly want a floral barrette."

He chuckles. "But then some kids were making fun of my family for only caring about horses, and instead of defending me, *she laughed*. She didn't know I was watching, but that was my first incident that raised a red flag. My second was when the teacher left the room for a minute to deal with something, and most of the kids started doing horrible things. Rifling through the teacher's belongings, trying to change their scores in her grade book, and generally making bad decisions."

"Okay."

"I told everyone to knock it off. Barrette-girl was busy trying to get her grade changed." He leans forward, bracing his hands on the table. "I think trauma situations are the only time we get the unvarnished truth about someone. So I'd rather date you now, under these circumstances, than go on a hundred dates with you back in New York where we eat fancy food and talk about nothing."

"I think I misspoke," I say. "I actually really like it here— the small town. People you know. Maybe it doesn't have the most gourmet food options, but people who care about you matter way more. I guess what I mean is, I don't want to be answering questions about who I hope dies and who lives on our dates. I wish we weren't in this situation at all." I sigh. "But if I have to be here, I'm glad it's with you."

He reaches across the table and holds out his hand, palm up.

I reach for it, dropping my hand on his warm one.

"I wanted a fry, but I guess this is fine."

When I try to yank my hand back, he laughs. "I'm kidding, Kat."

Kat.

With a name like Katerina, it's an obvious nickname. You'd think a million people would have called me that, but it's actually the very first time. My brother and Dad called me Rina sometimes. Everyone else has always used my full name.

But I love it.

The rest of the meal is practically perfect—from the tiny gathering of people all laughing and chatting at their own small tables to the perky, adorable waitress checking in on us in her bouncy, friendly way, to the way Gustav looks at me like I'm better than any food could ever be. . .I would live this moment over and over again for a very long time before tiring of it.

When the bell on the front door jingles, it barely even registers, until Gustav stiffens.

"What?" I ask.

He stands up then. "Grandfather. What are you doing here?"

28
GUSTAV

Three weeks ago, if someone earnestly told me that they believed a human could transform into a horse, I would've laughed until I cried. Two weeks ago, the only thing I cared about was the success of my IPO on Trifecta, the company I built myself.

Two hours ago, I had resigned myself to the loss of my company, and I had shelved my dream of inheriting my grandparents' empire. Being a Liepa—something I'd always half-despised—had taken over *everything*, and I knew that humans could turn into horses. In fact, I was falling for a human-horse myself.

I wouldn't have bet a single farthing on the odds of my maternal grandfather tracking down my father's Latvian relatives and locating me. But the one thing that even five minutes ago I felt was an utter impossibility was my grandfather wanting anything to do with me in light of my utter abandonment of what I'd spent the past decade building.

"I knew it would happen at some point, son." My grandfather sighs heavily and drops a wrinkled, gnarled hand on my shoulder. "It's in your blood, as much as I hoped it wasn't, and I can't blame you for my daughter's mistake."

Katerina has frozen like a baby deer facing an LED cannon.

"I've known about this old woman for longer than you've been alive, but I didn't figure you'd ever come all the way out here. In spite of my best efforts, I can't fathom why you're sticking around. But I waited, and you didn't come back on your own."

I lift my chin. "I'm not sure why you're here," I say. "But—"

"I'm here because there's no way I was ever going to hand my company over to that moron cousin of yours. I only used him to motivate you, Daniel. My birthday's in three days, and I want you to come home so I can announce that I've chosen you."

It's everything I ever wanted.

It's what I thought I lost when Grigoriy dragged me out of that lobby and Grandfather called to berate me for ruining the Black Rock meeting.

It's the gold ring I've been doggedly pursuing my entire adult life.

Only, now that it's here, being dangled right in front of me, I realize that it's not gold after all. It's barely brass, the kind that turns your whole finger green. The kind I should throw in the trash without a backward glance.

Even so, I can't help considering it, at least for a moment. With the kind of resources he's offering me, I could travel indefinitely. I could keep moving as long and as far as I wanted. I wouldn't be the czar of a powerful country or anything, but I might actually have more power and more reach than Leonid does.

I'd be free to move or travel anywhere I liked.

If Katerina would come with me, I could walk away from all this. Without fearing that I'm training, who knows? Maybe Leonid would let it all go. Perhaps, if he saw me living my best life, running a huge company, he'd see that I posed no threat to him. One of the few regions Grandfather has steered far away from is the Slavic countries. Nothing related to my father in any way was of interest to him. Unless Leonid saw my taking Katerina as some kind of threat, taking Grandfather up on his offer might solve all our problems. And I could actually protect Kat as I've longed to do.

"You'd be a Belmont in all the ways you always wanted," Grandfather says.

And that's the heart of it.

For more than ten years now, he's been dangling that over my head. My father's flawed. He's weak. He's greedy. He succumbs to his weaknesses over and over, and no matter how badly we needed him, his children were never a priority in his life.

But he always loved us.

His love was never contingent on our behavior, or our performance, or something as pedantic as having the right name. For eleven and a half years, Grandfather has known that his grandchild was waiting and desperately hoping for his approval. He knew it was all I really wanted, all I longed for.

And he withheld it to make me keep dancing.

Only now that I've slipped the leash is he finally offering me what I've longed for. Now that it serves him, he'll hand me the carrot I've been chasing.

But I see it now. I see what he's doing and who he is, and I won't be satisfied with it, not anymore.

I want more.

And I can't abandon Kristiana—never again.

No matter what Leonid decides to do with me, whether he might leave me alone or not, I doubt he'll simply walk away from my sister and her defiant husband. I doubt he'll leave Grigoriy alone, or my old family friend Mirdza.

I can't see the light in my own countenance, but I can imagine what it would look like if I were to smile at my grandfather, thank him for his offer, and return to New York City to kiss his ring at that party.

"No." I shake my head. "I agree with you that Prescott Belmont is a complete disaster, but I'm afraid I'll have to wish you good luck with him."

"You—what?"

"I waited a long time, desperate for you to say that I was competent and that you wanted me around," I say. "But now that you're here, still not quite saying all of that, but offering me what I wanted, I find that. . ." I spread my hands. "It's not what I want anymore."

Grandfather splutters.

"It's not that your company isn't amazing. It is. You're an excellent businessman with an eye for things that will take off and make loads of money. You're also a decent judge of character in a lot of ways, but you care about all the wrong things."

"I suppose," Katerina says, "that being an excellent CEO may not make someone the very best grandfather."

"Who's this?" Grandfather points.

"My girlfriend," I say. "Katerina Yurovsky."

"*She's Russian?*" Grandfather closes his eyes. "I should've known. And let me guess—she's the reason you just disappeared like that? She's gotten herself in some kind of trouble?" He glances down at her stomach, tilting his head sideways.

"She's not pregnant," I say.

"Be sure it's yours," he says. "They have tests for that these days."

Katerina laughs. "*It's* not anyone's. I'm not pregnant."

"That's a relief." Grandfather turns back to me. "I mean all of it. I'll put it in writing now." He waves his hand behind him, clearly gesturing at the Chief Counsel for Belmont Group. "Bring the shares."

"You're really not listening," I say.

"No." He slams his hand down on the table. "*You're* not listening."

"Sir." Tiny, ephemeral little Emery sidles past my large and overbearing grandfather and presses one hand against his chest. "I'm going to have to ask you to back up, and then I'm going to insist that you leave." She huffs. "Please."

My jaw hits the tiled floor.

"Who are you?" Grandfather's scowl could practically peel the old wallpaper off the walls. I'm actually nervous for the little girl who just intervened on my behalf.

"I'm the waitress for these two." She points at Katerina and me. "And as their waitress, I'm responsible for them having a nice meal." She leans a little closer and drops her voice. "Actually, my compensation relies on them having a good meal. Tips, am I right?" She sighs. "And you're just ruining everyone's night with your 'listen here' routine."

"Get out of the way, little girl." Grandfather frowns.

"When I was living back in New York City, I survived a year of junior high at a private, all girls institution." She raises her eyebrows meaningfully. "My freshman year in high school, I helped the horse doc break a mustang. That mustang is now my barrel horse." She drops one hand on her hip. "You don't scare me, old man. You're one tongue-lashing away from a heart attack. So, push me." She steps closer, her eyes flashing. "I dare you." She hisses. "Did I mention I know the sheriff? Because my great-uncle is always watching the Tonight Show right now, and he would be really annoyed if I had to call him down here because a non-customer was being belligerent in my place of business."

Grandfather swallows, his Adam's apple bobbing.

In all my life, I've never seen anyone shut Grandfather down—never. But watching a hundred-pound girl do it, well. The Birch Creek people are made a little different. It takes a few moments after Grandfather leaves for me to stop trembling.

The huge slices of apple pie Emery brings over do help. "On the house," she says. "I had a nasty father, you know. They only respond to bullies."

I tip Emery quite well, but on the way home, Katerina asks me a question. An obvious question. "Will your grandfather's appearance bring Leonid here?"

I'm so stupid that it's only occurring to me now.

Of course it will.

He knew my name was Daniel Belmont, and my grandfather may not be quite as high profile as the newly elected czar of Russia, but he's noteworthy. And there's no way he's not using credit cards.

My arrogant, irritating grandfather just blew our cover.

I think about our options the whole way home, but all this stupid drama ruined our date. That might make me the angriest of all. That, and leaving this tiny town that I'd never even heard of before we came. I'm even sad to leave the cantankerous old woman who shut the door in our face when we first arrived.

But when we reach Steve and Abigail's house, I know what we need to do. I cut the engine and turn to face my gorgeous girlfriend. "I'm going to use all three powers at once," I say. "Or you know, I'm going to try."

"What?" Katerina grabs my hand. "You can't do that. Just getting one new one is awful enough, but three?"

"Then you guys are going to do what I said. You're going to drive me around and around, taking turns sleeping and driving, until I wake up. Once that happens, I can learn to use those powers as we travel—stopping in empty fields or wherever we can to practice, staying ahead of Leonid. Once I'm competent, we'll stop and let him find us."

"Gustav," she says. "I don't like this plan at all."

"Who knows?" I ask. "Maybe when I take the other powers, I can stop Leonid from using them."

"Have you been able to stop Grigoriy or Aleks?" She frowns. "I feel like I'd have heard about that."

I shake my head. "Not so far, but maybe once I have control of all five, I'll be able to."

"Gustav," she says. "Let's talk to everyone about this. We can come up with a real plan."

But we've done enough talking. The one who has to do this is me, and I'd rather sleep as long as it takes in one fell swoop than slowly trying to integrate everything one after the other. "The hardest part was learning to use the powers together. I may as well work on all five at once."

Before she can argue further, I look at the cozy little house up ahead. The people who live here have done way more than they should have to help. We owe it to them to get out of here before things worsen.

"I've made up my mind," I say.

"Alright." Just like that, she stops arguing. She nods. "Tell me what I can do to help."

"I adore you," I say. "In case something goes wrong, I want to say that."

"I love you," she says. "I know it sounds stupid, because you don't know me that well yet, but—"

I kiss her.

It is dumb, for both of us.

I've known her for all of two weeks, and I disliked her quite a bit at first. But we've been through a lot, and I refuse to believe that bonds formed under stress are less real than those that are formed over bowls of ice cream and games of Uno. I think what I feel for her is honest, true, and valuable. "Thank you," I say. "For believing in me. For supporting me."

"Thanks for saving me from that marauding tractor," she says.

I kiss her again, and then I force myself to release her and climb out of the car. "Three at once." I inhale slowly. "Usually after just one, I'm really tired. Pushing past it for a short time is already hard."

"Maybe it'll help to focus on the things you're embracing," she says. "So look at that porch light. It beckons to me, you know. I can feel it, the electricity flickering through the wires. Those electrons, banging around. I know what it is now—I've spent more time doing internet research on lightning than anything else since waking up. Humans have figured out a lot."

A fly lands on my neck, and before I can slap at it, I decide to try something else. I focus on it, and I think about my forehead, and I imagine the energy balling up there, and then I try to punch through with that power as hard as I can, and I *zap* it.

It actually works.

The little bugger falls to the ground, dead. I'm a human bug zapper.

"I felt that." Katerina's voice is small and her eyes are round. "Like, a ripple in my connection. If I were asleep, I might have missed it, though."

"Should we wait for the middle of the night, then?"

She shrugs. "No way to know when he'll be distracted."

"I'll forge ahead, then." I don't see any fire anywhere, however.

"Hang on," Katerina says. "I'll grab some matches."

She darts into the house, probably thinking she can get in and out without someone stopping her. I'm not entirely sure. I'm also not sure how matches will help me, *per se*, since I'm supposed to be able to make the fire. I'm pretty tired, though, maybe from my new power, or perhaps because I spent so long working with both wind and earth today. I collapse on the porch swing while I wait for her to conserve what little energy I have. When she shoots back out, she's peering over her shoulder like a mouse darting away from a barn cat.

"What?"

She presses a finger to her lips and shakes her head.

Once she's closer, she whispers, "They're talking about us in there."

"Kat, the free world's fate is in our hands. I've just forced my ability to use lightning, and Leonid may now be able to find us. I hardly think—"

"They're placing bets on how long we'll date." She's fuming.

"Did anyone bet on all the way?"

She freezes then, looking up at me. "All the way?" She arches one eyebrow. "What does that mean, exactly?"

What could it mean? "That we'd stay together forever—get married?"

She inhales sharply, her mouth still slightly open. "Oh."

"No?" I shake my head. "Those idiots—"

But something drops down from the eaves above, zooming lower and lower, drawing near to Kat's head. I'm not sure what it is—a spider? A bee? Without thinking, without preparation, I wave my hand and fling it away with air, and then I incinerate it with a bright flash of fire.

"What was that?" Katerina's mouth gapes open. "You did it. You used a second power."

"That spider was huge." I yawn. "I think it was a spider. Did you see it?"

"A spider?" She shakes her head. "No, but I'm glad you got it away from me. I'm definitely not a fan, and that makes *two* bugs that have helped you tonight. I'm beginning to think all you needed all along was some insects."

"It's just water left." I sit on the porch swing, my eyes heavy, my limbs trembling. "But I'm not sure I can do it. I'm tired, and my head's already *pounding*."

"You have to," she says. "We'll drive you around until you wake up, but it'd be better if you could get them all at once. Way easier than having a whole extra blackout period."

"But water?" I shrug, closing my eyes and leaning against the side of the swing. "I don't even feel anything vaguely resembling that."

Katerina grabs my shoulder and shoves me. "Look. Gustav! Look!"

It's hard to force my eyes open—I'm so, so tired, but when I do, I sit straight up on the swing.

That stupid flaming spider set a pile of leaves ablaze, and now there's a robustly burning pile of detritus *right* next to Steve and Abigail's home.

My head's pounding like someone's inside my skull with a jackhammer, and my eyes feel weighted with trains, pulling, pulling, pulling them down. But I can't very well pass out while our new friends' house is about to burn to the ground. I clench my fists, I grit my teeth, and I focus as hard as I can.

Nothing happens.

The flames spread, hopping to the base of the porch.

Someone in the house notices, and people start to pour out of the front door. They're screaming. Someone's saying something about a fire extinguisher, and I know they have some kind of hose. It'll be fine, right?

It's fine. They'll get it put out.

Katerina stands up and backs toward the fire. "You have to save me," she shouts. "Gustav! Help!"

I can barely see straight—there are definitely two of Katerina, but I can't just let her walk into the fire. I have to do something. When I focus on the fire and trying to put it out, my hands burn. I'm sure there's something I could do, something that would. . .

"Water," Katerina's shouting. "I need *water*, Gustav."

Darkness clouds my vision, but her face is bright and crisp. Water. She needs water. I can sense it, vaguely, all around me. On leaves. In the ground. In the air.

That's when I realize that, unlike the flame, water can't be manifested from nothing. It can't just take over with one greedy spark. It has to be amalgamated from the tiny specks of water that exist all around me. Once I realize that, it's easy. So much easier.

I reach out, like Aleks taught me with earth, and I feel for the water that's close. That's when I feel the Birch Creek, the tiny but fierce creek that runs along the back of the property line, and I *pull*. I stream that water toward the blaze right behind Katerina, lighting her entire silhouette up so that it's red as flame, just like her gorgeous hair.

Her face relaxes, and the fire winks out, just as I lose my focus and the whole world goes dark.

❧ 29 ☙

KATERINA

Driving around constantly for days on end brings new meaning to the word tiring. It's practically impossible to sleep in the car, especially with seven other people, one of whom is quite large and also entirely unconscious.

When we turn on the news, it announces that Leonid Ivanovich, Czar of Russia, has decided to take a tour of the United States farm country. He's studying American agriculture to figure out how best to optimize Russia's ability to provide for its citizens. Yeah, right.

It's a clear lie.

He's coming for us.

And around the sixth day of driving, I start to worry about Gustav. Like, really worry.

He's barely breathing, for one.

He hasn't eaten or drunk anything for almost a week now, and the rest of us have been run pretty ragged. When I fall asleep, I dream that our car has broken down. That we can't find gas. Or that Leonid stops us in the middle of the road, torching all the fields and farmhouses on all sides.

"I think we need to find a hospital," I finally say. "It's been six days. He needs an IV or something."

"It's a magical coma." Kristiana's face is pale. "There's nothing a hospital will be able to do to help him." She purses her lips, and I can't help wondering whether she really believes that, or whether she's just worried that the hospital personnel will be even worse than the gas station attendants, who always eye us askance, peering through windows and around corners at the man who's passed out in the back of the car.

One of them is going to report us—it's only a matter of time.

If word of eight people traveling in the same high-end SUV, mostly Eastern European, makes it to the wrong people, we'll be in big trouble.

Perhaps most concerning is Aleksandr's declaration when we stop for gas at the beginning of day seven. "I'm running out of cash."

I'm not sure why it angers me so much that Kristiana seems far more alarmed about this than she is about Gustav's continued unconscious state.

But the real problems start on the morning of the eighth day. Grigory grunts as he's watching his phone screen, which isn't common. The man's inhumanly quiet and calm *all the time*.

"What?" I lean forward to peer over his shoulder.

He yanks out his headphones and turns his volume up. "Listen to this."

"Leonid Ivanovich, the current ruler of all of Russia and the country formerly known as Belarus, has taken a significant interest in a tiny town on the edge of the Utah-Wyoming border called Manila. He's decided to spend some extra time here, learning more about cattle ranching and alfalfa farming from the locals. When asked, he told reporters. . ."

"What?" All the blood has drained from Kristiana's face. "No."

There's a lot of murmuring in the car, but I can still hear his voice. His English tutor was British, and now that I'm learning to differentiate the various English accents, I understand a little more why he stands out here, in America.

"—the people of this area are so. . ." He pauses and looks right at the camera. "Well, they're just delightful. I can't get enough of their small-town mannerisms and the tight-knit friendships they've formed." When he smiles, my blood runs cold.

"We have to go back," I say.

"What good would come from it?" Adriana asks. "That's exactly what he wants us to do."

"Those people—what's he doing to them?" I think about Mister Steve, his kind wife Abigail, and Kristiana and Gustav's cousin, Amanda Saddler. She can't ever seem to keep her mouth shut. I can only imagine how well that's going over with Leonid. They'll all be charcoal by sunset tonight.

"First off," Aleks says, "We're at least twenty hours away, so nothing we do will be immediate. But second, Adriana's right. Going there is exactly what he wants, and while it pains me to see that he's figured out where we were, it won't help them for us to—"

"You're all cowards," I say. "You—"

My tirade's cut short when Gustav shifts into a massive, dark bay horse, his front hooves shattering through the window of the left side of our overpriced SUV. Unfortunately, when it happens, we're in the middle of a rather large city.

And people are videotaping us.

Hopefully no one believes it's real, because right after he shifts, Gustav wakes up.

GUSTAV

Waking up as a horse when you've gone to sleep as a human is probably never relaxing.

Waking up as a horse who's *inside* a car that's driving down the road is downright terrifying. My front legs are almost immediately sliced to ribbons as they plunge through the window of the confounded SUV. It's almost involuntary, thrashing around with my enormous body, trying to make room for myself.

Once I calm down enough to realize that I'm doing more harm than good, Aleks pulls the SUV over, and Kristiana and Katerina talk me through escaping the vehicle. It appears a tendon in my right front leg is severed, but thankfully Grigoriy can heal injuries that have just occurred.

Within moments, our only problem is that I can't manage to shift *back* into my human shape.

That, and our car is essentially destroyed.

"Leonid will know where we are immediately," Aleks says. "We need to buy a new vehicle—and a trailer—and get moving again right away."

"But you said we're out of money," Kris says.

Things are going really well.

We've at least escaped from the side of the road, walking a good ten miles down the side of the road as seven humans and a horse, and have found what appears to be an abandoned home near the edge of town. The grass is nearly dead, and yet, I find it oddly delicious. Probably because I haven't eaten in a week, but maybe because I'm equine.

Being a horse is straight up whack.

"How are we going to get him out of this form and back into his human one?" Grigoriy asks. "That should be our first order of business."

"Yes, thank you genius," Katerina says. "As always, the brain trust is working overtime."

Mirdza, who's usually pretty nice, looks ready to claw Kat's eyes out.

I try to tell them all to calm down and it comes out as a very loud, very concerned whinny. Kat pats my nose. I find myself leaning into her hand, like I really am one of these ghastly big beasts.

I hate it.

And I kind of love when she scratches the fur along my neck.

It's all very confusing. And the crappy, dead-brown grass is calling to me. While they argue, I find myself edging my way over to the brightest, shaggiest part of it. Once I start eating, my heart slows. My breathing steadies.

"—all it took was Kris telling us we could shift," Alexei says, "but she's tried that here, and it doesn't seem to help."

"Of course it doesn't help," Kat says. "He's her *brother*— he's the same bloodline. He shouldn't ever be stuck."

"Maybe it's because he's finally able to use all five powers," Kristiana says. "Maybe once his body fully recovers, he'll be able to shift back on his own."

"Yes," a new voice says from just behind me. A voice I don't recognize. "That's it—they figured it out."

I lift my head and whip it around.

The others are still arguing as if the strange woman didn't just speak. She's odd looking, to be sure. She's not tall or short, but she's *substantial* in a way I can't pinpoint. One moment she looks ancient, and the next, she looks quite young. She smells like that moment where earth meets the sky, and when rain on pavement meets a sunny day. Her eyes are unfathomable—dark, somber, hopeful, and bright all at once.

"Hello, Gustav. I've been looking forward to meeting you." She leans closer and drops a hand on the side of my massive cheek. "My missing puzzle piece."

I nuzzle her hand. I know there's not a treat there—that would be crazy. But then, like magic, there suddenly is. A big, sticky ball of oats and molasses.

It's better than any toffee, chocolate, or macaron I've ever tasted. I could eat treats like this all day. So of course she doesn't offer me any more.

No matter how many times I nuzzle her hand.

Jerk.

"You're all so much simpler as horses. I should keep you this way." She scratches the area underneath my massive, hot mane, and it's *heaven.*

I completely forget what everyone's arguing about, stretching out my neck and turning my head just a little sideways to really enjoy it.

"You can use all five powers now," the woman says softly. "And you can finally shift your form as well. It's scary and strange and you're not sure quite what to do, am I right?"

I freeze, remembering that we're all in big trouble. I turn back to face her with one big eye, wanting answers.

"It took me quite a while to figure out where they'd all gone. You see, my sisters and I split up the world long ago, and I really only have the jurisdiction to manage things in Europe and Asia." She snorts. "Baba Yaga, by the way."

Splitting up the geography of earth makes a strange sort of sense.

"My sister, Squannit, usually handles things on this side of the world. Like me, she goes by many names, but that's her oldest. She and I don't get along very well, so I don't visit often."

I'm not sure how to ask her to tell me more, but when I try, I make a weird whuffling sort of sound.

"I could spend a very long time talking about Squannit, including the horribly inappropriate relationship she had with one of the horsemen."

Horsemen? That reference causes me to snort, which blows snot all over Baba Yaga. She can't really mean the four horsemen of the apocalypse, right? Famine, pestilence, warfare, and death, from the Bible. That's insane, right?

Surely.

"Anyway, I know you have some decisions to make, so I just wanted to mention something important."

I really wish I could speak right now. I toss my head.

"Talking won't help. You humans always ask the wrong things." She purses her lips. "That's why I came while you think you're stuck."

Think? Am I not really stuck?

"Listen carefully, Gustav Daniel Liepa Belmont. More than anyone else, you should understand that life relies on balance. Parents must keep their children safe, and that requires rules, but for their children to grow and learn to handle life alone, they need freedom. Those two things can't exist in a vacuum. Where the one grows, the other shrinks."

I blink, and she rubs my nose.

"Good boy. At least you're listening." She drops her voice, as if the others might notice her if she makes too much noise. "All of life exists in such a balance, and our job—mine and my sisters'—is to help maintain that balance."

The balance between freedom and safety?

"Not freedom and safety, you simpleton, the balance between life and death. The balance between scarcity and abundance."

Whoa. She can hear my thoughts? Or was it an accident she replied to them?

She sighs. "Gustav, you are yourself already a balance of sorts. You've left the life you knew, the place you were raised, and now you've rejected the life you ran toward as well. You understand in a way that those others never will that life needs both a pushing force and also a pulling one. Growth only comes when there's resistance. If you truly eliminate the bad, the good ceases to have meaning."

But what does that mean? What am I supposed to do to Leonid?

"Leonid's beautiful and terrible. He's pure, and he's evil. He's dark and light all rolled together, just as his forefather was, and his problem is that he's not balanced in any way. Once day, he'll find his counterpoint. Until then, all you can do is contain him so he can't offset the balance of the earth too dramatically." She drops to a whisper. "Those kinds of imbalances always wake them up, and no one wants that, except maybe Squannit. They wreak enough havoc in their dreams. So I need you, my boy, to help contain the incomparable Leonid, alright?" She smiles, then, and it's one of the most stunning smiles I've ever seen. It's a study in contrasts.

The wrinkles of wisdom.

The tenacity of middle-age.

The hope of youth.

"I can't stay much longer, or Squannit, that sly vixen, will feel me and come after you for my sake."

Come after me?

"Trust me. She's not someone you want to anger. In fact, neither Squannit nor stupid Osiris ever would leave me alone about Rurik, and what they did was way worse."

Wait. Is she saying. . .

"If they find out you're here, or that the humans I gifted with powers are still mucking around, well. It'll get ugly. I can't protect you from them both, and I can't protect you from either of them here. Do you understand?" She looks around, then, as if she hears something on another plane. "They—I can't fight them. Not in America. You need to make sure you don't do anything really big or really stupid, not until you've gone home."

Home, as in Russia?

"Eastern Europe is best," she says. "Keep that in mind."

Good grief. Our existence is apparently not even legal, and now our creator might get in trouble if we make a mess over here where her contemporaries might realize we exist.

"Yes." She claps. "Exactly that. I knew you'd get it."

We're her bag of pot. Her dirty little affair.

"Not dirty," she says. "And certainly not pot." She shakes her head. "Just contain Leonid, and get him back home as quickly as possible. The longer you're all here, the worse it'll be."

Can I stop him from using his powers? That's what I need to know. And can I restore Alexei's magic?

Baba Yaga sighs, for all the world like I'm an errant toddler, yanking my diaper off and smearing the contents on the walls. "I already explained this. Your power came *after* his. That means that you can't stop him, not once he's been granted the magic. All you can do is contain him—wall him in. Got it?" Her head whips to the side, and her eyes widen. "You need to shift and get out of here, immediately. I'm not sure how long I can keep Squannit from noticing you."

And then, without any warning, she's gone.

One moment, she's here, rubbing my neck and patting my muzzle, and then she's just *gone*.

It never occurred to me that the person who *gave* us our powers wouldn't be able to help us if she wanted to. I thought she was fickle, but I'm beginning to think it's more that she's limited. When Mirdza told her story on the train, I thought it was callous of Baba Yaga to leave the woman and child to be protected by a crippled girl. But now, I wonder if she has to be careful what she does.

She knows too much about how things work, so she's limited in ways we aren't, but she did give me a clue. I may not be able to destroy Leonid, and I may not be able to steal his powers, but I can contain him, whatever that means.

While I was busy listening to Baba Yaga, the fighting among the others escalated. Kat's shouting in Kristiana's face when I turn back toward them. "He's not a gun to shove in Leonid's face. He's a person."

"Not right now he's not," Kris says. "And I think I know he's a person. He's my brother. You've known him for what? Like, two minutes?"

My forehead, where my magic usually kind of sits, feels empty. Nothing at all. But my heart, which usually beats like mad, feels large, slow, and steady. I wonder whether. . . I focus all my energy inward, and I think about how it feels to be *me*. I'm tall. I'm strong. I walk with long, slow strides. My heart beats in the center of my chest, not behind my front legs.

I think about how I felt when I kissed Kat, and how much I want to do it again. Then, like a jolt of lightning running through my entire body, I shift.

It's a brisk October day in I-have-no-idea-where, and I'm now standing entirely naked in a patch of scratchy grass.

"Bravo, little Gustav." Mirdza's smirking. "You grew up right."

"Not so little anymore." Adriana whistles.

I throw my hands up in front of my body, hunching forward a little, but it's too late. Adriana, Kris, and even Katerina have all spun around, and they're all staring at me, slack-jawed.

"Oh, come on, man," Grigoriy says. "All you have to do, if

you have your magic online, is think about what clothing you want to be wearing and it materializes with you."

"So all those times you were naked?" Kris is glaring at Aleks.

"I mean, most of them were because I had to be touching you to use my magic," Aleks says.

"Most?" Kris looks like she's going to tackle him.

"Clothes, guys?" I groan. "Come, now."

"They're back in the car," Alexei says. "So, I'm not sure. . ."

"Oh, for the love." Aleksandr shifts into a horse. Thirty seconds later, he's shifted back and he's holding a pair of jeans. He chucks them at my head.

"Jeans? That's the best you could do?" I'm grumbling, but I'm also stuffing my legs into the pants.

"It's hard to make clothing you're not wearing," Grigoriy says.

"I don't think I could even do it," Kat says. At least she has the decency to look apologetic about it.

"We do need to get some kind of new vehicle," Alexei says. "But what can we possibly buy for. . .how much did you say we have left?"

Aleks coughs. "Seven hundred and thirty-six dollars."

"Unless you idiots have lost my wallet, I'll buy it," I say. "Because while you were fighting, Baba Yaga paid me a visit, and I don't think we need to hide anymore."

"What?" Aleks looks around like she might still be hiding somewhere close. "When?"

"Just now," I say. "I'm not sure how none of you could see her. I'd like to master that trick."

"But when we reach Birch Creek," Katerina asks, "what will you do?"

"I'm not sure you can defeat him right now," Grigoriy says. "We should take some time first and—"

"I can't beat him," I say simply. "Baba Yaga already told

me—he's stronger. His line got the magic first, and she didn't say this, but I almost wonder whether he can choke me out if he tries."

"Have you lost your mind?" Kris asks. "Then why would we—"

"I have a plan, and you're going to have to trust me, for once."

$\mathfrak{H}$ 31 $\mathfrak{H}$

GUSTAV

My favorite part of horse racing was watching the jockeys breeze the horses in a circle before the race. I'd always pick which one I thought would win, and sometimes it was because I liked their silks.

Other times, it was the shiny coat of the horse.

As I grew older, it was the spring in the horse's step, or sometimes even the odds on the horse.

I was eight the first time my dad taught me to place a bet at a horserace. I still remember Dad handing me a fifty santïm note. I'd never held that much money in my hand. He walked me through placing my bets, more patient than I'd ever seen him as I told the Totes employee what I wanted to bet on.

The race was the most exciting one I'd ever seen, because I had money on horse number twenty-two. His silks were bright orange, and he had odds of eleven-to-one. Imagine my giddy joy when he *won*.

I wanted to go home with a fistful of santïm for my mother, but Dad insisted that I try again. By the end of the night, I'd lost every single lati I'd won, but I went home with a fifty santïm note clutched in my fist. I hadn't won, not according to Dad's criterion, but I'd contained Dad's desire to spend all the money we made.

I went home with the fifty he gave me—not a win or a loss. A containment. I have to pull off that same miracle again, and I think I can. Of course, not everyone has faith in me.

"I never liked you," Grigoriy says. "Not from the minute you tried to run from us in that lobby."

I roll my eyes. "I didn't try to run."

We're nearly to Birch Creek, after driving through the night, and the others still haven't agreed to my plan. Baba Yaga's words keep running through my head over and over.

Contain him.

Like my dad forced me to do with my money that night when I won big on my first bet, our job isn't to win. It's *not* to lose. They make me repeat everything she said at least three times, and I nearly have the whole thing memorized by now.

"She didn't say we couldn't kill him," Grigoriy says again.

"That's Leonid's problem," I say. "He thinks the answer is killing anyone who's bad. That can't be our solution, or we're the same as him."

"I don't think we should kill *everyone*," Grigoriy says. "Just him."

Katerina rolls her eyes. "Do you have rocks in your brains? Baba Yaga said—"

"She was afraid of someone," Grigoriy practically explodes. "Gustav said as much. She's covering herself, and I'm not going to let him wander off again just because he's her long-lost lovechild or whatever."

"The point," Kris says, "is that we're asking Gustav to confront him head-on, and he has a plan."

"A plan with a price that would be paid by *us*," Aleks says.

Kristiana sighs, because he's right.

"A plan that's the best idea I've heard," Katerina says softly.

No one argues with that.

"Fine, but if we do this, we kill him afterward." Grigoriy folds his arms with a huff.

"I agree," Aleks says.

"As do I," Alexei says.

"And me," Mirdza says. That one surprises me.

"Not that anyone cares, but I vote that he dies, too." No shock Adriana wants him gone. He almost killed Alexei and Grigoriy the last time they saw him, from what I hear.

"We'll have time to decide after seeing how he behaves," I say. "We can vote afterward, and we'll do what the majority demands."

That shuts them up, miraculously.

But when we reach Birch Creek, nothing goes as we expect. There aren't any roadblocks. There are no guards anywhere. In fact, we drive right up to Steve and Abigail's house, and it almost looks like there's a party happening. Amanda Saddler and her husband Tommy are here, judging by the big truck parked beside Abigail's SUV.

Several kids are darting around the swing on the front porch, playing some kind of tag-affiliated game.

But when we pull up and kill the engine, everyone freezes. I open my door and jump out. "Is everything really alright?"

"You came." Abby's not smiling, though. She looks a little ill.

"I'm so happy to see it." Leonid steps out from behind Steve, and I realize that he's grilling burgers on the side of the house.

Leonid's just standing around, grilling burgers.

No guards.

No Boris or Mikhail, at least, not that I can see. There's no one else here at all, other than our friends.

"Won't you join us?" Leonid's British accent is the only sign that he's not a local when he waves us over. And then in

Russian, he says, "You got here just in time. I was running out of patience, truth be told."

"Where's my brother?" Katerina asks.

"Boris and Misha are out back, playing a rousing game of horseshoes," Leonid says, still speaking in Russian. "If you've never heard of it, it's this strange thing they do here, where they try and throw a horseshoe as close to a metal stick as they can get it."

What on earth is going on?

Leonid's gaze shifts, his eyes turning toward me.

I'd have said that Katerina had the most stunning, the brightest green eyes I'd ever seen, but I'd never seen Leonid Ivanovich in person. His eyes are brighter than the grass in Easter baskets. They're the kind of bright that you really only see in CGI-enhanced movies or cartoons.

And he *is* annoyingly handsome—even more so in real life than he was on the television screen.

"You must be Gustav. You know, your friends here were *so sure* you'd come. I didn't have nearly the same faith that they did, but look! They were proved right after all." He smiles, and I want to strike him.

All you can do is contain him. Baba Yaga's words come back to me over and over.

I hope my plan isn't complete lunacy.

"Why are you just standing there?" Leonid gestures. "We've got food back here."

"How did you find out where we were?" I ask.

"You have your grandfather to thank for that. He's quite a man, you know. Self-made, or at least, mostly. He took his father's modest energy empire and turned it into something unique. I'm sure his disappointment when your mother fell in love with your father was truly deep."

If he thinks he'll taunt me into acting with rage over a few barbs aimed at my father, he's sorely mistaken. "My father disappoints everyone. It's what he does best."

Leonid steps closer. "You and I have more in common than I realized, Gustav. My father was a monumental disappointment as well."

"Yes, I imagine we could be besties in no time," I say.

"Sarcasm." Leonid nods. "It's the lowest form of humor, but bravo. If I were in your situation, I'm not sure I'd be cracking jokes at all."

"What do you want from me?" I ask. "Did you drag us here and threaten our friends just—"

"Ah, ah, ah." Leonid gestures toward Steve. "Where's dear old Amanda? Tell her to come out and say hello." He turns back toward me. "Friends? I think not. To me, these people are more like *family*."

And suddenly, I'm with Grigoriy. I want to kill him.

"Look. Here she is."

Mikhail has his arm run through Amanda's and he's walk-shoving her toward us, even as she stumbles.

"I'm sure you'll be alarmed to hear that her heart problem took a turn last week." He throws both hands up, palms out. "No fault of mine, I assure you. But the doctors say she hasn't got much longer to be with us." He clucks. "It's such a shame, but people cannot live forever, can they?"

She truly looks terrible. She's leaning on Mikhail like she'd collapse without his body as support. Her skin's pale, and her eyes aren't focusing properly.

Katerina and Kris both step toward Amanda.

"What do you want?" I ask again. "Just tell me."

"I could heal her," Alexei says. "If you just grant me my water powers for a moment, I'll heal her."

"Oh, but your darling Gustav now has powers." Leonid tilts his head. "I should so like to see him save his cousin." He looks around, a forced smile on his face. "I think we all would."

"But I can't," I start. "I mean, I don't know how—"

"It took me years to learn to heal things," Alexei says.

"And years beyond that to be capable of something like a delicate heart repair."

"Not a fast student, I see," Leonid says. "I was able to heal Grigoriy after mere minutes using water." He sighs. "I suppose not everyone's created equal, no matter what this misguided country likes to believe."

Alexei looks ready to strangle Leonid with his bare hands. "Just let me—"

"Let you?" Leonid laughs. "It's a *free* country here, or haven't you heard?"

"But you know I can't use my magic." A vein in Alexei's temple is throbbing.

"I can try," I say.

"You could kill her," Alexei says. "Her heart is leaking."

"You can feel that?" Leonid's eyes widen. "Spectacular. So you still have the affinity, just not the energy to do anything with it." He smiles. "That's even better, truly."

"What do you want?" Katerina's voice when she asks is soft. Like she's talking to an old friend who's lost his way.

His face shifts when he hears her voice. It hardens.

"Why did you travel this far?" Kat asks. "Why did you summon us here?"

"Have you ever had a gun pressed to your head, love?" Leonid takes three steps to a mesh yard chair and sits down. "Have you ever been afraid you were *about* to die?"

I glance at Katerina, looking for some kind of guidance, but she's frozen in place, her entire being focused on him and his taunts.

Leonid turns toward me, and he raises his eyebrows. "Oh, my. You two are dating." He starts to laugh, then, standing up and pacing. "You do not waste any time, do you, my dear?"

Katerina's cheeks are bright red.

"He's handsome. I'll give you that—you have consistently good taste." He sighs and taps his index finger against his lip. "What do I want? Everyone keeps asking, but I'm shocked that you don't already know." He folds his hands together, and then he throws them outward. "I want peace for all the world. Isn't that what everyone wants? Even Captain America, or was it Iron Man, who says, 'Peace in our time.'"

I blink.

Aleks frowns.

Grigoriy grunts.

"Say something that makes sense," Alexei says. "You already have Russia, and now also Belarus, apparently. Why come to America?"

"Because, dear Alexei Romanov, in my life, I've had many, many guns pressed to my temple. I've had people threatening me for my entire life. I intended to ignore you and your new, shiny puppet. I don't need to own the whole world, as I'm sure you can understand. But when I felt you load up a gun here in America, I couldn't just ignore it any longer, could I?"

A gun. That's me. I'm the gun.

Contain him. That's all we need to do. The plan will still work.

"I will swear never to leave the United States," I say. "I'll swear never to come to Russia, or even anywhere near it."

Leonid sighs. "So quick to roll over and expose your belly. So quick to make a deal." He steps closer, his bright eyes flashing. "You have mastered all five elements now, and like me, I suspect you can see what lies inside the human heart?"

I don't want to, but I find myself nodding.

"Bravo, really. I mean, you can't do much with it yet, apparently, but you did find your magic and subdue all five elements in under a month. It's impressive. You might one day be a worthy foe."

"Please." Amanda's voice is soft. I can barely hear her. "Please go and take your fight elsewhere. There are children here."

"Let me try to heal her," I say. "And let's do as she asks and let them go. This isn't their fight."

"Oh, but they made it their fight," Leonid says, "when they welcomed you into their home and helped in any way they could."

"That's right." Abigail's standing on the porch, scowling. "We may not have magic, and we may not even be related to any of you like Amanda is, but we will always oppose evil, wherever we see it."

Leonid claps. "See?" He shakes his head. "How could you not love them, these small-town folk? *Scrappy*."

"If you admire them, then do as she asks. Let them go."

"Now that you're here, I don't need them." Leonid beckons for Mikhail to bring Amanda close, and he drops his hands on her head. "I suppose, since it's either heal you or watch you drop dead in front of us, I'll go ahead and do it myself." He sighs. "Poor Alexei would, but he can't. You see, he's still powerless."

Amanda's arms flail, and her mouth opens, and she screams. I feel it, the pulse of water, the shot of life injected into her, and although I can't see it from here, I know he's doing something small, directed, and precise.

Almost as fast as she begins to scream, she slumps forward.

"Now, that pacemaker can't be helped, but you don't need it anymore. You should have a few more years left before everything else starts to give out, one by one." Leonid smiles. "I even cleared out the clogged valves and vessels while I was in there. See? I'm not the devil after all."

"I never thought you were," Katerina says.

He freezes for a moment, and he turns toward her slowly, his lips compressed. But then he shakes it off, his lips twisting into their sardonic shape again slowly. "Lying doesn't become you, my dear," Leonid says. "We all know you despised me—first and longest."

"You still haven't told us what you want," Kristiana says.

"You healed Amanda, which was a show of good faith, and now you'll let the locals go. But then what?"

Leonid tosses his head at Mikhail, and he and Boris step back. "You're right that they can all go. Let's talk when they're gone."

It takes a few moments, but eventually Amanda and Tommy, Steve, Abigail, Abigail's sister Helen, her husband David, and all the children have been loaded into their cars, and all that remain are Leonid, Boris, Mikhail, and the eight of us.

"Amanda's beyond the age where she can have children," Leonid says. "But I need Gustav and Kristiana both dead, and then I'll need Grigoriy and Aleksandr to surrender their powers, and we'll be done here."

Total and complete surrender. Those are his terms. I'm not shocked, but I am disappointed. I had hoped for something less. . .draconian.

"I'll think about your demands," I say.

The look Katerina gives me is, well, it's adorable.

"Alright," I say. "I've thought about them, and I'm afraid we can only agree to two of the three."

Leonid blinks. "Two of the three? Are you saying I can kill Amanda and you, but not Kristiana?"

I snort. "Hardly."

"What, then?" Leonid arches one eyebrow. "Because, honestly, I was just being polite. If you don't agree to my terms, I'll just kill you one by one until I can take what I want."

Aleksandr swears in Russian, and then he slams a tornado of dirt into Leonid's chest, sending him flying back. "You'll never kill my wife. Never."

These idiots are just incapable of sticking to the script.

Leonid, of course, fights back, shooting a strangely spiraling burst of water and fire at Aleksandr.

"Stop," I shout.

Everyone ignores me.

Grigoriy manages to knock the flame-water spiral off course with a gust of wind, but that sends it slamming into the side of Abigail's house. I cringe as a chunk of wall shears off, exposing the family room to the fall wind, debris immediately covering everything inside.

Boris brings his hands together, preparing to strike as well, I'm sure, but Katerina has other ideas. She shrieks, "You're such a total embarrassment," and launches herself at him. She starts pulling his hair, and electric bolts fly outward at strange intervals, one striking a tree and splitting it in half. Another leaving a dark mark on a large grey stone.

The horses in Steve's nearby paddock are racing around like mad.

Mikhail has joined the fray, slamming bursts of flame toward Aleksandr, most of which Aleks blocks with tiny tornadoes of dirt.

"Stop it now," I say, only this time, I put some force into it, and my words come out so loud that the ground shakes.

Everyone freezes.

"It's time," I say, using the same amplification.

Grigoriy and Aleksandr meet my eyes, and they nod.

Aleksandr starts, because he can't stand to be shown up, ever. "I hereby grant Leonid Ivanovich the right and ability to use earth."

"And I grant Leonid the right to use wind," Grigoriy says, never one to be outdone.

Leonid's eyes light up.

But this time, I'm the one smiling harder.

"Why?" Leonid turns toward me. "You know I'll kill you now."

"I think not," I say.

"No?" Leonid smirks. "Why ever not?"

"You've never come into two powers at once before," I say. "But let me tell you, as someone who managed to master three at once, you're about to go down—hard." I spread my hands out. "And all I have to do is stay alive until it happens."

Leonid's jaw drops, and he starts to fight like a cat in a bag, heading down to the river. Fire and water, lightning and earth stream at me simultaneously. This isn't someone who mastered his skills in a few hours or a few days.

No, Leonid knows what he's doing.

And Aleksandr and Grigoriy can no longer do anything.

But in his distraction, Leonid forgets to cut off Katerina, and she manages to keep Mikhail and Boris distracted. Either that, or they're afraid to really harm her.

I'm no mage, that's for sure, but I've gotten good at blocking, and the more attacks Leonid launches, the more exhausted he becomes, his eyes closing and then slamming back open. He droops and then straightens like a board, blinking rapidly. After a very focused and very concerted effort, he weakens fast. His movements slow. He struggles to keep his eyes open.

And then he passes out.

Katerina's chest is heaving, and a bead of sweat runs down the side of her face. "That was. . ."

"Brilliant?" I ask. "Well done?"

She snorts.

"You know you're impressed," I say. "Because it worked."

"I'm not only impressed." She steps closer and presses her hand to the side of my face. "I love you, Gustav Liepa. You're everything I didn't even know I wanted."

When Mikhail tries to flame us, I pull as hard as I can on flame, and his power winks out.

Katerina barks a laugh. "That—that was awesome."

"Now we're all powerless," Grigoriy grumbles.

"But," Aleks says, huffing. "When we kill him, we'll get our abilities back."

"True." Grigoriy stumbles forward, whipping out a long,

angry-looking knife that came from *who knows where*. The man always seems to have knives.

Without any warning, Grigoriy plunges it into Leonid's heart. The knife slides in easily, right up to the hilt, buried in his chest where his heart should be. But instead of jerking, or bleeding, or anything at all, something very, very strange happens.

The dagger *disappears*.

And Leonid shifts into a horse—a dark, rich, shiny chestnut with a narrow, perfectly proportioned stripe down his beautifully shaped face. He looks like he could be any racehorse Trifecta might have sponsored. He could be the one to watch for winning the Kentucky Derby, for heaven's sake.

The knife did nothing.

Grigoriy whips out another. This one's longer, and it looks even more wicked, with a serrated black blade. "Thinks he can shift to save himself, does he?" He plunges it toward Leonid again, very nearly in the same spot.

But this time, the knife stops, just outside of Leonid's body, vibrating. Grigoriy cries out and drops it, cradling his hand. He's swearing up a storm. Russian, English, and Latvian, all of them mixed up in a way that's almost poetic.

"What does that mean?" Katerina asks. "Why can't you stab him?"

"Contain him," I say. "That's what Baba Yaga said we must do."

"What does that mean?" Aleksandr asks. "Is she protecting him?"

"I'm not sure," I say. "But we have a week or so to figure it out."

❧ 32 ❧

KATERINA

Not five minutes after Leonid passes out, it starts to rain.

Alexei, Aleks, and Grigoriy race around, desperate to try and get the hole in the side of Abigail's house closed up. They're in the process of stapling a tarp up to cover the gaping hole when Gabe shows up on his bike.

"What are you doing here?" I look around to see whether his parents are anywhere close.

"I knew it." He pumps his fist in the air. "I *knew* you would beat him." He nods. "I'll go tell my parents."

Before I can stop him, he spins around and heads back down the road, pedaling furiously in the pounding rain.

No one seems to care about poor Leonid, who's now lying entirely unconscious on the ground in a puddle. Not even Boris and Mikhail, who are sullenly sitting on the ground, their hands ziptied behind their backs, have expressed any concern about what's to be done for their fearless leader.

"What should we do about Leonid?" No one answers.

"Hey." I grab Gustav's arm. "Leonid's lying in water, and if it keeps raining, I'm not sure he'll even be able to breathe."

330

"That would solve a few problems," Gustav says. "We can't stab him, but maybe we can drown him."

"We should add that to the list of options," Alexei says.

I'm happy they seem to be getting along, but this isn't exactly how I hoped it would happen. "Surely you can't mean to just leave him there." I can't help glancing back at where he's lying on the ground. He looks, for all the world, like he's dead.

"Not at all." Gustav's smile is warm when he turns around to face Leonid.

Finally, someone's going to at least move him someplace dry.

Gustav's brow furrows, and he lifts Leonid, making good use of what he learned about air, and starts floating him.

"So the strands of wind do work on him." Grigoriy drop his staple-arm from the side of the house to stare. "That's something you should add to the list."

"What *list*?" I ask. "What are you guys talking about?"

"We have a week, give or take," Alexei says, "to figure out how to kill him. Or barring that, to work out a way to contain him long-term."

I'm floored. They're supposed to be the good guys. "You can't really mean to kill him. I mean, I get why you tried in the heat of the moment, but now that it's passed, and he's incapacitated, there must be a better way."

Aleksandr sighs. "We aren't the imaginary 'Federation of Planets' or even a gutless organization like the United Nations. We have limited resources and an unknown amount of time before he's back up and running. Baba Yaga herself told us to contain him."

"But she didn't tell us how," Grigoriy says. "If she wanted us to keep him alive, she should've given us more information." He shrugs. "I mean to try every single way to kill that sucker that I can think of."

"Is this about getting your powers back?" I frown. "Because I understand the urge, but I went weeks without—"

"Spare me, princess," Grigoriy says.

I open my mouth to tell him where he can stick his terms of endearment, but Gustav's shoulders are slumped, and I decide to let this one go. My sweet and exhausted boyfriend dumps Leonid—or, you know, *horse* Leonid—in an empty pasture that at least appears to be relatively high and dry. He also sets him in the center of a small covered enclosure in the corner of the pasture.

It's not exactly a hotel room, but Leonid *is* a horse, and he did try to kill Gustav fifteen minutes ago. This is probably about as good as it's going to get.

The others are almost done securing the side of the house when Gustav gets a strange look on his face. A second later, the tarp they took such pains to secure is ripped away.

"Whoa," Grigoriy shouts. "What was that? Was that you, moron?"

But Gustav's smiling. And then, slowly, right in front of all of us, the chunks of splintered wood, the clumps of broken tile, the shards of shattered drywall, all float up into the air, and then they begin to slowly knit themselves back together.

Gustav's at it for nearly forty minutes, the last twenty of them with Steve, Abigail, and their entire brood standing behind him and watching, but when he's done, you can't even tell their house was hit in the first place.

"That was amazing," Gabe says.

"You saved us," Steve says. "Thanks."

"We put you at risk in the first place," Gustav says. "And to be honest, we aren't out of the woods yet."

We explain what happened with Leonid, and Gustav tells him where he put his unconscious form.

"The stallion paddock is the perfect place for him," Steve says. "And we know what to do with horses who don't behave around here. We'll help you any way we can."

"I don't want to kill him," Gustav says, "but it may be our best play."

"And if you decide against that, we'll help you come up with a way to keep him contained," Steve says.

Then they all go inside the recently repaired house to shower and clean up. Just like that, it's all settled.

I can't help walking across the big field to the side of their house and peering over the expanse of mostly-dead grass at Leonid's immobile form. He *did* want Gustav dead. He wanted Kris dead, too. He's definitely misguided.

A villain.

But I can't help feeling sorry for him.

Maybe it's that, if our roles were reversed, I'm not sure I wouldn't do the same things he's done. I can hate what he's done and who he's become and still lament that it's happened, can't I? Or does it make me a monster, too?

I'm not sure how long I'm standing there, but I'm soaked to the bone and shivering when a large, warm arm drops around my shoulders. "Kat." Gustav's large, warm mouth presses against the side of my face. "Come inside."

"I—yes. I should." I lean against his chest. "I know I should."

"Are you angry?"

I shake my head. "I'm proud of you. I'm delighted your plan worked. I'm sad it came to this, and I'm relieved that the largest danger is past. But. . ."

"You feel bad for him."

I shrug. "I'm sorry if that bothers you."

He drags me closer, and I turn so my face is pressed against his strong, wide chest. "Don't be. It's that compassion I first felt drawn to."

"Really?" I look up at him.

He drops a kiss on the end of my nose. "I've never said this to anyone before, but I love you, Katerina. Truly. I love you for your compassion. I love you for your forgiving heart. I love you for caring about people, even broken people like me." His arms encircle my waist and draw me in underneath his chin, even though I'm soaked. Even though I'm cold. Even though I'm broken.

"I just want you guys to focus on ways to contain him, if you can."

"You must understand why they're afraid," Gustav says. "If he wakes up and we can't contain him. . ."

"None of them have powers," I say. "I know. We already have our hands full, just keeping Boris and Mikhail under control."

"Well, I'm less worried now that they have no powers, but they are high-level Russian diplomats we're technically wrongfully detaining."

"Not that anyone would rat us out, but the world does know they're here."

"The Birch Creek people—" Gustav sighs. "I'm glad they're okay, but putting them at risk stresses me out."

We barely know them, but I already care about them all a great deal. "I know what you mean."

"We should get out of here as quickly as we can. We shouldn't let anything else bad happen to them because of us."

"Amanda's heart was repaired thanks to us being here, and you fixed their house," I say. "So it's not all been bad for them."

"I guess," Gustav says. "But still."

"Where will we go?" I turn and look up at him. "New York?"

"We?" His eyebrows rise.

"Where you go, I go," I whisper. "Unless you don't want me."

"Then I guess we have some things to talk about," he says. But he's smiling. "What do you want to do?"

"Once we deal with Leonid, I'll go anywhere you want.

New York. Latvia. Russia. Costa Rica. Iceland, though it sounds disturbingly cold, to be totally honest. You tell me, and I'll pack for it." Even thinking about a world where I'm not dealing with people arguing over what magic they have and what the world should look like, well. It sounds. . .unbelievably amazing. "But maybe whatever we decide, we start with a trip to Costa Rica. Or Hawaii. Or, ooh. I've always wanted to see Paris. I could eat chocolate croissants until I fall into a sugar coma and die."

"You know, I've never done much traveling. I always thought it was because I was too busy with school and work, but now I'm thinking maybe it was because I didn't have anyone to travel with."

"Oh?"

"Now that you mention those places, I can't think of much I'd rather do than go see them with you."

When he kisses me this time, I no longer feel cold at all. We may both be drenched and standing in the mud, but I've never been happier. The world may yet hold a lot of uncertainty and danger, but I'm finally facing it with someone I trust to have my back.

And it does make all the difference.

❧ 33 ❧
IZZY

When I found out that I didn't get into a single vet school, even my safety school, I didn't tell anyone.

I didn't tell my uncle, who's a vet. He spent summers teaching me horse basics. I didn't tell my step-dad who's a horse trainer. He knew just how much I wanted to go and taught me everything I know about horses. I didn't tell my boyfriend—he's already a vet, and not any old vet. A *rockstar* orthopedic surgeon people drive to see from miles around. But the real reason I didn't tell anyone is that telling them would mean I had to tell my mom.

I can't do that.

She was always there, at my side, making it possible for me to do whatever it took to achieve my dream. She drove me to my uncle's office day after day. She *married* a horse trainer who spent all his time teaching me everything with patience and kindness. Then she bankrolled all four years of my college education, lending assistance whenever I needed it.

She did all that so I could get in to vet school.

But I bombed the GRE. My GPA also slipped quite a bit in the past year, and now, it's too late. I'm doomed. My whole future's in question. The most painful part is that becoming a vet is who *I've always been*. If I'm not going to go to vet school, who am I? What's my purpose?

What's my value?

If I didn't have such an amazing boyfriend, I might think I had no value whatsoever.

So now I'm driving home like some kind of criminal, trying to screw up my courage to ask Mom and Steve for a loan, because thanks to an unscrupulous jerk at work, my boyfriend's in a bind. He needs my help, and I don't have any other way to come up with the hundred thousand dollars he needs to clear his name.

I already checked with the bank.

Without some kind of collateral, there's no way they'll give me a loan, which means I'm totally stuck. My only option right now is to beg Mom for a loan so I can bail Heaston out of jail and help pay for his defense.

How the other docs in his practice could just turn on him like that is unconscionable. My fear is that Mom and Steve haven't been the *most* supportive of me dating someone who's almost ten years older than me. Hearing he needs to borrow money—even though it's just short term— is going to be. . .uncomfortable.

I considered telling them I needed the money for vet school.

But what if I never get in? Then, even after Heaston pays me back, I'd have to tell them that I'd lied. Nothing could be worse than that.

When I reach the ranch, it's super wet and muddy. It looks like it rained ten inches in the past twenty-four hours. I'm pulling Steve's little two-horse trailer behind my truck—I borrowed it to take a horse he'd been breaking to a client who lived near me the last time I went out. Now I'm returning the trailer, finally, not that he'd ever ask me to bring it back, but I know it's more annoying for him to have to use his slant load for little trips.

I've barely pulled up when I hear a bizarre, high-pitched scream coming from the rarely used stallion pasture. I didn't think he had a stallion right now, so I'm a little surprised. I should go right in and get things over with, but I've always been a bit of a procrastinator, and a new horse is a draw of its own.

Before I can rethink it, I'm already jogging out to the far pasture, ready to check out the new guy.

I'm usually a grey girl. Give me dark greys with lots of dapples or bright greys that are nearly white. Sure, they're a hassle to keep clean, but they've always spoken to me—all that light and bright energy.

But when I set eyes on Steve's new chestnut stallion?

I could almost weep, he's so beautiful.

Boy, he looks mad, though. He's prancing back and forth, wearing the earth down in a long, furrowed path, his nostrils flaring, his mane rippling like shining mahogany satin.

"Look at you." I stupidly reach my hand through the extra tall fence.

He snaps at me.

I laugh. "You're a feisty one. I like that."

Oliver, one of Steve's grooms, happens to be walking by. "You shouldn't reach through the wire. He's headed for the kill pen. He's just here until they can arrange transport."

My jaw drops. "The—what?"

"Apparently he's a total maniac." Oliver arches one eyebrow. "After watching him for an hour, I don't even fault the owner. He's *nuts*."

As if on cue, the massive stallion rocks back on his hind legs and rears straight up, screaming like the devil himself.

"Still. The *kill pen?*" I sigh. "What a shame."

"They say he can't even be approached, much less ridden," Oliver says.

He's not even broke.

Ugh, what a waste.

"At least they could geld him first," I say. "Maybe he'd calm down."

If anything, that almost makes him scream louder. He rears back again, and this time when his hooves strike the ground, mud sprays in every direction. He immediately goes back to pacing, almost as if he can understand what we were saying.

"You shouldn't be killed," I whisper. "Someone should save you."

He freezes, and he turns toward me, sniffing the air.

I reach my hand through the fence again, prepared to snatch it back quickly, but he trots over, looking like he's hanging suspended in air between every hoof strike against the ground. It's hard to look that regal when every step squelches, spraying wet earth in all directions, but somehow, he manages it.

He looks like a hundred thousand dollar horse.

Which is how the idea takes root.

A stupid idea.

Monumentally stupid.

I mean, stealing a horse is always a horrible idea. Really, really bad, but if they're going to kill him anyway. . . Then I'm not really stealing him. Right?

"You can't be that bad, right boy?"

He presses his nose against my hand.

I brace myself to be bitten, but he never bites. His nostrils flare, but he snorts, and then he settles a little, shifting and bumping my arm with his huge face.

"What's your name?" I ask.

As if he can tell me.

He makes the dragon sound I love so much from horses, the snort that sounds supercharged and repeats in quick succession.

"How about Drago?" I ask. "You remind me of a *dragon* among horses, and I might be about to do something really crazy."

He whinnies then, long and loud, but he still doesn't snap at me.

"Let's see," I say. "I wonder if we might get along. Do you think I could break you and turn you into something worth a hundred thousand bucks?"

As if he's answering me, he shuffles and bumps my arm again.

"It would be better than dying, at least," I mutter. "I'll leave this up to fate. If I can manage to halter him and lead him into the trailer without anyone finding out. . ."

I wait until Oliver's gone.

Mom and Steve are probably eating breakfast. They could be out any time, though, and it takes me almost three minutes to find an unclaimed halter at the back of the tack room. I'm not even sure it's big enough for his huge stallion head.

When I walk up to his enclosure, my hand's trembling. Can I really do this, steal a horse that's slated to be killed? Not tell anyone I'm even doing it?

I mean, Oliver could say I was here, but maybe he won't think to.

Maybe I'll get this shining chestnut god back to Heaston's place and start breaking him before they figure out where he's even gone. If I can. . .if I could sell him for a decent chunk of money, maybe I won't need to tell Mom and Steve that I even need money. Maybe I can help Heaston on my own.

That would be better all around.

"This is the test," I whisper to myself again. "If I can halter him and he loads, then there's a chance."

When I open the stallion enclosure, the chestnut stallion's waiting, head down, polite and patient. He looks totally different than the stallion who was screaming earlier. I slip the halter over his head easily, which is good, because it's barely big enough for me to clip it at all.

"You might need a draft size halter with that massive head of yours. At least warmblood would be better. Sorry this one's so small, big boy."

His soft whuffle sounds almost like a laugh.

I rub his nose, and then he leads right along beside me like a little doll until I reach the trailer. He balks once, but the second time I ask him to walk in, he clops his way right into the center of the trailer. "It's three hours to get to my place," I say. "You'll be there before you know it, I swear. And then tomorrow, once you're settled in, we'll get to work."

This is probably the most insane thing I've ever done in my life, but when your whole life has come off the rails, maybe you need something insane to get it back on track.

Or at least, I sure hope so.

*** I hope you really enjoyed reading My Wild Horse King! The next book, My Trojan Horse Majesty is up for preorder already.

If you liked the Birch Creek Ranch characters but haven't read that series yet, it's written under my B. E. Baker (women's fiction) pen name. You can grab The Bequest now on any retailer of your choice, OR you can get a whole series bundle for substantial cost savings on my website. www.BridgetEBakerWrites.com (Psst. You can also sign up for my newsletter there so you don't miss updates or "deals.)

There will be ONE final book after the fifth one, My Death Horse Overlord, and it will feature another Birch

Creek Ranch character. <3 I'm hoping to get My Trojan Horse Majesty out early, but it should be out early 2025 at the latest.

If you haven't tried my Dragon shifter series yet, WHY NOT? The third book for that one is coming in October of this year. You can start with Ensnared now.

ACKNOWLEDGMENTS

My husband puts up with a lot. After 46 books, he knows what he's in for, but he's such a great sport. My kids are just right after him in terms of supportiveness, and my mom is barely behind the rest (and only because she had the audacity to have more children, who also demand some of her attention. The nerve.)

I'd like to REVERSE CREDIT my animals who all try their hardest to make sure I never write again. The dogs incessantly beg for food and face scratches. The horses continually injure themselves in idiotic ways causing me to bandage and apply ointment and schedule vet visits allllll the time. You guys are the worst, and I love you the very most.

And as always, MY READERS are the best. You guys support, buoy me up, drum up excitement, drown me in praise, and check in when you find minor typos or inconsistencies. I love you forever and a day. Thank you for allowing me to have my dream job and pay for my dream life by loving my fictitious people as much as I do. From the BOTTOM of my heart, thank you thank you thank you. And if you're not in my Facebook reader group yet, or on my newsletter, WHY NOT? Come join us! (Bridget Baker Binge Readers Recovery OR sign up for the newsletter at www.BridgetEBaker Writes.com) XOXOXO

ABOUT THE AUTHOR

If you've made it this far (book four of the strangest series out there), you probably already know the author of these books is a shameless shredder of the wall between fiction and the author writing it. I have too many kids. I have way too many pets. And my husband is just EXTRA. (He has to make up for his lack of hair.) I love God, I love learning, and I love my people (which includes my readers...)

ALSO BY BRIDGET E. BAKER

The Dragon Captured Series: (dragon shifter romance!)

Ensnared

Entwined

Embroiled

Embattled

The Russian Witch's Curse: (horse shifter romance!)

My Queendom for a Horse

My Dark Horse Prince

My High Horse Czar

My Wild Horse King

My Trojan Horse Majesty

The Magical Misfits Series: (paranormal humor!)

Mates: Minerva (1)

Mates: Xander (2)

The Birthright Series:

Displaced (1)

unForgiven (2)

Disillusioned (3)

misUnderstood (4)

Disavowed (5)

unRepentant (6)

Destroyed (7)

The Birthright Series Collection, Books 1-3

The Anchored Series:

Anchored (1)

Adrift (2)

Awoken (3)

Capsized (4)

The Sins of Our Ancestors Series:

Marked (1)

Suppressed (2)

Redeemed (3)

Renounced (4)

Reclaimed (5) a novella!

A stand alone YA romantic suspense:

Already Gone

I also write women's fiction/romance books under B. E. Baker.

The Scarsdale Fosters Series:

Seed Money (1)

Nouveau Riche (2)

Minted (3)

Loaded (4)

The Finding Home Series:

Finding Grace (1)

Finding Faith (2)

Finding Cupid (3)

Finding Spring (4)

Finding Liberty (5)

Finding Holly (6)

Finding Home (7)

Finding Balance (8)

Finding Peace (9)

The Finding Home Series Boxset Books 1-3

The Finding Home Series Boxset Books 4-6

The Finding Home Series Boxset Books 7-9

The Birch Creek Ranch Series:

The Bequest

The Vow

The Ranch

The Retreat

The Reboot

The Surprise

The Setback

The Lookback

Children's Picture Book

Yuck! What's for Dinner?

www.ingramcontent.com/pod-product-compliance
Lightning Source LLC
Chambersburg PA
CBHW021227060726
47590CB00005B/1665